SHE NEEDS

BY
SUE MacKAY

A FATHER FOR POPPY

BY
ABIGAIL GORDON

MILLS &
BOON

With a background of working in medical laboratories, and a love of the romance genre, it is no surprise that **Sue MacKay** writes Mills & Boon® Medical Romance™ stories. An avid reader all her life, she wrote her first story at age eight—about a prince, of course. She lives with her own hero in the beautiful Marlborough Sounds, at the top of New Zealand's South Island, where she indulges her passions for the outdoors, the sea and cycling.

Abigail Gordon loves to write about the fascinating combination of medicine and romance from her home in a Cheshire village. She is active in local affairs, and is even called upon to write the script for the annual village pantomime! Her eldest son is a hospital manager, and helps with all her medical research. As part of a close-knit family, she treasures having two of her sons living close by, and the third one not too far away. This also gives her the added pleasure of being able to watch her delightful grandchildren growing up.

THE FAMILY SHE NEEDS

BY
SUE MacKAY

First published in Great Britain 2015
by Mills & Boon, an imprint of Harlequin (UK) Limited,
Eton House, 18-24 Paradise Road, Richmond, Surrey, TW9 1SR

© 2015 Sue MacKay

ISBN: 978-0-263-24697-1

Harlequin (UK) Limited's policy is to use papers that are natural,
renewable and recyclable products and made from wood grown in
sustainable forests. The logging and manufacturing processes conform
to the legal environmental regulations of the country of origin.

Printed and bound in Spain
by CPI, Barcelona

Dear Reader,

Many years ago I moved from Auckland to the small rural town of Motueka—talk about a culture shock! But once I got my head around no traffic lights, and all the apples and kiwifruit anyone could wish for growing everywhere, I quickly discovered some of the most wonderful people and made a lifelong friend there.

When I wanted to tip Karina Brown out of her usual Auckland haunts and into somewhere that could nurture her I naturally chose Motueka, and let the locals work their magic on her, too. And then along comes Logan Pascale—and if ever there's a man who needs help it's him. Of course it's Karina who really gets him back on his feet, with her big heart and a ton of love to share.

I hope you enjoy following these two on their journey to happiness.

Cheers!

Sue MacKay

To Jacqui.
Thank you for the keys to your house,
a sympathetic ear, lots of advice I mostly ignored,
and the best ever parties. It might've been
a long time ago but I've never forgotten.

Books by Sue MacKay

Praise for Sue MacKay

CHAPTER ONE

'I'M AFRAID IT'S a no from this bank, Miss Brown.' The manager stood abruptly, indicating the interview was over.

Karina gritted her teeth to hold back a sharp retort. Miss Brown? In a town where everyone from millionaires to bag ladies was on first-name terms, she had just been insulted. She'd lived in Motueka for a little under a year but no one called her *Miss* anything. She was Karina Brown. End of. Had been since the day she'd left Auckland in a blaze of flashing media cameras and pushy reporters shoving microphones in her face as they demanded answers to questions she'd had no intention of answering. The day she'd gone back to her maiden name and left her old life behind to go and reinvent herself.

'Thank you for your time, Mr Pederson.' She gave the same back through clamped jaws.

Rising from the chair, she was astonished to feel her legs shaking. Smoothing down her knee-length pencil skirt and tugging her shoulders back tight inside her tailored jacket—not worn since Auckland—Karina strode out of the bank manager's office with all the aplomb of her old persona. She would *not* grovel for the money she desperately needed to buy the other half of the house—not yet. Being told no just increased her determination to achieve her goal.

'How'd that go?' Rebecca called, only loudly enough for her to hear.

Crossing to her friend, who was more commonly known as Becca, despite her name badge, stationed at the bank's customer service desk, Karina shook her head. 'A big fail. Apparently I'm not a good prospect for lending money to.'

Ironic, considering her background. Once upon a time several hundred thousand dollars had been chickenfeed to her. Nowadays she lived on the wages she earned as a nurse at the medical centre she jointly owned in the small rural town of Motueka, far removed from that glamorous life. She had a tiny nest egg, put aside for rainy days, but nothing big enough to buy out Logan Pascale.

'Don't you dare think like that,' growled Becca.

'I showed him the property valuation and suggested I could spread the loan out for thirty years.' She'd be sixty-four and nearly ready to retire by then, but it would be worth it.

Becca leaned closer. 'It shouldn't mean a thing, but half the problem is you're not a local. Here, coming from the Big Smoke up north is like coming from another country.'

'I've heard that enough to know it's true.' But it didn't explain the malicious gleam in Pederson's eyes as he'd told her no. He'd been enjoying himself at her expense. 'Bet he's looked me up online.'

'Are you sure you want a mortgage hanging over your head? Couldn't you ask someone in your family for the money this once?'

'What?' Karina shuddered. Prove to her father that what he believed had been right all along? That she couldn't make it on her own? 'No!' she barked, too loudly.

Becca wouldn't understand her need to stand on her own two tiny feet and do what was right for a little boy who relied entircly on her for everything.

'I can't do that,' she reiterated, more quietly. This was the toughest test she'd faced so far in her stand to be independent. *So suck it up and beat the odds.*

'I figured that'd be your answer, but don't let your pride get in the way of what's right.'

Jeepers, Becca, be blunt, why don't you?

'Anything I do will be what's right for Mickey.'

Mickey. The boy she loved as if he were her own. As one of his two guardians, she intended doing everything within her power to make sure she kept the only home he'd known. She'd promised his parents no less.

'How *is* that bundle of mischief? I haven't seen him for days.'

'Mickey's cool.'

Damn, but this was hard. She also needed to keep everything exactly as it was for herself. She'd crafted a new life in which she was in control and happy, in a quiet, comfortable way.

'Just the usual hiccups. Not enough honey on his toast and me putting the wrong shirt out for him to wear to kindergarten.'

'I bet you give him everything he wants.'

'How can I refuse when he gives me that gappy grin? But this morning he was very clingy and didn't want to go to kindergarten. Most unusual. Said his tummy was sore.'

'Did you insist on him going?'

Karina shrugged. 'Jonty's looking after him while I'm here.'

Becca returned to the original problem. 'What are you going to do about buying out Dr Pascale now?'

'Know a millionaire with lots of cash stashed under his bed?' A few hundred thousand was all she needed but, hey, in for an apple, in for a sack full of dollars.

'You want a sexy hunk to go with those millions?'

'Rich *and* sexy? All in one package? What's the catch?' Because she'd had that package and knew the pitfalls all too well.

'I don't know any guy around here fitting the description.' Becca grinned.

'Just as well.' Karina smiled back, thankful that her friend hadn't pointed out which of them actually knew the most millionaires.

'You still don't want to put your toe in the dating pond?'

'That's the last thing I want. I'm enjoying being in charge of my own life. Why would I want to give that up to be told which functions to attend and who to invite to dinner?'

Becca chose not to answer that. Instead she went with 'Heard when the good doctor's actually arriving?' A gleam of excitement lit up her eyes.

'Not a dickey bird. I don't even know if he's left Africa yet.' Hopefully he was still out in the wilderness, working with people who needed his medical skills. 'The longer I hear nothing, the longer I've got to come up with a solution for the house.'

But the days were running out—fast.

'Wonder what he's like? Even if he doesn't have millions under his bed he could be sexy.'

'Like *that's* going to make a difference to anything.'

The situation was complicated enough, with them sharing guardianship of Mickey and having joint ownership of the house and attached medical centre. They'd never met, which suited her perfectly. She'd kept everything ticking over since Maria and James had died. Dr Pascale hadn't made it home for his brother and his sister-in-law's funeral—hadn't talked to Karina at all, even by phone. Their only communication had been through the lawyers acting for the unusual partnership put in place solely to protect Mickey.

When a letter had arrived from the estate lawyers stating that Dr Logan Pascale wanted to sell the property and invest the money for Mickey's future, she'd felt a familiar punch in her stomach. Only this time she refused to fold. This time she would stand up to anything being thrown at her and would not be told what to do. Mickey shouldn't be moved away from all his memories of his parents.

When Maria and James had approached her about becoming a guardian if the unthinkable happened, she'd promised to do everything to make Mickey happy. Maria, her best friend ever, had hugged her and said that was exactly why they were asking. Now she had a promise to keep.

Putting that aside, Karina said, 'Guess I'd better be

getting home.' She turned to stare out through the glass doors and shivered at the sight. 'It wasn't raining when I walked up here.' Though the sky had been grey and threatening. 'My car needs two new tyres.' It sat in the driveway going nowhere in the meantime.

'I'd offer you my truck, but my brother's borrowed it.' Becca handed her a large umbrella with bright blue logos splashed across it. She winked. 'Compliments of the bank. They're only for our most important clients.'

Karina couldn't speak for the sudden lump in her throat. *Thank you*, she thought as she stared at this woman who'd unexpectedly become a good friend. *Thank you*. Hopefully Becca understood.

The wind blew rain into her face as she headed down High Street towards home. Home, Mickey, the surgery: her life. The life she liked to think she controlled.

'Mostly…' she muttered as the rain got worse.

Within minutes her skirt was soaked and her blouse was getting damp down the front. Her jacket hadn't been designed to be closed across her breasts. Very classy, but totally impractical for her newer, more prosaic lifestyle. She hurried along the footpath, quickly giving up on avoiding the puddles. She'd have jogged all the way, but given she was wearing three-inch narrow heels—all to impress an unimpressionable goat of a banker—she figured that might be a little crazy even for her.

The cooler air did nothing to chill her anger at being refused a loan. She should have asked on what grounds she'd been turned down, but giving Mr Pederson the pleasure of knowing he'd upset her hadn't been an option. Now she'd have to think of another way to raise the capital. *Oh, yeah, like how?* Short of selling herself down at the wharf, there weren't any ideas shining out at her.

Shoving the disappointment and her sense of unfairness down deep, where she kept insurmountable problems, she focused on reaching home as soon as possible. Before lunch she needed to change Jonty's wound from when he'd fallen in the chook pen and caught his forearm on a stake.

Dear old Grumpy Jones. Secretly, she adored Jonty. Underneath all that griping he was such a sweetheart, and so helpful. Without him she'd never have got the garden dug in time to plant spuds and onions. He'd complained about it with every turn of the soil, but when she'd tried to wrest the spade from him he'd given her an earful.

A gust of wind slammed into her and caught the umbrella, turning it inside out. The heavens poured water onto her carefully styled hair and turned her blouse see-through. So much for trying to look half-decent for once. Of *course* the bank's umbrella was rubbish. Went with the miserable manager's image.

Locking the gate at the bottom of her driveway, she turned for the house and groaned. The hole in the asphalt had overflowed, sending water streaming out to the road. Water, water everywhere…

'It's so tempting.'

Despite her angst with the world she felt a flicker of mischief unfurl deep inside, and she raised a grin. Might as well get some fun out of the day and act like the delinquent Mr Pederson believed her to be. This hopelessness needed stomping on—and stuff the shoes. It was doubtful she'd be wearing them again anyway.

Karina breathed deep and leapt into the air to land in the shallow hole. Splashes of murky water shot in every direction, including up her legs. Up, down, splash, splash. She pretended the tears leaking from the corners of her eyes were from pure pleasure, and not exasperation at her inability to fix the current crisis.

'I want to do that!' Mickey yelled from the veranda.

'Come on, then.'

So the sore tummy had recovered. She watched anxiously as he leapt off the steps and charged towards her.

'Go easy,' she muttered. She hated that he believed he was invulnerable. But she also acknowledged that his condition mustn't hold him back.

Splash. Mickey's round face split wide into a grin. Bending his knees, he bombed his feet into the deepest water he could find. His shrieks filled the air, and soon Karina was laughing hard. To hell with banks and money and everything. *This* was what life was about: enjoying the little things, and especially having fun with this boy she loved so much.

When Mickey was totally soaked she grabbed his hand and started for the house. 'Let's get into dry clothes and then I'll make us hot chocolate drinks.'

'Can we?' Mickey shouted. *'Really?'*

'I reckon.' She bounded up the steps and kicked off her shoes. 'Is Mr Grumpy here or out in the shed?'

'Inside our place.'

She untied Mickey's laces and tugged his shoes and socks off. 'Straight to the bathroom, please. Get out of those clothes while I find you some dry ones.'

'What about my hot chocolate?'

'After you've changed.'

She ruffled his hair and gently pushed him inside, before banging the door shut behind them. Dropping her sopping bag and the useless umbrella into the bucket in the corner, she spun around to head to her bedroom and pulled up short at the sight of a man walking towards her.

'Who are you?' she gasped, though from the way goosebumps were lifting her skin she already had an inkling. So much for hoping he was weeks away. But, hey, it was that kind of day.

'Logan Pascale.' The long and lean, tanned man held a hand out to her. 'You're Karina Brown?' His eyes were very wide, and definitely not focused on her face.

Automatically putting her hand in his, she tried to lock eyes with him, but he was staring at something below her chin. When she followed the direction of his gaze she gasped again. Every last scrap of her clothing was wet, clinging to her like plastic wrap, and her blouse was more see-through than if she'd worn nothing. Her breasts pushed hard against her bra...her very lacy, transparent bra.

Open up, floor, right now. Gobble me up.

When nothing happened she dredged deep for what little pride she could muster. 'Yes, I'm Karina.' She lifted her head to study the stranger who held the future of Mickey's home in the warm, strong hand she was still holding. Snatching her hand free, she stepped back and returned to scrutinising him.

'Jonty let me in. He's popped home for a moment.'

Despite the chill settling over her due to all that wet-

ness, warmth eased through her body, touching her
tummy, her toes, her face. He might be too lean for
her taste, but her body didn't seem to care if the way
it responded when she looked at him was an indicator.
His face was gaunt, as if he needed feeding up. But
those eyes were what really caught at her. Piercing, yet
guarded, while also holding a hint of humour and compassion. A disturbing mix.

Oh, man, this was so *wrong*. The guy should come
with a warning label. *Don't come near unless you hold
all the aces*. She was short on aces today. Worse, she
couldn't stop staring.

Tall… Okay, anyone was tall compared to her. Oh,
and he had the most gorgeous crop of overlong black
hair, while his day-old stubble made her mouth water.

'Karina, I want my clothes!' Mickey yelled.

'Coming,' she called back, far more quietly.

'I'll wait for you in the kitchen,' her distracting visi-
tor told her. 'Want me to make that hot chocolate I heard
you mention?'

'With marshmallows, ta.'

He was already acting as if he lived here. She
shrugged. *Get over it*. Logan Pascale owned half the
place; he could come and go as he pleased. Was that
good or bad? That warmth he'd engendered evaporated,
leaving her shivering with cold and apprehension as she
opened drawers to find Mickey some clothes.

Logan did hold all the aces. He wanted to sell the
place she'd made her home and had believed she'd live
in for many years to come. He had as much right to
make decisions about the property and Mickey's future
as she did. But had he even heard of joint decisions?

Her sigh was filled with annoyance and frustration of the most irritating kind. If he thought selling up would help his nephew's cause then he didn't know damn all about Mickey.

But of course he didn't. Visiting briefly once a year meant he hardly knew his nephew. Hadn't seen the day-to-day growing up stuff, didn't know what he liked and hated, wouldn't understand how the Down syndrome affected him.

No doubt Logan intended getting things done fast so he could fly away again, leaving her to cope with the mess he'd created.

Well, think again, Pascale. I'm made of stronger stuff. You won't get away with it. I've grown a back-bone because of men like you. Men who charm women out of their three-inch-high shoes all because they have a hidden agenda.

CHAPTER TWO

LOGAN DRAGGED HIS eyes forward and headed to the kitchen. His mouth twisted into a tight smile. He might have stopped staring at that bundle of unbridled energy, but her image still seared his brain. Her small body, with those clothes moulded to each and every curve, those enormous eyes the colour of the hot drinks he was about to make blinking out of that elfin face.

From the little he knew about her he understood that she'd walked away from an extremely comfortable life and all that entailed. He certainly hadn't been expecting to be surprised by her energy for life. When he'd first seen Karina carrying on in the driveway, before Mickey had joined her, he'd thought she was a teenager playing hooky from school, not the qualified nurse taking care of his nephew.

He'd felt a delicious shock when he'd realised those curves certainly didn't belong to a teenager, but instead to an all-grown-up woman. A very tempting grown-up woman. It wasn't difficult to imagine running his hands over that body. *Damn it*. He couldn't afford to get sidetracked, even for a few hours. He might have been living the life of a monk lately, but that would have to continue at least while he visited Motueka and sorted out Mickey's future—starting with making arrangements to sell this place.

'Kar—ina, where are you? I'm ready.'

Did Mickey ever talk in fewer decibels than a jet on take-off?

'Coming, kiddo.'

At least Karina replied quietly, in a soft, almost caressing tone.

Caressing. As in stroking, touching…

Logan stomped through to the kitchen, where everything appeared spotless. Nothing like what he was used to in the over-used, under-tidied kitchens of Nigeria, where all energy went into helping people rather than putting things away in cupboards only so that someone could remove them again moments later. This was kind of a nice change. Homey.

Whoa. They were going to sell this place. Getting comfortable and cosy wasn't an option.

He had no difficulty finding chocolate to go into the milk he'd put on to heat. A stack of bars stood right beside the tin of drinking chocolate powder in the pantry, along with packets of marshmallows. He popped a marshmallow in his mouth as he stirred the milk, savouring the sweet burst of flavour on his tongue.

Karina bounced into the small space, using up what little air there was, bumping him with her elbows or hips every time she moved—which was constantly. While those curves were now hidden under trousers and a chambray shirt, he knew they were there. Her hair was damp and curls were beginning to fly, adding to that waif-like appearance.

'Will you look at that?' She nodded in the direction of the window. 'It's already stopped raining. Put on for my benefit, was it?' She came closer and peered into the pot. 'Looking good. Pour Mickey's before it gets too hot. He doesn't like waiting for it to cool.'

Trying to ignore the scent of roses and damp hair wafting around her, Logan reached for the mug she held out. 'Sure. He's grown heaps since I was last here.' *Concentrate on Mickey and the perfume will eventually evaporate.* He hoped.

'Kids do tend to grow and change quite a bit in a year.' She placed two more mugs on the bench. 'I presume you're joining us in our hot chocolate moment?'

'Might as well.'

There hadn't been a hint of sting in her words, and yet the guilt they caused tightened his gut enough to ache. He hadn't been the best uncle, or brother, over the years. He knew that more than anyone.

'I would've been back nearly two months ago except for an exceptional circumstance.'

Why justify himself to this woman? It was none of her business. Except...

'I'm sorry you've had to shoulder all the responsibility for Mickey since James and Maria died.' Not to mention the medical centre that had been James's pride and joy, and had seemed too dull to *him*.

She shrugged. 'No worries.'

'Understatement your thing, is it?'

This house had had more than its share of problems due to lack of maintenance over the years. The lawyers had made sure he knew about every last fault. At least that was something he could, and would, fix. He had an appointment at two o'clock to talk to a real estate agent and get the property on the market. Getting it up to scratch was part of his agenda over the next few weeks.

'Not that I'm aware.' Karina opened a tin from the pantry and placed some cookies on a plate. 'I'm sorry you missed the funeral. We held off as long as possible, but no one could track you down.'

Wow, she had a way of ramping up the guilt without even trying. His gut wanted to regurgitate that marshmallow.

'There are often days—weeks in the rainy season— when all contact with the outside world is lost.' He wasn't going to mention that, where he'd been at that critical time, contact with anyone had been impossible.

A small hand rested on his forearm, orange-tipped fingers splaying lightly on his shirtsleeve. Each fingertip was a heat source, tripping through his chilled body and reminding him of easier times. Carefree times.

She said quietly, 'I wasn't having a poke at you. I understand the difficulties. James mentioned how hard it could be to get hold of you in Nigeria.'

If only the reason had been that simple. His eyes locked with hers, saw nothing but genuine sympathy there. Sympathy that should be tightening his shoulders and making him prove he didn't need it but was instead undermining his determination to remain aloof and do what was needed as quickly as possible before he headed back to a world he understood.

But he didn't understand it. Not any more. Strange how the easy look in Karina's eyes made him long for a break, here, in this quiet town where people really were safe. To be able to take each day slowly, get his

body back in shape, his head thinking straight, and
to get to know his nephew. Time even to get to know
Karina Brown.

Jerking his arm away, he snapped, 'If it had been at
all possible to get here I would've.' He drew in a deep
breath, tried for calm. 'But it wasn't possible.'

If he'd stepped one foot outside his prison hut his
body would have been riddled with bullets and he'd
have been left to the flies and the vultures.

Hot milk splashed on the bench as he poured the liq-
uid into the mugs.

Karina deftly wiped up the spill before dropping
two marshmallows on top of each drink. 'Mickey, sit
up at the table. You can have one cookie before lunch.'

She perched on a chair beside the boy, holding her
mug in both hands, her gaze thoughtful. Was she trying to believe he'd been telling the truth?

'How did you get on at the bank?' he asked, in an
attempt to distract her from his apparent failings as
an uncle.

'How did you know that's where I was?' She shifted
on her chair, began twisting the mug back and forth between her hands.

'Jonty mentioned it when I introduced myself.'

'That surprises me.' She sighed, then stood up
abruptly. 'I'd better go see if I'm needed before surgery closes for lunch. Keep an eye on Mickey, will you?'

Oh, no, you don't.

Logan cut off her mad dash by taking her arm and
holding on until she turned to look up at him. 'I've been
over there. Everything's under control.'

'You checked up on my surgery?'

Could those eyes get any bigger? 'Isn't it *our* surgery?' he asked quietly. 'I wasn't checking up on anything. I was introducing myself.'

The air hissed over her bottom lip as she sagged in on herself. Pulling her arm away, she dropped onto the chair she'd hurriedly vacated.

'Yes, I went to the bank. No, they won't lend me the money I need to buy you out. Any further questions?' she snapped.

He lifted out another chair, flicked it around to straddle it, and folded his arms over the top. 'Why do you want to buy me out? Doesn't it make sense to sell this rambling old place, with its huge grounds, and buy a new, comfortable, easily kept home?'

'No. It. Doesn't.'

The words fell like heavy weights between them.

'This is Mickey's home, the place where he remembers his mum and dad. I will *not* take him away from here. He gets upset enough as it is some days.'

'I see.'

'Do you?' Those perfectly shaped eyebrows lifted. 'What about the surgery? If we sell the house, where's that going to be relocated?'

'I'd have thought that'd be the last thing you'd want to be bothered with. I know you struggle to keep a GP full-time.'

She could have told him what he already knew, that she'd managed with locums so far. But she didn't. Instead she went for his throat. 'Unless you have plans to take over?'

Logan stood up so fast the chair knocked against the table. 'Are you out of your mind?'

Him? Working in a small town, dealing with the everyday stuff of colds and stomach bugs and high blood pressure? Signing on for ever?

'That would not work. Believe me.'

He strode over to stare out of the window onto the drive, with its hole that needed repairing, and swore silently. Not in a million years. He wanted to be with people who had no choices, who were forever grateful for any little help they got. People who came and went so quickly they didn't cling to his life.

Mickey banged his empty mug on the table. 'I want to play with Mr Grumpy.'

Karina didn't move, almost as though she hadn't heard Mickey. Even if the neighbours probably had.

Logan turned. 'Who's Mr Grumpy?'

'He teaches me things.' Mickey slid off the chair and picked up his mug to bang it on the bench. 'Doesn't he, Karina?'

'Yes, he does, sweetheart.' She stood up. 'And I should've changed Jonty's dressing before now.'

Definitely looking for an excuse to escape him.

'Can it wait a few more minutes and I'll come with you?' When she looked at him with astonishment, he hastened to add, 'I take it Jonty and Mr Grumpy are one and the same.'

Karina's lips twitched. And sent his hormones into a little spasm. She really was seriously distracting.

She told him, 'Yes.' And then, turning to Mickey, said, 'Mr Grumpy should be in the potting shed, planting the tomato seeds. If he's not you come straight back here and we'll find him together. Okay?' She held her hand up, palm out.

Mickey high-fived it. 'Okey-dokey, hokey-pokey.'

Logan watched his nephew racing from the room and felt his heart stir just a tiny bit. Having Down syndrome wasn't holding the kid back from enjoying himself.

'Does he understand fully what happened to his parents?'

Sadness filled Karina's eyes. 'As much as a kid his age can. Sometimes he asks when Daddy's coming home from work, or if Mummy's going to make his dinner. There are nights when I find him crying into his pillow. But then I've found him doing that when he's lost his favourite toy, so I could be completely wrong and he hasn't got a clue why he now lives with me.'

'From what my parents told me, you had a lot to do with him before the accident.'

Not a stranger, like him. Guilt raised its head again. Mickey hadn't remembered him this morning. No surprise, considering he'd been about three the last time Logan had flown in for a quick visit. Thank goodness James had had the good sense to make Karina joint guardian with him. Even if she wasn't family in any DNA kind of way, the boy had a firm constant in his life and wasn't coping with a man who preferred working and living in exotic places. Make that who had *used to* prefer.

Mickey needed security—he needed the same people in his life day in and day out, to see the same kids at play-group every time he went. He certainly wouldn't get that tagging along with his uncle to desolate places on the African continent. Besides, that wasn't an option after what had happened on his last tour. Far too dangerous.

Karina spoke quietly. 'I'd been working here for a

few months when the accident happened.' She blinked furiously. 'Mickey and I were great mates even then.'

'Coming from Auckland to such a small place must've taken some getting used to.'

'It was refreshing.' She picked at a spot on the table. 'Maria and I met in Auckland while doing our nursing training and became firm friends. Inseparable at times.'

She raised those beautiful eyes to his face and the sadness spilling out made him want to wrap her up in his arms and hold her tight.

He didn't. Because he mightn't be able to let her go. Because he needed to be held, too. Because he should have been here for Mickey, and even for Karina.

'You were Maria's bridesmaid. I vaguely recall a wedding photo.'

'Hardly a bridesmaid when those two went out to lunch and came back married. They dragged me along, saying they had a surprise.'

'There was a guy there as well.'

'The law requires two witnesses.'

The words were flat. Her face had gone blank, her eyes expressionless.

The devil got hold of his tongue. 'Who was he? I didn't recognise him as one of James's friends.'

He'd recently gone weeks without talking to anyone, bar demanding to be freed, and since then he'd apparently lost the ability to be circumspect.

'My ex-husband.'

Never had he heard so much emotion in two little words. Anger, disappointment, despair, hurt, and a whole lot more. Something beyond his shoulder seemed to fascinate her for a long, drawn-out moment. Then she blinked.

'We split very suddenly and I wanted a change of environment. Staying on in Auckland no longer worked for me.' She continued spilling her guts. 'About that time Maria decided to be a stay-at-home mum and asked me to fill her place at the surgery. I think she made that up, because she'd been managing very nicely until then. But I arrived here within days and I'm not likely to leave again.'

'Only now you've got a wee boy.'

And a big heart. She didn't appear to be struggling with everything she did, and yet her days had to be close to chaotic at times—especially given that Mickey needed a lot of attention with his condition.

'A boy I'd do anything for.'

He got the message loud and clear. *Don't mess with Karina. Or Mickey.*

'So what do you do for a social life in Motueka?' Might as well ask anything that came into his brain while he had her talking.

Karina shrugged. 'Friday night drinks at a bar on High Street with a friend is more than enough for me. As I've no intention of marrying again I'm not joining the dating circuit.'

Unbelievably honest.

'I can understand that.'

Way too much information, Logan. He knew from the slight widening of her eyes that she'd read between the lines of his simple statement and understood he was as uninterested in finding a soul mate as she was. He'd seen far too many relationships bite the dust in Africa.

Commitment to the health organisation left little time for anyone or anything else.

Karina said, 'You want to sell this place?'

She was forthright. He'd give her that.

'Yes.'

He'd be the same.

'Why?'

'I've seen the builder's report the lawyers have had done. This place needs major repairs and maintenance, which won't come cheap—especially for a property nearly eighty years old. A comfortable house with no financial worries for you seems a good idea. Though what you'd do for jumping puddles I'm not sure,' he added, forcing a smile.

A smile that she chose to ignore as she stood up, stretching as tall as possible on her toes, which still left her well short of his chin. 'Haven't you left something out?'

'Like what?'

Those eyes that had entranced him now appeared to be ready to slice him to shreds. He was about to get an earful. Her cheeks were reddening, her mouth tightening.

'The bit where you will then be free to fly off into the sunset, knowing there's nothing here for you to worry yourself over. Your nephew will be well cared for, and he won't miss out on a thing because there won't be any repairs to pay for. You'll have done your bit for your family.'

His family? Yes, she certainly knew how to twist the knife. As he opened his mouth to explain that his nephew was better off being with her, she cut him off and added to his distress.

'I will never sign any sale agreement you draw up. *Never*. Get it?'

Her forefinger stabbed his chest—hard. Strange how he wanted to wrap his hand around that finger and kiss the tip.

She hadn't finished. 'This is Mickey's home until the day he doesn't need one any more.'

She couldn't have put it more bluntly than that. Yet he sensed a well of emotion and need behind her statement. What for, or why, he had yet to figure out. He'd also have to work harder on persuading her that his way was best for all of them. And the reasons she believed were not necessarily behind his thinking. Though she wasn't entirely wrong about those either.

CHAPTER THREE

OF ALL THE stubborn, thoughtless, selfish men in the world, Logan Pascale had to be top of the pile. Karina bit down on the words threatening to spill off her tongue and headed out to the shed to find Jonty. The stubborn, thoughtless, selfish man followed her.

'I need to replace that dressing for you,' she informed the older man down on his knees trying to unscrew the broken handle of a spade. She'd do her best to ignore Logan for now.

'They don't make these handles like they used to,' Jonty grunted.

Beside the old man Mickey sat on his butt in spilled potting mix. 'I'm helping Mr Grumpy.' He reverently held a pair of pliers in his hands.

Jonty didn't look up as he said, 'I don't need the dressing changed. There's nothing wrong with this one.'

The bolt suddenly flicked free and spun across the floor.

Mickey crawled after it. 'I got it.'

Karina squatted beside Jonty. 'You don't want to get an infection.'

'Pish. I'm healthy. No infection's coming near me.'

The second bolt was giving him as much trouble as the first.

Logan hunkered down on his haunches opposite them. 'How'd this break?'

Go away and leave us be. Her teeth snapped shut, sending vibrations through her skull.

'Damned rocks,' Jonty griped.

Karina wasn't giving in. 'Let me see that arm, please.'

The old man glanced at Logan. 'Women, eh? Bossy creatures—think they know best.'

Logan laughed: a warm sound that briefly lifted her black mood.

Then he won points by saying to Jonty, 'I know what you mean, but in this instance I think Karina's right. An infection in your arm could be debilitating for some time. You might have to delay finishing that digging.'

Jonty's knuckles were white as he tried to budge the bolt. 'I guess.'

'Here. Can I get that?' Logan asked in an offhand manner that made it easy for Jonty to accept his offer.

'You do that while Miss Bossy, here, does her nurse routine.'

Smothering a smile, Karina removed the dressing and cleaned Jonty's wound. It would have been better doing it inside, but Jonty would never agree. 'It's looking good. You were very lucky not to have that spike go any deeper.'

'I got two dozen eggs this morning,' he muttered.

Good, there'd be some spare to trade for fresh bread at the bakehouse down the road. 'They're laying well, considering it's winter.'

'There you go.' Logan handed back the screwdriver and a few screws.

'You look like your brother.' Mr Grumpy squeezed Logan's shoulder. 'Sorry about James, lad. We miss him and Maria around here.'

Weren't men supposed to be reticent? Mr Grumpy had said more words in the last ten minutes than he often uttered in a whole day.

Karina taped on the new dressing and gathered up the old one. 'There you go.'

'Thanks, lass.'

'Is Mickey okay with you until I've got lunch ready?'

Jonty rolled his eyes and took the spade minus its handle back from Logan.

'That's a yes, then.'

She thought Logan would remain in the shed, but he was quickly on his feet to go with her.

The problem with walking towards the house after having heard Logan mention maintenance was that she looked hard at the weatherboard walls and window frames. The paint was peeling in places, and some of the boards did show signs of rot. The putty around the glass panes had cracked and in places had fallen out completely.

'Yeah, it does need an overhaul,' she admitted grudgingly under her breath.

The guy had supersensitive hearing. 'A major undertaking, involving a lot of time and effort to restore the whole building.'

She spun around, skidding on the sodden grass. His hand quickly caught her arm, steadied her, then instantly dropped away.

Rubbing the place where those strong fingers had gripped, she raised her head and told him, 'Think about how wonderful this old building could look with a new coat of paint and those windows picked out in a shade of green to fit in with the grounds.'

The large grounds in which the lawns were mowed once a month, whether they needed it or not, summer and winter. And in which the trees should have been pruned and the wayward hedge needed cutting off at the roots.

Logan's eyebrows were in danger of disappearing under that mop of dark hair. His flat mouth quirked up into an annoying smile. 'You have a wonderful imagination.'

'What are your plans? Are you in town for long?'

'As long as it takes to make you see reason and get this place on the market.'

He didn't half labour the point. The breath she dragged in chilled her bottom teeth. 'Then you'll be here a long time.'

Could she ask him to leave his half of the money in the property as a loan to her? No, she couldn't. She'd only just met him, but she was over his incredulous glances already.

'I'll buy a lotto ticket tomorrow.'

'Why not go easy on yourself and accept that selling is the right thing to do?'

Logan held open the back door and indicated she should go ahead of him. Heading directly to the bathroom, she dropped the small bag containing Jonty's old dressing into the bin. Her head spun with retorts but she managed to keep the brakes on her tongue. He didn't—and wouldn't—have a clue how important a refuge this house was to her. Here, she was in charge and her opinion counted. Here, her family and her ex didn't tell her what to do with her days.

Back in the kitchen, she got out the bread and margarine, some hardboiled eggs and lettuce, and began making sandwiches. The clock didn't stop for Logan. She needed to get back to work.

When he parked his butt on the corner of the table, looking as if he had no intention of moving until he got his point across, she knew a moment of fear. What if he won this crazy battle and the house was sold out from under her? Would it be so bad to live in another house in Motueka? *Yes, it would.* Jonty wouldn't be next door, griping and grumbling at her while he watered her vegetables, or complaining that he hated boiled carrots more than tinned peas and yet eating every last mouthful on his plate whenever she cooked his dinner—which was most nights else he'd starve. He'd never learned to cook; his late wife had been old-school and believed that was her role.

Another argument against Logan's plan to sell was that the medical centre would have to shift. Or, worse, close down, forcing the patients she'd come to know to transfer to other centres.

Surreptitiously studying this stranger as she spread margarine, it shocked her to realise that he looked as though he belonged here. He had every right to be here. No denying that, much as she wanted to. But looking as if he fitted right in—that was too much to absorb. So she wouldn't. She'd carry on the fight in the hope that eventually she'd get it through his very handsome skull that she meant every word she uttered.

Starting with: 'You honestly think I should walk away from this?' She waved her hand in the direction of the surgery through the wall. 'Tell all the patients, "Sorry, but we're not interested in looking out for you any more"? People don't like change, Logan.'

'Are you sure it's not you that dislikes change?'

This man went straight for the heart of the matter every time.

She pretended she hadn't heard him. 'Especially the older folk. They know their doctor and nurse, and they trust them to know their backgrounds without having to delve into files for an answer about who their son is or where their grandchildren live. That sort of thing distresses them.'

'Except the current locum's only been here three months and plans on leaving within the next three. Where's the continuity in *that*?'

He didn't miss a trick, which sucked big-time.

'I won't change my mind.' Her voice was rising and she didn't care. This man riled her.

'I'm getting the picture.' He folded his arms over his chest, the movement diverting her gaze from his inscrutable face to those muscles that underscored the polo-necked jersey he wore.

'So am I,' she muttered, not quite sure whether she was referring to his stubbornness or his mouth-watering chest.

Either of them was a problem. Logan was nothing like his brother in physical shape or appearance. James had been of average height and had carried a bit more weight than was healthy. But he'd had an open face and oodles of kindness and generosity. She wasn't sure where Logan was with those characteristics.

'Where are you staying while you're in Motueka?'

'Here. That's if you don't kick me out on the street. I like the spare room at the back of the house.'

Wanting to say no to that idea didn't mean she could.

'There's no space to swing a cat in there.' It was tiny and filled with cartons that needed to be gone through. 'It's also an ice box, being so far from the fire in the lounge and the heat pump in the hall.'

But she knew nothing about this man.

'It will suit me perfectly.'

'What's wrong with the room next to Mickey's? It's bigger and warmer.'

Why make him comfortable? If he didn't like the room he might leave earlier than planned.

'I figure I'll be out of your hair down there.' His eyes zeroed in on the sandwich she was making. Avoiding eye contact? 'I noticed all the cartons. I'll shift them into the other bedroom after lunch.'

'They're full of James and Maria's personal belongings. I haven't had the gumption to go through them. Anyway, I thought you should be the one to deal with James's stuff.'

And I'll keep putting off sorting through Maria's until finally I can do it without instantly bursting into tears. If only I could throw everything away untouched.

'I probably should.' Logan sounded equally reluctant to tackle that issue. Which she couldn't fault.

'I'll try to get around to it before I head away again.'

Since Logan seemed intent on steamrollering her

opposition to selling they'd be at loggerheads the whole time and he'd probably be glad to leave sooner rather than later. Behind her back she crossed her fingers.

'The wardrobe's locked. It's the only way to keep the door from bursting open and spilling files and books across the room.' She tried one last time. 'You sure you don't want the other room?'

Those smoky grey eyes roamed the kitchen before returning to her. 'The small one's fine. Better than some places I've been lately.' He sucked a quick breath on that.

'I'll find some linen.'

'Karina, I don't expect you to run around after me. I'll make my own bed.'

'What *do* you expect of me, then?'

'To seriously consider my proposal to sell. In fact, you might as well come with me to see the real estate salesperson.'

'I what?' The knife slid out of her fingers and clattered onto the floor. 'Haven't you listened to anything I've said?'

'Have you listened to *me*?' he asked, in a cool, calm tone.

What would rattle this man? Except for those moments when his eyes had looked everywhere except at her he'd remained in control, no matter what she'd said. Which was warning enough. She knew controlled and controlling men better than most.

'I've heard every single crazy idea you've come up with so far!' she yelled.

Get a grip. This is not the way to deal with him. Think about Mickey. That's it. Sweet little man that he is, he needs you to bat for him, but sensibly, not like a shrew.

She tried to rein in her anger. 'Maybe it would be better if you stayed in the motel down the road.' It didn't come out quite as calmly as she'd hoped, but it was an improvement.

Logan remained perched on the edge of the table, totally unperturbed at her outburst. 'I want to have as much time as possible with Mickey before I head away again.'

She pounced. 'And when might that be?' Now she was repeating herself.

'Probably not as soon as you'd like.'

Did his lips twitch? She'd swear they had, which was kind of deflating . If she wanted to be treated fairly then she had to do likewise.

'I'm making one rule. We don't talk about selling while you're staying in this house.'

'Karina, apart from seeing Mickey and sorting out some legal stuff with the lawyers over James and Maria's wills, the only purpose of my visit is to sell. See it from my point of view. I can't do a thing to help you around the house when I'm overseas. If you're living in a new home I won't have to worry about that.'

'I see.'

He sounded too darned reasonable. Didn't mean she was prepared to change her mind, though. Was she being selfish? Not at all. For her, this wasn't about repairs and maintenance—it was about having a home. Not a house; a home. She'd had houses, mansions, and she knew how cold and impersonal they could be. She'd come to Motueka to turn around her life and find out what she really wanted for herself, and she had created a little world right here that would suit her for years to come. The thought that Logan wanted to take that away frightened her.

'I don't want you worrying about me. I'm not your concern. Only Mickey is.'

'The way I see it, if you're happy then so is my nephew.'

'Then you've nothing to worry about. I'm happy living right here.'

Her tummy tightened. *Huh? It's true. I am. Aren't I? I was until this morning. And I will be again, the moment Logan understands he's wrong about this.*

'And if you're really worried about the medical centre and the house, why don't you move here permanently? You could share in making Mickey happy. He'd love to have you around the place.'

Logan didn't bat an eyelid, didn't have a fit as he had earlier when she'd suggested the same thing. 'Give me some time to catch up on what happened with James, and get to know Mickey properly, and I'll postpone that appointment with the agent.'

'You're bribing me now?' She found a small smile for him. 'Stay one month and I'll listen to you at the end of that. I'm not saying I'll go along with your plans, but we'll discuss them then.'

And I'll spend that whole month showing you why you're wrong. I'll also be busy finding the funds to buy you out.

'Fine.'

Another twitch of those lips. Had he read her mind as easily as that?

Leaning back against the bench, Karina fought the need to study him while he stared at his feet. The expression on his lean face was sad and worried, as if he didn't know where to go with any of this after all. *Well, blow me over, rover. This guy has some serious issues.*

Folding her arms under her breasts, she tried to deny the compassion building up for him. She couldn't let it rule her head. Instead she needed to focus on what was best for Mickey. And then for her.

One thing was for sure: Logan Pascale would not be good for her. At all. Yes, but he would be great for one little boy who struggled to understand why his mum and dad didn't walk in through the door at the end of the day as they'd used to.

Logan wanted to laugh, which was a surprise in itself. Karina was as transparent as clear water. He knew he was going to be hounded over the coming weeks. He should go and book into a motel immediately. But he'd play the game. He'd only been in this house a couple of hours and already he didn't want to leave. The building was old and draughty, the windows rattled when the wind gusted, there was a bucket in the laundry, catching drips, and the carpets were threadbare. But, as Karina had said, it was a home—not just a house with two people rattling around in the vast spaces.

'Lunch is ready.' Karina pushed a plate laden with sandwiches across the bench towards him.

'Want me to get Mickey?'

She nodded. 'And Jonty.'

'Why am I not surprised?'

Filling the kettle, she shook her head at him, those curls flying around her face and causing his gut to clench.

'He looks after my gardens and hens and I give him some meals. Green dollars.'

'Yeah, sure. Nothing to do with a kind heart or friendship?' He couldn't resist winking as he stood up, ready to stride out of the kitchen.

What a woman. Too darned diverting for his own good. Mickey and his eager smiles had already caught at him, so throw in Karina with her exuberant, even fiery spirit and he was knocked off his feet. He hadn't experienced anything so normal in a long time. He didn't want to now.

In Africa he knew his role—understood that there were no long-term connections with his patients, the women he worked with, the places he lived and worked in. He was there simply to help people less fortunate than him who needed his medical skills. Plain and simple.

Apparently others had thought he could also provide a source of money for their militant operations. Their illegal activities. The militants had got the wrong end of things when they'd kidnapped him, believing he was the son of a wealthy English lord. That lucky guy had been whisked away to safety the moment the CEO of the African Health Organisation had realised what was going on.

No wonder this place felt like a slice of heaven with its everyday normality.

Logan knew he was being a pain in the proverbial by choosing a room that Karina obviously preferred him not to have, but it suited him perfectly. He might have explained that after sharing cramped quarters with his colleagues for as long as he had he relished the idea of having space to himself. What he wouldn't tell her was that he had to have privacy at night.

Sweat popped on his brow. Karina was right in that he should find a motel, only not for the reasons she'd been espousing. One night here and she'd be kicking him out anyway. Not to mention the awkward questions she'd be asking if he had his usual problems.

He focused on the mundane, hoping the other, darker thoughts bothering him would fade for a while.

Instead of going to get Mickey to come for lunch, he said, 'I was under the impression Mickey went to kindergarten all day?'

'He usually does, but a sore tummy kept him at home this morning.' Karina lifted one shoulder. 'After that puddle-jumping I'd say he's fit to go this afternoon.'

'Want me to drop him off?'

'Sure.'

'What time do you finish work?' he asked when he returned with Mickey and Jonty in tow.

'Five-thirty, give or take.'

'Then you come home to cook dinner?'

Karina nodded and smiled. That smile pushed the darkness inside him further back.

'I hope you're happy with risotto?'

'Sounds good to me.'

'Mickey usually gets dropped off at the surgery about four. If you want to spend time with him you can collect him then.'

Her smile expanded, sending a flood of heat right

down to the tips of his toes, heating all parts of his body on the way.

'He'd love that. You're family, Uncle Logan.'

His head dipped up and down in agreement as he swallowed the crazy need for her she'd inadvertently cranked up all too easily even while she'd been so ruthless in her comments about what he wanted to do to her haven. Again, Karina hadn't held back on pressuring him, but he was getting used to her forthrightness. If he used it wisely it could save them both a lot of the trouble that ducking and diving around their problems would cause.

'Mickey mightn't understand, but I'm right beside him all the way.' His mouth lifted into a small smile. A rare occurrence recently. 'But you have a point. I'm not used to small boys.'

'I'd have thought many of your patients would be small boys. Boys of any size and age, really.'

'I used to kick a football around in the dust with plenty of young lads, but somehow getting to know Mickey seems daunting.'

Terrifying, even. There wouldn't be any second chances. He had to get everything right from the get-go. There was a lot riding on that—things like Mickey living a happy childhood despite losing his parents.

Karina laughed, and it was as though the sun were in the room with them. Her face had that cheeky, fun quality she did so well. That wild hair was a riot of curls now that it had dried. What would it feel like to run his fingers through those coils? To feel them spring against the palms of his hands?

'Right,' she said. 'That's you sorted. Unless you'd prefer Mickey gives kindergarten a miss and stays with you?'

'What do four-year-olds like to do with their afternoons?' Damn, he hadn't meant to say that out loud.

'Believe me, Mickey will order you around and run you ragged.'

Did she have to look so pleased?

Unfortunately Karina's smug look had turned out to be justified. Logan grimaced as he sidestepped another spray of muddy water Mickey sent his way. What was it with small boys and puddles? The rain might have stopped hours ago, but the water swamping the lawns hadn't drained away and didn't look as if it would any time soon. Another problem that needed looking into. Like that hole in the driveway, which definitely had to be sorted.

'I want to see Karina.' Mickey stood before him, staring up with those eyes that reminded him so much of James.

James. His older brother. Logan's heart squeezed tight. They hadn't been close, but they'd always known the other was there if needed. Hence the guardianship thing. He'd been touched when James had asked him, yet he'd thought he should have asked Mum and Dad. Apparently they'd believed Mickey needed younger guardians. They also hadn't been comfortable at the prospect of living on remote Stewart Island with Mickey.

If he ever needed urgent medical attention, getting off the island wasn't as simple as getting on board a boat and starting the engine. Weather ruled down there. It was a place his parents had fallen in love with, and they'd moved there the moment he'd finished school. It wasn't a place he'd ever thought of as home.

Logan sure as hell hadn't expected to take up the role of guardian so soon, if ever. It was only supposed to be insurance—the kind you took out but never used. If he'd known what would happen only weeks later he'd have told James to find someone better suited. Not that his brother would have listened.

A small hand wrapped around his fingers. 'Karina's at work.'

'Yeah, buddy, I know. So we'll have to wait to see her.'

Mickey shook his head. 'No. I want to see her now. I need to go pee-pee.'

'I'll take you inside.'

Mickey's head turned from side to side. 'No. Got to go to work.' He began tugging at Logan's hand. 'Come on.'

A cheerful-looking man glanced up from the counter as they walked in the front door of the medical cen-tre. 'Hi, Mickey. Sounds like you've been having fun.' Then his gaze swooped to Logan. 'You must be Logan. I'm David Maxwell, the current locum. Sorry I missed you earlier.'

'Hey, good to meet you. I never had any intention of dragging you from your patients when I dropped by. I was just eyeing the set-up.' Logan held out his hand. 'This little guy wants the bathroom. Apparently you've got a better one than what's at home.'

David chuckled. 'What we've got is Karina.'

So Mickey and Karina had bonded completely. That was good for the little fellow. He was very lovable. Even after a few hours Logan knew leaving him again wouldn't be as easy as he'd expected.

'How does he cope when he's at kindergarten?'

Karina answered from another room. 'There are good days and there are not-so-good ones. His teacher's quite strict, but sometimes I go and get him and then he sits in here with me and his colouring-in book.'

'I need pee-pee, Karina!' the subject of their conversation yelled.

In the waiting area people laughed.

David grinned. 'You'd better hurry, Karina. It's looking a bit urgent out here.'

She appeared in an instant. 'Come on, Mickey.' Then over her shoulder she muttered to Logan in a very cheeky tone, 'Think you dodged a bullet?'

He shuddered. Karina's bullets would be comparatively harmless compared to the real thing. 'Apparently you're a dab hand at this.'

'You'll keep.' She flapped a hand at him before following Mickey down the hall.

'Keep?' David asked in a hopeful tone. 'You're not looking to hang around permanently, by any chance?'

Hating to disappoint another person already, he shrugged, but finally had to be honest. 'No, my contract's still running with the organisation I work for.'

'Motueka isn't just a quiet town in the back of beyond. There's always lots going on.'

That hope was fading.

'After the places I've been, it's fair heaving. If I ever did come back permanently I think I'd prefer living and working in a place like this. Big cities don't hold any attraction for me.'

If he ever came back? Why would he? What was here for him?

A little boy who had yet to call him Uncle? A boy who needed a man in his life?

A feminine laugh floated down the hall from the direction in which Karina had disappeared. Okay, there might be another attraction, but he couldn't change his life plan for a woman.

'Life plan? More of a total stuff-up.'

'Sorry?'

He'd forgotten David was still standing there, looking hopeful and resigned all at once. 'Talking to myself. Not a good look.'

'I guess you've got a lot to sort out at the moment, without me dumping the surgery problems on your shoulders. We can have a chat in a few days.' Then he looked worried. 'You will be here for a while, right?'

'Right.'

Exactly how long was 'a while'? This was another round of questions he wasn't dealing with very well. Harmless enquiries and yet they ratcheted up the tightness in his arm muscles, in his chest.

Glancing around, he saw people in the office, the waiting room, the hall: all innocent of anything but normality. Normality he struggled to fit into. By the toy box in the waiting room a toddler lunged for a wooden truck and shrieked at the top of his lungs.

Logan knew that the ear-piercing, gut-tearing sound came from the little boy. Knew it. But somewhere in his head he was hearing one of his fellow hostages as she was beaten, screaming her fear and rage and pain.

That same fear, rage and pain thumped at his temples.

Suddenly he was so tired he could barely stay upright. Exhaustion gripped him, drained his body of every drop of energy. Exhaustion that sleep would not fix. Only exercise might.

It was happening again. He couldn't blame jet lag. That might be compounding the debilitated state he found himself in, but it wasn't the cause. That remained back in Africa. In the form of dangerous men armed with machine guns and the inability to listen to reason. Men who thought the quickest way to riches was holding innocent people to ransom.

'Are you all right?'

David was staring at him with that same wary look he'd seen in his colleagues' eyes all too often since he'd been freed.

'I'm fine.' His voice rasped with tension. 'I need some fresh air. Tell Karina I've gone for a walk, will you?'

Tell her I'm sorry I'm leaving Mickey with her while she has to work. Tell her I apologise for coming here before I'd managed to quash the demons lurking in my skull.

He ran for the door.

CHAPTER FOUR

KARINA ROLLED OVER in bed and held her breath. Something had woken her. But what? The house creaked as usual, but otherwise everything seemed quiet. She must have been imagining things. Punching her pillow into shape, she curled up on her side and closed her eyes.

There it was again. A low moan—followed by a cry.

Slipping out from under the warm bedcovers, she shoved her feet into slippers and pushed her arms into her thick robe. Out in the hallway she listened for a minute but heard nothing. Had Mickey called out? Carefully opening his door, she checked him over but he was sound asleep.

Karina returned to her room as a cry cut through the quiet, lifting the hairs on her neck. It came from further down the hall. Logan? Had he fallen and hurt himself?

Outside his door, she hesitated. If the noise hadn't come from in there, she'd look a right idiot, bursting in and waking him. Leaning her ear to the door, she heard mutterings from the other side. It sounded as though the man talked in his sleep. She smiled. Who knew what she might learn if she felt inclined to listen in? Straightening up, she began to turn away. There was still that noise to check out.

'Don't touch me, you pig!' Logan shouted.

At least she presumed it was Logan, even though his voice was pitched higher than usual and filled with hate. Was that fear in those words? It sounded as if he needed help. What if someone else was in the room, attacking him?

Flinging the door wide, she flicked the light on and stared around the room. Nobody but Logan. He lay sprawled across the bed, the sheets wound around his legs, his arms thrashing against the mattress at either side of his hips. His skin glistened with sweat, and yet he was shivering. His eyes were wide, staring at the ceiling, then at her, then cruising the walls. Back to her. Not seeing her or seeing anything. As though he didn't know where he was.

'Who are you? Get out of my hut.'

Oh, my God, he's having a nightmare.

Wary of those flailing arms, she reached to touch his shoulder. 'Logan. Wake up. Logan. You're having a bad dream.'

She shook him gently. His arm swung up and out. Karina stepped back, felt his fist graze her thigh. This time she snatched at his arm, held it tight against her body, shook him as gently as possible.

'Logan. Wake up. It's Karina. You're in Motueka. You are safe.'

Was this the right thing to do? Should she be trying to bring him round more slowly? But how?

'Did you say Karina?' Logan blinked at her. Then

looked around the room, tried to peer past her. 'Where did you say I am?'

'You're at James's home. Remember? Where Mickey lives.'

In her tight grip his arm began relaxing, the tension slowly ebbing away as reality dawned in those gunmetal-grey eyes.

He said nothing, continued to stare at her, not quite believing her.

'Motueka. Mickey, Karina.' She enunciated slowly, clearly, hoping the significance of those words would reach him.

Did this have anything to do with his sudden mood change that afternoon? David had told her Logan had become agitated and taken off for a fast walk. When she'd asked him about it later he'd fobbed her off with some nonsense about needing fresh air. As if the air in the back yard where he'd been playing with Mickey had been stale and old?

Lowering his arm to his side, she spoke quietly, so as not to disturb him unduly. 'Logan, I'm going to cover you with the quilt. It's freezing in here and you've got goosebumps on your arms.'

He also had scars on his chest and his ribs were too close to the surface. Not enough muscle or fat covered him. As if he'd been ill. What had the nightmare been about? Was it linked to the state of his body? What would he do if she gave in to the need to hug him to her? To kiss away that pain darkening his eyes to the colour of cold slate? If she ran her fingertips over those purple lines on his skin, would he yell at her?

Carefully keeping an eye on him, in case he hadn't

completely returned to wakefulness, she retrieved the quilt from the floor and covered him right up to his chin. 'There you go. I'll flick the electric blanket on for a bit. It'll warm you faster.'

Logan wanted to curl up and die—or at least to hide under that quilt so Karina never saw his face again. He'd just blown everything. She'd never leave Mickey with him now. Not even for five minutes. She'd think he was a veritable nutcase, and she'd be right.

But hiding was pointless. She'd seen too much already. Next the questions would start. Why? When? How often did these nightmares occur? Questions he'd never answer. The shrink had told him they were part of the process and to accept them—to talk about them, even. Eventually they'd stop.

Eventually couldn't come soon enough. He was adamant he wouldn't talk about them. Especially not to Karina.

Slowly he raised his eyes to her face and saw nothing but concern glittering out at him. Concern for him? He did not want that, so he went on the attack and grabbed her hand. 'Did I yell out?'

She nodded. 'A couple of times.' Bending down, she fluffed around at the side of the bed until he heard the switch for the blanket click on. 'Don't worry about it. I always sleep with one ear open, listening for Mickey.'

'You didn't need to come into my room. I'm not exactly a child.'

He was upsetting her, but how else to divert those questions that must be burning her up?

Her usually open countenance shut down, and her

concern was withdrawn as her face tightened. 'I came in here because I thought maybe you'd fallen and needed help. That's all.'

'Can you turn the light off?' He dropped her hand as quickly as he'd caught it.

'Sure.'

The dark held all kinds of terrors but he needed to hide his eyes from her all-seeing gaze. Thankfully even with the light off the room was still partially lit from the hallway. Perfect, really. Half-light kept the demons at bay and saved what was left of his pride.

Karina asked from the doorway, 'Want a cup of tea?'

'No. Thanks.'

'I'm going to make one for myself.'

'Karina—' His tongue flicked across his lips. 'I apologise for any inconvenience.' He looked at the wall on the other side of the room. 'I don't know what happened.'

Lying didn't come easy, but what else was he supposed to do?

He wasn't fooling her at all. He'd bet his debatable sanity that she knew this wasn't the first nightmare he'd had. His recovery from this episode screamed *Been there, done that—often.*

Her smile returned, as it always did. If he'd learned anything about Karina since arriving it was that she smiled a lot. Except when she talked about her ex-husband.

'Sure you don't want a drink of some sort? Hot chocolate?'

Karina's voice penetrated his topsy-turvy mind, helped bring him further back to the here and now of the pokey room that was temporarily his bedroom until he could persuade this woman to sell.

'Treating me like one of Mickey's playmates now, are you?' The smile he gave was as false as most elderly people's teeth, but acting normally was beyond him at the moment. When she didn't answer, he said, forcing more lightness into his voice, 'Hot chocolate would be good. Three marshmallows this time.'

'Be back in a few minutes. Don't fall asleep while you're waiting.'

'That's not going to happen any time soon,' he muttered.

Experience told him he'd lie awake for hours, fighting sleep and the evil that waited there for him. Those scumbags had a lot to answer for.

The moment he was alone he hauled his aching body out of bed and pulled on jeans and a sweatshirt. He was cold, yes, but more than that he'd seen Karina's eyes slide across his chest. He'd seen her assessing the way his ribs poked out, seen her gaze stutter on those raw scars crisscrossing his torso. He did not need reminding of how he looked after weeks of surviving on one plate of gruel a day. He knew. He did not need to see the scars to remember the pain of being slapped with a machete. It had been weeks since he'd studied his body in a mirror. It would be months before he looked again.

God, his legs were wobbly. He sank back onto the bed, felt the warmth seeping up from the electric blanket. Luxury. A simple thing and yet he began to thaw, in his muscles and around his heart. *Thank you, Karina.* Maybe his wariness of people might take a backward step in this crazy, mixed-up home where genuine kindness was the order of the day.

Karina heard Logan poking at the fire in the lounge and took his chocolate drink and her mug of tea in there, careful not to switch on the main light as she entered. As much as the chocolate tempted her with its sweet smell she had to be kind to her hips occasionally.

'Here you go.' Placing the mug on top of the firebox, she turned to head back to bed. There were a million questions buzzing around her skull but she knew better than to voice them.

'Stay while you drink your tea…'

The hesitancy in Logan's voice spoke to her in a way his usual in-control tone could not have.

'Sure.' Sliding into one of the two armchairs placed at either side of the firebox, she leaned back and propped her feet on the wood basket. It was kind of cosy with the half-light and the quietness of the house. She loved night-time. The dark had always been her friend—like a child's comfort blanket. In the dark she made the most sense of all her problems.

Logan blew on his drink. 'I'll move to the motel tomorrow.'

He sat on the edge of the other chair, leaning his elbows on his knees, the mug held between both hands. The sweatshirt he'd pulled on might cover the chest that had drawn her attention all too easily, but even covered and in the semi-dark the view wasn't half bad.

'Stay here, Logan. The motel's proprietors won't make you hot chocolate at one in the morning.'

He chose not to answer. Did that mean he agreed

but hated to admit it? If so, then he was telling her the nightmare would reoccur.

'So...' She sipped her tea and looked to lighten the tension that was turning his knuckles white. 'Tomorrow being Wednesday, Mickey has gym time at three-thirty. Want to take him?'

'I guess I'll have mastered the pee-pee trick by then.'

'There's no trick. But you might have to be firm about not bringing him to me. He's taken to you quite quickly, but I'm still the main constant in his life. Anything new makes him seek me out.'

His smile was wan, but at least he tried. 'Is he likely to cause a scene if I insist on taking him to the bathroom?'

'Possibly. I can be there if you want. I take an hour off on Wednesday afternoons.'

'How do you do it? You don't appear to be asleep on your feet, yet you should be. You make me tired thinking about everything you manage to fit into your day. Did Mickey always go to kindergarten full-time?'

The questions were coming thick and fast—possibly in an attempt to distract himself from that nightmare.

She explained how things worked around here. 'It used to be mornings only, but now he's older and I'm working full-time, he goes all day. He loves socialising with other kids, and he has a best friend, William.'

'You said something about listening out for Mickey during the night. Does he wake a lot?'

'He's getting better. At first, after James and Maria died, he'd wake three and four times. Now it's barely that often in a week.'

Logan chewed his marshmallows and blew on his drink. 'I haven't had this since I was a kid.'

'It's one of those comfort drinks, isn't it?'

'Yes.'

Oh, cripes. He'd be thinking she was treating him the same way she did Mickey, when he had his waking moments. 'I didn't mean—'

'I like comfort drinks.'

'Good.'

What else could she say? Did he like comfort hugs? Sexy hugs?

Wash your mouth out, Karina Brown.

Why? She'd love nothing more than to feel those strong arms wrapped around her, holding her against that chest. Even looking out of condition, his chest tempted her—sad puppy that she was. It had been a long time since a man had held her because he cared about her.

Yeah, and if Logan did hold you, what then? You'd stand there pretending you weren't horny as hell? Because you would be. Parts of your body you'd forgotten existed are already heating up with desire.

No, she wouldn't have the strength to step back and pretend she could take or leave his hug. It would be impossible not to give in to the unusual sensations that had been assaulting her from the moment she'd first set eyes on him.

Logan asked, 'How do you feel about being a full-time caregiver to Mickey? It can't have been easy, stepping up when you were single and not used to parenthood.'

Right. So he wasn't thinking of anything hot and sexy.

Giving herself a mental shake, she answered the

question and ignored the other part of what he'd said. 'There wasn't time to think about it. I got the phone call about the accident and went immediately to collect Mickey from the babysitter they'd left him with that night. From that moment on I've been his mum. And dad. Surrogate, maybe, but there's no one else.'

He needed a real father on hand. A male role model. Preferably a permanent one who didn't disappear to the other side of the world for a year at a time.

'Your parents have visited twice, staying a few days. They're great with him.' And with her. Adele and Mark Pascale never made her feel uncomfortable about raising their grandson, instead encouraging her with everything.

'How did you feel when Maria and James asked you to be a guardian? Did you realise what it would entail?' Logan spoke softly, as if aware that he might be stepping outside the boundaries of where their relationship allowed him to go.

She could ask him the same question. The only difference being that he was family while she wasn't. It was a bit strange.

'At first I was shocked. Then I felt honoured. But, hey, I never expected I'd actually be stepping up to do it.' Even now, the fact that Maria and James had asked warmed her, especially on the days when she doubted her ability to do a good job. 'As to your other question— yes, I was fully aware of what looking after Mickey meant.' Another gulp of tea. 'I have never regretted signing those papers. Not once.'

'I didn't mean to suggest you might have. I apologise if you got the wrong idea.' Logan looked uncomfortable.

'Were you comparing my reaction to yours?' Might as well be blunt.

'I guess. It was easy to say yes because, like you, I believed I wouldn't be needed.' He locked his eyes on hers. 'I'm just being honest.'

Karina shook her head at him. 'You're a great uncle, even agreeing to look out for Mickey. I know James was thrilled. He knew you wouldn't say yes for the hell of it, that you'd have thought it through.'

'It's uncanny that they organised the guardianship only a few months before the accident.' Sadness leaked out of those eyes still focused on her.

'I understand a lot of parents do it these days.' Sadness gripped her as well. 'But you're right—the timing was impeccable.'

'Sounds like my brother. He never left anything to chance.'

At last he looked away, to stare at the wall again. He'd gone from a nightmare to talking about this. *Not good.* Time for her to lighten the mood or neither of them would get any sleep tonight.

'So, tomorrow you're going to gym practice, where the mums will love you.' Maybe she should tag along after all. Huh? Was she feeling a twinge of envy over other women enjoying Logan's company?

'Why?' He looked puzzled.

Didn't he get how good-looking he was? 'A new man in town never goes amiss.' She dropped her feet to the floor. 'Time I hit the sack.'

Logan's eyes widened, but thankfully he remained quiet.

Shoving herself upright, she headed for the door

and solitude. She needed to think about Logan and this funny hitch in her breathing whenever she looked at him.

She didn't want another man in her life. Ian had soured her for that, with his infidelity and his other family on the side; a family he'd seemed more tied to than her. She did owe him in a way, because he'd woken her up to herself and made her see how compliant she was to his demands, which in turn had made it easy for him to control her so thoroughly. Just like her dad had done all her life.

She'd become aware of what she wanted out of her life which was not a grand lifestyle, nor a career-driven one. She'd realised she wanted to earn her own way, make her own decisions whether they be about what to have for dinner or where to live. And here she was. Happy and being strong.

'Goodnight,' she called over her shoulder, and refused to acknowledge the fact that Logan was watching her as she fled the room. Refused to admit to that glimmer of heat that had lit up his eyes when she'd mentioned going to bed.

Neither of them needed to get close to the other. He obviously had more than enough problems of his own without adding her to the mix.

Knock, knock. 'Karina? Wake up.'

Karina dragged her eyes open. 'Logan?' *What now?* Had he had another nightmare? The bedside clock showed five-oh-five.

'Can I come in?'

Her door was already opening.

'Of course.'

Her thick brushed cotton pyjamas gave her all the decency she could wish for, and would definitely smother any residual heat he might have felt a few hours ago when she'd left him in the lounge.

She found her bedside light, flicked the switch, blinked in the sudden yellow glare. 'What's the problem?'

'We've got a patient waiting in the kitchen. Steve Garrett.'

'Steve? What's he gone and done this time?'

Logan handed her the robe from the end of her bed. 'Slipped on ice outside the fish factory and twisted his ankle. He was heading home after the night shift.'

'Ice?' Rain yesterday…frost today. 'At least we'll have a fine day.'

'He seems to be a bit of a toughie. Doesn't want to go to hospital for an X-ray.'

'That's Steve. Hates a fuss. He'll be wanting to get strapped up so as he can go home and get some sleep before he takes over looking after the kids while Faye goes to work.'

Shoving her freezing feet into her slippers she tightened the belt of her robe at her waist, picked up her cell phone and the keys to the surgery and headed for her door, brushing Logan's arm on her way past.

'Welcome to general medicine, Motueka style.'

Logan strode along beside her. 'I was surprised when I opened the door to his knocking.'

'How come you heard him and I didn't?' So much for thinking she was a light sleeper.

'I was still in the lounge.'

So he hadn't gone back to bed. 'Hope you kept the fire going. Eighty-year-old houses lose their heat real fast.'

Shouldn't have said that. He'd file that small piece of info away to bring out when their arguments over selling or not selling stalled.

Steve sat at the dining table, his face screwed in pain as he stared belligerently at his right foot. He looked up the moment they walked into the room. 'Sorry to barge in like this, but you know how it is.'

'Sure do. How are all those kids? Keeping you busy?'

'Running me ragged, more like. Can you strap this foot so's I can work tonight?' He straightened up on the chair, sucked in a sharp breath. 'I'm not feeling so flash.'

'What's not right? Something apart from your ankle?' She pulled out another chair. 'Put your foot on that.'

'My chest hurts when I breathe deep.'

'Tell us more about that tumble you took.' Logan picked up Steve's arm, placed his finger on his wrist and began taking a pulse.

'Not much to tell. One moment I was walking to the car, the next I was flat on my back. My right side's sore. Must've landed that way.'

'You didn't twist sideways? Hit your chest or shoulder?' Karina asked as Logan continued counting the pulse rate. 'You might've pulled a muscle around your ribs.'

'Could've. I don't know.' Steve held his breath as she began levering his boot off.

'Sorry. This is going to hurt a bit.'

'Just do it.'

Logan stopped counting. 'Pulse is fine. Let me look at your eyes. Pupils all good. Karina, can I get a stethoscope from the surgery? I'd like to be certain that we're only looking at a pulled intercostal muscle.'

'Let's move over there. We're going to need tape to strap this ankle anyway.' Karina crossed to the door that led through to the surgery and tugged the keys from her pocket. 'Leave this open in case Mickey calls out.'

'You really should have an X-ray,' Logan told Steve once they were settled in the nurse's room.

'I walked on it to get here, didn't I?'

'You call that walking? I've seen ducks crossing the road more elegantly than the way you hobbled through here.'

Karina opened the store cupboard to retrieve a roll of elasticised tape.

Logan nodded at Steve. 'I'm not going to ask how you got to the house. It's best I don't know that you drove that vehicle I heard pulling up at the gate minutes before you banged the front door down. But I'm thinking you're right—a broken bone would be giving you far more grief.'

Karina began winding the tape around Steve's swollen ankle and foot. 'If you change your mind, give the surgery a call and David will organise an X-ray in Nelson.'

'Pull your jersey and your shirt up,' Logan instructed when he'd found the stethoscope. He listened to Steve's heart, then gently felt his ribs and sternum. He was thorough and careful. 'Does it hurt when I touch here? Or here?'

Steve shook his head. 'No. Only when I breathe deep, so I'll give up breathing for a bit.'

'Good idea. Do you want some painkillers to see you through the day?' Logan put the stethoscope down on the desk.

'No, I'll be right, thanks, Doc.'

A small smile lifted the corners of Logan's mouth. 'You do realise that the treatment for a sprained ankle is to keep it raised for at least a couple of days?'

'Yeah, sure. No problem.'

Karina chuckled. 'Which means you'll carry on as usual.'

'You honestly think my kids are going to let me lounge around all day?' Steve shook his head at them. 'You have no idea. They'll be running wild within minutes if they know I can't catch them.'

Karina shivered in the doorway as she watched Logan walk down the drive with Steve, ready to grab him if he slipped again. Not that Logan would necessarily stay upright himself if that happened. Jack Frost had been heavy-handed this morning, leaving a thick layer of glistening ice. Mickey would have a blast later, jumping on all those puddles in the lawn to smash the ice layer on top.

Walking back to the kitchen, she looked down at herself and smiled. With her pyjamas and slippers she definitely didn't look elegant—something she'd used to be known for. Funny how in Auckland she'd never even owned a pair of pyjamas, preferring instead lacy negligees, and yet here she didn't care a scrap for anything that wasn't warm and practical for getting up to Mickey.

It went to show how removed from life as she'd

known it she'd become. Had she spent too long here, hiding away, not being forced to partake in that relentless round of socialising her family was famous for? Who cared? She was very happy with her lot.

She certainly didn't miss having to have her makeup on, her hair styled, and being dressed immaculately before Ian got up.

She heard the front door close. Logan had returned. She'd liked watching him in doctor mode: so gentle and careful, yet thorough. He could no more help himself when it came to looking out for someone than she could stop worrying about where to find those thousands of dollars she needed.

What had gone wrong to cause his nightmares? Because she knew as sure as she knew that Mickey was four that he'd had others. While he'd been distressed when she'd woken him, he hadn't been shocked. Once he'd come out of it he'd known what to do to get back to reality quickly.

If only there was a way she could help… But even if there was, Logan wouldn't let her near. He stood tall and proud, and just acknowledging that she'd witnessed him in that distressed state must be annoying the hell out of him.

Logan shook his head. Motueka wasn't the sleepy hollow he'd expected. He still couldn't get his head around Steve just knocking on the door, though it made sense in a roundabout way, with the only alternative being a long drive to the Nelson Emergency Department.

Steve had told him Karina had delivered their last baby after his wife's waters had broken while they were at the park. Karina had been there. The baby had been in a hurry and she'd stepped up.

'She's one in a million, Doc. Don't you go messing with her or talking her into leaving.'

He'd told Steve, 'I'm not taking Karina anywhere.'

Karina would never consider leaving Motueka. She didn't even want to shift to another house, warmer and easier to look after. In her mind Mickey belonged here.

What was it like, knowing where you'd be in twelve months' time? In twenty-four? What was it like waking up in the same house, with the same person, day in, day out, month after month? To feel safe all the time? He guessed he'd never know. Not while there were so many people who needed him back in Africa.

In the kitchen, Karina had switched the kettle on. 'Tea and toast, I reckon. It's not worth going back to bed now. Mr Grumpy will be over soon.'

A wave of guilt rolled through Logan. He'd been one reason she'd lost sleep. A motel for the rest of his stay would be best, but he couldn't find any enthusiasm for the idea.

'It's barely gone six. What's Jonty doing out and about at this hour?'

'He used to be an apple orchardist, and they're always up before the sparrows, especially in spraying season, when they need to be ahead of the wind. Old habits haven't gone away just because he's now living in town.'

She tugged the fridge open, peered inside.

'I guess…'

He still woke before four every morning himself, as he had in Africa. Back in New Zealand, in the deep of winter, he still couldn't get past that hour. If he went to sleep at all. Knowing no one would attack him in the middle of the night didn't mean he sometimes didn't lie awake, waiting for it to happen.

'I know it's early, but do you feel like poached eggs on toast? I've got the munchies.' Karina raised an eyebrow in his direction.

'I'm starving.'

Another habit he hadn't ditched: eating whenever he could because he didn't know when his next meal might turn up. The shrink he'd seen a few times after being released had told him that would eventually change back to normal, once his brain accepted that all the food he could possibly need was available any time he wanted it.

'Where do you put it all?' Karina asked, her eyes skating across his body.

Of course she'd seen him half naked and knew how thin he was under the loose sweatshirt.

He forced a grin. 'I got lucky when metabolisms were being handed out. Mine's fast and furious.'

'Sure.'

So she didn't believe him? *Sorry, that's the best you're going to get, lady.* But he'd give her a half-truth. 'Working in some of the places I do, you soon learn to grab whatever's on offer because there can be many hours between meals if it's chaotic—which it usually is.'

'Why Africa?' She collected eggs and bread, got out a pan and filled it with hot water and added a splash of vinegar. 'It's a long way from home.'

'I went to England first.' *Why had he said that?* 'My mum's English.' *Motor-mouth. Stop.* She'd met Mum, so would know that. 'I have a British passport and I decided to do some post-grad work in London.' *Oh, hell.*

'I didn't know that.'

Why would she? 'Don't tell me you and James never had any heart-to-hearts about his wayward brother?'

Her cheeks reddened, making her prettier than ever. 'He talked about you sometimes; usually after too many whiskies.'

'Ouch.' Logan sucked in air through gritted teeth.

Karina laid a hand on his shoulder. 'Don't take that as a poke for not being around. James knew you were doing what you loved.'

She looked so earnest, so concerned for him. Not to mention downright cute, all wrapped up in her thick robe and with those fluffy slippers that looked like stuffed possums on her feet. He felt his body tilting towards her, as if he were being drawn into a vortex. A vortex he had no idea how he'd get out of if he fell over the edge.

He pulled back a step. Then another. And soon there was enough distance between them for him to stop being so distracted.

She'd turned away to drop bread in the toaster. He watched her hungrily. Every movement, every breath. She was beautiful. Not so much in the traditional physical sense of the word, but in her heart. In the way she helped others, always giving, sharing, trying to allay anxieties. She'd smoothed away his guilt over James, for now at least. She was very dangerous to his equilibrium.

Another step back. 'Thank you for telling me that.'

'How many eggs?'

'Two.' He opened a cupboard and found the biggest array of tea he'd ever seen. 'Which flavour do you want?'

'Plain old gumboot variety, first thing.'

Her lips lifted into a soft smile. And turned his stomach into a riot. *Get over yourself. The woman only smiled, like she does with everyone.*

'Gumboot tea.' He dredged up a chuckle. 'My grandma used to call it that.'

'So did mine. She made pots of tea so stewed you could stand a spoon in it.' She shuddered.

'What time docs Mickey get up?'

'After seven. Fingers crossed.'

'It's all go from then on?'

'He's got more energy than I know what to do with. Thank goodness.'

'You worry about his health?'

He placed two mugs at the breakfast bar and went to the drawer to get the cutlery out. Why wouldn't she worry? She'd recently lost her best friend. She understood the precariousness of life. Was that the real reason why she didn't want to move? Had she hidden herself away here?

'Too much, probably. Down syndrome brings its own set of problems.' She winced. 'He's been lucky so far. I'm probably looking for trouble we don't need.'

Seemed that was second nature to her. 'I know he had to have heart surgery for Persistent Ductus Arteriosus soon after he was born. While James sat at Mickey's bedside he often emailed me about his terror that his boy wouldn't survive the after-effects of the operation.' He'd felt close to James then, wishing he could help in some way.

'Poor little mite. It must've been hideous. Thankfully there've been no lasting problems.'

'You could consider he's had his share of complications pertinent to the condition and now he's got a straight run ahead of him?'

Karina's eyes met his. 'You reckon? Not very medically technical, that approach.'

'No, and nor is worrying about what he *might* get.'

She smiled. 'Thank you. Glad to have you on my side. Now, enjoy your breakfast.'

'Kar—ina.' An ear-shattering yell came from down the hall. 'I'm up!'

Her eye roll was over-the-top and funny.

'So much for seven o'clock.' She pushed her breakfast aside and stood.

Logan leapt up and pressed a hand on her shoulder, pushed downwards until she sat. 'Let me get him. You eat your eggs.'

The surprise on her face was worth the million questions rolling through his tired brain about what to do with Mickey.

'Just give me a few pointers. Do I get him dressed for the day or are dressing gown and slippers all right for now?'

She shook her head as she smiled. 'Mickey will let you know.'

CHAPTER FIVE

ON HER WAY back to work after lunch two days later, Karina diverted to the driveway to take a nosy at the hole Logan had managed to make many times bigger than the mere nuisance it had previously been.

'What was wrong with filling it with some of that gravel piled out the back?'

'Don't interfere with a man's work,' Jonty growled as he struggled to shovel dirt into a barrow.

Logan stopped digging and wiped the back of his hand over his damp forehead. Why did he do that? It was diverting; it drew her gaze to his mud-smeared face. He looked exhausted and had done since first thing that morning, when she'd found him in the kitchen making porridge.

'Something I remember from childhood. Gran's oats covered in brown sugar and cream.'

When he'd smacked his lips she'd wanted to laugh, but the breath had hitched in her throat as his tongue had slid across his bottom lip. She'd had to turn away and look for the bread to make Mickey's toast, otherwise she'd have reached across and traced the outline of his mouth. That would have been just great for on-going relations.

As far as she knew he hadn't had a nightmare last night. But judging by the shadows under his eyes he must have sat up all night trying to hold them in abeyance. He couldn't keep doing that. She'd explain later that it was okay if he woke her. Not that he'd like that one little bit.

Logan caught her attention. 'There's a drainage problem that's caused seepage. That in turn has undermined the driveway. We're fixing it properly to prevent it happening again.'

What was wrong with it just being a hole that filled with water every time it rained?

'It's grown a bit bigger every time we've had heavy rain, but it's not like it's a huge problem.' *Yet.*

'Relax, Karina. Jonty and I'll get it sorted. It's not going to cost you a thing.'

So he knew where her real concern lay. Of course he did. Hadn't her visit to the bank been the subject of their very first conversation? 'Thanks.' *I think.*

Then Jonty got in on the act. 'When are you taking your car in for those tyres?'

Damn him for asking in front of Logan. Keep this up and Logan would be thinking she was too incompetent to be raising his nephew. If he didn't already.

'I'll get around to it over the next few days. No hurry.'

Except she needed to get the groceries in, and there was a trailer-load of firewood to be collected from Becca's brother's place.

Logan folded his hands across the end of the shovel

handle and dropped his chin on top. 'You shouldn't leave your car unroadworthy. What if something happens to Mickey? What if it's raining when you take him to gym practice?'

'Haven't you got a vehicle somewhere we could use? Don't tell me you came over by bus?'

'Yes, I have a rental four-wheel drive. It's parked outside the gate.'

She'd seen the vehicle by the kerbside for a few days but hadn't thought anything of it. 'Good. Have I got some chores for *you*!'

I'll ignore that smile that's got my knickers in a twist. What was it about this man that had her hormones sitting up and taking notice when she definitely didn't want to be interested? Who was in charge of her body's reactions anyway? Logan or her?

He shrugged and banged the shovel into the hole. 'Sure. Any time.'

Nothing wrong with his hormones, then.

Jonty had been standing there listening to this conversation, his eyes flicking between her and Logan, a hint of mischief in his gaze. As he opened his mouth, Karina wanted to put her hand across it to stop whatever he was about to say. But he surprised her into silence.

'Get your car along to the tyre shop on Greenwood Street tomorrow and my nephew will change the tyres.'

'I'll arrange a time later. Thanks, Jonty.' *After pay day next week.*

Jonty was pulling his cell out of his pocket and punching some numbers. 'Tomorrow,' he growled at her. 'Kevin—Karina's car needs some tyres for her warrant. Do it tomorrow, will you? Yep. I'll tell her. Put it

on my account.' Snap. The phone was off. 'He'll pick
it up before he opens at eight.'

'Jonty, you can't go paying for my tyres.' How embarrassing. Her eyes shifted sideways, locked with Logan's steady grey gaze. There was no condemnation
there, only understanding.

Jonty growled. 'I'll pay for whatever I like. Before
eight o'clock. Don't forget.'

'I won't.' She reached over and wrapped her arms
around the generous old man. 'Thank you so much.'

Jonty pulled out of her hug. 'Don't get all silly, girl.
It's only so as you can get supplies in for our dinners.'

She laughed. 'Then I'll make your favourite pudding
for tomorrow night.'

Logan paused with a shovelful of mud and stones.
'Can I ask what that might be?'

'Apple and raspberry pie with lashings of ice cream.'
She'd picked and frozen raspberries from the garden
during summer, so that there would be a steady stream
of pies over winter.

Logan winked at her. 'Vanilla ice cream?'

'If you're lucky,' she said. 'I'd better get to work before they send out a search party. Jonty?' She tapped
her friend's shoulder. 'I really do appreciate what you're
doing for me.'

'Get to work, girl, and stop your blathering.'

Jonty and Logan were laughing together as she
crossed the lawn. Now that he'd retired Jonty must miss
male companionship after years of employing many
local men.

Mickey seemed to have hit on the male bonding thing
too. It had been almost impossible to drag him away

from the men and inside for lunch. And when it had come time to go to kindergarten he'd refused, thrown a rare tantrum. That had startled Karina into giving in far too easily. She was torn between being consistent in her parenting and letting him spend time with Uncle Logan. Tomorrow she'd get him back on track.

Karina sighed away a sense of being on the outside of things. The guys were happy doing man stuff. Nothing to get her knickers in a knot about.

Walking into the clinic, Karina made for the nurses' room, only to pause at the door of David's consulting room. 'Hi. Are you all right?'

David was behind his desk, leaning with his forehead in his hands. The face he turned towards her was green. 'Not really.'

Crossing to him, she was startled to see his rubbish bin placed strategically at his feet. 'Want to throw up, do you?'

'Yep.'

'What else? A fever? Stomach cramps?' Her hand touched his forehead. 'You've got a temperature.'

'My kids came home from school the day before yesterday with the Ds and Vs. Guess they've passed it on.' He groaned and held his breath. Then said, 'It was so sudden. I was fine before lunch.'

'What did you have for lunch?'

'Pumpkin soup and toast.' He shook his head carefully. 'Not the culprit.'

'Guess not. You'd better go home and get into bed. If you stay here you'll pass it on to patients and staff.'

What about the patients he'd seen earlier? Had they already caught the bug?

'The waiting room's full.' David groaned again.

'I'll ask Logan to fill in for you. After I've phoned your wife to come get you.'

'She can't leave the kids home alone.' He reached for the bin and Karina stepped back as he heaved.

'Then I'll take you. Just stay in here until I get back.' She placed a box of antiseptic-infused tissues on the desk at his elbow. 'I'll be as quick as I can.'

Back outside, she called, 'Logan, we've got a problem. David's been taken ill and the patients are backing up already. Can you help out?'

He was a partner in the clinic, after all.

'Sure. Sorry, Jonty, we'll have to leave this for now.' Already Logan had placed the shovel on top of the wheelbarrow and was striding towards the house. 'Karina, tell David I'll be there in ten minutes. I need to clean up and change into something a little more presentable.'

'Mickey, you're going to have to go to kindy now. Uncle Logan's going to work.'

'No!' Mickey screamed, and ran to hide in the garden shed.

'What's that about?' Karina stared after him.

Logan shrugged. 'I'd say he's happier playing at home, that's all.'

Jonty headed for the shed. 'I'll sort him. You get him some clean clothes.'

Karina followed Logan to the back door. 'Can I use the four-wheel drive to take David home?'

'Keys are on my bed.' He sat on the top step at the back door to tug off the now filthy work boots that had used to belong to James. 'What's David's problem?' he asked as she stepped past him.

'Probably a twenty-four-hour tummy bug. He says his children came home with it two days ago. I did hear about something doing the rounds yesterday, but this is the first I've seen of it. I hope Mickey hasn't caught it from one of his playmates.'

'Nothing wrong with his energy levels all morning.' Logan stood up and went inside in his damp socks, leaving wet footprints on the clean vinyl of the laundry floor and all the way through the kitchen.

Karina pulled a face at his back. She'd washed the floors only that morning, before going to work, and now there was a trail of size-twelve outlines cutting across the middle of them. She guessed that was what having a man living in the house meant.

Mickey fought her as she removed his soiled clothing and pulled on a new set. 'Why can't I stay with Mr Grumpy?'

'Because I said so.' *Huh?* She glanced over her shoulder, looking for her mother, who'd used that exact expression and tone to her so often as she was growing up.

Wherever the words came from, they worked. Mickey quietened down and helped pull his sweatshirt on. When his head popped through the top she grabbed him into a hug, placed a hand on his forehead to check his temperature and gave him a kiss.

'That's my boy.'

When Karina returned to the medical centre after dropping David and Mickey at their destinations, she found everyone quietly waiting for their turn with Logan. According to Leeann, the receptionist, he'd

explained the situation to them and was now busy fa-
miliarising himself with the computer system in the
consulting room.

Leeann had made tea and coffee for those patients
who wanted it. 'Keeping them happy!' She grinned at
Karina.

'Go, you.'

She found Logan in David's room.

'Anything you need a hand with?' she asked.

'I can't find the lab forms.' His brow was furrowed,
making him look studious. He'd scrubbed up darned
well, looking very debonair in a crisp white shirt.

Leaning over his shoulder, she showed him which
file he needed and watched until he opened it. His hair,
hanging over his collar, was damp from his hurried
shower. He smelled of soap. How she managed not to
run her hand over his head she'd never know. Stepping
back quickly, she drew oxygen into her lungs and tried
to act as if she felt light-headed every day.

'Karina? You're not feeling ill, too?'

The concern in his tone would have been warming
if it hadn't embarrassed her because of what she was
thinking.

'I'm fine.' When he narrowed his eyes she sped to
the door and escape. 'Call me if you need anything.'

She'd be hiding in her room, folding towels and or-
dering swabs, hoping Logan didn't twig to her completely unprofessional behaviour.

To be reacting to a man at all was unusual for her.
To be doing so at work, when he'd stepped in for her
colleague, was wrong. Her phone rang, thankfully

diverting her from all thoughts of Logan and on to laboratory results.

The problem with that was hearing that young Sarah Griggs's haemoglobin was far too low, and the blood film suggested severe iron deficiency. Now Karina had to discuss this with Logan in between John Gainsborough getting a repeat prescription for statins and Colleen Murphy limping badly from a pulled muscle at the back of her knee after a rough netball game.

'The lab's running tests on Sarah's blood for iron levels and will send them through the moment they're ready,' she told him.

'With a haemoglobin of seventy she needs a blood transfusion, not to mention finding the cause of her anaemia.' Logan brought up Sarah's file on the screen. 'She doesn't appear to have any previous history of iron deficiency. I wonder what her diet's like? She seems too young for a bleeding ulcer, but it's not impossible.'

He ran through the options and asked a couple of questions about whom to contact at the hospital for follow-up tests.

After showing him the contacts list, Karina said, 'I'll tell your next patient there'll be another delay.'

Logan had to phone Sarah's mother pronto.

The afternoon progressed with everyone feeling they were continuously taking two steps forward and one back. By the time Logan saw his last patient out, Karina knew he was shattered. Those shadows under his eyes were now big black patches, while the lines defining the corners of his mouth appeared deeper. Her heart squeezed. Lack of sleep was catching up with him.

Quietly she said, 'Time to lock up and go see Mickey. He'll be beside himself with wanting to be with us.'

Jonty had collected him from kindy and was staying with him.

Logan's dark, thick eyebrows rose as if she'd made a blunder, but all he said was, 'I'm surprised he hasn't been banging the door down to get in here to find his Karina.'

'And his Uncle Logan.'

'He hasn't called me that yet. I doubt he understands the concept of what an uncle is.'

Karina nudged him towards the door. 'Let's get out of here before the phone rings again.'

It had been quiet for at least five minutes. Unbelievable.

Punching in the security code, she told him, 'Mickey knows more than you realise. James spent a lot of time explaining where you fitted into his family.'

'Of course he did. What was I thinking?'

He tried to stifle a yawn, but in the light flooding the yard from the high-intensity security lights Karina saw the telltale strain of his mouth and jaw.

She slipped her arm through his and headed for the back door. 'Roast chicken for dinner. Hope you like it?'

'Sounds delicious. I haven't had a roast for years.' He pressed her arm against his side. 'Why are we out here when you've got an internal door between the surgery and the private part of the house?'

'The insurance company demands that door stays locked. Anyway, I prefer keeping both domains separate. Home and work.'

'Fair enough.' He opened the back door and stepped back as Mickey rushed past him and leapt at her.

'Kar—ina, where've you been? I don't like kindy any more.'

Whoomph. Karina gasped and staggered backwards as a tornado of arms and legs wrapped around her. 'Sweetheart—steady.'

What was this about kindy? Usually he couldn't wait to get there.

'Careful, my boy.' Logan's hand spread across her back, pressing forward to keep her upright. 'You've got to be gentle with ladies.'

'He does?' She blinked up at the man and leaned harder against his warm hand.

He instantly dropped his arm and muttered, 'Basic training in the male-female relationship. Always look out for the lady.'

Thankfully Mickey squirmed to get down just then, distracting her so that she didn't have to think of a reply—if one was needed.

'Logan, can we dig some more on the drive?'

'It's *Uncle* Logan, Mickey. And no, it's too dark and cold to be outside. We'll get back to the job at the weekend.'

'I want to do it now.'

'No, Mickey, we can't.'

'Why not?'

'Because it's late and I'm tired.' Logan's jaw was tense.

Mickey stared at him. 'You have to go to bed.' Then he wandered away to watch TV.

Karina headed for the kitchen, tossing over her

shoulder at Logan, 'Go easy on him. He's still trying
to get his head around the concept that Mummy and
Daddy aren't here to play with him.'

He followed her. 'I'm a doctor, and I understand totally what's happened to them, and I still can't get my
head around it. James was thirty-seven, with a son to
live for. I'm two years younger and running solo. Life's
very unfair.'

'It's incomprehensible.' Without thinking she placed
her hand on his forearm, her fingers pressing into his
jersey-clad muscles. 'That's how it is at times.'

Logan leaned back to peer down at her. 'You haven't
had an easy time of things, have you? In your own life,
I mean?'

She couldn't answer around the tears suddenly blocking her throat so she backed away, opened the oven to
check on the chicken and the vegetables. Everything
was browning perfectly and the succulent smell of roast
meat filled the air. Thank goodness for oven timers.

Above her head, Logan murmured, 'I'll set the table.'

'Don't forget Jonty,' she managed.

He was in the lounge, watching the news and keeping an eye on the fire.

'Karina?' Logan hadn't moved away. 'I'm sorry if
I've inadvertently upset you.'

Closing the oven door, she headed for the freezer to
get a packet of peas. 'No problem.'

Where had those tears come from? It had been a long
while since she'd shed tears for her broken marriage.
Coming home after a hectic day at work, with Logan
beside her, Mickey eager to see her; all had conspired
to give her a sense of longing so deep it frightened her.

Longing for what she'd once thought she'd have with Ian. Longing to love someone, to be loved in return. A deep yearning for a baby. A family of her own. Which was plain stupid. She had a child—a boy who needed her so much it hurt at times. Mickey was her family.

'It's me who should be apologising. I don't know where that sadness came from.' *Liar.* She did know; but not why now, here, with Logan. She felt lost. She hadn't done lost for a long time.

Catching her elbow, Logan turned her to face him. 'Don't ever apologise for your emotions. Especially not to me. You are entitled to cry, to feel sad, angry, or whatever grips you at that moment. You don't always have to laugh and smile.'

His rare soft smile said he totally understood.

'Thank you.'

She had to push him away right now, this instant, because with every minute he was moving closer and closer to overtaking her heart.

She straightened her back and stomped to the pot drawer. 'That roast's calling.'

'My stomach just sat up in anticipation,' Logan said on his way past to the laundry with a dirty tea towel. Then he was back, asking, 'How long's the roof been leaking in that room?'

The stains on the ceiling were in varying shades of murky brown from the many times rain had come through. 'Since before I moved in.'

'I'll put that on the list of jobs to do.' He headed to the dining room.

Forget feeling lost—try angry.

'Put it on the list?' She snapped her fingers. 'Just like

that. Get the job done; tick it off the blasted list. Call the real estate agent, find a buyer, kick Mickey out of his home. Oh, no, you don't, Logan Pascale. No, you damn well don't.'

'Smells delicious.' Logan placed tablemats on the table, found cutlery and set out four glasses. He was beyond tired and knew if he didn't get some sleep tonight he'd be a basket case tomorrow.

There was no response. Karina seemed too busy stirring the gravy and holding a conversation with herself. What had got her all antsy now?

'Kar—ina. I want a hug,' Mickey demanded. 'I've been good.'

She spun around and her face lit up, banishing the unexpected anger blinking out of those big brown eyes. 'Come here.' Her lips softened into a smile as she hauled Mickey up into her arms.

Logan ached to wrap his arms around them both and hold them close. To protect them. Instead he stepped around them and headed for the room that was temporarily his bedroom to dump his wallet and phone. Their voices and laughter followed him down the hall.

Karina. He'd seen her pain in her tight body, heard it in her tear-filled voice, known it in the desolation echoing through her words. A broken marriage and the loss of Maria would have taken a toll. Throw in the added responsibility for a young boy who wasn't hers and no wonder she had her moments of feeling down. She came across as strong, but occasionally he glimpsed turmoil in her gaze. Was he adding to that by being here? By wanting to improve her situation in his own way?

Logan's hands curled into fists. He cursed the militants who'd kept him from returning in time for the joint funeral. He could have helped Karina—stood by her as she hurt.

He felt sweat beading his brow as once again he ran through the day he'd been kidnapped, searching for anything he could have done so that he might have made it back to New Zealand in time. Again there was no lightbulb moment to show how he could have done anything differently. Face it: with an Uzi jabbed into his back there really hadn't been any other way of reacting except to move in whatever direction he was ordered.

Which only made him more incapable than he'd believed he was. Unable to save himself or either of his colleagues who had also been dragged away to be dumped in huts in the most hostile place he'd ever had the misfortune to be.

'Uncle Logan, here's my storybook.'

Logan blinked, shook his head to block those hideous memories from becoming a full-blown storm in his brain, and dropped to his haunches to eyeball Mickey. 'What did you call me?'

'Uncle Logan. That's who you are.' The boy nodded seriously. 'My daddy's brother.'

'Yes, Mickey, I'm your uncle. How cool's that?' He held his hand up to high-five him. Mickey slapped him in return and warmth stole into Logan's heart for this tough little guy. 'It's cool being uncle and nephew.'

'Do it again.'

'What are we agreeing on this time?'

Mickey's small hand barely covered his palm. 'Everything.'

'I see there's some serious male bonding going on here.' Karina stood in the doorway. 'I hate to break up the fun, but Mickey, you need to wash your hands for dinner.'

'Come on, Uncle Logan. Wash your hands or Karina won't let you eat.'

'Does he get the bossy thing from you, by any chance?' Logan asked as he stood up.

She gave a wary smile. 'Of course.'

'Actually, I think he's got James's genes there.' He casually dropped an arm over her shoulders, half expecting her to pull away.

Which she did. Tugging free to move into the hallway, her face tightening.

'Karina? What's wrong?'

She was definitely going a bit remote on him.

'Not a thing. Truly,' she added when he locked eyes with her. 'I'm wondering how David's getting on and if he'll be at work tomorrow.'

He knew that was quick improvising, but if she wanted the subject changed he'd play the game. 'Why not leave him be? I'll cover for him until he's back on his feet.'

'You realise he'll be getting his hopes up that you might decide to stay on and take his place permanently?'

'When you tell David I'll cover for him again, you can throw in a bit about me heading back to my other job as soon as I'm fit enough.'

Damn, damn, damn. His mouth had got away on him.

'You're not fit?'

Of course she'd instantly pick up on his blunder. '"Worn out" is the non-technical term.'

Would he get away with that?

Her eyes filled with disappointment. 'Sure...' She shrugged. 'I guess it must be exhausting, working in extreme heat and without the usual backup that modern hospitals provide.'

He saw behind her attempt to get him to speak about his life in Africa. She wanted to know why he was unfit, why he had nightmares, why he wasn't rushing back to his job for the next few weeks.

'At least I get down time. Unlike you. You go from one job to the next, never taking time out for yourself.'

'Mickey isn't a job,' she snapped, the disappointment shadowing her eyes quickly replaced with annoyance. 'I'm a normal person, going to work at the medical centre and coming home to look after my boy and do the usual household chores.'

'You've made a haven here, but how long do you think you can go on living like this? Pretending it's normal? Because it's not, whichever way you look at it. You've had someone else's child thrust on you. You've got a medical surgery to keep running and you're not a doctor. And we won't even mention this house.'

Triple damn again. Talk about motor-mouth. Exhaustion did that to him time and again.

Karina snapped, 'You're a fine one to talk. Why do you spend your life in the remotest of locations? Out of touch with your family?'

She leaned back against the wall and folded her arms, pushing those tantalising breasts up and out. Breasts that were rising and falling rapidly as her breathing tempo ramped up. Breasts that pushed at the front of her white blouse and drew his gaze, making him temporarily forget what they were arguing about.

Her foot tapped the carpet. Logan shivered. For a guy who preferred his own company and didn't do heart-to-heart conversations, this strange sense of loss just because Karina had gone quiet on him as she waited for an explanation he couldn't give came out of left field.

She could have rubbed his nose in the fact that half the responsibilities around here were actually his. But she hadn't.

Lifting his eyes, he met her steady gaze. 'I left New Zealand because I didn't feel connected to anything or anyone.'

No, that wasn't one hundred per cent correct, and somehow he knew Karina would see through any attempts to gloss over things in his usual careless way. Unbelievable, but he found he didn't want to lose credibility with her.

'My family were all busy doing their own thing. I decided to go to London for post-grad work. That's where I heard about the African Health Organisation and immediately applied to work for them. Something clicked. I wanted to help people who were desperate. I've never gone without life's basics, and a part of me has always been about making sure others have the same advantages.'

Her stance softened a fraction. Those arms dropped to her sides and she straightened up again. 'You didn't think you'd be able to help people in your own country?'

'Of course I did. But on the African continent illness

and need is on such a huge scale. There's no welfare system for the poor and desperate.'

He pushed away from the bench he'd been leaning against.

'Shouldn't we be feeding Mickey and Jonty?'

'As opposed to telling each other a little about ourselves? Yes, you're probably right. But, Logan, I think you're wrong. There are many people in this country who could do with your skills.'

Logan didn't want to argue with her. 'I'll tell the others dinner's ready.'

He needed to get away from her for a moment—to break that thread of contact that had him telling her things he'd never talked about, not even to the shrink.

What was it about Karina that had him prattling on so much? She didn't need to know about his current situation. Nightmares excepted. She had enough of her own hassles to deal with.

Remember that next time your tongue starts getting away on you, Logan. Forget that at your peril.

Telling Karina the nitty-gritty of his life was allowing her too close—something neither of them needed.

So when he returned to the dining table with Mickey in hand he said something that would keep her at a distance. 'Have you ever thought about where you might like to live if this place sells?'

'Not once.'

'I hear there are some new subdivisions going on, with big homes being planned.'

'I've got a big home.'

Ice would have been warmer.

Logan deliberately dug a bigger hole. 'A sprawling,

ramshackle building that needs painting, insulating and refurbishing?'

'Mickey, don't put your knife in your mouth.' Karina watched the boy with an eagle eye, and totally ignored Logan.

Jonty concentrated entirely on eating, shovelling his food in as though he didn't know when he'd next eat.

Logan forked up a mouthful of chicken and mushroom and chewed thoughtfully. The problem with getting what he wanted was that it wouldn't necessarily make him any happier. Less so in this instance. He had pushed Karina away, but now he desperately wanted her back on side, laughing with him, not looking at him as if he intended stealing the roof from over the head of the person she loved.

His belly soured. He knew with absolute certainty that he'd hurt Karina if he carried on with his plan before coming up with a better idea for her future— one that suited her. Even he finally understood that she meant it when she said she wasn't leaving easily.

He had some serious thinking to do.

After dinner.

As a yawn opened his mouth he grimaced. Make that after a good night's sleep.

At least with this level of tiredness he should manage to sleep right through and not have a nightmare.

But then Jonty joined in, first banging his knife and fork down on his now empty plate, then asking, 'What are you up to, Pascale? Selling? Over my dead body, lad.'

Logan swallowed his mouthful. The day just kept on getting better and better.

CHAPTER SIX

'GET AWAY FROM ME,' Logan snarled.

The gun barrel was whipped across his back. Shafts of pain zapped through his body. No one believed in moderation around here. The only language these men used was violence.

'I need the toilet. Get it? Moron…' Logan muttered under his breath.

A large man shoved at his shoulder hard, so he stumbled against a tree. Pain grabbed his calf muscle, where a wound from a machete festered.

'Don't touch me!' Logan spat at his assailant.

A hand gripped his forearm, shook him. 'Logan.'

'Ah! You've finally learned my name. Leave me alone.'

'Logan.'

That pesky voice persisted.

'Logan, wake up. You're having a nightmare.'

What else could being used as a punch bag by these thugs be?

'It's me, Karina. You're safe. You're at James's house. Wake up.'

The shaking at his forearm grew stronger, more

insistent. He opened his eyes barely enough to see what was going on. Karina? A nightmare?

Reality slammed in. Another nightmare.

Slowly, slowly, the evil in his skull faded and he felt safe enough to open his eyes fully. Karina sat on a low stool beside his bed, her hand still holding his arm. Her lovely face oozed concern. In the half-light from the hall she appeared smaller, softer, less than the energy-packed woman she really was.

He shoved upwards to sit with his back against the pillow. Sweat rolled between his shoulder blades, poured from his brow into his eyes, the salt stinging.

'I got you up again.'

Her smile was blinding because it was for him. 'No, Mickey did that. He needed to go pee-pee. Too much water before he went to bed.'

'Thanks for waking me.'

He'd deliberately sat up most of the previous night so he'd be so tired tonight he wouldn't have a nightmare. Showed how much he knew.

'Want a hot chocolate?' asked the soft voice that banished the harsher ones in his head.

'Love one.'

'I'll be right back.'

Karina leapt up and headed for the kitchen, taking the warmth with her.

Logan shivered, ran his hands up and down his arms, trying to heat his icy skin. When that didn't work he scooped up his sweatshirt from the floor and pulled it on before finding his jeans. He was done with sleeping.

'Why are you getting up?' Karina asked from the doorway.

He glanced over his shoulder at her. 'I always do when this happens.'

Her eyes were wide as she stared at him. Make that as she stared at his backside, if the direction of her startled gaze was anything to go by. So she'd got an eyeful? Didn't look as if she thought the sight was too bad.

She lifted her head and locked on his eyes. Her cheeks heated up a cute shade of pink. 'Um…that milk will be ready.'

She was gone, her feet slapping the carpet as she ran down the hall. She'd left the milk heating unwatched? That was unlike Karina.

He followed, stopping when he saw her making her tea, not his chocolate. That sat waiting, ready, on the bench. So she hadn't left the milk where it could boil over.

The tension in his gut began backing off. He'd got under that smooth skin and tipped her world a little bit upside down. Cool. He liked that.

Whoa. No, he didn't. What had happened to staying clear of all involvement? Hadn't he talked himself through this earlier in the day? He could not afford to get close to Karina in any context of the word.

Pulling on an unemotional, uninvolved, just-a-friend kind of face, he picked up the mug of chocolate and watched as she dunked the teabag again and again.

'That's going to taste revolting if you keep mauling that bag.'

Flick. The teabag and the teaspoon landed in the sink. 'You should go back to bed with your drink. It might relax you enough to fall asleep.'

Exactly. He wasn't ready for another round with the guerrillas. 'Think I'll sit by the fire for a bit.'

Nodding, as if she'd expected him to say that, Karina headed for the big room. 'I'll throw some wood on the fire.'

Following slowly, he sipped his chocolate and watched the sway of her hips under that thick robe. He relaxed some more. She did that to him without even trying.

When she'd finished stoking the fire she turned to him with a smile and he said, 'I like it when you smile.' It warmed him and curled his toes. Not to mention tightened his groin.

The situation just kept getting more complex by the day. So he shouldn't now be running his finger down one of those bewitching pink cheeks.

'I'll make a deal with you. I'll smile more if you do. At least ten times a day.'

Putting his mug aside, he reached to cup her chin, tipped her head back further, all the better to see every expression flitting across her face. 'I don't smile enough?'

'Nope.' She'd stopped smiling. Instead she looked sad. For him?

He bent his head closer to that tantalising mouth, grazed his lips across hers. 'I'll try harder,' he murmured.

Karina whispered something he didn't catch as he touched her mouth with his, pressing harder this time. She obviously hadn't said stop, because right at this moment she was pushing her warm body against his hungry one.

He responded by increasing the pressure of his kiss, and when her mouth opened under his he slipped his tongue inside that sweet cavern and tasted her. When Karina danced her tongue across and around his mouth he lost all sense of everything except this wonderful woman his arms were suddenly wound around. She was exquisite: delicate yet strong, soft yet fiery, sweet yet acid.

A low growl slid across his bottom lip. Karina jerked back, taking that sumptuous mouth with her. Her eyes were filled with some strange emotion he didn't dare put a name to in case it echoed his own need. Her tongue traced her lips where moments ago his mouth had been, as though she was savouring him.

Then she tamped down hard on all his heat and the sensations racing through his body.

'Logan, we can't do this.'

'You're right—we can't.'

But they just had, and he wasn't ready to stop, no matter how sane and sensible that might be.

She continued as though he hadn't spoken. 'It won't solve a thing. Will make everything worse, if anything. We want different outcomes with this house, with Mickey's living arrangements, with my life. We need to keep talking, get to know each other so we understand where we're both coming from and where we're headed.'

She dropped into one of the armchairs.

Damn, she was so right in one way. But he sought oblivion from the nightmares and where better than in Karina's arms? Unfortunately it seemed Karina could haul the brakes on far easier than him.

'I was getting to know you just then.'

He sat opposite her. His mouth still felt the impression of her lips, still tasted her. Still wanted more of her.

Her face hardened. 'Don't be flip.'

'I wasn't. That's how I feel.'

'Tell me about your nightmares.'

Restless, he stood up to move closer to the fire. His skin still held a chill, his feet needed to be moving.

Karina sipped her tea, both hands wrapped around the mug. 'You said something about a gun the other night. Tonight you swore and mentioned going into your hut. You were very angry.'

She'd got that right. Angry and unable to do a damned thing about it. Not during the nightmare, nor when it had been for real. He'd been caught up in something so big it had been terrifying. The vulnerability he'd known had unnerved him. No wonder he got angry. That worried him. Sure, he could get fired up, like anyone, but it was always short-lived. It wasn't this gut-deep, almost out-of-control conflagration that consumed him.

Another sip of tea and she was saying quietly, 'Have you talked to someone about them?'

Them? The nightmares? Or the men who'd done this to him? The shrink had told him only time and talking would help. The horror was locked in his head, sometimes getting as far as his throat, where it blocked off all the words pushing to spew out. Except when he slept. Then he seemed to be able to articulate some of his anger.

'Yes.'

'Did it help?'

'No.'

Yet sitting here with Karina, watching her as she relaxed into her chair, he could feel the red-hot coils in his gut loosening, cooling. She'd done him more good than anyone else had.

The next words he uttered slipped out before he'd finished thinking them. 'You've got the biggest heart I've ever known.'

'That's one way of telling me to mind my own business.' After a long moment she said tiredly, 'I think it's time I tried to get some sleep.'

As in going to bed. Her bed. Alone. Where he couldn't hold her or kiss her. Wise woman.

'Karina?' he called softly as she reached the door. 'I'm not ready to talk. Yet.'

But maybe the day would come when he could—with her.

Karina slid into bed and punched the pillow so it would mould around her neck and keep the cool air out. Closing her eyes, she waited for the sleep she doubted was there for her.

She'd pushed Logan too hard with her questions, as though his kiss had given her the right. Her fingertip outlined her bottom lip. *Why did I stop kissing him?*

Because there was too much between them—too much in his past, too much everything—to be getting so close to each other. Because, for her, a kiss was more than a smacking of lips. Kissing a man meant something. That man had to touch her in some indefinable way—and Logan did exactly that.

Considering her stance on men these days, her reaction didn't fit with her need to be independent. And from the few things he'd let slip she doubted Logan wanted a long-term relationship.

His silences were full of stop signals, and yet she kept finding another question to ask, and another. The guy hurt so badly at times that the pain poured out of him. When he came out of those nightmares his eyes glittered with anger and fear and vulnerability. He'd hate it that she saw the vulnerability. He was a man's man. He took pride in his strength, wouldn't expect to be bested by anyone. Yet she knew someone had got the better of him.

Who? Why? Where? In Africa, obviously, because he'd only been back in New Zealand a week and this wasn't new. He had the jaded appearance of a man who'd been through these nightmares many times.

From that blank expression when she'd asked about them, she wasn't about to find out anything enlightening any time soon, if at all. Everyone was entitled to privacy, but her heart ached to be able to share, to take away some of that pain.

Not going to happen.

And that kiss…? Her lips softened as her forefinger again traced their outline. As far as kisses went it hadn't been earth-shattering, but it had been damned close. Logan's mouth on hers had warmed her right to the tips of her toes and made her happy. And excited. For someone intent on a solo life her world had been tipped sideways in a very disturbing way.

'Kar—ina.'

Mickey.

She sighed as she shoved herself out of bed and groped around in the dark for her slippers and dressing gown. Mickey was quite capable of going to the bathroom on his own. The hall nightlight kept darkness at bay.

'Coming, sweetheart,' she called quietly.

'I need pee-pee.' Mickey was rubbing his eyes with his fists and looking absolutely adorable when she flicked his bedside light on.

'You'll have to cut back on drinks before bedtime if you're going to keep waking up like this.'

Once in the bathroom, Mickey was happy for her to go and straighten up the mess that was his bed. A restless sleeper, Mickey always managed to tangle his sheets and duvet, and to lose his pillow down behind the headboard.

'I'm finished.' Mickey appeared at her side. 'I want a drink of water.'

'Not a good idea. You'll want to go pee-pee again.'

'I'm thirsty.'

'How thirsty?' She felt his brow. No temperature. His face was its usual colour. Had he contracted that tummy bug? 'Do you feel all right?'

'Yes, very good. Can I have my water now?'

'Get into bed and I'll get it. A very small glass.'

Along the hall she peeked into the lounge and spied Logan, sprawled out in the armchair, those long legs stretched close to the firebox. A gentle snoring filled the quiet.

'Not returning to your bed again?' she whispered. 'Is this your way of fighting the nightmare's return?'

What would he do if she kissed his cheek or brow, like she did Mickey? She'd never know.

Returning to Mickey's room, she found him sound

asleep. Tucking the sheets up over his shoulders, she gazed down at him. He was so cute it broke her heart. So far he hadn't had to deal with any trouble from other kids about his Down syndrome, but the day would come and she wanted him to be strong and happy, so that he could cope with any teasing he might encounter.

Back in bed, she let her worries about finding the money to buy out Logan fill her mind. What with David getting ill and the surgery overly busy, she hadn't got around to phoning any other banks to make appointments with their managers. She'd start first thing in the morning. If that failed she'd have to come up with another solution.

Like what? her brain taunted.

The most obvious answer would be to call her father and tell him she would use some of her trust fund after all. But, despite having a sensible reason to do that, she wouldn't. It would be tantamount to admitting she couldn't manage without her family's wealth. No. She'd find another way.

'Pee-pee, Karina.'

Alarm bells began beeping. Mickey used to have urinary infections regularly, but not lately. Three times in one night was not like him. Did he have an infection? Poor little man didn't deserve one.

It was nearly six and there didn't seem any point trying to snaffle half an hour's shut-eye. In the kitchen she made a cup of tea and sat at the table, opening yesterday's mail. The power bill was higher than usual, but then she did use the clothes dryer during winter. The rates bill was there. Thank goodness for Jonty taking care of her tyres. He'd saved her heaps.

Maybe Mr Bank Manager did have a point. She *wasn't* a good risk for a loan. But she could and would always pay her way, no matter how hard it got. Coming from a background of endless money to spend on absolutely anything that took her fancy, learning to save should have been difficult for her, but it hadn't. In Motueka she didn't need loads of new clothes, didn't go tripping off on exotic holidays. Life had become simple, and she loved it.

Sure, there had been days when it had frustrated her that she couldn't just hop on a plane to somewhere warm, or cool, or whatever her mood wanted at the time. But she'd soon learned she didn't need any of that to make her feel good about herself. Realising that Ian had had too much control over her and she was now free had done that.

But right now she did need money, and she wasn't as free she'd like. She was tied to doing what Logan expected if she didn't find that pot of gold, didn't make him see there were other solutions than the one he was hell-bent on.

'Hey, you're up early.' Logan strolled into the room, looking all mussed up.

'I think Mickey's got a urinary infection. He's been up to the bathroom three times.'

'I'll check him over when he next wakes up. He hasn't got a fever, has he?'

She shook her head. 'Didn't seem to.'

'Has he had an infection before?'

'A while back.'

'Okay.' Logan filled the kettle and spooned instant coffee into a mug.

Karina watched him from under lowered eyelids. He'd easily made himself at home. Did that come from living and working in so many different locations? Would he fit in anywhere? Or was it because this was the nearest to his own home he had? If so, did that indicate he might change his mind about selling?

That would mean having him in the house more often. Could she remain impervious to him then? Would she be able to turn away when her mouth cried out to be kissed? When the heat spreading down her body demanded physical release?

She doubted it. So he had to sell to her.

She eyeballed the man causing these problems. 'Would you give your share of this place to me as a loan? I'd get proper papers drawn up and make regular payments into your account.'

Did she have to sound like she was begging? Yeah, she did—because she was.

Logan straddled a chair and studied her. Probably trying to go from Mickey's pee-pee problem to could he lend her a few hundred thousand dollars within minutes.

Huffing out the breath she'd been holding, she started again. 'Of course I don't know your circumstances, but if you don't need the funds you'd get from selling, then it makes sense for you to lend it to me. A win-win answer.'

'When did you come up with this idea?'

Heat crept into her cheeks. 'Just now.'

'So you haven't thought it through?'

'What's there to think about? A loan with you is no different to a loan with the bank. I'd pay the going interest rate.'

That gorgeous mouth she'd kissed last night actually

softened into a small smile as he kept on watching her. 'Why did the bank turn you down?'

'None of your business.'

Except it was if she wanted to borrow from him.

'Sorry, I take that back. I think the manager didn't like me, or he has a thing against lending to women. I have a small nest egg that I try not to touch except in dire emergencies.' She'd managed to save some of her wages before she'd moved in with Mickey. A deep breath in. 'But the account I use for day-to-day expenses is kind of empty.'

'Explain "empty".' That smile hadn't disappeared. Yet.

'My wages from the medical centre go in every fortnight and by the time the next pay day comes round I've used most of it. If not all of it.'

'What about the weekly amount from James and Maria's estate to cover Mickey's expenses?'

'The lawyers told me I'd have to wait for that until probate had been finalised.'

'That was done a month ago.' Logan's eyebrows rose in a disconcerting fashion and his mouth flattened with annoyance. 'You weren't told that?'

'I thought the lawyers would phone, or at least send a letter about it. It's hard. I don't want to seem to be waiting for James and Maria's money. It's not like Mickey's going without anything. The lawyers might think I'm a greedy cow if I ask.'

She'd made a vow never, ever to ask for money again and that meant from anybody. Unless it was a loan.

'Why am I not surprised at that answer?' The

annoyance vanished and Logan's mouth widened into a heart-stopping smile, astonishing her.

'You think I'm a push-over, don't you?'

'You're a dedicated, big-hearted, caring woman who puts everyone before herself. Nothing wrong with that. But you also have to be practical. James would be angry if he knew you weren't getting the funds available.'

Did he have to sound so reasonable?

'It's not about whether you think you can manage. James can't be here for Mickey, but he made damned sure he could provide for him in the advent of a disaster happening—as it did.'

'I hadn't thought of it like that.'

'I'll get on to the lawyers today.'

His tone told her that those lawyers were going to wish they'd been paying her for weeks.

'Thanks.'

This conversation hadn't resolved the house sale issue, but she knew when to stop pushing. There were still more than three weeks to come up with a solution.

Standing up, she placed her mug in the sink. 'Time I got ready for the day.'

Logan stood up too. His knuckles under her chin tipped her head back, so she had to look directly at him. 'About me lending you the money...? I didn't say no. Or yes. But if I do agree I won't be asking you to pay me any interest.'

Her mouth fell open. Not a pretty sight. 'But—'

His thumb slid across her jaw. 'We're supposed to be waiting a month before discussing what's happening with this place, remember?'

Sucker punch me, why don't you?

'You're right. I made that request. I guess I'd better stick to it.'

'One other thing, Karina. Have you thought about what you'll do when you meet someone you want to marry? Would you expect him to fall in with your plan to live here for the foreseeable future?'

'Me? Get married again?' She pulled away from that tender thumb to gape at the man. 'That *so* is not going to happen.'

'Come on. You can't know that. What if you meet someone tomorrow and fall in love? You're telling me you won't want to get married again? Or at least have a live-in relationship with him?'

Disbelief glittered out at her.

'That's exactly what I'm saying.'

'Your marriage break-up must have been horrendous for you to still feel like that.'

He stood watching her. Seeing what?

'It broke my heart.' *And it made me think hard about myself.*

'I guess that's not easily forgiven or forgotten.'

'No, but I don't blame him for everything. I let him control my life just as my father had conditioned me to do.'

Genuine kindness showed in Logan's eyes, causing a small lump in her throat that she had to clear before continuing.

'I come from money; went to the best schools, became a fashion icon, had the society wedding. All for nothing.'

Now Logan looked confused. 'So why are you trying to raise money from the bank to buy me out?'

'I walked away from it all.'

As his mouth opened with what was probably another question she held her hand up to stop him.

'What Ian did was wrong. But there was a silver lining in a convoluted way. I'd trained as a nurse but never got to put it into practice. I'd had my fun, but then it was time to fit in with the family line and become the perfect wife and hostess. My sister revels in all that.'

'You never did?'

'That's why I can't hold it against anyone. I always complied, but the day I learned of Ian's duplicity I learned there was more to me. A part I'd never explored. The person I wanted to become. And here I am.'

'I'm more than impressed. It must've taken a lot of guts. But that's no surprise. You've got that in spades.'

Her head jerked back a notch. 'Thank you.'

His simple yet empowering statement went a long way to reminding her that, yes, she *was* strong—could do whatever she had to for Mickey. Which meant fighting this man to keep Mickey's home.

Ironic, really.

'I'm glad you told me. It helps—'

'Kar—ina, I peed in my bed.'

She winced. 'Nothing like a dose of reality to get the day moving.'

'Go have your shower. I'll take care of this.'

Logan headed for Mickey's room, not pausing to see if she agreed.

She couldn't fault him, really. Except for one thing. He liked being in charge, too. Then again… Her fingers touched her lips where he'd kissed her last night. He was nothing like her ex at all.

CHAPTER SEVEN

'I DON'T WANT to use the potty.' Mickey stamped his foot on the bathroom floor.

Karina ached to pick him up for a cuddle, but that wouldn't help get the urine sample she needed to send to the lab. 'I need you to.'

There was a knock on the door and Logan asked, 'Can I help?'

'Yes.' Maybe Mickey would listen to him. 'I've got a problem.'

'So I heard.'

Logan's smile lightened the tension in her tummy.

'Along with everyone else in the street.' He hunkered down to Mickey's level. 'Hey, buddy, I want you to do your pee-pee in the potty this time so I can get it tested. If I don't do that then we can't make you better. Understand?'

'But I'm big.'

'Yeah, I know. But sometimes even big boys have to do this.'

'What about you?' Mickey eyed him suspiciously.

'Yeah, if I had to.'

'I don't want Karina watching.'

Phew. Progress. 'I'm out of here. See you over at the medical centre in ten. Mickey, Mr Grumpy's taking you to kindy. Be good for him, please.'

'What's that lad yelling about this morning? Doesn't he know he's got a quiet button?' Jonty stood on the back porch with his car keys dangling from his fingers.

Karina grinned. 'Good luck with that. Logan's getting him sorted.'

'You all right? You've got black puffy bits under your eyes.'

'Charming.' She'd applied more layers of make-up than sensible this morning, and obviously they hadn't hidden a thing. 'Bit of a sleepless night.'

'I saw the lights on during the night. Everything all right?' he asked.

Telling him about Logan's nightmares wasn't an option, but… 'You've got a rollaway bed in your back bedroom, haven't you?' She'd seen it when she'd been over at his house one time.

'Want it?'

'Can I borrow it for a few weeks?'

'I can only sleep in one bed at a time.'

'Thanks, you're a treasure. I'll get Leeann to help me carry it over at lunchtime.' She wasn't having Jonty lift it. He'd argue, but sometimes he had to remember he was eighty-two.

'Tell Logan to do it. He might need fattening up, but he's a man under those fancy shirts he wears.' Jonty stomped down the steps. 'Going to give those ruddy hens a talking-to. Only got six eggs this morning. Stupid females.'

That was why she loved Mr Grumpy. She never knew

what was going to come out of his mouth next, but it would always be entertaining.

'I'll sort the bed.'

No way would she ask Logan to get it. He'd want to know why and then he'd refuse, saying it was totally unnecessary. But now she'd got the idea of setting a bed up for him in the lounge, she wasn't backing off. Next time he had a nightmare and wanted to sit by the fire he'd be able to lie down and hopefully fall asleep. He'd argue, but if the bed was in place and made up, then there was nothing he could do except ignore it. Which, when she thought about it, was exactly what he'd do.

'Can't say I don't try.'

Ice cracked under her shoes as she carried the washing basket to the line. She tipped her head back and the clear blue sky made her smile. It was going to be a cracker of a day, even if she was wearing thermals and thick tights.

By the time she'd hung the washing Mickey was calling from the porch. 'Can I knock on the washing?'

She felt the first towel she'd hung up. 'It's not hard yet. Give it a bit longer.'

'Here I come! Watch me, Karina.'

Mickey loved it when the washing froze solid on the line. And, honestly, she'd been excited the first time it had happened. They didn't have frosts like that in Auckland. Maria had laughed at her for getting so excited, calling her a big kid.

Maria. 'I miss you,' she said out loud. 'If only you were here to help me sort out what I'll do if Logan gets his way with the house.'

But then if she were here, the problem wouldn't exist.

Air caught in her chest as Mickey slid towards her. She whispered to Maria, 'Your boy is growing taller every day. You'd be so proud of him.'

She smudged an errant tear off her cheek, and probably wrecked her make-up.

'Knock-knock, who's there?' she asked Mickey.

'Jack Frost,' he answered as his little knuckles tapped a towel, then a pillowcase. 'He hasn't done it right.'

Karina laughed despite her sadness. 'Give him a chance. The washing's only been hanging a few minutes.'

'What's so fascinating about the washing?' Logan asked as he approached, looking heart-stoppingly gorgeous in a blue-and-white checked shirt and the navy jersey he must have bought when he'd arrived back in the country.

Should she tell him that the price tag and garment label were hanging down his back? Nah, not yet.

'This isn't any old washing, is it, Mickey?'

In a rush of words Mickey explained about the knock-knock game, and looked disappointed when he couldn't demonstrate what he meant.

'Come on, Uncle Logan. I want to break some ice.' He ran towards a frozen puddle.

Karina watched him and a big sigh puffed across her lips. 'I love that boy so much it scares me.'

Logan took her elbow and turned her in the other direction. 'I know. It's apparent in everything you do with him. He's very lucky he's got you.'

'He'd have been luckier still if he hadn't needed me. Or you.' *Sniff. God, don't cry now—not when Logan's right beside you.*

'Hard, isn't it?' His fingertips pressed gently into the crease of her elbow. 'You're surrounded by memories of Maria. What's good for Mickey isn't easy for you.'

Did he have to be so accurate? How the hell was she supposed not to cry now?

By sucking it up, breathing deeply and concentrating on that crack in the path until this moment of self-pity faded. That was how. She shouldn't be feeling sorry for herself. She was alive and well, and she had Mickey to care for. And she was tough. Or getting there, anyway.

Logan murmured, 'You're allowed to have down days.'

'Sure.'

But why today? Why now, when she'd just been laughing with Mickey? Why this moment, when Logan knew exactly what was going on?

He was too damned kind and understanding, despite his determination to do things his way. He was getting to her. In ways she'd never expected any man to reach her again. He was reminding her that her body was capable of loving a man, of being loved back. Unfortunately it couldn't be Logan who'd break through her barricades. He was on a mission. And while it included her, that was only to make sure his nephew's life ran smoothly. And his.

Tugging her elbow free, she stepped away, putting space between them while avoiding his all-seeing gaze. Somehow she managed to dredge up a smile that gave away nothing of what she really felt.

'You're supposed to cut the labels off a jersey before you wear it.'

Leaning towards her, he ran a finger along her jaw, making her gasp as shivers ran through her.

'Can I trust you with the scissors when we get inside?'

Wiggling a splayed hand back and forth, she said, 'You won't know until I'm done.'

Then she all but ran for the surgery, determined to get away from that vexing finger that had sent heat to her core, melted her in ways she'd never melted for any man before. Not even Ian.

The waiting room was overflowing with patients.

'Seems we've got an epidemic on our hands,' she said.

'The phone hasn't stopped ringing since I unlocked the door,' Leeann told them. 'The stomach bug's responsible for about a quarter of today's appointments, and the flu's doing the rounds.'

Karina groaned as she delved into one of Leeann's drawers for scissors. 'Fingers crossed none of us catch any of these things.'

Leeann said, 'I take it David's not coming in today?'

Logan answered her. 'I told him to stay home. He's over the worst and just needs to get around to eating again, but no point in him rushing back. I'm happy to work another day, and then he's got the weekend to fully recover.'

Another day working with Logan. That wasn't so good for her equilibrium. This attraction she felt for him tended to trip her up.

Deal with it. Be professional. It's only for one more day.

Yeah, and then they'd go home together, eat dinner with Mickey and watch TV until bedtime. Very cosy.

The end of the month couldn't come fast enough, so she could get him out of her system and on his way. If only she didn't need to delay the situation about the house. Which reminded her...

'I've got to make some phone calls.'

Karina headed to her room and began dialling. She'd try all the banks before considering fishnet stockings, a minuscule black leather skirt and a walk along the wharf after dinner.

With two appointments arranged for early next week she headed out to the waiting room.

'Robyn Jenkins? Come through.'

Robyn was instantly on her feet and following Karina to the nurse's room. 'Thanks for putting me first. I'm going to be late for school as it is.'

'How's William? I'd intended ringing to see if he could come and play last weekend, but something always cropped up.'

Robyn's son William and Mickey went to the same kindergarten and loved playing together.

Robyn shook her head, then groaned.

'What's up?'

'Nothing. A bit of a headache.'

Karina studied the thirty-nine-year-old as she took a seat. Robyn was here for her regular blood pressure check-up. 'Where's this headache?'

'Behind my left eye.' Robyn rolled up her sleeve, ready to have her blood pressure read. 'Is Mickey enjoying kindy?'

'I think so.'

I don't want to go to kindy.

'William can't stop talking about Ben.'

'Ben?' Karina asked.

'The new boy,' Robyn explained. 'He joined a few weeks ago and William seems very taken with him.'

Maybe that explained Mickey's not wanting to go to kindergarten. William had a new friend and Mickey felt left out. It was inevitable, Karina supposed. William was highly intelligent for a young boy, whereas Mickey had learning difficulties.

The relief at finding a possible reason for Mickey's angst about kindy was enormous.

'Right, Robyn, how long have you had this headache?'

'Since before I left home.'

'What about your eyesight? Any blurriness? Double vision?'

Robyn started looking worried. 'Funny you ask that. I had to keep blinking to see properly as I parked the car. I'm not seeing too straight now either. The headache's getting worse. Like *bad*.'

Karina didn't want to panic Robyn. 'Stay there. I won't be a moment.'

At Logan's door she knocked.

'You're needed urgently.'

Logan joined her immediately. 'What's up?'

Quickly filling him in, she asked, 'Could it be a brain aneurysm?'

'It's possible. What's her history?'

'High blood pressure treated with statins. I'll read her BP now.'

Logan strode into her room, crossing immediately to Robyn. 'I'm Logan, standing in for David. Karina tells me you've got a sudden, sharp headache and double vision. Anything else out of the ordinary?'

He didn't muck about.

Karina wrapped the cuff around Robyn's arm and felt her trembling.

'I feel a bit sleepy.' Robyn blinked again and again.

Logan asked, 'Have you been taking aspirin in the last day or two?'

'No.'

'Any other drugs apart from your statins?'

'No.'

'I'm going to examine your eyes.' Logan looked around for an ophthalmoscope, opened the drawer Karina indicated. 'Try to hold as still as possible. The light can be annoying, I'm sorry.'

'BP's high.' Karina wrote down the figures and showed him.

Pulling out a chair, Logan sat opposite a now very distressed Robyn. 'I don't want you to panic but you're going to hospital.' He looked briefly to Karina. 'Can you call an ambulance? Stat one.'

As Karina picked up the phone and punched triple one, Logan returned his attention to his patient, acting and sounding like the complete professional he was, showing no signs of urgency when he must be desperate to have Robyn on her way to hospital.

'The sudden sharp headache, double vision and what I see in your eyes suggests to me that you might be having a small bleed on the brain.'

The last of the colour in Robyn's face drained away. 'Am I going to die?'

'You've come in very early on, which is good. In

hospital they'll do a CT scan and some blood clotting tests to find out if it is a bleed or not.'

Logan spoke slowly and softly, pausing after each sentence for Robyn to ask questions, but she appeared too busy digesting what was happening.

After organising the ambulance Karina said, 'Robyn, do you want me to ring Tony so he can go with you?'

'Please. And the school won't know where I am either. I should be there by now.' Tears spilled down Robyn's face.

'I'll call them. I won't say anything other than you're too unwell to attend today. Tony can keep them posted.'

Out in Reception Karina told Leeann what was happening before asking, 'Can I borrow you to help me shift a bed at lunchtime?'

'No problem.'

Going into the doctor's consulting room, she found Luke Browning—still waiting for Logan to finish his check-up. 'Won't be too long now, Luke.'

'No worries. I've got all morning.'

'How are those babies? Still waking you and Liz for feeds throughout the night?'

Luke and his wife had finally had triplets after their third IVF treatment, and they had to be the most loved babies on the planet. Karina had lots of cuddles with them whenever they came in for check-ups, and every time she wondered if she was wrong to think she could stay single and not have children of her own. But she loved Mickey as though he were hers. So what was her problem?

The sound of a siren cut off any further conversation. Karina met the paramedics at the back door and took them directly to her room, where Logan gave them the rundown while she helped Robyn onto the stretcher.

'Take care.'

Minutes later the medical centre returned to calm, and Logan picked up from where he'd been interrupted, but it was well after midday before they caught up with their patient list. Fortunately it was mostly a day of flu and tummy bugs and drug prescriptions and nothing else eventful.

Karina felt drained of energy and it was barely lunchtime. Getting up to Mickey so often had caught up with her.

Logan paused in the doorway to Karina's domain at the surgery. Sitting at her desk, hunched over a file, she looked tiny. With her big heart and exuberant personality he sometimes forgot how small she was. Even in his less-than-fit state it would be easy to scoop her up into his arms and hold her against his chest, kissing her senseless before exploring every inch of skin on that to-die-for body. After he'd carried her to his bed, of course.

Bed. With Karina curled into him.

Bed. *Duh...* That was why he was here. 'Why did I just see a bed being taken across our lawn and into the house?'

The stunned look on her sweet face told him she hadn't known he was there.

'What?'

Then that cute pink filtered into her cheeks. Embarrassed? Or guilty?

'Who was carrying it?'

'Mr Grumpy and a wheelbarrow.'

She leapt out of her chair. 'That man needs telling off. I told him not to do it. It's too heavy for him.'

'I don't believe it. You told Jonty not to do something? Talk about challenging him. He was always going to do it from the moment you opened your mouth.' He grinned at her mortification.

Her pearly whites showed between her lips as she sucked in a breath. 'Guess my brain was in sleep mode.'

Sleep... Bed... *Go, damn it.* His brain was fixed on sex—with Karina.

'You haven't answered the question. There are more than enough beds in our house. Why another one?'

The pink shade darkened to a rosy red. Those teeth dug into her bottom lip so hard it must hurt.

'It's going in the lounge.'

That drove away all thought of sex. 'You're setting up a bed for me to sleep on in front of the fire?' Like *that* was going to happen. Damn her for interfering. These were his nightmares, his problem. Not Karina's.

'Yes.'

Defiance glared out at him from under those long eyelashes to which she'd applied a load of mascara.

'Don't bother making it up. I won't use it.' If he lay down there he'd have a nightmare just as surely as he would back in the bedroom.

Tidying the files into a neat pile, Karina pushed out from the desk and stood. 'Lunchtime. Do you want soup and toast?'

Even as she asked she was heading out of the room.

Following her, he shook his head at her back view. 'You're avoiding the subject.'

'Not at all. But we've only got half an hour before we need to be back here. I can't sit around talking all day.'

'Why do you do this? Switch off when the conversation isn't going your way?'

It was like trying to discuss the house with her— impossible. When Karina made her mind up about something there was no getting through to her that there might be another solution. One that suited both of them.

Of course she didn't bother answering his last question.

As he reached the back porch Jonty was just leaving. His face was pale and he was yawning.

'Are you all right?' Logan asked. Had that bed weighed too much for the stubborn old man?

'Of course I am.' Jonty shuffled down the steps and began to stomp away.

'Jonty, there's a stomach bug doing the rounds. If you're feeling ill it would pay to have a check-up in case you've caught it.'

'Don't need no doctor. When you get to my age all they do is find too many things wrong with you and try to make you eat rabbit food and drink nothing but water.'

Logan stepped back onto the path. 'Come with me to the surgery while everyone's at lunch.'

'This thing that's laying everyone low... It's a twenty-four-hour bug?'

'Yes, with another day thrown in to get over it.'

'Then I ain't got that.' Jonty turned towards the gate that led to his house.

Oh, no, you don't.

'Let's go. I'll just take your temp, and I promise not

to tell Karina to put your food through a blender before serving it.'

'Huh. That girl will do whatever she chooses, whether you or I like it or not.' But he changed direction, now aiming for the surgery.

Jonty wasn't getting any argument from him about Karina.

In the consulting room he said, 'Right, park your backside on that chair. Do you feel nauseous?' When Jonty dipped his head in acknowledgment, he continued. 'Any fever? Sweats? Day or night?'

'Some.' Jonty turned his hat over and over in his gnarled hands.

He's afraid. He thinks he's got something serious and doesn't want to know. At his age who can blame him?

'What else?' Logan lounged on the end of the desk, as if he had all the time in the world to listen to this old guy.

'My gut hurts lots and the toilet stuff's not so good.'

'Any blood in your stools?' When Jonty raised an eyebrow in question he gave a more basic term for stools, then asked, 'Is it black?'

'A bit.'

'Up on the bed now and I'll check your stomach.'

Jonty stared at him, that hat almost spinning now. 'I don't want you finding anything I can't deal with. You understand?'

'I do. Completely. But let me put it this way—what if you've got something easily treatable?'

'What are my chances? I'm too old these days.'

Logan put up a smile. 'You're also fit and very alert.'

Faded green eyes met his gaze and finally Jonty said, 'Thanks, lad.' He clambered onto the bed. 'Don't take too long. I've got to pick up those pipes so we can fix the drive in the morning.'

Logan warmed his hands under hot water, mulling over Jonty's symptoms and which tests to order. Those tests would be the hardest to obtain. Jonty would fight him all the way. But he had an ace up his sleeve. Karina. Jonty's Achilles' Heel. He adored her as much as she did him. He might grizzle about it, but they'd get those tests done if she told him to.

Listening to Jonty as he listed his symptoms of stomach pain, dark stools, weight loss and tiredness, Logan began considering Crohn's disease.

'Ever have any mouth ulcers?'

'One or two.'

'Right…' Now he knew which boxes to tick on the lab form.

It was late afternoon when Karina tracked him down in the tea room, getting a coffee. 'Mickey's very quiet since he got back from kindy. I hope he's not sickening for something.'

The boy was sitting in the corner, colouring in a picture of an elephant, and his desultory manner underlined Karina's comment. Still…

'Stop worrying. If he's crook we'll know soon enough. There's one plus. His urinary frequency seems to have stopped.'

'How can I not worry? Tell me that, Logan.'

He didn't get a chance.

Leeann strode into the room, saying to Karina, 'Becca phoned and said to remind you it's Friday night.'

'I'll call her back and tell her no.' Karina looked despondent.

'What does Friday night have in store?'

'Drinks at the pub. But I'm too tired to be bothered today.'

'Well, I'm not. It sounds like the best idea in ages. We've had a big day, so let's go unwind for a bit. Who normally looks after Mickey when you go out? Jonty?'

She looked stunned and she dipped her head.

'Come on, Karina.' He dropped an arm over her shoulders, squeezed her gently against him. 'It will be good to have some adult time.'

Leeann hadn't finished. 'Becca also said, Karina, that you should bring the doctor everyone's talking about.'

Logan laughed. 'There you go. I'm officially invited.'

'Wait till I see Becca,' Karina snapped as her face coloured a beautiful shade of red. 'I'm going to kill her. Slowly. Painfully.'

'You sure know how to make me feel wanted.' Logan dropped his arm and picked up his coffee. 'Just as well I've got a thick skin.'

'He's yummy!' Becca leaned close to Karina the instant Logan stood up to go for another round of drinks. 'No wonder you didn't want to bring him along for the rest of us to get to know him.'

'I didn't want to bring him because I have him in my face twenty-four-seven as it is.' She winced at her own unfairness. 'I just wanted some time to think without him there, to not think about anything except having some fun.'

'You're not seriously telling me you don't have fun with the yummy doctor?' Becca laughed. 'Come on, Karina, you're not made of ice.'

Her face flushed. 'Unfortunately.'

'Aha, so you *are* interested in him?' Her friend looked too darned delighted with that.

'Here you go, ladies.' Logan placed replenished beers in front of them and took his seat next to Karina. This time he managed to place the length of his leg against hers.

On her other side she got one of Becca's elbows in her ribs. 'Nice...'

'Shut up,' Karina whispered back, and adjusted her chair to put space between her and Logan. Picking up her drink, she tried to focus on the crowd and who was there that she knew.

Logan leaned closer. 'You any good at pool?'

'I know one end of a cue from the other.'

'She'll beat the pants off you,' Becca's brother informed him.

'Let's give it a whirl.' Logan stood and reached down for her hand. 'I haven't played for a while, but I bet I can beat you.'

'Now, there's a challenge.' Tugging her hand free of his, and feeling the instant cool where his fingers had been, she strode across to the table and began setting it up.

'Heads or tails?' He stood beside her, flicking a coin up and down in his right hand.

'Heads.'

The coin slapped onto the back of his hand. 'Heads it is.'

Karina chose a cue and went to the end of the table. Bending over to line up with the triangle of balls, she mentally crossed her fingers that she wouldn't make too much of an idiot of herself, then aimed the cue ball to break up the triangle. She could play, and sometimes she even won, but a champion she was not. As her first shot showed.

Hard as she tried, she couldn't ignore Logan when he nudged her aside.

'Let me show you how it's done, girl.'

Rolling her eyes, she laughed. 'You don't have a problem with self-belief, do you?'

'I'll have you know I beat the Nigerian health centre staff every time.' He winked. 'The fact we used sticks for cues and apples for balls had nothing to do with it.'

He sank three balls before missing a difficult shot.

'What did you use for a table?' Lining up her next ball, she leaned over the edge of the table for better access. The resounding *thunk* as the ball hit the side of the pocket and dropped in made her chuckle. 'Take that.' *Thunk*. 'And that—and that.'

'A tin table with hats nailed to each corner.'

Laughter bubbled up just as she moved her cue. It slewed sideways and she missed her target. 'Look what you made me do.'

'Excuses, excuses. Again, let me show you how it's done.'

'Smarty-pants,' she coughed out around her laughter.

Then she got an eyeful of neat, butt-filled pants as he leaned so far over the table it was a wonder his feet remained on the floor. The laughter dried up; as did her mouth. *Oh, my.* Now, there was a sight for sore eyes. Any eyes.

'Looks like the drinks are on you.'

Logan's voice penetrated the heat haze in her brain.

'Why?' A glance at the table gave her the answer. 'The best of three?'

She began emptying the pockets and putting the balls back into the wooden triangle.

'You're on. But first I need my beer. It's hot work, playing nice to a lady.'

'That was nice? Distracting me and then sneaking balls into pockets when I wasn't looking?'

Don't ask me where my gaze was.

'All part of the plan. Win by means foul or fair.' He brought their beers across. 'Get that inside you and see if it doesn't improve your eyesight.'

Did he know how he'd distracted her? He couldn't. He'd been facing the other way. He wouldn't have known she'd been interested in his derrière. She studied him over the rim of her beer bottle. He looked decidedly cocky. Maybe he'd planned it all along. Well, two could play that game.

'Your break.' She nodded to the table and waited impatiently as he broke the triangle, then went on to pocket five balls.

'See if you can beat that.' He grinned as he straightened up.

Quickly averting her gaze from his backside, she grinned back. As she'd decided: two could play that game.

Studying the balls on the table, she found the one

she wanted to drop first and walked along to the side, where she leaned as far across as possible without losing her balance. *Thunk.*

Her opponent was silent, and she didn't dare look around to see if she'd distracted him as neatly as he had her.

Finding another suitable ball to aim for, she once again arranged herself over the table and sank it. When all the balls were gone she turned to him, smoothing down the top that had somehow ridden above the waist of her trousers, and said airily, 'We're equal.'

He blinked and shook his head. 'You think?'

Oh, I know.

But she kept those words to herself.

CHAPTER EIGHT

'ANOTHER PERFECTLY CLEAR DAY.' Karina stretched her
arms above her head as she peeked out of the window
on Saturday morning.

Logan's mouth dried as her breasts were pushed
higher. When she bent at her waist, leaning first to the
right and then the left, her arms still high, she looked
so lithe he wanted to grab her and slide his hands over
each and every tempting curve, from those breasts down
to her bottom.

That bottom had grabbed his attention last night as
she'd sprawled across the pool table to reach a ball. He'd
been blindsided by the curvy vision that had totally distracted him and lost him the second and third game.

She straightened and faced him. 'Did you go back
to sleep after your hot chocolate?'

Talk about a passion-killer. Another nightmare had
brought her to his room at three in the morning. He'd
have been happy to have her waking him for pleasure,
but not to drag him out of hell. *Be grateful she did.*

'No. And before you ask, I didn't use that bed.' When
he saw a question forming on her lips he held a hand
up. 'Sleep's highly overrated.'

Instantly he wished back his thoughtless retort. Hurt blinked out at him from those chocolate eyes. In trying to deflect her questions he'd upset her.

'I'm sorry. That was uncalled for. Can I ask you not to talk about my nightmares if I promise to stop coming out with half-baked comments like that?'

The hurt faded and a half-smile touched her mouth. 'Sure. I'm not really a nosy person, but I do like to help where I can.'

'Unfortunately you can't fix me.'

Though he wished she could. But for that to happen he'd have to tell her about the PTSD and watch any respect slide out of her eyes. It shocked him how much he never wanted to lose that.

Changing the subject before she could ask why she couldn't fix him, he said, 'Did Mickey sleep through?'

'Not a peep. I wonder what the other night was about?'

'Just one of those things. I'm glad the results came back negative for an infection.' Seemed Mickey was over that episode. 'What do you do on the weekends?'

'I coach Mickey's football team, but we've got a bye today.' She sipped her steaming tea. 'Hey, why don't we go up to the Mount Arthur car park? Mickey hasn't seen snow.'

From Africa to Mount Arthur? From forty-plus degrees to something barely above zero? Different. But didn't he want different? There weren't likely to be any guerrillas hiding in the trees there.

'How are your snowman-building skills?'

'Non-existent. But I've got carrots and bananas in the pantry.'

'What for?'

'The nose and mouth.' She gave him that impish smile. 'Whatever else were you thinking?'

He hadn't been thinking. That was the problem.

'Shall we see if Jonty wants to join us? We were going to finish the drive today, but he might like this better.'

'I'd forgotten about that. It's a great idea. He might forget worrying about his health for a while.'

'He *is* worrying, isn't he? Not that he'll ever admit it. Do you think he'll go to those appointments at Nelson Hospital that I've arranged? He was very unhappy about them. Should I offer to drive him over next week?'

It wasn't as though he'd be working, and he might be able to call in at the reclamation yard for a window frame to replace the existing one in the laundry that dry rot had wrecked.

'I reckon he'd go with you. He told me you remind him a lot of James, and they were close.' Karina touched his forearm with those orange-tipped fingers. '*Were* you two alike?'

'You mean you haven't worked that out yet?' He smiled to lighten the question, in case she was still wary of him. She could change attitude quickly.

'You're more stubborn than James. Far less likely to change your mind once you've made it up.' That elfin face turned cheeky. 'And James would never have dug up that driveway, or considered painting the house. That's manual work, and he hated getting down and dirty.'

'True... Strange, when both our parents are hands-on kind of people.'

'They absolutely love living on Stewart Island, don't they?' Karina shivered.

Warmth snuck in under his ribs. 'Yep. It's about as remote as you can get, unless you go to the Chathams. The weather's extreme, the fishing's amazing, and they don't ever want to leave.'

'Have you visited?'

'Often.'

He drained his mug and went to rinse it under the tap. 'What time do you want to head away?'

'Ten? The roads won't be quite so icy then.'

'We'll take the four-wheel drive. It's a lot safer on the terrain we're going to, even if you do have new tyres on your car.'

Karina pulled a face. 'Where would I be without Jonty?'

'I'll go and ask him what he wants to do.'

'I haven't seen him out and about yet. If he's not in our yard he's usually in his shed.'

'You're not thinking something's happened to him?'

He felt a twist of worry for the old guy. Already Jonty had made an impact on him, had him caring. That was the problem with staying too long with people.

'I'm probably overreacting.'

'On my way.' Logan opened the back door and reached for his boots.

A shot rang out. He dropped to the porch floor, rolled sideways and looked around the yard. Where had that come from? Who was out there? His gut tightened as his ears strained for any sound, his eyes scoping the yard.

'Stop. Go away, you bastards.'

'Logan? What are you doing? Are you all right?'

Karina loomed over him.

'Get down!' As the order slid across his tongue he heard a motor, then a car speeding down the road, back-firing repeatedly. Expletives formed but with a herculean effort he managed to keep silent.

'Logan? Talk to me. You're freaking me out.' Karina crouched beside him. 'What happened? Did you slip?'

His chest rose as he filled his lungs. *One, two, three, four.* It would be easier to lie. 'I thought I heard a gunshot,' he muttered. Truth was hard, but he had to try it.

'You've been shot at? In Africa?'

Those eyes were filled with disbelief. Or was that shock?

He nodded and sat up. The porch was freezing. Quickly getting to his feet, he picked up the boots he'd dropped. 'Yeah, Nigeria is a fun place to work—believe me.' Shoving one foot into a boot, he tugged at the laces and tied a knot.

'Were you ever hit? Shot, I mean?' The question was quiet, and filled with loads more questions.

'No.' Logan straightened and looked directly at Karina. 'No.'

That wasn't a lie. A dead hostage was no use to anyone. The guns had been pointed a metre either side of him, their bullets kicking up the dust close enough that he'd felt the grit on his legs, the warning explicit. *Don't think you can get away.*

Logan looked deep into Karina's eyes, saw nothing but her big-hearted concern and felt his heart roll.

'But you had a bad time?'

'Yeah, Karina, I did.'

Then he bent and brushed his lips over hers to stop

her talking. Except the instant his mouth touched hers he had to have more, had to lose himself in her. His arms came up and wrapped around her, hauling her warm, compliant body close against his chilled, frightened one. He could forget the horror while Karina deflected it.

He deepened his kiss. Karina returned it, meeting each of his moves with one of her own. Then her arms slid around his neck and pulled him even closer, and he felt safe. Warm and cared about and safe.

'Good morning, you two. Hope you've given Mickey his breakfast?'

Karina jerked out of his arms and spun around to stare at Mr Grumpy as though she'd never seen him before. Her fingers were pressing her bottom lip as if she was trying to keep that kiss there.

'Mickey?' she squeaked.

'Is having a lie-in.' Logan stood behind her, his hand on her shoulder, and eyeballed Jonty, who had a stupid grin on that wrinkled face of his.

'You won't be interested in doing any more digging this morning, then.' Jonty clomped up the steps to stand right in front of them.

Logan relaxed. 'I was on my way to see you.'

'Humph,' Jonty grunted.

Ignoring the interruption, Logan continued, 'We're heading up Mount Arthur—taking Mickey to see the snow. Do you want to come?'

'Why the heck people like rolling around in that stuff is beyond me.'

'Come on, Jonty. It will be fun. Can you picture

Mickey throwing snowballs?' Karina had finally found her voice.

'Unfortunately, I can. What time you leaving?'

Karina gave him a quick hug. 'Ten o'clock. I'll pack a lunch and some drinks.'

Jonty stomped back down to the path. 'None of that lemonade stuff for me. Hot tea is the only thing.'

'Guess that's a yes, then?' Karina called after him, and then turned back to Logan.

Her face was his favourite colour—pink. Her eyes were filled with mischief and wonder. Then she leaned close and traced her finger over his chest.

'I'm sorry you had a bad time. Let's have some fun today.'

He just had. What could be more fun than kissing a hot woman? He hadn't enjoyed himself so much in a long time. Which showed how much he'd lost his grip on reality.

He had no right to be kissing his nephew's guardian. It would only set up difficulties for further down the track. What if they disagreed on Mickey's education or health plan? How could they resolve things amicably if they'd briefly got too close and personal? How did parents deal with these situations? *Parents*. He was not nor ever likely to be a parent, given his penchant for working in inhospitable places. He was a guardian. Full-stop. But that meant giving the same love and care and concern, didn't it? Like a parent.

Logan swore silently. He was caught whichever way he looked at it. Sighing, he gave up his one-sided argument. 'Want me to get Mickey up? Give him the good news?'

'Sure. There are plenty of thick clothes on the bottom shelf of his closet.'

Karina turned to go inside.

Who'd have believed something as ordinary as a car driving by could have led to him kissing her? Though he was glad she'd stopped pushing for more answers than he was prepared to give, he felt they'd crossed a line in their relationship. No longer were they only Mickey's guardians at loggerheads about where he'd live. Those problems remained, but now Karina knew a little of what drove him and he knew how far she was prepared to go to look out for those she cared about— a very long way.

He did not need or want that from her. The things that had tipped his world upside down, including James's death, were his to absorb and cope with alone.

Karina sat up front with Logan, giving him occasional directions as they drove through the valley alongside the Motueka River. Frost glittered on the grass in the paddocks and on kiwi fruit vines while the sun made a feeble attempt to warm the world.

She tried to ignore that kiss. Failed. If only that kiss had a future. But it had come out of a moment of shock on her part and fear on Logan's. His fear had been quickly followed by embarrassment, and then he'd kissed her. To erase that fear? Or in the hope of diverting her so she'd forget what she'd seen?

'What's snow?' Mickey shouted from behind her.

'It's like ice, only all mashed up. Like if I put it in the blender to whizz round and round.'

Logan flicked an amused glance her way. 'Where do you get these ideas?'

'Have you got a better way of explaining it?' Her smile was teasing, taunting him to come up with something.

Which he damned well did. Too easily. 'It's like hard ice cream, buddy, but it doesn't taste half as good.'

'Yippee! I'm going to have ice cream all day!' Mickey yelled.

'Shh, you're giving my eardrums a hard time.' Karina looked around and shook her head at the excited wee guy. 'Mr Grumpy's probably wishing he'd stayed home right about now.'

'No, he isn't. He's having fun with me.' The decibels dropped infinitesimally.

Jonty winced and rubbed his ears. 'What did you say? I've gone deaf.'

Mickey knew a cue when he got one. He yelled, 'You and me are having fun!'

'Mickey,' Logan growled in a low tone. 'Stop shouting. There's no need for it.'

'I like yelling.'

'Stop right now. It's not nice.'

'Okay.' That was said with much less energy.

Karina let go the breath she'd been holding. 'Phew,' she whispered. 'Thought we were in for an argument.'

'Who makes the snow?' Mickey asked next, without deafening anyone.

Logan shot her a grin. 'Answer that one.'

She pulled a face at him and launched into an explanation. 'It's part of the weather. You know how rain comes out of the clouds? Well, snow is like frozen clouds that land on the ground, but it's thicker than rain.'

'Very good,' Logan muttered.

'Can I jump and splash in it?'

'You can jump in it, and you'll get wet, but it won't splash. It's good for making snowmen. We're going to build one today.'

'Can I build my own?' The yelling was back.

'Quieter, buddy. And yes, you can. Mr Grumpy's brought along a sled for you to ride down the slope on, too.' Logan turned up the mountain road Karina pointed to. 'Here we go.'

Karina immediately asked, 'Isn't riding a sled dangerous?'

'What's the worst that can happen? He'll tip over, for sure, but you said there aren't any cliffs, and the slope's not steep. It's good for him to push his boundaries in a safe environment.'

This was why Mickey needed his Uncle Logan around. 'I suppose…'

Looking out at the snow-covered trees, Karina felt a small fizz of excitement in her veins. She hadn't done anything like this for so long.

Behind her, Jonty said to Mickey, 'It's going to be freezing cold and you'll soon be wet as a fish. The way those two up the front go on, anyone would think this is fun.'

Smiling, she glanced across at Logan and saw him smiling too. Impulsively she touched his arm, and spoke quietly enough that only he could hear. 'Knew he'd be thrilled to come.'

'Exactly.'

'It's rude to whisper in front of others.'

'Yes, Jonty.'

Finally Logan pulled the vehicle into a parking space and looked around. 'Appears half of Motueka's here.'

'Definitely the place to be.' There were children in every direction, and adults trying to keep up with their offspring. 'Let's get amongst it.'

Mickey ran straight for the biggest mound of snow he could see and jumped into it. His look of astonishment when his feet disappeared was priceless. Karina clicked her camera madly, afraid to miss any of his antics.

'Come on. You're missing out on the fun.'

Logan reached for the camera but she ducked out of his reach and clicked a picture of him. Just for the record. Nothing to do with capturing that beautiful face and its rare happy expression. 'Go and jump in with Mickey. I'll get a couple more shots, then join you.'

'Silly fools. They'll get soaked.' Jonty stood beside her.

'That's why there's a bag of towels and clothes for everyone in the back of the car.' She snapped more photos—plenty of Logan as well as Mickey. It was a golden opportunity to take Logan's picture without having to explain why.

Jonty put out his hand. 'Give me that fandangled thing. I'll take the snaps while you join in the circus.'

'Okay. Do you know how to use it?'

'It's a camera, isn't it?' His gnarled hand closed around the small device. 'Which button do I push?' Five minutes later Jonty declared, 'I know what I'm doing, girl. Leave me to it, will you?'

The photos probably wouldn't be great, but what did

it matter? She'd have memories of today, and she could take more pictures later on.

Bending down, she scooped up a handful of snow and shaped it into a ball. 'Hey, Mickey, look at this.' Taking careful aim, she lightly threw the ball at his middle.

Mickey whooped and shouted, 'I want to do that. I'm going to make the biggest.'

He made one so big that when he tried to throw it the ball landed on his feet.

'Here, buddy, make smaller ones so that you can throw them at Karina and make her laugh. Like this.'

She got pelted, with all three males ganging up on her. Jonty had given up being photographer to join in the fun, even laughing once when he got a direct hit from Mickey.

'I liked the sled best.' Mickey hung on to Karina and Logan's hands and swung between them two hours later, as they made their way back to the car park and a late lunch. A smile lit up his face, and his eyes were bulging with excitement.

'Even when you tipped over and got your head buried in the snow?' she asked. Her heart had stopped for a moment, but Mickey had come up laughing and demanding to fall off again.

'I tasted the snow. It's yucky. Not like ice cream at all. What's for lunch? I'm starving.'

'I've got bacon-and-egg pie.'

By the way all the faces lit up she knew she'd won some points. She wouldn't mention the cream dough-nuts she'd bought from the bakery until Mickey had eaten his pie, otherwise he'd go straight to the second course. She was spoiling him—spoiling them all, really—but what the heck? In these chilly conditions people needed food in their tummies, and why not have something naughty but tasty?

Though if Logan was right, and Jonty had Crohn's, then he needed to be warned that he shouldn't eat too much of that sort of food. *Damn*, she should have thought about that and brought something more suitable.

'Watch out!'

The shout came from behind them.

Logan snatched Mickey and leapt sideways in one smooth move. She jumped after them. A young boy on a snowboard shot past. Looking around for Jonty, she saw he was further over, well out of danger. Shuddering, she muttered, 'Idiot. He shouldn't be doing that in a crowded area.'

'I think he might've lost control further up and doesn't know how to stop.' Logan held Mickey in his arms as they watched the boy finally crash to a stop in a large snowdrift. 'He seems to have survived unscathed.'

A loud voice indicated that the boy was getting a telling-off from his father. Karina grimaced. 'Parenting never stops.'

'A lifetime commitment,' Logan said, then asked, 'Where's that lunch? I'm in need of a hot drink, too.'

She heard the shiver in his voice. 'Guess this is a shock to your body?'

'You're not wrong there. But, hey, I'm enjoying it.' He grinned at Mickey, who was still in his arms. 'What about you, Mickey? Isn't this awesome fun?'

'Yip. My nose is cold.'

The food went down fast as everyone was ravenous. But standing around devouring pie and doughnuts had them feeling the cold too much.

'Do we head home now or have some more games in the snow?' Karina wondered aloud.

'I want to ride on the sled again.' Of course Mickey would fight the going home suggestion.

Logan placed the sled on the snow. 'Come on. I'll pull you to the top.'

Karina trudged along beside them. 'You're going to sleep well tonight, my boy.'

At the top they turned the sled around and Mickey clambered on, standing up on his feet. 'I'm going to do the same as him.' He pointed to an older boy on a snowboard.

'No, Mickey. Sit down.'

Too late.

The sled was already moving down the slope and Mickey was struggling to keep his balance. Logan leapt after him, jogging alongside the sled, ready to catch him if he slipped.

Swallowing the worry tightening her tummy, Karina walked down behind them, watching like a mother hen over every move Mickey made.

Things were going perfectly until the sled bounced over the end of a ski as its owner hurtled across in front of Mickey. The sled slid sideways fast, tossing Mickey into the air.

'Mickey!' she screamed, and ran, each step sinking into the snow.

'Kar—ina.' He rolled over in the snow and stared around. 'Kar—ina!' he yelled.

She and Logan reached him at the same moment and dropped to their knees at his side. Logan put a hand on his chest, his fingers making quick work of checking him over.

'You're all right, buddy. Just a wee cut on your chin.'

'I don't want a cut. It hurts.' He rubbed his chin, and when his fingers came away red he shrieked.

Karina reached for him, bundled his little body up in a hug. 'Shh, sweetheart. It's all right. You just had a little crash.'

You're never going to ride a sled again.

Mickey cuddled in tight, crying and hiccupping against her chest. 'I was going good like that boy.'

Logan collected the sled and laid it beside them. 'You were doing great, buddy. It takes practice to be perfect.'

'I don't want to do it now.'

Logan pulled a small ball of twine out of his pocket. 'Fair enough, but how about you sit on the sled and I'll tie this rope to the end so I can keep you from going too fast?'

Mickey shook his head. 'I might fall off again.'

'Not if I've got hold of you.'

Karina stood up, Mickey still in her arms. 'It's—'

'Give it a go, Mickey.' Logan cut her off. 'If you don't like it we'll stop.'

Wriggle, wriggle. Mickey wanted to get down. She locked eyes with Logan as she lowered the boy, shook her head at him.

'Back on the horse,' he said quietly. 'He'll be fine.'

I worry far too much. Yeah, she got it. But mothers, even surrogate ones, were allowed to.

Of course it was an uneventful trip back to the car

park, where Jonty stood, stomping his feet and muttering about silly people who didn't know when they'd had enough fun for one day. He took the sled and headed for the four-wheel drive.

Logan lifted Mickey to hold him in one arm, took Karina's hand with his free one and said, 'Let's head home. I think we've all had enough excitement.'

She didn't pull her hand free. It felt so right to be close to him after the day they'd shared. Later on she'd probably regret this, but now she wanted to be a part of someone.

'Hey…' Logan stopped a few metres short of his vehicle and turned to face her. 'You're one hell of a woman.'

Then those lips she was getting to know and enjoy captured her mouth again. His tongue slipped inside and she tasted him.

All too soon he pulled away. 'Come on. Jonty will be keeping score if we're not careful.'

CHAPTER NINE

By the end of the next week Karina had two bank loans on offer to consider, and a driveway that no longer flooded in a downpour. That had been proved already, when the frosts had moved over for a weather bomb that had brought more rain than anyone had seen in years. She also had a vase of colourful winter roses on the dining table from Logan and Mickey, for giving them such a fun day out on the snow.

The arrival of the beautiful flowers at the surgery had had Leeann staring in amazement and Karina's stomach fluttering like a butterfly in the breeze. Ian had used to have his secretary send her flowers every Friday afternoon, but those elaborate floral displays had never warmed her soul. Nothing like these, with their handwritten note from Logan.

On her way out of what had used to be her bank for the last time, having closed all her accounts and transferred her funds to the new bank she'd finally chosen, she saw Becca.

'I can't believe Logan's been here nearly two weeks already.'

'And...?'

Karina's heart sank. What could she say? Kisses didn't count as world-changing events, and nor did the numerous hours she'd wasted thinking about Logan. It seemed Logan didn't know when to back off out of her head space.

She cut Becca off at the pass. 'And nothing.'

'He came to Friday night drinks.'

'He wanted a break from everything.' *Don't ask what 'everything' involves.*

'He had a great time playing pool with you.' Becca grinned wickedly. 'He hardly took his eyes off you. If I wasn't the generous-hearted woman I am I could've been insulted.'

Unfortunately for her friend, Karina didn't want to talk about the man who was haunted by something so terrible he relived it almost nightly in his sleep.

'Look, he's here for Mickey and they're getting on so well. It's "Uncle Logan this…", "Uncle Logan that…"' Mickey would be heartbroken when Logan left, but that was out of her hands. 'And Logan's offered to give David a break by working mornings all next week.'

'That's kind, but do you like him? Think he's sexy?'

'A bit.' She'd never been able to lie. 'All right—a lot. He's caring and giving, and a lot sexy. But he's leaving in little more than two weeks, so I can't afford to play around with him.'

As long as it's not too late and I haven't already caught the Logan bug.

Because he'd sneaked into her heart a little bit while she'd been busy making him hot chocolate. She cared about him and for him, and at the moment that was survivable. She would miss him when he left, but her heart would be intact.

Really?

Of course. Absolutely of course.

Becca watched her far too closely. 'Bringing him along for drinks again tonight?'

'Drinks? Is it Friday already?' She slapped her head. 'How could I forget?'

'This Logan's seriously distracting you.'

'He could look after Mickey while I join you. That's why he's here—to bond with his nephew, not to go out with me.'

His eyes were sometimes filled with laughter and happiness and at other times were bleak and desperate, but whenever he was with Mickey his expression was always bright. She wouldn't think about that deep, hot look he wore around her.

A text message hit her phone. Digging deep in her bag, it took her a moment to find the phone amongst all the junk that somehow seemed to accumulate when she wasn't looking.

Are you coming home for lunch? We're missing you. Logan.

'Got to go. Seems my men need me.'

Becca had the nerve to laugh. 'You're hooked! Your men? That's brilliant.'

Karina opened her mouth to refute it, but snapped her lips shut. How could she explain that whatever affected Mickey affected her? Make that whoever had anything to do with her boy touched her. Nothing to do with her heart and Logan.

Tell that to the birds.

Saying, 'I'll text you about tonight,' she left her friend, still laughing, and headed for the car to go to the supermarket. On the way she replied to Logan.

Why's Mickey at home? He should still be at kindergarten.

Logan came back instantly.

The teacher called, said he was upset.

Why does my boy suddenly hate kindy when he's always loved it? Is Logan playing the 'Uncle' card too hard? I should never have let him stay home that first day. She laughed softly. *Listen to me, sounding like a mum—a mum in all but DNA. Cool.*

When she let herself into the house thirty minutes later she found Logan and Mickey lying on the rollout bed in front of the fire. Her feet turned to lead even while her throat ached with emotion. Mickey's small body was curled in against Logan, his cute face pale and his eyes closed. Logan's arm was wrapped around his nephew's body, holding him close, protecting him. They looked perfect together.

Slashing at the tears on her cheeks, she crossed to stand beside the bed. Whatever Mickey was unhappy about, she'd never forget this picture. He belonged in Logan's arms.

When she opened her mouth Logan raised a finger to his lips. 'Shh. He's only just fallen asleep,' he whispered.

Nodding, she quietly asked, 'Want anything? A drink? Lunch?'

'A cup of tea wouldn't go amiss. And a sandwich.'

He looked so hopeful she wanted to laugh.

'You eat like a horse, yet it doesn't stick to you. If I ate half what you do I'd be enormous.' She squinted at him. 'Actually, your face has lost some of that gauntness.'

'So I'm gaunt? Charming.'

Glancing at Mickey, she felt the fun go out of her. 'He's obviously tired, which isn't normal.'

Logan winced. 'He's peed a lot this morning, so I've collected another specimen to send off.'

She shivered, forgot to whisper. 'You don't think this is the start of something worse? An underlying illness?'

Panic flared, rapidly drying her mouth, cranking up her heart-rate and crunching her stomach.

'Karina, take a deep breath and listen to me.' He no longer whispered either.

His calmness had her instantly taking that breath. 'I know I worry too much, but I can't help it.'

'Despite the urinary frequency and tummy aches, I don't believe he's ill. He's tired, but think of the energy he's been expending in the snow and helping me and Jonty with the digging. There's plenty of colour in his face. Nor is there too much,' he added, when her mouth opened to ask exactly that.

Forcing the panic down, she acknowledged that Logan was more qualified medically than she'd ever be. If he wasn't overly worried maybe she shouldn't be either. 'Is it because he's getting close to you and will do anything to stay home with you?'

A rueful smile told her he knew the problems that he would cause when he left. 'Sorry, but I admit I'm enjoying being with him.'

Good. And bad. Another person in Mickey's life who would leave.

'I'll get that tea.'

'And a sandwich?'

Placing the steaming mug and a plate stacked high with ham sandwiches on a stool within easy reach of Logan a few minutes later, she told him, 'I'm due back at work. Anything else I can do before I go?'

Shaking his head, he whispered, 'I've got it covered.'

'I'll pop over when I'm not busy.' Then she couldn't help herself. 'You're really bonding with the wee man.'

'Not quite how I thought it would go down.'

The look of love he gave Mickey grabbed at her heart.

'You must be doing it right if he's relaxed enough to go to sleep with you.'

Usually if there was even a hint of distress the only person Mickey had wanted since he'd lost his parents was her. But that had been changing over the time Logan had been here. She should feel a twang of jealousy that he was so comfortable with Logan, but all she knew was relief. Things were looking up as far as this relationship was concerned.

Mickey and Logan were playing Snakes and Ladders when she got home. The dinner she'd prepared earlier was heating in the oven, and Jonty was watching the news.

Karina sighed. 'That's what I call domestic.'

Logan raised his head and locked eyes with her. 'Are we going out for Friday night drinks?'

'I guess…' Honestly, she'd prefer to stay home and keep an eye on Mickey.

'Jonty's prepared to look after our boy.'

Our boy? That sounded as if they had a family thing going. 'How's Mickey now?'

'I don't want you to go out,' Mickey answered her. 'My tummy's sore. And my head—'

Logan cut in. 'Haven't you spent the last thirty minutes complaining because you're starving and don't want to wait for dinner? Not to mention being a gymnast on the couch?'

'Stay home with me.'

'No. Karina and I are going out and you will be good for Mr Grumpy. Do you understand?'

'Yes, Uncle Logan. But—'

'Dinner's ready!'

Karina cut him off and hurried to dish up for him and Jonty. She and Logan would eat when they returned.

But Logan changed that.

'Is there a Thai restaurant around here?' he asked as they finished their beers.

'Just along the road,' Karina informed him. 'It's really good, what's more.'

'I'm drooling at the thought of a hot red curry. Want to have a meal there?'

'I'd love it, but what about Mickey?'

'I'll ring Jonty and see if he's okay to stay on for a

bit.' He held his hand up in a stop sign. 'I won't be asking if Mickey's well. Jonty's raised his own kids. He'll know if there's anything we should be worrying about.'

'Okay.' She forced herself to relax by breathing deep yoga breaths, dragging the air all the way down to her tummy, where it mixed with the beer and sent bubbles up her throat. *Great*.

Becca did her usual elbow-nudge thing. 'You're going on a date! How long's it been?'

'For ever,' she answered without thought. *Wait up*. 'It's not a date. We're both hungry, so we're doing something about it.'

'The food warming in your oven at home would do that,' Becca pointed out.

'I guess…' It was a date. *Oh, my God*. 'I don't do dating.'

'You do now. And you couldn't have picked a sexier guy if you'd checked out every male in Motueka.' Becca grinned. 'No, I'm not interested. He's too brainy for me.'

Logan snapped his phone shut. 'Sorted—let's go.'

Becca wrapped her arm around Karina in a hug and whispered, 'I want every detail.'

'This satay is superb.' Nearly an hour later, Karina licked her lips of every last dot of sauce. Becca was going to be annoyed when she told her that. And about the delicious entrée of crumbed squid rings and spring rolls. 'How's that curry?'

'Heaven.'

She'd figured it might be, since he hadn't said a word since his first mouthful.

'And the wine's not bad either. Hope you're up to walking home, because driving's out.'

Logan topped up their glasses from the bottle he'd ordered.

'Two weeks ago I stomped home in a right snot on three-inch heels—tonight's not going to be a problem.' She had on her favourite boots. 'Not a drop of rain in sight either.'

'No puddle-jumping, then?'

'You spoilt that when you fixed the drains.' She smiled to take any perceived sting out of her words, then changed the subject. 'Where did you do your training?'

'I followed James to Christchurch, which is just up the road from Ashburton, where we grew up. I had some half-baked idea that we could flat together, become best buddies and all that. Didn't factor in that he already shared a flat with five other guys. But I soon teamed up with some other students and had a blast.'

'There's something about getting away from home. It changes you for ever.'

Except her father had insisted she return to the fold the moment she had her nursing qualification in her hot little hand and she'd complied. How different would her life have been if she hadn't?

Logan started telling her about some of the pranks he'd got up to as a student. The wine ran out so they walked home, still talking about themselves.

For Karina, the best part was having Logan's arm around her shoulders, holding her close to him. Her arm around his waist soaked up every movement, and had her dreaming of her bare arm against his skin. Her blood sizzled with desire.

I'm on a date. Yeah, and very shortly I'm going to be home, tending to Mickey and cleaning up the kitchen after Jonty. Hey, Cinderella, where's the pumpkin?

Their date came to a jarring end the moment they walked in the door. Mickey and Jonty were arguing over who'd cheated at Snakes and Ladders. Was that even possible?

Karina shook her head and lifted Mickey up into her arms. 'Bedtime for you.' Tears streaked his sweet face and shadows underlined his innocent eyes.

'Don't want to go to bed,' came the inevitable reply.

'Want and get are two different things.'

He was exhausted. Overtired, as it turned out. Sleep did not come easily, so that by the time he did finally succumb more than an hour had passed and all the heat that had fired her body had buttoned off. Not that it would take much to fire it up again.

In the lounge, Logan and Jonty were talking about the rugby game on TV. Deflated further, she turned away, headed for the kitchen and the mess on the bench.

So much for a hot date. She'd overreacted to the intimacy of sharing a meal and being held close to Logan on the walk home. Of course he wasn't interested in anything that might make life difficult between them when they dealt with the house, the surgery and Mickey's future.

Angry at herself for even considering that they might have an interlude that was about them and nothing else, she banged pots and plates into the sink and turned the tap on so hard water drenched the front of her top.

* * *

Logan stirred the pumpkin soup he'd found in the freezer and checked the oven temperature. He'd found heat-and-eat buns right next to the container of soup. Everything was all set for when Karina came in from the surgery for lunch, which should be any minute now if they closed on time. It being Saturday, and theirs the only surgery open today, they might be overrun with patients.

He was getting a kick out of doing things with and for Karina. Like last night at the Thai restaurant. They'd been so relaxed together it had been marvellous: sharing those entrées and watching her perfect teeth bite into the spring roll he offered her. He'd been turned on all the way through the meal.

But that was nothing compared to the tension tightening his muscles as they'd walked home. *All* his muscles, which hadn't made for comfortable walking. It would have been all too easy to stop and kiss her senseless. Hell, he'd wanted to kiss her right from the moment they'd left the house, heading for the pub. Her perfume had filled his vehicle, teasing and taunting. Her hands moving in the air as she'd chattered non-stop had had him aching to feel them on his skin.

With every step he'd wanted to stop and wrap Karina in his arms while he devoured her with kisses. But a little voice at the back of his head had prevailed. What if Karina took him too seriously? Thought they might have a future? Believed he'd change all his plans and stay on here with her?

Even then he'd been unbelievably close to giving in

to temptation. Then they'd walked in the front door and had been confronted with the chaos that was Mickey.

Mickey hadn't wanted anything to do with anyone except Karina, which had left him out of the loop, so he'd joined Jonty in the lounge. In hindsight that had been a good thing, because it had given him time to cool down and realise what taking Karina to bed would have done to their relationship. He wasn't prepared to make a mess of that just because he desperately wanted her. Not when he had to negotiate a truce on what to do with the house and the surgery.

The back door opened and a blast of cold air smacked into the kitchen, bringing him fully alert.

'Something smells delicious.' Karina skipped into the kitchen.

'I've been raiding your freezer.' When her eyebrows rose he added, 'Soup's the only thing on a cold day.'

'I was hoping for something warm.'

Warm? You're hot.

As she looked around, worry creased Karina's brow. 'Where's Mickey?'

'In the lounge, making a chart to keep score of who wins the most Snakes and Ladders games.'

While Karina went to see him Logan opened the oven and placed the buns on the rack. 'Five minutes until lunch is ready,' he called after her.

'Mickey says he's hungry. Again.' She smiled from the doorway, where she stood with their boy in her arms.

'Hope you don't mind, but I also got out a beef casserole to thaw for dinner. I haven't had anything like that since I was last at Mum's, and the moment I saw the container my stomach started doing a loop-the-loop.'

He began ladling soup into bowls.

'Go for it. Does this mean I'm not on dinner duty tonight?'

She sat Mickey on a chair and lifted his hair off his forehead, her hand automatically stopping to feel his temperature. She had all the instinctive parenting skills necessary, though she should relax a bit.

'I'm a genius at heating pre-cooked meals.'

Her smile widened, then slowed. 'Some of Jonty's tests have come back. Looks like you're on the right track—though the faecal occult blood result isn't back. His white count's slightly elevated, with a predominance of neutrophils, including band forms.'

'That'll be because of the numerous mouth ulcers. What about his B12 and folic acid? Iron?' Logan placed a bowl in front of Mickey. 'Blow on it first. It's hot.'

'Iron borderline normal. B12 and folate low.' Karina picked up one of the remaining bowls and settled at the table. 'Funny how I didn't notice he was losing weight until you said something.'

'You often don't when you're around someone all the time. Eventually it would have dawned on you. He says he's lost seven kilos since Easter.'

'Did he say why he's been taking so much aspirin?'

'Headaches, stomach pain, sore knees. The aspirin could've exacerbated the stomach problem and given him ulcers there too.'

Flicking the hot buns onto a plate, Logan placed them on the table and sat opposite Karina. This was cosy. A man could get used to it.

'Careful, Mickey.' Karina pushed his bowl closer to him.

'How do you think Jonty will cope with a strict diet regime?' With Crohn's disease some foods were definitely off the menu, and Jonty would have to work out which were the trigger food groups peculiar to him.

'He's not called Mr Grumpy for nothing.'

'True.'

The soup was delicious and required total concentration.

'From the way that's going down, I'm guessing it's also been a while since you had soup.'

When he raised his head he found Karina watching him with questions in her eyes. 'I'd forgotten how tasty something as simple as pumpkin soup can be.' Had he deflected those questions? What did she want to know this time?

He soon found out.

Karina licked her spoon until it shone, then asked, 'Are you looking forward to going back to Africa?'

He shivered. 'Yes.'

'I'm getting mixed messages.'

Too damn observant. That was what she was. *Come on. Think of something to say that won't reveal the truth but isn't a lie. Come on*, he repeated in his skull.

'I'm happy to go back. There's so much to do there. It's never-ending.' As her brow furrowed he knew she wasn't buying into his explanation. 'I haven't been in NZ long and I still need to unwind completely.'

He also needed to be here. Mickey was getting used to him, wanted him in his life. That had to be good, but it also complicated everything.

The furrows remained in place. 'Will you go to the same base as last time?'

Try as hard as he might, he couldn't prevent the shudder that rocked him, and she saw it, those eyes widening ever so slightly.

'No,' he muttered, and pushed off his chair to get more soup in an attempt to shut her up without growling at her. Offending her was not on his agenda. He liked her too much. Besides, they had to get along for Mickey's sake. 'I'll probably go to Uganda next time, even though I haven't quite finished my last contract.'

'Will it be another twelve-month stint?'

'They usually are.' He had yet to discuss his deployment with his boss. Hopefully by then he'd be able to say with full confidence that he'd got over the kidnapping.

She stood beside him, holding out her bowl for more. 'That's not exactly what I asked.'

He knew that. His shoulders rose and fell as he ladled soup into her bowl.

Back at the table Karina eyed him as he sat down. 'I know I'm a pest, but I have to look ahead. Knowing if you'll be coming home to see Mickey during the next year will make it easier to tell him what to look forward to.'

Her honesty could be a pain, but he couldn't fault her reasoning. 'It wouldn't be fair to leave you on your own with Mickey longer than a year.'

Even that was too long to expect Karina to hold the fort. But twelve months back in that stinking heat, wondering where the next attack might come from, fear-ing being taken and locked up again, wasn't going to be a picnic either.

'I'm quite happy with the situation, but it worries me that it's not always easy to contact you. What if something goes wrong? Like Mickey getting seriously ill and my needing you?'

Nurses and doctors were known to look for all sorts of illnesses when it came to their own kids, and there was no denying that, to Karina, Mickey was her own. But…

'Mickey's doing great. I suspect the headaches and tummy aches are about attention-seeking.'

As she tapped her bottom lip repeatedly with her spoon he wanted to hug her tight, kiss away those worries screwing up her eyes. He wanted to make everything easier for her.

'How would you feel if I was living here? Was available all the time? Would that make you feel I was infringing on what you're doing with Mickey?'

Now, where the hell had *that* come from? Next she'd be thinking he planned on staying around.

Her spoon clattered into her bowl and her chair tipped back as she raised startled eyes to meet his gaze. 'You're not serious?'

That hurt. 'What if I am? Mickey's as much my responsibility as yours. Besides, I'm not looking forward to leaving him for so long.'

So she didn't want him here, didn't want to share parenthood. She'd had it her own way too long.

'Sorry, that came out all wrong,' she backpedalled. 'It would be great for Mickey if you lived in Motueka.'

'But apparently not in the same house as the two of you?'

That hurt too. He'd become used to Karina being around all the time. He liked sharing meals and looking out for Mickey with her, and had enjoyed working alongside her in the surgery. Seemed she didn't think the same. Of course she was right. Sharing a house really wasn't wise. What if, despite her protestations, she did meet a man she wanted to settle down with? It was bound to happen one day. She was too attractive to remain single for ever. He'd be like a spare wheel around the place. *Come on...* He'd hate it—and he had no right to that emotion.

Karina might be sneaking under his radar and touching his heart, but he wasn't about to run with that. She'd already been hurt badly by her ex and she didn't need a basket case next time around. Nor did Mickey need the fallout a broken relationship would bring if it didn't work out between them.

Standing, he gathered up the empty soup bowls and took them to the sink. 'You're safe. I couldn't stay still in one place long enough to make a life for myself here.'

She didn't need to know that he'd begun to feel that this might be the place where he could let go of the fear and grab at the sense of belonging that sometimes caught him. Whether that was the location and its townsfolk, or just two people in particular, he still didn't know. But, as he didn't usually go looking for places to leave his heart, he suspected it was Karina and Mickey who'd weaved their magic around him, causing this disturbance to his head and his heart.

* * *

Karina couldn't get Logan's words out of her head.

'How would you feel if I was living here? Was available all the time?'

He had refuted them almost immediately, but it had been as though he was testing her: seeing what she felt about the idea.

Well, buster, the answers to those vexing questions are entirely up to you. She flicked the towel she was folding, getting a small satisfaction out of the snapping sound it made. *I can't tell you what to do with your life.*

Logan living here would be the best thing for Mickey and the worst for her—even if he lived in another house. Already she'd grown too close to him, and she wasn't looking forward to the day he left.

Male laughter reached her from the direction of the shed, where Logan and Jonty were sanding the frame on a set of windows they'd bought at the demolition yard in Nelson during the week.

Another maintenance job being attacked; another thing soon to be ticked off Logan's list. He seemed to be getting immense enjoyment out of doing these jobs, saying on more than one occasion that it was great seeing the results of his hard labour.

'What's hard about it?' Jonty had asked one time when they'd all been in the garden. 'It's what real men do.'

Logan had laughed at Jonty's poke, no doubt safe in the knowledge that the old man was more than happy to work alongside him.

You're all man—right down to the tips of your toes. She'd had to slam her mouth shut on the words.

Logan was comfortable showing his softer side. He spent hours with his nephew and had been more than happy to step up when needed in the surgery. Oh, and he had a chest and a butt that were definitely real man.

But she didn't know what to make of Logan's query about him staying around. She'd be absolutely thrilled, she suspected. He was impossible to ignore, despite her best intentions. He was knocking away at the barriers she'd hoisted around her heart. Often she found herself thinking about him at times when she had no right to be—times when she was meant to be reading patient notes or making sense of Mickey's erratic behaviour, which she hadn't been able to find an answer for even by searching the net.

Logan. Get out of my head. Now. Stay away.

See? She didn't want him moving here permanently.

Yeah, I might, though.

What if she was falling in love with him?

Then he's got to go. No argument.

He mightn't be anything like power-hungry, control freak Ian, but she'd loved Ian with all her being and she suspected that was how she'd love Logan if she allowed him into her heart.

That was how she loved Mickey.

That was how she loved. Full-stop.

With a child, that was okay. Parents loved unconditionally and took the knocks along the way.

But to love a man like that again, knowing full well how painful it would be at the end, would be utterly foolish. She wasn't ever again going down that black hole. And the only way she could be sure of that was by not getting involved with Logan.

Logan might be wonderful with Mickey, but he also liked to be in charge, liked controlling everything around him. Such as selling the house. In his book he was right: no argument. Just like her ex and her father. She was never again going to be that person who did as others bade in the hope that they'd love her more.

No, siree. I know how this unfolds. I give in once, the second time is easier, and so it goes.

Love Logan or not, she wasn't getting involved with him.

CHAPTER TEN

A SHOUT WOKE Karina from a deep sleep.

'Here we go again…'

She rolled out of bed and groped for her robe and slippers as another cry ripped through the house.

'Logan?'

These nightmares weren't getting any less frequent.

In his bedroom, she went through the routine of shaking him awake and making him aware of where he was, and who with, before turning to head to the kitchen and the chocolate and milk.

'Don't go. Stay here with me for a bit.'

Logan's voice was raspy with sleep and whatever had disturbed him.

'It doesn't help, going to the lounge. The nightmares follow me.'

Sitting up, Logan shuffled sideways, making a space on the bed for her.

As he tapped the mattress beside his hip he added, 'I won't bite.'

He leaned back against a pillow, looking exhausted and nothing like a man who might have light entertainment on his mind. Karina's eyes followed his hands as they tugged the bedcovers further up his chest. He'd taken to sleeping in a tee shirt and shorts, but no clothing or bedcovers could blot out the image she already held of his body.

Easing down, she swung her legs up and stretched them alongside his—except hers barely reached past his knees. 'I'm nothing like my mum and sister. Too short and not thin enough.'

Logan stared at her unglamorous pyjama-clad pins and picked up her hand to fold his strong fingers around hers. 'You've got curves in all the right places, and for the record curves are not to be sneered at.'

He squeezed her hand.

'Thanks…I think.'

She felt the shivers still passing through him intermittently. *What were the nightmares about?* she asked herself for the hundredth time. It was the one question she'd never verbalise. The look in his eyes when he came awake after one was not something she wanted to be responsible for bringing back.

'I was kidnapped for ransom. In Nigeria. By guerrillas.'

Karina gasped, shocked at his disclosure and stunned that he'd read her mind. Squeezing his hand in return, she felt increasing shudders rock through him, and moved sideways so that her shoulder rubbed against his upper arm.

She finally managed a lame, 'Logan, that's absolutely terrible.' What could she say? 'Why did they take you?'

'Money. They came into our quarters in the middle of the night and took three of us at gunpoint. That's why I didn't make it home for the funeral. I had no idea James and Maria had died until after I was released.'

'Why didn't we hear about this in New Zealand? Surely it should've made headline news?' Reporters weren't known for their discretion. Not the ones she'd dealt with, anyway. 'Your parents don't know, do they?'

'No.' Logan shivered again. 'Because of my English passport my director didn't dispel the notion that I was British, so I guess the local media missed that a Kiwi had been taken. Secondly, I was mistaken for the son of an English lord who was working at a neighbouring camp. Only after the man had been sent out of the country undercover were the guerrillas informed they held the wrong man.'

For someone who didn't ever talk about this he suddenly seemed incapable of stopping. Karina held his hand and waited, wondering if he even realised he was telling her this stuff.

'I got lucky,' he said angrily. 'Luck being relative. Six weeks after we were captured I saved a child who'd fallen in the river we were camped by. Technically the lad had drowned, but I was able to revive him. Turned out he was the leader's only son. After a further two weeks of hanging out in a hut I was sent away with a man from a neighbouring village. At first I thought he was going to knock me off and leave me to the hyenas, but after four days I began to hope. Hope's a strange thing. It grips you, teases, taunts, screws with your mind. We walked all night and most of the day, lying up under any tree we could find when the temperatures were unbearable. By day six I was getting so weak I doubted I'd make it to wherever we were headed, and then suddenly there was a small town on the horizon. After that everything was a blur until I found myself back at base.'

'Thank goodness.' Her thumb traced back and forth on the back of his hand. 'What about the other two? You said they took three of you.'

'Still in captivity, last I heard, but negotiations are underway with the US government.'

She shivered. *Unbelievable.* It was like something out of a movie: over-dramatised and unrealistic. Except this was true.

'Those scars on your body…?'

'The brutes enjoyed whipping us with the flat side of a machete. The slightest pressure either way and our skin would be sliced. Infections were rampant.'

Admiration for him ramped up, filled her heart. How did anyone come through all that and still be a kind, caring person like Logan was? Here he was, getting to know his nephew, working hard to improve the house for her—whether they sold it or stayed. Yet he said he would return to that area. *Crazy.* Why would he?

Turning, she saw wariness in his eyes as he watched her. Was he searching for disgust on her part because he felt he'd failed somehow? He'd be looking a long time.

Laying her head on his shoulder, she wanted to weep for him, but knew better. He'd hate that. She asked, 'How long after reaching your base did you leave Nigeria?'

'Three days. I was sent to hospital in California to be checked over and to talk to the shrinks.'

'Then you came home?' Did Motueka feel like home to him?

'Home… It's not a word I use often. I've always focused on being wherever I'm needed and not on putting down roots.'

Unbelievably sad. She'd had problems, but she had always known where she belonged. 'And now?' she asked softly.

'I haven't a clue. I still need to help people. That's in my psyche. But do I do that in Africa or Asia? Or right here in Motueka? I haven't a clue,' he repeated.

'Go easy on yourself. Sort those nightmares out first.' She leaned harder against him.

Logan wrapped his arms around her and brought her even nearer. His chin nestled on her head. Strands of her hair lifted with each of his breaths, then floated back down onto her cheek.

This felt right. If she pressed her cheek hard against his chest she felt his ribs, and now she understood why they stood out as they did. He needed feeding up. Under her ear, his heart beat fast. Occasionally a shiver still shook him. Lifting her hand, she touched his chest, his chin, paused. Pulled back and snuggled close again.

They stayed like that, listening to the house creak as outside the night air cooled down towards freezing point. Then Logan moved carefully. His lips brushed her forehead, trailing feather-light kisses from one side to the other and then down her cheek to her chin and along her jawline. Over her throat, moving slowly downward to the V in her pyjama jacket, his breath so soft it caressed her.

Her breathing faltered around the lump of desire suddenly blocking her throat. Lifting her hands, she slid her fingers into his thick, dishevelled hair and massaged his skull with soft circles, holding him against her breasts.

Logan groaned and pulled away to tug her down the bed until she was on her back. His fingers shook as he tried to deal with the buttons keeping her chest covered. 'Help me here,' he muttered through gritted teeth.

With a hand on his chest she pushed him away and sat up to shuck off her robe. About to attack the buttons on her top, she paused, drinking in the sight of Logan's chest as he hauled his tee shirt over his head.

'Karina?' The shirt landed on the floor. He was staring at her with such hunger in his eyes.

'Do you want to stop? Say so if you do.'

Her eyes tracked the outline of his ribs and moved over those muscles as she shook her head, not trusting her voice. To hell with the buttons. She jerked her top over her head and then lay back to lift her butt and slide her pyjama bottoms down past her thighs.

Logan returned to where he'd left off; kissing a trail between her breasts, moving to one breast to tease her until she thought she'd scream with need, only have her other breast put through the same tummy-tightening, heart-cranking sensations. Her muscles grew tighter and tighter. Her centre was wet.

Her hands flailed against the bed as she tried to reach for him. 'I have to touch you!' she cried.

'No. Not yet. One touch and I'll be gone. Let me give you this.'

'But I want to feel you. My skin on your skin.'

It was torture to lie there, being made love to without giving something back. She wanted Logan to feel what she was feeling, to share the sensations pouring through her, yet he didn't seem to think he was missing out.

'Your turn's coming. You'll get more than a handful, I promise.'

Again that beautiful mouth shifted its centre of attention, this time trailing more of those delicious kisses over her stomach before moving ever downward, until he reached the hot, molten apex at the top of her legs. Any thoughts about what she should be doing to Logan were lost as he went from kissing to licking and all too quickly drove her to the brink with a gripping need clawing through her.

Just when she knew she couldn't take any more without exploding into a thousand pieces, Karina moaned. 'I need you inside me.'

Logan hesitated. 'Do you have a…?'

Karina shook her head. 'It's okay. I have an IUD.' She'd had it fitted while she was married, as Ian hadn't wanted to start a family.

Logan rose above her to kneel between her legs, his reaction to her big and beautiful. She reached for him, slid her hands over, around his length. And cried out. *Beautiful.*

Logan lowered his body and pressed the head of his erection to her. Her hands stroked until he pushed inside, deep within her heat. As he filled her she nearly wept with joy and love. When he withdrew to drive inside again her breathing caught, her lungs stalled, her muscles quaked with need. Then her climax cracked, whipped through her, taking over and blotting out all thought, leaving only exquisite sensations rocking through her.

Slowly Karina's breathing came back to something like normal, as did her heart-rate. Logan lay sprawled half across her and she held him tight, making the most of this moment. His chest rose and fell rapidly. Sweat glistened on his back. She tugged at the bedcovers. In the chilly night air it wouldn't be long before they were cold, despite the heat between them.

She wanted to laugh and to cry, to be quiet and to talk. She wanted to repeat what they'd just shared, yet was worried it might not be the same. She couldn't believe that making love after all this time could be so wonderful, that she'd been wrong to think she would never know a man again.

'Thank you,' she whispered.

'That should be my line,' he gave back, and carefully rolled over to pull her in against him, spooning them together, his arm wonderfully heavy on her waist, his hand splayed across a breast.

'We can share it.'

Her mouth was swollen and tender as she smiled into the semi-dark. Her fingers traced her lips. *I feel whole—like a part of me that I didn't know was missing has been given back.*

But she was wise enough to know that this night had not changed anything. She still intended staying on in this house. Mickey still needed her to fight for what he required. Logan hadn't emptied his skull of those demons plaguing him.

She might be feeling languid and filled with warmth right at this minute, but it was only an interval, brought on by a nightmare and her unexpected need to get close to Logan just once.

Her eyes drooped closed and she snuggled further into the warm body at her back. She'd enjoy the moment and stretch it out for as long as possible.

Logan held Karina like a delicate gift, never wanting to let her go. He didn't know if it was in his power to lift his arm and set her free. Not that she was trying to move away. Quite the opposite.

This was a precious time; an intimacy beyond making love. Their sweat-slicked bodies locked together as they cooled, their hearts slowing as that intense, mind-blocking release eased off. Of course he wanted to do it again, but not right at this moment. Now he wanted to treasure this amazing woman who'd shown the tormentors in his head where they could go—for a while at least.

'You sent them packing,' he murmured.

'I'm glad. Now we know there is a cure.'

He chuckled softly. As if it was going to be that easy. But he didn't even mind so much at the moment. Around Karina, anything seemed possible. Even slaying dragons would be doable.

'I've moved on from hot chocolate.'

'You can have both.'

She said nothing else for a while, and he began to think she'd fallen asleep. Then...

'You gave me back my heart.'

'Your ex bruised you that badly? He stole it and never returned it when he left?'

Was this the first time for her since her marriage had fallen apart?

'I thought I'd given him so much of myself there was nothing left for anyone else. Now I'm not so sure.'

Her voice had got lower and lower, and he strained to hear her clearly.

'Karina, like I said: you're a beautiful woman with a big heart.'

She'd done so much for him, right from the day he'd turned up here, full of ideas about what they should be doing with the house and the surgery. Despite their disagreement about the property she hadn't flinched at extending him a hand.

Under his arm she tensed.

'Karina?'

Silence.

'Hey, I didn't say that earlier just so I could have sex. I'm not saying it now because I'm grateful. I believe it. Truly believe it. Okay?'

Had her ex told her how lovely she was to get his own way? While all along he'd been bonking his other woman on the side?

'Okay.'

The tension relaxed and she wriggled against him, that perfect backside rubbing where it counted and causing him to bite down on the need springing to life and tightening his manhood again.

She stilled. Of course she'd have felt his reaction. Kind of hard to miss.

He grinned. He was probably crazy not to be acting on it—he would do so shortly—but holding Karina in his arms had to be the best thing to happen to him in a long time. He continued holding her, burying his face in her silky hair, breathing in her scent. Sex and sweat and woman. He'd be a millionaire if he knew how to bottle that. But he didn't want to share it. This was his moment; their moment.

Carefully pulling the covers up to their necks, he shifted to get more comfortable. There were still hours left to enjoy before they had to get out of bed. He should be shivering from the cold, but he was warm for the first time in months. Sure, he'd been hot beyond comprehension out in the middle of Nigeria, but this warmth was inside him, heating the corners where he'd shoved his fear and vulnerability and cold anger. This warmth was all down to Karina.

He could get used to it. Which was why he wouldn't repeat it. There'd only be one night with Karina. It wouldn't be fair on either of them to continue being intimate for the remainder of his time in Motueka and then for him to walk away as though it didn't matter. Because it would. He'd have nudged aside one set of problems for another. But staying on permanently wouldn't work. He still had to face down his fears.

He shuddered. That day seemed to be racing at him and he was so not prepared. Despite tonight, and making love with Karina, the fact was those evil men did dominate his head, his life. He knew he had to prove they hadn't won, that he could banish them for ever.

He needed to get back to being normal. That wasn't going to happen while he was shut away in small-town New Zealand. No, that required a visit to what was for him enemy territory. Another shudder. Then and only then did he stand a chance of making a life for himself. Maybe even a life that included a family.

He already had Mickey. Karina would complete the picture.

But he was getting way ahead of himself. They'd made love once and here he was thinking too far ahead. Just because Karina had him beginning to feel whole again, it didn't mean she might contemplate a relationship with him. She'd made a niche for herself with Mickey, and she certainly didn't need a shell of a man living with them.

So he'd enjoy this moment. Holding Karina, feeling complete, even knowing it couldn't last, meant everything to him. She'd done so much for him in her kind and generous way.

Now he had to do something for her.

Unfortunately he knew exactly what that was.

CHAPTER ELEVEN

KARINA SANG UNDER her breath as she hopped out of the shower. Singing out loud would only bring complaints. But, damn she felt good this morning. Nothing like good sex—no, make that very good sex—with Logan to make the day wonderful.

It's six a.m. and the rain's bucketing down, and I'm on top of my world.

Uh-oh. Rain.

Where were the buckets?

Pushing into her robe, she dashed to the laundry and hastily placed buckets under the drips, took another to the bedroom next to Mickey's and placed it under the newest problem.

'When did that leak start?'

Logan leaned the shoulder she'd kissed so thoroughly during the night against the doorframe, his hands in his jeans pockets, feet crossed at his ankles, sexy stubble on his chin. He looked like a very tired movie star.

'Last night too much for you, lover-boy?' She flicked a finger under his chin. Heat sizzled through her veins as that stubble softly rasped her skin. Tingles licked the base of her spine.

He caught her finger to run his tongue over the tip. 'Are you avoiding my question?'

Her happiness slipped a notch. 'There was a damp patch on the carpet after the last rainfall.'

'I guess you'll be buying more buckets this week, then.' He didn't look so happy either. 'You should've told me.'

This was why they shouldn't have slept together.

'Let's make tea and toast. I'm hungry.' All that exercise had used up last night's dinner. She pushed past him. 'You must be, too.'

She'd noticed while exploring his body during the night—how could she not?—that his ribs didn't stick out quite so much as that first time she'd seen his chest.

Breakfast was quiet until Mickey woke up. When he protested loudly about wanting to stay home again her heart wasn't in trying to reason with him. Instead she picked him up, took him out to the car and buckled him into the seat; surprising herself as much as Mickey.

He yelled at her all the way to kindergarten, so by the time she got to the clinic she had a pounding headache to go with her darkening mood.

All morning Karina was aware of Logan's voice through the wall as he talked to his patients, and it reminded her of him talking dirty as they'd made love. Had sex. They had not made love. That would mean they were going somewhere with this, and anyone with half a brain only had to look into Logan's eyes and know the only place he was going was out of here and far away.

He was still haunted by what had happened and his

way of clawing back some control in his life was to organise hers.

Voices intruded from outside. Workmen with ladders and tools were striding along the path.

'What the—?' Leaping up, she ran for the door and charged out onto the lawn. 'Excuse me. Who are you?'

One of them stopped and stared at her. 'Mrs Pascale?'

Not likely. 'Karina Brown. This is my property. What are you doing here?'

'Seems there's a mistake. I thought this was Dr Pascale's house?'

'It is.' The man himself came up behind Karina. 'I'm Logan Pascale. You're Harry?'

'That's me.' He jerked a thumb over his shoulder. 'This the roof you want looking at?'

Harry Whoever flicked his gaze back and forth between Karina and Logan.

'That's right.' Logan stepped around her. 'Come in and I'll show you where it's leaking. I'd like you to check the whole structure while you're at it, and give me a quote for both repairs and a full replacement.'

Karina seethed. 'Excuse me?'

'Be with you in a moment,' Logan called over his shoulder.

Oh, boy, you are so going to regret this.

She charged after him. 'What happened to talking to me about any repairs?'

'I didn't realise I had to run absolutely everything past you.'

'It should've been a reasonable assumption. I do live here. All the time. Unlike you. I have every right to know what's going on with my home. I also think it only fair if I have a say on the decisions being made.'

'I only talked to the roofing company this morning, and we have been rather busy in the clinic.'

Karina came close to stamping her foot. Close, but she didn't. 'You've obviously been thinking about it before this morning.' A picture of him leaning against that doorframe flashed into her head. 'You could've told me about this instead of giving me a hard time about buckets. Is this how I'll learn you've contacted a real estate company too? They'll just turn up with their listing pads in hand and go through my home as though they own it?'

'Cut it out. It's a huge step from roofing to selling.'

'So you're not getting the house ready to sell?'

Logan's eyes narrowed. 'We're having that discussion at the end of my stay, remember?'

'So it's fine for you to prepare the house for sale, but I'm not supposed to think about it or, heaven forbid, even mention what we might do?'

She'd come full circle—had swapped one control freak for another. And here she'd been thinking she'd made progress in the standing on her own two feet stakes. *Idiot.*

'Karina, breathe deep and calm down. We—'

The heel of her shoe was buried in the soft ground as she gave in to the urge to stamp her foot. '"Breathe deep", he says. Like it works for you. *Not.* Anyway, I don't want to calm down. I want to tell you exactly what I think.'

Those grey eyes became the colour of cold steel. 'I'm listening.'

'From the moment you arrived I've been hearing what you plan to do with Mickey's home and the clinic. Not once have you said, *Let's discuss our options*. Oh, no, you want the whole package wrapped and sealed so you can go away again with a clear conscience. You think that's the best thing for Mickey—and for me. Well, I'm telling you, buster, you are *wrong*. I am not moving. *Ever*. Nor is *my* boy.'

Anger and pain shot through those eyes and she knew she'd gone too far. Mickey was in his care too. Except she was the one who'd be here day in and day out, every month of the year and beyond.

'Finished?'

As if she'd trust that calm tone. 'I don't care if the roof leaks, or the carpet needs replacing. It doesn't matter if I have to juggle locums to keep the surgery running. This is my home. You can't sell it out from under me. Us, I mean.'

Hot tears ran down her heated cheeks but she didn't care. He could think what he liked about them as long as he got the damned message.

'Leave me alone. Leave us to live quietly and happily, as we were before you arrived. I don't need you interfering and telling me what to do.'

'You have to start facing reality.'

'Yours? Or mine?' she snapped.

He stood tall, staring down at her. Some of those lines around his mouth and eyes had filled out over the weeks he'd been here. *Huh?* Why was she thinking about that now? Then he got her full attention.

'I think it's a good idea if I move out for the rest of my stay in Motueka.' Light glinted off those steely eyes.

'I agree.'

But what scheme would he be cooking up when he had more time on his hands? Who would wake him from those nightmares? She opened her mouth to say that if he stayed they'd work something out. Stopped. Pressed her lips together. Maybe they wouldn't. It was too late. Putting everything off until the end of his stay had been a mistake.

'I'll come see Mickey every day.'

'Of course.' She didn't expect any less of him.

'I'll get my things at the end of the morning session.'

'Right.'

He spun away, turned back. 'I'll pick Mickey up from kindergarten today and take him with me until dinner time. Is that okay with you?'

'Yes.'

God, now they sounded like a divorcing couple, fighting over the kids.

'This might be for the best anyway. He's getting too close to you and his little heart is going to break when you go. Moving out of the house will soften that blow.'

For Mickey and for her.

Logan's cheeks paled. 'I get it. I've stayed too long. But he *is* my nephew. I *am* his family.'

The longing lacing his words stole into her heart, slowed her anger.

He reached a hand out and ran a finger over her chin. 'This isn't over, Karina.'

'I think it has to be.'

She should be grateful he was on the move, but she couldn't explain the way her heart thudded wildly as she watched him cross to the corner of the house and disappear around the back. He really was leaving, and taking something of her with him—a piece of her heart. At least it was a piece and not the whole package. It felt beyond hard to watch him go, but it would have been a lot worse in another week.

Toughen up. Take everything on the chin. Get back to life as you know it.

Quiet and happy. Lonely and boring. At least she'd know where she was. Or would she? Just because Logan was no longer staying here it didn't mean he wouldn't be hatching plans. Didn't mean she'd switch him off, out of her system. Impossible after last night, after knowing his body, knowing how he moved when he came inside her.

The sound of screeching tin had her turning her head in the direction of the roofers.

The house would feel empty, but at least it would be dry.

Logan swore as he tossed his few clothes into a hold-all. What the hell had happened? One minute everything had been hunky-dory, the next he was out on his butt. Not that he could blame Karina for that. He'd put his hand up—said he was going. But she'd been quick to jump down his throat with all her unfounded accusations.

Now he had to find a motel room that was far enough from humanity that no one would hear him calling out in his sleep. Not everyone would be as patient and understanding as Karina. No one would care like she did. He'd gone two nights without a nightmare this week. A first. All down to Karina.

Outside, he went to talk with Harry, agreed on a price for a new roof, and walked down the drive to his vehicle, refusing to look back. Somewhere behind him Karina would be nursing a patient or making a sandwich or drinking tea. What she wouldn't be doing was wishing he'd stay.

Karina, I've fallen in love with you, somewhere between your puddle-jumping antics and last night, when I held your naked body tight against mine. Leaving is breaking me, but staying will break you. I'm not the right man to love you. You need someone willing to face his demons like you've done: bravely and without fanfare.

So he had things to do for her, to get the show on the road. Chucking his bag onto the back seat, he climbed into the vehicle and scrolled down the contacts list on his phone.

'Uncle Logan, have you come to get me?' His favourite little man ran at him an hour later. 'Pick me up.'

Logan obliged. 'Want to go for a ride to Nelson?'

Mickey's yells of excitement brought his teacher racing outside. 'What's going on? Is Mickey all right?'

'He's fine, Scarlett. I'm taking him out of kindergarten early today.'

'He's been missing a lot of kindy since you came on the scene.' Scarlett shrugged. 'You do a lot with him. He adores you.'

'The feelings are reciprocated.'

But give it another week and the boy might hate him. He squeezed Mickey tighter, breathed in his boy smell, and looked upwards. *James, he's a cracker kid.*

Tell me how to do the right thing. Hell, tell me what the right thing is.

'Where's Karina?' Mickey asked as he drove out of town and onto the causeway heading to Nelson. On one side of the road were apple orchards, on the other a tidal estuary.

'At work.'

She enjoyed her job, and her enthusiasm for her busy life seemed endless, but could that be a cover for the hurt underneath? He'd begun to appreciate her need to make a haven from where she could look life in the eye.

'Why isn't she coming with us?'

'She's letting us have man-time together.' His nephew had latched on to Karina like a lifeline. *Well, duh, she* is *his lifeline. So get it sorted, get it right for her, make her life easier.*

His foot pressed harder on the accelerator. The lawyers were waiting.

The house was cold when Karina let herself in after work. The day had dragged, her body ached, and tears had regularly threatened but thankfully hadn't spilled. She couldn't have David or Leeann asking what was wrong, or the patients fussing over her.

In the lounge, she cursed. The fire hadn't been set. There was no kindling chopped, nor any wood in the basket. Those had become Logan's jobs over the time he'd been here, and obviously they hadn't been foremost in his mind when he was walking out.

Trudging outside to the woodshed, she picked up the hatchet and began splitting pine for kindling. Dinner. *Yeah, well, so what?* The chicken she'd planned on bak-

ing could stay in the fridge. About all she could face
was toast. It wouldn't hurt Mickey this once.

'Let me do that. You're going to lose a finger unless
you start watching what you're doing.'

She leapt up, dropping the axe at her feet. 'Don't
creep up on me.'

Sadness leaked out of Logan's eyes. 'Let's not play
those games. Mickey's inside, looking for you. I'll bring
the wood in and be on my way.'

Gulp. He had a point. She had lashed out thoughtlessly.

'Thank you.'

'Karina, we went to Nelson.' Mickey's short arms
wrapped around her thighs. 'It took a *long* time.'

Placing kisses on his head, she lifted him to stare
into his sweet face. 'You're home now.' She loved him
so much it terrified her.

'Logan took me to a big building with lots of windows. The lady gave me a lemonade drink.'

'That was nice.' Where had Logan gone? To see his
real estate agent? *Yeah, I bet he did. Of course he wants
this house sold ASAP now that he's moved out.*

About to storm outside and give him a piece of her
mind, she hesitated. *Slow down, think it through.* It
wasn't as if he could sell without her signing papers
for the trust lawyers. She'd wait and see what he said.

He said absolutely nothing about his jaunt over to
the city.

'I've brought in enough kindling and wood for the
rest of the week.'

*Don't say a word. See if he'll talk about the house,
or the surgery. Anything.*

'Thank you.'

'See you tomorrow, Mickey.'

And he walked out.

That went well.

She snatched bread out of the pantry. A can of baked beans. Mickey's favourite dinner.

'I'm hungry.'

Right on cue.

'Set the table, then.'

He put three mats up, then three sets of cutlery. 'Where's Uncle Logan gone?'

That was the thing. She didn't know. Not that it was a problem. She had his phone number if she needed to get in touch.

'Into town, sweetheart.' *Please don't ask me anything else.*

'Will he be back to put me to bed?'

Did she want a tantrum? Or peace and quiet while they ate?

'Let's hope so.' Not quite a lie, but close enough to crank up the guilt.

Thankfully Mickey shrugged and dragged a stool over to the sink, filled three glasses with water. But when she tried to undress him for bed it was a different story.

'Where's Uncle Logan? I want him to read to me.'

'He's in town, sweetheart. Now, let's get your shirt off.'

'No.' He ducked out of reach.

Damn you, Logan Pascale. 'Mickey, come here. Now.' She gritted her teeth and counted to ten. Stood up. 'Right. Get into bed. Clothes and all.'

She was done arguing.

'Why won't he help me?' Mickey bit his bottom lip and blinked as tears rolled down his face.

'He's busy.' She tentatively made to lift his shirt and was surprised when he let her. 'Where did you get those bruises?'

Her heart stilled as she studied the purple marks on his upper arm. Three dark marks about the size of a fifty cent piece. Too uniform for a bleeding disorder, surely?

Mickey shut his eyes. 'Don't know,' he whispered as he reached for his pyjama jacket to pull over his singlet.

'Did you bump into something at kindy, sweetheart?'

He nodded slowly and climbed into bed.

'You need to watch where you're going.'

After tucking him into bed, she read him stories until he fell asleep. Dropping a kiss on his forehead, she clicked off the light and headed to the lounge, curled up into a chair.

Where are you staying, Logan? In the firebox flames flicked against the glass, sending a warm glow over the tiles. *Will the motel proprietor look after you when the nightmare strikes?*

Tears spilled over and poured down to drip off her chin.

Can you bring back the pieces of my heart you've stolen? I can't let you keep them. This wasn't supposed to be so hard. *When did I fall for you? Was it that day I came home to find you lying in front of the fire, holding one tired little boy? Or the morning you brought me a cup of tea in bed because I'd got up to Mickey three times and to you once during the night?*

Could it have occurred during one of those night-mares, when anger and fear had glittered out of his grey eyes as he returned from that place of horror he went to in his sleep?

It didn't matter. It had happened. And she needed to do something about it. Pull up the barriers and protect what was left.

Her heart stuttered. *Too late*, her head screamed.

With an exasperated sigh she threw herself out of the chair and went to make hot chocolate. The heck with her hips. This was a serious situation and only chocolate would help. That or Logan apologising and then sitting down with her to talk through everything.

The spoon scraped against the bottom of the pot as she absently stirred the heating milk. Her hand shook slightly. How would she cope if the house was sold? Could she make a haven in another place? There'd been so many changes over the last few months. She wasn't ready for any more.

Suddenly she was afraid. Afraid of starting again, of finding that some of those things she'd strived to put behind her had come back to torment her.

Logan Pascale had already changed things by being—Logan. She'd been unsettled from the moment she'd first laid eyes on him. She'd begun to want, to wonder, to hope, to feel. There was more to life than what she had. She could have it all and survive hap-pily. But only if she was prepared to step off the edge and give it a go.

There was the crux of the matter. She was not going to take a risk with her heart, her life, her everything ever again. It had been a lonely battle since Maria had died, but she couldn't let that rule her head. So, even loving Logan as she did, she had to keep him at arm's length. No, make that at the end of a rainbow. Unattainable. Out of temptation's way.

She had to ask him exactly what he was up to. His answer should dampen the fire in her belly.

Picking up the phone, she tapped Logan's number.

'Karina.'

'Do you like working in the clinic? Are you tempted to stay on permanently?'

Silence, then the sound of a chair being moved. 'That's why you've phoned?'

'Yes.'

Silence. Then, 'I can't.'

More silence.

She finally gave up waiting for him to expand on that. 'So you're determined to return to Africa?'

'Yes.'

That was all she got. *Yes*, with a load of caution behind it.

'Why?' She could also do short and to the point.

'It's where I work.'

'Oh, come on. You sign up for one contract at a time, not indefinitely.'

Dislike for herself rose and soured her mouth, but she had a battle to fight and listening to her heart right now would not win what she needed from him.

Then Logan said, 'The doctors at your local hospital work from one contract to the next, too. That's how it's done. They still say they work in Nelson, or wherever.'

True.

'Aren't you worried you might get kidnapped again? Or worse?'

Her heart squeezed so tightly she feared she was having a cardiac incident. A medical one, not a romantic one. She did not want Logan facing danger again. He might not be quite so lucky next time.

'Of course I am—even when the odds are against it.'

She shut her eyes against the pain in his voice, against his courage and his need. Her chest rose and fell as deep, slow breaths filled her lungs, dribbled out. *I need to support him and let him go without laying on guilt for doing what he wants.*

So all she had to do was tell him to go, as she'd wanted to do all along, and yet something held her back. Her obstinate heart?

'I think I understand.'

'Do you? Really?'

His scepticism drove her to say, 'You're braver than me. By a long way.'

Hiss. The milk had boiled over. She swore. 'Sorry— got to go.' *Click.* End of conversation. *Wipe, wipe—* milk everywhere. Damn, damn— sob. Rinse, squeeze the cloth—sob, sob.

Tossing the cloth in the sink, she headed to bed for a long, sleepless night.

Somehow they had to work together in the morning. Could she pull a sick day? That would work. Not.

CHAPTER TWELVE

KARINA SURVIVED THE morning by avoiding Logan as much as possible. Later she barely coped when he returned Mickey to her at dinnertime, and struggled with Mickey's tears and tantrums when Logan walked out through the door to go to his motel.

When Mickey refused to get undressed for bed she knew with absolute certainty that she had to walk away and let him have his way. She was in danger of screaming at him. And she'd never forgive herself if she let the despair that had dogged her all day form into words to lash him with. None of this was Mickey's fault.

'Go to bed in your clothes,' she said, and pulled the covers down.

Mickey climbed into bed and turned his head away.

'Goodnight, sweetheart.'

Silence was his answer. Had he been taking lessons from his uncle?

She cleaned up the kitchen, folded the washing, got some mince out of the freezer for tomorrow night's dinner, sat at the table with the mail, pushed that aside and got up. Turned off the lights and went to bed. Her body ached with tiredness. Her head was about to split in half. Her stomach was a knot.

She lay on her back, staring at the darkened ceiling, waiting for sleep to creep in and give her some relief from her thoughts for a while. Waited and waited.

'Karina...' Mickey stood by her bed. 'I'm lonely.'

You and me both, my boy.

She tossed the covers back. 'Come on, get in. We'll cuddle down together.'

She wrapped her arms around his body and held him close. And finally nodded off.

To dream of a hot, sexy man with demons in his head and concern for others in his heart...

'Wake up, Karina.' Mickey ran a finger over her eyelids.

Rolling over with a groan, she stared at the digital clock. Seven-thirty-five. What had happened? She never slept this late.

'Come on, sleepy head. Time we were up and about.' She pushed out of bed, feeling as if she'd done ten rounds with a heavyweight boxer. Except she'd never make the end of one bout. 'You have your shower first.'

'I don't want a shower.' Mickey still wore his clothes, and his flushed face was screwed up ready for an outburst.

'Okay, sweetheart, here's the deal. You can't go to see Uncle Logan if you don't shower.'

Since when had bribery become a part of her repertoire?

'I'll find you your favourite sweatshirt while you're getting clean.'

Blackmail as well?

He slid off the bed, thumping onto the floor. 'You can't come in the bathroom.'

Since when?

'Promise to wash your face, behind your ears and between your toes? And all parts in between?'

'Will Uncle Logan check?'

'Absolutely.'

Mickey dashed down to the bathroom, suddenly eager to get in the shower.

She could kill for a cup of tea and some headache pills. Not necessarily in that order.

She found Mickey's clothes for the day. Guilt at her handling of his reticence over showering bothered her. Using Logan as a bribe hadn't been right, but it had been the only thing to come to mind. Unfortunately the chances of Mickey forgetting by the time he saw his uncle were about zero. She'd deal with Logan's re-action when it happened.

She opened the bathroom door enough to slip the clothes through, then closed it and went to the kitchen to poke through the cupboard for painkillers.

'Where are they?'

Shifting recipe books, packets of antibiotics for Mickey's previous infections, she couldn't find what she wanted. They'd be in the bathroom cupboard.

'Go away!' Mickey shouted.

She'd completely forgotten she was banned from there. 'Sorry, Mickey, I'm going—'

His little torso was black and purple with bruising.

'Mickey? Sweetheart? What's happened?'

She knelt in front of him, took the towel out of his hands and began drying him ever so gently as she stud-

ied every part of him. Had she discovered the reason
he hadn't wanted to undress for bed?

'I'm sorry.'

He was sorry?

'This isn't your fault, Mickey. You haven't done anything wrong.'

If he'd fallen he wouldn't have bruises on both his
stomach and his chest, his back and his thighs. *Leukaemia.* The word landed in her brain like a bomb.
Leukaemia. The dreaded disease that many children
with Down syndrome contracted often first appeared
as bruising due to low platelet numbers.

Leukaemia—with all its treatments and tests and
transplants and—

I'm going to throw up.

Not in front of Mickey. Swallowing the bile, she
struggled to get her stomach under control. Sweat broke
out on her brow and upper lip.

'I haven't been naughty, Karina. Promise.' Fat tears
ran down his face.

'I know you haven't,' she croaked, before dropping
the towel and placing the softest kiss on each cheek.
'You're my man, and my man's good. Let's get you
dressed and warm, then we'll call Uncle Logan.'

She wanted to hug him tight but didn't dare. What
if she added to those bruises?

'Will he be angry at me?'

'No way. He loves you.' What was this about?
'Mickey, did someone hurt you?'

'No—o.'

Holding him carefully against her, she stood up.
'Let's get the phone.'

'I'm not going to hospital,' he hiccupped against her neck. 'I don't like being sick.'

'I know, sweetheart. I really do.' *Right now it's the last place I want to go too, but it's where we're headed.*

Logan answered on the first ring. 'Karina? You okay?'

'You need to come home and see Mickey. Urgently.'

'What's up?'

'He's covered in bruises. They're everywhere. What if it's AML?' The fear that had started in the bathroom bubbled up, almost overwhelming her. 'Logan!' she cried. 'He's so small, he doesn't need this.'

'Karina, stop it. You're panicking.'

Great for him to say when there was a tremor in his voice.

'There could be any number of reasons for the bruising. Not only acute myeloid leukaemia.'

Hearing him enunciate those dreaded words made her skin chill.

'The front and back of his body are covered.' She kissed the damp head nestled against her. 'He needs you.' *Damn it.* 'I need you.'

'Hang in there. I'll check him over, then if it's necessary we'll take him to hospital, get the specialists on to it immediately.'

Hurry up and get here. I need your strength. I can't do this on my own. Oh, no, Maria and James. Maria, I'm so sorry. Your baby's sick. I've let him down by not keeping him healthy.

Even though she knew perfectly well that no one could prevent leukaemia striking, the guilt was crawling through her frozen body.

I am so sorry.

'This is so hard, Logan. What if—?' She couldn't finish the sentence. Her throat was clogged with un-shed tears.

'One thing at a time, okay? Unlock your door for me.'

'Mickey hid it from me.' She turned the lock to open. 'He refused to get undressed last night, slept in his clothes. Then he got into bed with me. I wasn't allowed to see him in the shower.'

Now she was blathering. Worse, she couldn't stop.

'If I hadn't gone in to get some pills I mightn't have known for another day. What sort of mother does that make me?'

'The best.'

A familiar hand touched her cheek in a caress, then removed the phone from her ear.

'The very best.'

Her eyes widened. 'That was quick.'

'I was walking out of my room the moment I heard your voice.' Logan turned his focus to Mickey. 'Hey, buddy, how's my boy?'

'I don't want to go to hospital, Uncle Logan.'

Logan raised an eyebrow in Karina's direction.

She shook her head. 'I never mentioned hospital.'

Logan held his arms out to Mickey. 'Can I hold you and get a hug, buddy?'

Mickey unwound his arms and reached towards Logan.

Logan held him as tenderly as he would the finest crystal. 'Let's go to the bathroom and you can show me your tummy.'

Karina held her breath, but the fight seemed to have

gone out of Mickey. He cuddled close to his uncle and said nothing.

Karina didn't breathe again until Logan had done a short but thorough examination of Mickey's torso.

'These bruises could've been made by impact. With what? That is the question. But I'm not certain about anything. Best we go to Nelson ED and get some blood work done.'

'I'll get his jacket and shoes.' She had to get away from those trusting eyes Mickey had locked on her. 'I won't be a moment.'

She sat in the back of the car with Mickey in his car seat beside her. She couldn't take her eyes off him, as if she might be able to keep the baddies at bay if she didn't look away. His little hand gripped hers so tightly she'd probably never get the feeling back and she couldn't care less.

The trip took for ever, and yet they seemed to pull up in the hospital car park almost before they'd left Motueka. Logan carried him in to the ED and after a short conversation with the nurse on the reception desk they were shown through to Dr Cavanagh, a paediatrician.

Mickey started crying. 'I want to go home.'

'Shh, sweetheart. We're going to make you better.' *I'm not making promises I can't guarantee.* But, damn, she wanted to. Anything to take that misery away from his beloved face.

Karina took him from Logan and paced up and down, leaving the doctors to their discussion.

Then… 'Hello, Mickey. I'm Paddy—a doctor like your uncle. We're going to go into a little room so you can show me your tummy without everyone else seeing. Okay?'

His manner was so gentle Mickey didn't protest.

It didn't take long—as if Mickey had worked out that if he did what he was asked he'd get out of there quicker. Even when Paddy took some blood samples he only squeezed his eyes shut and turned his head into Karina's breast.

'Go get a coffee in the canteen. I'll be along the moment I know the answer to these.' Dr Cavanagh held up the blood tubes and a form.

'How do I sit here pretending my world isn't imploding?' she asked Logan ten minutes later, when he placed a mug of tea in front of her and put down a juice for Mickey.

It took for ever until Paddy strode through the canteen, a smile on his face. 'White cells, platelets and haemoglobin all normal—the rest will take longer. But we've ruled out the main players in AML.'

Tears of relief streamed down Karina's face, and when she glanced at Logan she saw pools of moisture in the corners of his eyes. Taking his free hand in hers she stood. 'Come on, Mickey, we're taking you home.'

Paddy cleared his throat. 'Actually, as we still don't know what caused those bruises, I need you to stick around a bit longer. In cases like this there are certain procedures I need to follow. Mickey, is it okay if I ask you a few questions?'

Mickey nodded and gripped Karina's hand.

'Mickey, has anyone been hurting you?' Paddy asked him gently.

Logan looked shocked. 'Are you suggesting he's being pushed around at home?'

Karina felt the bottom fall out of her world when only seconds ago she'd started to feel relief and hope. Did the doctor think that she'd been hurting Mickey?

'It's okay, Mickey,' she whispered, feeling sick to her stomach. 'You can tell the truth. Has anyone been hurting you?'

Slowly, Mickey nodded again. 'Ben.'

Ben? Suddenly her conversation with Robyn flooded back to her.

'Is Ben the new boy in your class?'

Mickey sniffed. 'He says I look funny. If I try to play with him and William, Ben pinches me and tells me to go away.'

All the arguments about his not wanting to go to kindy came back. 'I thought Mickey was being clingy and wanting to hang around with Logan when he refused to go to kindy.'

She looked to Logan, saw anger and compassion warring for supremacy in his eyes. Not anger ather, surely? Yes, she'd made a mistake, but—

He tucked an arm over her shoulders. 'We've been worrying too much about the medical and not enough about the human factor.'

Phew. She relaxed against him. 'Why would a kid do that to a sweet wee boy who never hurts anyone?'

Paddy intervened. 'You'd be shocked at how much of that I see in here. Now, go home, take some time to make your lad feel safe and secure about the world out there, and give yourselves a break. It's a rare parent who looks for bullying straight away. I'll call you as soon as I have those other results.'

So they weren't out of the woods yet. Karina smiled her thanks for this man who'd dropped everything to see Mickey, even when he was obviously asleep on his feet after a night shift.

Logan shook his hand and took her elbow. 'Let's go. What do you reckon, Mickey? Want to see Mr Grumpy?'

'Do I look like an idiot, Uncle Logan?'

Karina's heart froze. 'No, you don't,' she growled, then softened her tone. 'No, you are not an idiot, Mickey. You're the best little boy in the world.'

'You're awesome, buddy.' Logan's arms came around them both, held them as he breathed through the anger tensing his body. 'And I thought what happened to me in Nigeria was bad,' he whispered against her ear.

Back home, they left Mickey with Mr Grumpy, after he'd eaten baked beans on toast for a late breakfast, and headed out to see his kindergarten teachers. Paddy had called to tell them the other tests were normal.

'You were right. I worry too much about the wrong things. I should've listened harder to Mickey.'

Logan took her hand as they walked up the path to the kindergarten. 'Blaming yourself is a waste of time. You're a great mother to him. Just keep believing that.'

The teachers were shocked, but admitted that they had noticed changes in Mickey's attitude and how lately he'd often avoided going out to play at break time. They hadn't made the connection between Mickey's behaviour and Ben joining the class, but when William and the other children were questioned they admitted that they had seen Ben hurting Mickey.

The teachers assured Karina and Logan that they'd speak to Ben's parents and it wouldn't happen again.

'How could they not have noticed?' Karina snapped as she buckled her seatbelt for the short ride home. 'We'll take Mickey out of here and enrol him in another kindergarten.'

Logan shook his head slowly. 'I don't know… This'll happen again wherever he goes. He's different, and kids always pick up on that.'

Feeling let down, she rounded on him, only to have him hold his hand up.

'Hear me out. He needs to learn to stand up for himself—not to run and hide.'

'Sure, Logan, and how's he going to do that?'

'I'll be there for him; with him. I'm going to kindy every day until he feels comfortable, and then I'm going to keep talking to him about what happened so he never again thinks he has to hide anything from us.'

Huh? 'What are you talking about? You're leaving in a week.'

'I'm staying. Permanently.'

Logan hadn't thought it through, but the moment the words left his mouth he knew it was true. Here in Motueka, with Karina and Mickey, he'd found what he'd been looking for most of his adult life.

A hand pushed at his shoulder.

'Stop it. You can't go from selling the house and the surgery and bailing out to suddenly telling me you're staying. Do you ever consult with other people before you make decisions that might affect them?'

She was peeved.

'I'm not selling the house or the surgery. I sorted it all with the lawyers yesterday, in Nelson.'

'That's not answering my question.'

She locked her eyes on him and waited, her fingers tugging at the hem of her jacket.

He'd done what she wanted, hadn't he? What was there to discuss?

'Is it all right with you if I'm a permanent fixture in my nephew's life?'

Disappointment replaced her annoyance. 'You know it is. What's not all right is the way you go about doing things that involve me. I've spent my life falling into line to suit first my father and then Ian. I am *not* going to do it for you. Ever.'

So she thought he was a control freak? 'I was trying to do the best for you both.'

'Take me home. I'm done here.' She turned to face the front, her shoulders tight, her hands still fidgeting. 'I'm done with you.'

His heart curled up tight, painfully. Until she'd said that he hadn't realised how much he'd been hoping she cared for him.

'I'm still not going away.'

'Mickey will be thrilled.'

Did Karina want him gone so she could bring Mickey up on her own? He doubted it. She'd phoned him the moment she found those bruises, had turned to him for help. She was tough on the outside, but underneath was a softie who sometimes needed to be able to lean on someone. *Him.* He had to be her backstop. He couldn't handle it if she found someone else to fill that gap in her life.

Could he win her heart in the months ahead? It wouldn't be easy, but the reward would be worth all the waiting.

Karina stood in the doorway of what had briefly been Logan's bedroom. Her heart thudded against her ribs. Tears blocked her throat. Logan sat on the floor with Mickey kneeling beside him. In front of them was an open carton of James's belongings. Photos covered the carpet, many of them torn or crinkled from being screwed up. The photo of James in Logan's hand was shaking.

'That's my daddy.' Mickey tapped the picture. He rummaged through the others. 'And here's Mummy. She's pretty.'

'Yes, buddy, she is.' Logan's voice sounded full of tears. He was focused on the picture of his brother, drinking in every pixel.

'I want them to come home now.' Mickey picked up some more photos.

Logan ran a hand over Mickey's head and down his back. 'You and me both, buddy.'

Tears spilled down Karina's cheeks. 'And me,' she whispered.

'Hey.' Logan looked up. 'We're doing a bit of sorting here.'

'Sure.' She took a step into the room. 'I had to put the photos away. They got too much for a certain boy. He wasn't coping.'

'Hence the damaged ones?'

She nodded. 'That's why there's only the one on the wall in his bedroom.' Out of reach of Mickey.

'Karina, can I put Mummy and Daddy in my bedroom now?'

'Yes, sweetheart, you can.'

Hopefully enough time had passed that he would no longer get too distraught every time he looked at the photos. She moved closer and squatted down beside Mickey.

'You choose which ones you'd like.'

'Uncle Logan's staying with us.'

Her gaze instantly fixed on Logan. As in staying in this house? Or in Motueka? 'You've explained?'

'Of course. But I didn't say exactly where I'd be living.' His eyes never wavered. 'I can find a house close by.'

'Or you could move in with us.'

How would she cope? How could she not? She loved him. Loved *them*. They were a family unit, put together under unusual circumstances, but that didn't mean the love wasn't real or strong or good.

I love them both so much it hurts.

She loved Mickey; always had and always would. She loved Logan: always would. She'd done what she'd sworn never to do again: fallen in love. Fallen for Logan. Surprisingly, that didn't feel like a problem right now. He might act first, tell her later, but he always had her concerns on his radar, looking out for her and Mickey.

Was she going to ruin a chance at happiness by being pig-headed? He hadn't brushed her aside when she'd complained he should have discussed everything with her. He'd been at the front door as fast as possible when she'd phoned in a panic that morning. What more did she want?

For Logan to love her.

She stared at him. Would he ever feel for her what was tightening her chest, speeding up her heart for him? Did he get tingles at the base of his spine every time she walked into the same room? Tingles she'd come to accept as her Logan barometer?

Only one way to find out all the answers.

The air was suddenly chilly, but her blood was warm, her heart heated. 'Hey…' She leaned across and took his face in her hands, kissed him full on the mouth.

'Tell me I'm not dreaming,' the man holding her heart whispered.

Her reply was to kiss him some more.

'I could get to like this.'

Now he took charge of the kiss, deepening it and sending hot need flowing through her body.

Finally she pulled her head back, just enough to see into his eyes. 'I know I'm all over the place about what I want, but I'd be happy if you stayed here. Permanently. With us. For Mickey. For me. I love you, which is why I got huffy with you. I didn't think I could take a chance on happiness, but now I know I can't do anything else. You've found a way into my heart. Not sure how, but you have.'

Her lips pressed together in a rueful smile. She could go on and on, but he'd probably do a runner from the madwoman.

Logan reached a hand around one of hers. 'I'm not going back to Africa. After this morning I know I don't need to. I have you. Nothing, no one, is half as scary with you at my side.'

'Kar—ina. You want a photo?'

'Sure do, sweetheart. You pick one for me.'

She slowly slipped out of Logan's hold, unwilling to leave his warmth and strength, but knowing those would always be there for her, whenever she wanted them. She just knew it.

'Karina…' He pulled her back to him. 'I love you, too. You're amazing, the way you've accepted who I am, the mess I've been. I doubt I'd have begun to recover without you there for me. But most of all I just love you—everything about you.'

Her heart swelled and more tears flowed—this time for joy.

'Thank you,' she croaked.

This time she'd got it right. She knew it from the bottom of her heart.

Logan stared down at a picture of his brother and sister-in-law. 'I wonder what those two would have to say about this.'

'I think Maria would be laughing fit to bust. In the nicest possible way, of course.'

'James would tell me to grab life and live it with you and Mickey.'

One month later…

A handful of people were gathered in the lounge at the old house in High Street. Karina looked around, smiling at everyone.

Mickey's grandparents, Adele and Mark, were smiling nearly as much as she was. David and his wife and Leeann and her partner were chatting together. David was more relaxed now that he could share the clinic's workload with Logan, and no longer talked of moving away. Becca stood in the middle of the room, watching everyone as if she was the boss around here. All dressed up in a figure-hugging suit, looking stunning, she had a new boyfriend at her side who looked as though he never intended letting her get away. Jonty, dressed in his Sunday best, stood with an excited Mickey.

This was what life was all about—what she'd been searching for most of her life. Warmth and happiness.

'I'm sorry your parents couldn't be here.' Logan spoke quietly to Karina as they waited for Becca to start the proceedings.

So am I.

'Don't be. It's their loss, not ours.' Karina refused to let her mum and dad hurt her again, especially today of all days.

She had Adele and Mark now. They made her feel welcome and loved, with no pressure about how she did things—including raising their grandson—with the kind of family love she wanted and revelled in. But it was only a drop in the bucket of love she received from Logan every minute of every day.

She glanced down at the simple cream silk dress she wore and knew nothing but happiness. It was a beautiful outfit. One she'd wear again and again when she and Logan went out for an intimate meal. Her life had been turned around.

Becca approached with a huge I-told-you-so smile. 'Ready?'

Karina laughed. 'I've been ready for weeks.'

'Then let's do it.' Logan took her free hand and locked those beautiful grey eyes on her.

Becca turned to face their guests. 'I know the marriage celebrant isn't supposed to cry, but this is my first wedding, and Karina is my best friend, so you'll have to put up with a few tears as we go through the ceremony.'

Jonty grumped, 'Get on with it, girl. Lunch is spoiling.'

Karina's heart squeezed. Here it was. The moment she joined her life with the best man ever. A man who'd always look out for her and Mickey, who wouldn't deliberately break her heart or trash her love. A man she'd give her life for, who would share raising Mickey, would cherish for ever.

In one hand she gripped Logan's fingers tightly. In the other she held a bunch of the first of the season's daffodils, grown and picked for her by Jonty. The spring flowers spoke of new beginnings and brighter days to come.

Leaning close to Logan, she whispered, 'I love you.'

'I know,' he whispered back, with a cheeky glint in those eyes she adored.

Eyes that expressed so much of who Logan was. She'd seen pain and fear in them, anger and stubbornness. She'd also read love and wonder and care and concern for her and for Mickey. Those eyes had led her to this moment.

'Becca, we're ready,' she said around a big smile. She was done waiting. 'Do it.'

She mightn't be concerned about lunch, but she sure was bursting to become Karina Pascale.

Mickey stood beside Becca, his cute little face so serious it must be hurting him.

'I've got the ring in my pocket, Uncle Logan.'

Maria, you'd be so proud of your wee man. He looks gorgeous. He's growing up fast, and he's absolutely devoted to Logan. I wish you could see him right this minute, standing proud and tall for us.

Tears ran down Karina's cheeks. 'And we haven't even started!'

Becca took the hint, cleared her throat and began.

'Love. That's what brought Karina and Logan together. First their love for Mickey, then their love for each other.' She swallowed hard. 'The day Karina said she had to get home to her men I knew she was a goner.'

The room was quiet, as though the few guests were holding their breath for fear of missing a single word.

'These three people have a very special relationship. Today I'm marrying Karina, Logan *and* Mickey. They will look out for each other in the good times and the bad times; they'll always be there for each other. Their love will conquer everything as it's already shown us.'

Becca turned to Karina, tears glistening in the corners of her eyes.

'Karina Brown, will you take this man to be your lawful wedded husband?'

Her throat ached, her eyes moistened as she looked into Logan's eyes, but her voice came through loud and clear. 'Yes, I will.'

'Logan Pascale, will you take this woman to be your lawful wedded wife, and look after her every minute for the rest of your life?'

Karina grinned. Her friend was nailing him. She winked at her man.

His fingers squeezed hers. 'Yes, to both questions.'

'Mickey, can you pass Uncle Logan the ring please?'

Mickey solemnly placed the ring in Logan's hand.

Karina's hand shook as Logan slid the band of gold on to her finger.

'I love you, Karina, more than life itself.'

Becca nodded. 'I declare you married. Logan, feel free to kiss your wife.'

'Like I need telling twice.' He leaned close. 'Love you, Mrs Pascale.'

Then his mouth claimed hers amidst cheers from their family and friends, who were raising glasses of champagne in their direction.

Of course Mr Grumpy had the last word.

'Now we can eat.'

* * * * *

A FATHER FOR POPPY

BY
ABIGAIL GORDON

First published in Great Britain 2015
by Mills & Boon, an imprint of Harlequin (UK) Limited,
Eton House, 18-24 Paradise Road, Richmond, Surrey, TW9 1SR

© 2015 Abigail Gordon

ISBN: 978-0-263-24697-1

Harlequin (UK) Limited's policy is to use papers that are natural,
renewable and recyclable products and made from wood grown in
sustainable forests. The logging and manufacturing processes conform
to the legal environmental regulations of the country of origin.

Printed and bound in Spain
by CPI, Barcelona

Dear Reader,

Hello once again. In this book, *A Father for Poppy*, I have left Heatherdale for a while and chosen another delightful place to set this story—namely, The Cotswolds, where in a famous eye hospital two people who have lost contact meet up again and make up for lost time as they find a deeper meaning to their relationship.

I hope that you will enjoy getting to know Drake and Tessa, with romance in the air once more.

Do you believe, as I do, that love makes the world go round?

Abigail Gordon
(From Marple Bridge, where the river bends.)

For my dear friend Jill Jones.

Books by Abigail Gordon

**Visit the author profile page
at millsandboon.co.uk for more titles**

CHAPTER ONE

THEY HAD MADE love for the last time with the evening sun laying strands of gold across them. It had been as good as it had always been—sweet, wild and passionate. But there had been sadness inside Tessa because deep down she'd known it was the end of the affair, although neither of them were prepared to put into words that it was over.

It had been the agreement when they'd met—no commitments, take what life offered and enjoy it. Wedding rings were a joke, brushed to one side with babies and mortgages. Having spent her young years amongst her parents' quarrelling, unfaithfulness and eventual divorce, she was wary of the kind of hurts that a gold band on the finger could bring.

So she'd kept her distance from the men she'd met until Drake Melford had appeared in her life and everything had changed. He hadn't asked anything of her except to make love and when they had it had been magical. There had been no suggestion of any kind of commitment and in the beginning she'd been totally happy.

The attraction between them had been intense. So much so that when they'd been together at either of their apartments they'd made love on the rug, the kitchen table, and even once on a park bench in moonlight when the place had been empty, giving no thought to the future. Only the present had mattered.

So what had gone wrong? Something had changed the magic into doubt and misgivings, telling her in lots of ways that it was over, and whenever she'd wanted to ask Drake what was happening to them there had been the 'no strings' pact that had made the words stick in her throat.

Her only comfort had been in knowing that she wasn't competing against another woman, that it was his career that was going to take him away from her, and ever since then Tessa had kept the memory of that time buried deep in one of the past chapters of her life.

But a fleeting glimpse of the back of a man's neck and the dark thatch of hair above it as he'd got into a taxi outside a London railway station had been a reminder that anything as memorable as the time she'd spent with Drake Melford would never stay buried.

She brushed a hand across her eyes as if to shut out a blinding light. It wasn't the first time she'd given in to wishful thinking, and she knew how hard she had to fight to keep sane once the raw and painful memories were allowed to intrude into the life she had worked so hard to build in Drake's absence.

She groaned softly and an old lady next to her in the taxi queue asked, 'Are you all right, dear?'

Managing a smile, Tessa told her that it was just a stitch in her side instead of a thorn in her heart.

It was a Friday. She was in London for an important meeting and at the moment of seeing the man at the front of the queue getting into the taxi her thoughts were on what lay ahead and any surprise announcements that might be made.

She'd travelled up from Gloucestershire, where she was employed for the yearly AGM that was held in the city, and intended on staying the night at a hotel and catching an early train back in the morning.

Horizons Eye Hospital was on the edge of the elegant town of Glenminster, with the green hills of the county looking down on it, and was renowned for its excellence in specialised treatment. Tessa was employed there in a senior management position and was deeply committed to every aspect of it.

She'd heard it said that the health service had more managers than doctors. Though she, of course, respected the fantastic work done by the medical teams, at least a doctor didn't have to get up in the middle of the night when a patient who had arrived with valuables in their possession and asked that they be put in the hospital safe was unexpectedly being discharged and wanted their belongings returned to them. As the only key holder, this meant a deal of trouble for Tess.

It had also been said that she must wish that her position there was more connected with healing than organising. But Tess had always believed that a clean, healthy and efficient facility with good, wholesome food did as much for a patient's recovery as the medical miracles performed there.

As her taxi pulled up outside the building where the meeting was to take place, she was remembering a veiled comment that the chairman of the hospital board had made to her.

The top consultant of the hospital was retiring, so would be saying his goodbyes at the AGM, and the chairman had remarked that, much as the hospital was already famous, the man who was to replace him was going to take it even higher on the scale of excellent ophthalmology. When she'd asked for a name he'd just smiled and said, 'All will be revealed at the AGM.'

And now here she was, still too bogged down with the past to be curious about the present, until she walked into the conference room and realised that this time she hadn't been wrong in thinking she'd seen him. Drake Melford was there, chatting to some of her colleagues in his usual relaxed manner. It was history repeating itself.

Tessa turned quickly and made her way to a powder room, where a face devoid of colour stared back at her from the mirror. She closed her eyes, trying to shut out what she'd seen out there, telling herself that she should have known it was Drake that she'd glimpsed at the taxi rank.

She'd caressed his neck countless times, pressing kisses on to the strong column of it, raking her fingers through the dark pelt of his hair... But the meeting was due to start any moment and the chairman would not be expecting her to be skulking in the powder room.

The hospital board was already seated around a big oval table when she went back into the room, with Drake, the chairman and the retiring consultant seated centrally. When he saw her, Drake felt his heartbeat quicken and wished that their meeting—after what felt like a lifetime of regret—had been a more private one.

But a part of him knew it was better this way, as a casual meeting of old friends, rather than... Rather than what? he asked himself.

As she eased herself into a seat at the far end of the table, Tessa listened to what was being said as if it were coming from another planet.

The chairman was making a presentation to the retiring consultant, who was following it with a short farewell speech, and then Drake would be introduced to those who would be working with him at the famous hospital.

He received a warm welcome from the chairman, who described him as a local man, top of his field in ophthalmology, and who, having fulfilled his obligation to a Swiss clinic, had agreed to accept the position of chief consultant at the Horizons Hospital.

There was loud applause. Tessa joined in weakly. Then Drake was on his feet, speaking briefly about the pleasure of being back in the U.K. and how he was looking forward to being amongst them. For Tessa it was like a dream from which she was sure she would awaken at any moment.

After that, routine matters were discussed and soon the assembled members retired to a nearby hotel where an evening meal had been arranged for all those present.

So far the two of them hadn't spoken, but when she was chatting to one of the members of the hospital board, Drake went past with some of the bigwigs and called across, 'Hi, Tessa. You're still around, I see.'

She made no reply, just smiled a tight smile at the thought of being referred to as part of the fixtures and

fittings. It was hardly the reunion her fevered brain had
imagined during all those nights of tossing and turning.

As the evening wore on it seemed that quite a few of
those at the meeting were booked in at the hotel for the
night, Drake amongst them. Every time she thought of
him being under the same roof she had to pinch herself to believe it.

Leaving most of them settled in the bar after they'd
eaten, she went to her room and tried to come to terms
with the day's events. The first time she'd met him
had been mesmerising and today had been no different, though for a different reason, she thought, lying
wide-eyed against the pillows.

The most mind-blowing thought was that after three
years of being denied his presence, she would now be
seeing him on a daily basis. How was she going to
cope with that? Their agreement had made it easy for
him to leave her when the opportunity for a promotion
had landed at his feet, and there had been no word of
any kind from him since he'd left. Not one. And now
they would be colleagues again. Tessa groaned into
her pillow.

Drake had gone to his hotel room shortly after her and
there was no smile on his face now. When he'd received
the offer to work in Switzerland everything else had
faded into the background. It had been a chance to improve his expertise and he'd been so keen to get over
there he had given no thought to what he and Tessa had
shared, so obsessed had he been with his own affairs.

It had only been as the months had become years
without her that he'd realised what he'd lost in his arro-

gance. Too much time had passed for him to get in touch with her again, and he had felt...what? Regret? Shame?

For all he knew, she might be married with a couple of little ones, he'd told himself whenever the desire to be with her had surfaced. He'd hoped it wouldn't stop him from making amends if the opportunity ever presented itself, and almost as if the fates had read his mind had come news of the vacancy at Horizons Hospital. Discovering that Tessa was now a senior manager at the hospital was only an additional bonus, he told himself.

He'd been anticipating her arrival at the meeting and observed the dismay in her expression when she'd seen him. There would be no warm welcome or happy reunion.

Then, fool that he was, he had made it a certainty by the patronising manner in which he'd greeted her when the meeting was over, as if she had been stagnating while he'd been on top of the world. Some of the Swiss Alps had actually seemed like the top of the world, but he'd had no chance to explore them because he'd always been too busy fulfilling his contract. He could no longer deny that he had been hoping for a different homecoming, and was plagued by flashes of memory of how things had once been between them.

In her room just down the corridor Tessa was also remembering when she and Drake had first met. It had been at a hospital staff meeting when he'd come to talk about some advances he had made in his work.

She'd arrived not intending staying long as her job was in Administration, but had been curious to see the man who was making a name for himself in eye surgery.

He'd been chatting laughingly to a group of nurses who'd been hanging on his every word as they'd waited for the meeting to begin, and Tess had been struck by dark good looks.

Having seen her arrive, he'd stepped to one side to get a better look and from the way his glance had kindled she'd known that he'd liked what he'd been seeing. Slim, elegant, with hair the colour of ripe corn, and wearing a black suit with a white silk top, Tessa Gilroy had been used to the appraisal of the opposite sex, but had rarely allowed it to proceed further than that. Her job had taken up most of her time and she'd accepted that.

But the stranger, tall and straight-backed with eyes of warm hazel and a thick, dark pelt of hair, had seemed different from any man she'd ever met, and when he'd been introduced to her as Drake Melford she'd known why.

His name had been mentioned frequently in medical circles because he'd been new, different, with a vivid, unorthodox approach that had got results, and she was to find that his attitude towards her would be the same.

Their only contact on that occasion had been a brief handshake on being introduced, and when the meeting had ended she'd left, leaving him encircled once again by admiring medical folk.

Her doorbell had rung at six the next morning and she'd found Drake Melford on the step. 'I couldn't sleep for thinking about you,' he said. 'Can I come in?'

Barefooted in a white cotton nightdress, she nodded and stepped back to let him pass, as if welcoming a man she barely knew into her apartment at that hour was something she did all the time.

She made a breakfast of sorts and they ate without speaking, eyes locked over every mouthful of food, and halfway through he pushed his chair back, lifted her up into his arms and carried her into the bedroom.

The first time they made love was rapturous. She was so in tune with his desires and the magic of his presence that it felt as if she had been waiting all her life for him to appear in it.

For the rest of the time it was slower and more sensual, and when at last Drake lay on top of the silk coverlet with his arms behind his head, he said with a slow smile on his face, 'Wow! I haven't felt like this in years, Tessa. You are incredible.'

It was then that they made the pact, still drowsy with fulfilment but not so sated that they couldn't think straight.

They would take it as it came, they agreed. No ties, no commitments, no promises. There would be no babies or mortgages.... An open-ended affair.

And when Drake got dressed after that last time and slung his things into a couple of suitcases Tessa watched him in mute misery, eyes shadowed, mouth unsmiling. She didn't speak because there was nothing to say. It had been what they'd agreed from the start...no ties.

But one of them had discovered that they didn't want it to be like that any more and it hadn't been him. She'd fallen in love with him, totally and for all time, and to find him back in Glenminster and part of her working life was going to take some adjustment.

Whether Drake's life had changed since then or not,

she didn't know. But hers certainly had, because now there was Poppy. Poppy was the small bright morning star that Tessa had adopted after getting to know her while she'd been in the children's ward in Horizons. On the strength of that, Tessa had done two of the things that they'd vowed to steer clear of all that time ago: allowed a child into her life on a permanent arrangement and taken out a mortgage.

She had moved out of the apartment where she'd lived and loved so passionately, bought a cottage built of golden stone not far from the hospital and life had been good again because there'd been love in it. A different kind of love, maybe, but love nevertheless.

Drake was standing by the window of the hotel room, gazing out to where theatres and restaurants were sending out a blaze of light onto the main street.

In the background was the everlasting drone of the traffic that would be far more noticeable when daylight came, and was a far cry from the silence of the mountains and the soft white snows of Switzerland.

But his yearnings weren't for those. He'd left Glenminster without a second thought three years ago with an easy mind, because Tess had seemed willing enough to keep to the pact they'd made on the night they'd met.

So why was it, he asked himself, that the moment his contract in Switzerland had come to an end he'd caught the first London flight available to be there for the meeting? And why had he hired a car to take him directly to the place where they'd lived and loved until his ambition had come between them?

It wasn't like he'd been expecting Tessa to be all

dewy-eyed and panting to take up where they'd left off three years before. If he had, she would have soon put that misconception right when she'd seen him at the meeting and observed him so joylessly that the attention he'd been receiving from everyone else had seemed claustrophobic.

If she was going straight home in the morning, would she let him give her a lift? he wondered. For all he knew, she might be turning the occasion of the AGM into a shopping trip or a theatre break and he could hardly go knocking on her bedroom door to question her plans after three years of silence and all that had passed between them...

He had planned on making an early start because he had to find somewhere to live when he got to Gloucestershire. He wanted to be settled into some kind of accommodation before appearing at the hospital in his new role on Monday morning. So it would seem that unless they met at breakfast their first proper encounter would be at work, under the eagle eyes of their colleagues. It was hardly ideal, but they were professionals and they would make the best of it.

It turned out that Tessa was already in the dining room amongst a smattering of other early risers when he went downstairs at six o'clock the next morning, and before he could give it another thought he stopped by her table and said, 'I've got a hire car and will be leaving shortly. Can I give you a lift to Gloucestershire?'

'No, thanks just the same,' she told him levelly, in the process of buttering a piece of toast. 'I have a seat booked on an early train. The taxi that I've arranged to take me to the station will be here soon.'

'Are you still at the same address?' he asked casually, letting the rebuff wash off him.

'No, I've moved recently,' was the curt reply, and then to his surprise she followed up with 'If you haven't got any accommodation arranged, there is the house in the grounds of the hospital that the retiring consultant has been living in.

'The property was bequeathed to Horizons in the will of some grateful patient and is now vacant. I'm sure it could be made available to you if you wished.'

Drake was frowning. 'I don't want any fuss, Tessa, I'm here to work.' He realised his tone had come across perhaps a little harshly, so he added, 'But I suppose living so near work could be very useful.'

In truth, he was amazed. After her tepid reaction to his return he hadn't expected her to do him any favours. He was the one who'd been a selfish blighter all that time ago and anyone observing them now would find it hard to believe they'd been lovers.

'I will most certainly look into that,' he assured her, dragging his mind back from the past.

Meanwhile, Tessa's only thought was whether there would be anyone sharing the place with him if it was available.

It was an old house that its previous owner had cherished, with high vaulted ceilings, curving staircases and spacious rooms all furnished with antique objects, with its biggest benefit being that it was only a matter of minutes away from the hospital for the consultant in charge when needed.

'Now that you mention it, I seem to remember something about being offered it when I accepted the position,' he said, 'but I had so much on my mind at the time I'd completely forgotten about it. So thanks for that, Tessa.' Could he sound more like an idiot? Drake thought to himself.

She shrugged as if it were of no matter. 'You would have heard about it sooner or later.'

'Yes, well, thanks anyway,' he told her, and as a member of the dining room staff came to show him to a table, added, 'Until Monday morning, then.'

She nodded and turned back to her tea and toast, hoping that she hadn't given any sign of the fast-beating heart that the turmoil inside her was responsible for. Having already settled her account, when her taxi arrived she left the hotel as swiftly as possible, and without a backward glance.

So far so good, Drake thought sombrely as he watched her go. At least they were on speaking terms *and* Tessa had taken the trouble to tell him that his accommodation arrangements might soon be solved. But who was it that *she* had moved house for?

She wouldn't have left her beloved apartment for no reason, and he could hardly expect that her life had been on hold while he'd been away. She'd watched him leave that day without a murmur. Or could it have been that he hadn't given her a chance to get a word in with his obsession about the job in Switzerland, and the opportunities for developing new techniques it had presented?

But he'd made his choice and paid the price. It had been over then and nothing had changed. It wasn't like he'd returned to Horizons for her. He'd wanted the job—and to see her for old times' sake, not to rekindle what had once been between them.

But that wasn't to say that he'd forgotten the passion they'd shared, or how it had felt to lie in each other's arms. So much so that he hadn't slept with anyone since, hadn't found anyone he'd wanted to share that with. Now that he had some distance, he could see that what they'd had was without equal—but he didn't regret taking the Swiss job, which had developed his skills and offered him a once-in-a-lifetime opportunity. Now, for better or worse, he was back and he couldn't deny that a part of him was curious to see if there was anything left of it.

He could tell from Tessa's manner that his return hadn't sent her into raptures—far from it—but perhaps beneath her frosty reception she was as curious as he to see whether any of the old passion remained. The old Tessa certainly would have been.

On the train journey home Tessa rang her friend Lizzie, who was Poppy's childminder and the only person she would entrust her adopted daughter to stay with overnight, and was told that she'd been fine. A little bit weepy at bedtime but a couple of stories had made her eyelids start to droop and then she'd slept right through the night.

'I should be with you by lunchtime and will come straight to your place,' Tessa told her, but Lizzie suggested bringing Poppy to the station to meet her, knowing how she would be longing to see her again. Tessa was anxious to hold her little girl in her arms again, and thanked Lizzie, who was mother to two cute little ones of her own. But when her friend asked if the meeting had justified the long journey and overnight stay in London, Tessa could only reply that it had been full of strange surprises.

She didn't regret refusing Drake's offer of a lift home, even though it would have been faster. The thought of being in close contact with him for three to four hours had been inconceivable.

Until yesterday he had been out of her life completely and now he'd come back into it with the same ease as when he'd appeared at her door at six o'clock in the morning an eternity ago, and now she was wishing him far away… Or was she?

With Drake back in her life he would no longer be a shadowy figure from her past. She would be able to see him and hear him, but would also have to keep him at a distance.

Her life had been transformed with Poppy in it. The little one had been in care, waiting to be adopted after losing her parents in a car crash, and when she'd been brought into Horizons soon after with a bleed behind her eye from the accident, Tessa had been drawn to the solemn little orphaned girl and had spent much of her free time beside Poppy's bed.

'*You* are just what the child needs,' her social worker had said.

'What! A single mother!' she'd exclaimed. 'Hardly! My life has never been planned to include children.'

But the seed had been sown and the more she'd thought about it the more she had known that she wanted to take care of Poppy. So the proceedings to adopt had begun, with every step along the way feeling to Tessa more and more that it was the right thing to do. If she needed any confirmation of it, the happy little child that Poppy had become was proof.

If Drake had any recollection of the pact they'd once made, he was in for a surprise, she thought, and as the train left the station on the last leg of her journey home she was wishing that he had stayed in the place that he'd been so eager to go to, because now she had her life sorted.

They were waiting for her on the station platform, Lizzie holding Poppy's hand tightly as the train stopped, and when she saw her, the little one cried, 'Mummy Two!' It was the name that Tessa had taught Poppy to call her so that 'Mummy One' wasn't forgotten, and as she held her little girl close her world righted itself.

'So where are the boys?' she asked Lizzie, whose twins were the same age as Poppy.

'They are at home with their daddy. He's taking a few days' leave from work so I didn't need to bring them,' Lizzie explained, as she pointed to where her car was parked. As they walked towards it she asked, 'So what went wrong while you were in London, Tessa? You didn't sound very happy when you phoned.'

'You aren't going to believe it when I tell you,' she told her. 'Guess who is taking charge at Horizons from Monday?'

'I haven't a clue. Who is it?' she asked.

'Drake is to be the new chief consultant. Drake Melford!'

'What?' Lizzie cried. 'He's back here in Glenminster? How do you feel about that?'

'Honestly, I'm shattered at the thought. My life is

sorted, Lizzie. I'm happy as I am with Poppy and my job. They fill my days.'

'Have you actually spoken to him?'

'Yes. He's on his way here in a hire car and offered me a lift, which I refused...needless to say.'

'And he's taking over on Monday?'

'Yes, giving me no time to compose myself after our London meeting,' Tessa replied, looking down at Poppy, who was holding her hand tightly, 'but nothing is going to interfere with my life and Poppy's. Drake will be in my working life—that I can't help—but for the rest of it he will be just as much out of it as he has been during the years we've been apart.'

Her first thought on awakening on Monday morning was that she would be in the same place as Drake today. Indeed, it was a while before she could focus on anything else. For not only would she be in the same place as Drake *today*, she would be for the foreseeable future. While their professional goals would be aligned, she could imagine him making his entrance into the life of Horizons Hospital with his usual charm and confidence, while she would be struggling just to keep afloat.

But at least she wouldn't be on the wards or in Theatre, where he would surely be. That would be intolerable, so if the chance came to stay in her office all day she would take it. *Coward*, she couldn't help but think.

What about all the other days when she would be out there, arranging and improving the standard of care that the hospital provided for its patients? She couldn't hide in her office every day.

She'd risen through the ranks because of her ex-

pertise, efficiency and professional manner. She had
years of experience, having worked in a similar capacity on cruise ships, and wanting to revert to dry land
for a change had gone into hospital administration. She
couldn't help but wonder how her life would have been
different if she'd never met him, if she'd stayed on cruise
ships perhaps.

But there was no point going over what couldn't be
changed. And, anyway, she could never regret the road
that had brought her darling Poppy into her life.

Her friend Lizzie lived on the other side of the hospital, at the edge of a town that was endowed with the
beautiful architecture of bygone days and wide shopping promenades. It was an arrangement that suited
both mothers. As well as putting Tessa's mind at rest,
knowing her little adopted daughter was cared for by
someone she could trust during working hours, it provided Lizzie with an income of her own and gave the
two friends an excuse to see each other very often.

Tessa had to drive past the hospital to get to Lizzie's
and as she took Poppy to be dropped off she saw what
must have been the hire car that Drake had indicated
when he'd been offering her a lift at the London hotel.

It was parked amongst other staff cars and she wondered where he had stayed over the weekend, and how
she could possibly be so disinterested after the way
she'd adored him. Had her feelings eventually turned
to pique because she'd been discarded so thoughtlessly
for a promotion and a trip to Switzerland?

When she arrived at her office, which was part of
the hospital's administration complex, her secretary,
middle-aged Jennifer Edwards, was already there and

eager to inform her that the new senior consultant had called to say hello on his way to the wards and what did she think of that?

'I don't think his predecessor even knew we existed,' Jennifer said in a tone of wonder, and Tessa's hopes of a busy day in the office without sightings of Drake began to disappear. But Jennifer went on to say that he'd stopped by to explain that he was calling a meeting of *all* staff who were free to attend at five o'clock that afternoon and hoped that the two of them would be there.

'But will you want to stay behind?' she asked Tessa, knowing that normally she would be setting off to collect Poppy at that time.

It was a tricky question. Her dedication to her job demanded that she be there to support the new head consultant, and deep down she knew that if it wasn't Drake she would be phoning Lizzie to explain that she would be a bit late. She'd already been away from her little one for part of the weekend on hospital business and felt that she had given enough of her free time, but Tessa knew that was just an excuse. It would be worse if Drake thought she was being difficult because he had come back into her life unexpectedly—perhaps she should go to the meeting just to show him that he was fine. *Stop it, Tessa*, she told herself severely.

She was free of the spell he had cast over her. And she wasn't going to the meeting. If they didn't speak today she would explain tomorrow that she'd had another commitment that had been equally important.

It had been a hectic day, Drake thought, as he made his way to the main hall of the hospital at five o'clock, but it was to be expected with patients and staff all new to him…with the exception of one.

Would Tessa be there when he spoke briefly to his new team? He hoped so. There was no way he would want to cause her pain or embarrassment, but they were adults—and professionals, for goodness' sake—and could surely behave that way.

If his restlessness and discontent while he'd been in Switzerland had been because he'd made a big mistake by not cementing their relationship, there was nothing to indicate so far that *she*'d been missing *him*. If she was now living with someone else, he had only himself to blame.

He was crossing the hospital car park to get to where the meeting was being held and caught a glimpse of her in the distance, about to drive off into the summer evening. He quickened his step but she was pointed in the opposite direction and as the car disappeared from view he had his answer.

She had better things to do, it would seem, than stay behind to hear his few words of introduction to the staff. It was going to take more than just showing up, or his charm, to get to know her again. Did he even want that?

Minutes later he faced a varied assembly of the work-force and with complete sincerity assured them that every aspect of the day-to-day challenges that Horizons Hospital was confronted with would have his full attention. Relieved that the meeting at the end of their working day had been brief yet reassuring, most of them went on their way, leaving just a few who wanted to meet the new chief consultant.

CHAPTER TWO

AFTER THE LAST of the staff members had left Drake's thoughts turned to food.

He was starving, and the thought of relaxing over a meal in a good restaurant in the town centre had no sooner surfaced than he was on his way there.

He had to pass a park on the way and happened to cast a glance at a certain bench that had memories of a time that was as clear in his mind now as it had been then. Did Tessa remember? he wondered. Did she think of it each time she passed this spot?

As he drove along a country lane not far from the hospital he unexpectedly found his curiosity satisfied about where she had moved to. It was in the porch of a cottage by the wayside that he saw Tessa, and he almost ran the hire car into the hedgerow in his surprise.

She was chatting to a guy of a similar age to himself and as he drove past Tessa reached out and hugged him to her. Drake's first thought was that this had to be the man who had replaced him in her heart. His second thought, which took a while to summon up, was, So what? But at least he knew now where she was to be found out of working hours.

As for himself, he'd wandered into the house in the hospital grounds that she'd mentioned, after remembering the keys on his desk and the chairman's note offering him the use of it, and thought it wasn't his type of place. It was too drab and he thrived on light and colour. But he had already decided that its proximity to Horizons would be perfect in an emergency, so was going to take advantage of the offer. He'd look for something else when he had time.

The food was fine when he found a restaurant that was his type of place; it battened down his hunger with its goodness, but Drake hardly noticed it. He'd got the job of a lifetime back in his home town and a place to sleep that plenty would die for, yet he wasn't happy.

It had been a mistake to come back to where he and Tessa had been so besotted with each other, so right for each other in every way. He'd had three years to realise in slow misery that he'd thrown away a precious thing without a second thought to satisfy his ambitions, and would have been even more selfish if he'd expected that time might have stood still where she was concerned.

She was just as beautiful now as she'd been then, but there was no warmth in her towards him, and as the night was young—it was barely seven o'clock—he decided to call on her on the drive back. If possible, he would wipe the slate clean by apologising for his past behaviour and assure her of his intention to stay clear, with the exception of their inevitable coming face to face sometimes in a professional capacity at Horizons.

* * *

When Tessa opened the door to him the shock of what he was seeing rendered him speechless. Standing behind her on the bottom step of the stairs and observing him unblinkingly was a small girl in a pretty flowered nightdress with hair dark as his own and big brown eyes.

'Who is *she*?' he questioned, standing transfixed in the doorway.

'She's my daughter,' Tessa told him. 'Her name is Poppy.'

'How old is she?' he asked hoarsely.

'Three.'

There was a pause. 'Is she mine too?' he asked in barely a whisper as the colour drained from his face.

She shook her head and watched the dark hazel of his eyes become veiled. 'Who *is* her father, then?' he choked, as the small vision on the bottom step rubbed her eyes sleepily.

'Poppy is my adopted daughter,' she told him. 'Her parents were killed in a car crash and we got to know each other when she was brought into Horizons with a bleed behind her eyes from the accident.

'She was with us for quite some time and we became close. I used to sit beside her whenever I got a spare moment and take her a little surprise every day. In the end I applied to adopt her and was successful. So there you have it. No cause for alarm.'

Turning, she scooped Poppy up into her arms and held her close. As their glances met she told him, 'Poppy has brought joy into my life.'

'Yes, I'm sure that she must have,' he said flatly, turning to go. But then thought that before he did he might as well ask another question that could have a body blow in the answer. 'So is the guy I saw leaving earlier her new daddy?'

'No, of course not,' she replied, her voice rising at the question. 'There are just the two of us and we're loving it. The man you saw was the husband of my friend Lizzie who minds Poppy while I'm at work. When I picked her up this evening we left her doll behind, and he brought it, knowing that she would be upset without it.'

'Ah, I see,' he said, and added, with a last look at the child in her arms, 'I'll be off then, to let you get on with the bedtime routine and maybe see you somewhere on the job tomorrow.'

'Yes, maybe,' she replied.

She was relieved to see him go. Her heartbeat was thundering in her ears, her legs were weak with the shock of his surprise call, and she didn't know how she was going to cope with having Drake so near yet so far away in everything else. He probably thought she was crazy to be taking on the role of mother to someone else's child.

As he walked down the drive to his car she couldn't let him go without asking, 'Did you find somewhere to stay?'

He turned. 'Er, yes. The keys for the mausoleum, along with a welcoming note to use it if I so wished, were waiting for me, and as it's so near where I'm going to be working, and I didn't feel like looking for anywhere else, I took advantage of the offer.'

'You don't sound too keen on the accommodation,' she commented.

'It's a roof over my head, I suppose, but it's rather dark and dreary. I'm more into light and colour, if you remember.'

She remembered, all right, remembered every single thing about him from the moment he'd knocked on her door early one morning until the day he'd packed his bags and left. But the memories had been battened down for the last three years and she wanted them to stay that way.

He had his hand on the car door and as he slid into the driving seat and waved goodbye, she carried a sleepy Poppy up to the pretty bedroom next to hers. Looking down at her, the feelings that being near him had brought back disappeared as her world righted itself again.

Tessa didn't sleep much that night. She usually went to bed not long after Poppy to recharge her batteries for the next day, but not this time. Her moments of reassurance when Drake had gone and she'd carried Poppy up to bed hadn't lasted.

She kept remembering how his face had changed colour from a healthy tan to a white mask of disbelief when he'd thought that Poppy was his, and when she'd told him that she wasn't, she could tell that he'd thought she was crazy to adopt a child. Clearly nothing had changed with regard to what he saw as *his* priorities, and they obviously didn't include parenthood.

Why did he have to come back into her life and disrupt her newfound contentment? she thought dismally as dawn began to filter across the sky.

In her role as health and safety manager Tessa went round the wards each week, chatting to patients at their bedsides about what they thought of the food, cleanliness and general arrangements of the famous hospital, taking note of any comments that were made. The morning after Drake's surprise visit it was down as her first duty of the day.

As she made her way to the children's ward, where it would be parents she was chatting to rather than the small patients, one of the nurses who had been there when Poppy had been admitted caught her up on the corridor and asked when she was going to bring her in to see them.

The plight of her small adopted daughter had pulled at all their heartstrings when she'd been admitted frightened and hurt after the car crash that had taken the lives of her parents. But Tessa had experienced a strong maternal feeling towards the little orphan that had made the promises she and Drake had made to each other seem selfish and immature.

At that time she'd had few expectations of ever seeing him again, but she'd been wrong and thought guiltily that she should be happy for the hospital's sake that he had taken over, instead of complaining about the effect he was having on her life.

'I'll bring Poppy the first chance that comes along,' she told her. 'It is just that the days seem to fly.'

On the point of proceeding to wherever she was

bound, the nurse said, 'What about Drake Melford? Wow! If I wasn't so fond of my Harry I'd be tempted. That man is every woman's dream!'

He was certainly that, Tessa thought, and when she looked up the man himself was moving quickly along the corridor in their direction and the nurse made a swift departure.

She felt her shoulders tensing, but then reminded herself it was Drake the surgeon coming towards her, not the dream lover of the past, and with a brief 'Hello, there,' he was gone.

Drake had driven the short distance back to the hospital car park the night before in a state of amazement. The scene he'd just been confronted with at Tessa's cottage had revealed that the person she'd moved house for was a parentless child, a small girl without a father. *He* could hardly get his head around what was certainly the last thing he'd expected to find on his return to Glenminster.

A husband and a child of her own wouldn't have been too much of a surprise, but the dark-haired little tot at the bottom of the stairs had been nothing less than a shock to his system, and after seeing Tessa in the corridor just now, he had to admit that he was still reeling.

She had done the rounds of patient appraisals and been closeted with the laundry manageress for the rest of the morning. Then, after a bite of lunch, she'd spent the rest of the day in her office, dealing with the demands of the busy eye hospital, and it wasn't until Tessa was leaving at the end of the day to go to collect Poppy that she saw Drake again on his way to Theatre. He nodded briefly in her direction, but instead of accepting thankfully that it was a sign he was keeping the low profile that she wanted from him, Tessa was filled with sudden melancholy.

It came from the memory of strong passions and their fulfilment in a relationship that for her had been transformed into a love that was strong and abiding, and not according to the promises they'd made to each other when they'd first met. If she'd told Drake back then how she'd felt he would have seen it as not keeping to her part of the pact they'd made and so she'd stayed silent.

And now when he had finished for the day, whenever that might be, he would be alone in the huge house that he had reluctantly opted for, while she would be alone in her living room, Poppy asleep upstairs. It was a matter of minutes between their respective homes, but an unimaginable distance in every way that mattered.

Why couldn't he have stayed away, she thought anxiously as she set off to Lizzie's, instead of coming back to awaken memories from the past that she'd finally been able to put aside because her life had been made liveable again since she'd adopted her precious child.

She'd seen his expression when she'd explained who Poppy was, as he'd observed her at the bottom of the stairs, and he'd actually gone pale.

Yet there was no one better than Drake for bringing a smile to the face of a frightened young patient in the children's clinic, having them laugh instead of cry while he was making a shrewd assessment of their problems.

They'd been in a similar professional situation when they'd first met. He'd been on the staff of a less famous place than Horizons but had been moving up the ladder fast, already a name that was well known in the profession, and she'd been employed as a mid-level manager where she was now, which had brought her into his line of vision when he'd been the speaker at Horizons that night.

His had been a personality that had drawn her to him like a magnet. From the moment of their meeting she had been enraptured, and, being just as much a free spirit as he was, had thought that the pact they had made would survive any hazards or setbacks.

But lurking in the background had been his ambition, his determination to be at the top of his profession, and he'd gone and left her to pick up the pieces, taking her silence on the matter as her acceptance of the open-ended arrangement they'd agreed on.

Tessa had been thankful they hadn't lived together, had each kept their own space, that there had at least been one aspect of his going that she hadn't been left to face.

As days had turned to weeks and weeks to months she had felt only half-alive until Poppy had become part of her life and her own unhappiness had seemed as nothing compared to what had happened to the little orphaned girl.

When she arrived at Lizzie and Daniel's to collect her after each working day, she felt joy untold to hold her close and know that she was hers.

'So how has another day with Drake around the place gone?' Lizzie questioned when she arrived.

Her friend had been there for her during the long months after his departure, and knowing how much

Tessa had been hurting, she had admired her when she'd adopted the small girl that she was holding close.

'Not bad' was the reply. 'I've seen him briefly a couple of times but not to talk, so I guess he's getting the message.'

'And are we sure that it is the right one?' Lizzie questioned, raising an eyebrow.

'Yes,' she was told firmly.

'Good for you, then. He hasn't brought anyone with him…maybe a wife or fiancée?'

'It would appear not,' Tessa told her, and went on to say, 'I haven't told you, have I, that when Drake called last night and saw Poppy, he asked if she was his. Something that would never have been on his agenda, and he seemed quite overcome with relief to be off the hook when I explained that she wasn't.'

'So nothing changes, then?'

'No, it would seem not. And now that he's taken over at Horizons I'm just grateful that I'm not on the wards or in Theatre. With my job our paths won't cross that much.' She smiled and took a breath. 'He's living in the big house in the hospital grounds at present and not liking it all that much, which I can believe. He is too much of a socialising sort of person to enjoy living on his own in that sort of place, but once he gets into his stride we shall be seeing the real Drake Melford.'

Later that evening, sitting alone in the cottage garden with Poppy fast asleep upstairs, Tessa was watching the sun set over the hills that surrounded the town in a circle of fresh greenery and letting her mind go back to that other time when its golden rays had embraced her and Drake on their last night together.

She'd vowed then that never again would she leave herself open and vulnerable to that sort of pain and loss, and had kept to it, relying on a polite but firm refusal when other men had sought her company.

There had been no expectation in her to hear from Drake again so she hadn't been disappointed. But a part of her was still hurt that he hadn't even dropped her a quick line to let her know how the new job was going, if nothing else.

Then out of darkness had come light. Poppy had come into her life and she'd begun to live and love again, and nothing was going to interfere with that, she vowed as the sun began to sink beneath the horizon.

On Saturdays she took Poppy to see her maternal grandfather in the town centre. Tessa had met him at her bedside when the little girl had been brought into Horizons after the accident, and had been aware of his frustration at the thought of his granddaughter being taken into care because he was too old to look after her.

When Randolph Simmonds had heard some time later that the smiley blonde hospital manager loved Poppy and wanted to adopt her, he had been overjoyed and looked forward to their weekly visits.

He had an apartment in a Regency terrace overlooking one of the parks not far away from the town's famous shopping promenades, and always on Saturdays insisted on taking them out for lunch and afterwards driving them up into the hills, where pretty villages were dotted amongst the green slopes.

Randolph was due for eye treatment soon in Horizons and his first question when they arrived on the Saturday was whether the new fellow had arrived yet, as he wanted Drake Melford to be in charge of any surgery that might be necessary.

'Yes,' Tessa told him. 'He has been with us a week, but, Randolph, you need to be on his waiting lists, or do you have an appointment to see him privately? Drake is extremely busy.'

'Oh, so it's Drake, is it?' he said, twinkling across at her. 'You're on first-name terms?'

'I knew him way back before he was so much in demand, though he was already making a name for himself,' she explained flatly. 'I hadn't seen him for quite some time until the other day.' Then she steered the conversation on to a different topic. 'Do you want me to sort out an appointment for you privately? Or you can see him through your optician or GP, if they think it is necessary.'

'You could make me a private appointment if you would,' he said immediately. 'I'm getting too old to be shuffling around waiting rooms and clinics.' With his glance on Poppy, who had gone out into the garden to play, he asked, 'How is the little one? Does she still cry for them in her sleep?'

'Not so much,' she told him. 'I've taught Poppy to call me "Mummy Two" so that your daughter isn't forgotten, and she seems happy with that.'

'And maybe one day there might be a "Daddy Two", do you think?' he questioned.

'There might, but don't bank on it,' she told him. 'The three of us are happy as we are, aren't we?'

He sighed. 'Yes, you were heaven-sent, Tessa.'

* * *

When they went for lunch to Randolph's favourite restaurant Tessa was dismayed to see Drake seated at one
of the tables. But, she thought, having already promised
to speak to him on Randolph's behalf, and not looking
forward to any kind of one-to-one discussions with him,
it seemed an ideal opportunity to put forward the old
man's request.

'Isn't that the man himself?' Randolph exclaimed. 'I
saw his picture in one of the local papers.'

'Yes, that's him. I'll introduce you while he's waiting to be served and you could mention an appointment
now if you like,' she said, as they approached his table.

'Yes, why not?' he agreed.

Drake had seen them. He rose to his feet as they drew
near and Tessa saw that his glance was on Poppy, who
was holding onto her grandfather's hand and looking
around her.

'This is a surprise, Tessa. I wasn't expecting to see
you here,' he said, with a questioning smile in Randolph's direction.

She ignored the remark and changed the subject by
saying, 'Can I introduce Randolph Simmonds, Poppy's
grandfather?'

As they shook hands the old man said, 'We have
just been discussing my need for a private appointment
with you, sir, which Tessa was going to organise, and
here you are.'

It was a table for four and Drake pointed to the three
empty seats and said, 'Why don't you join me for lunch
and tell me what it is that you want of me.' Beckoning

a nearby member of staff, he asked them to bring a child's chair for Poppy.

Tessa felt her heartbeat quicken. This wasn't what she'd expected, but there was nothing she could do about it now, and while Poppy's grandfather was engaged in explaining his eye problems to Drake she talked to Poppy and pretended that she wasn't shaking inside.

Until Drake's voice said from across the table, 'I've just been explaining to Mr Simmonds that I'm going to do as my predecessor did before me and use the same facilities that he had put in place for his private practice in the big house in the grounds. So, yes, I will ask my secretary to get in touch with him first thing on Monday morning, if that will be satisfactory.'

This is ludicrous, he was thinking. Across the table from him was the woman he'd once romanced and made love to in a torrent of desire and had had it returned in full, and they were behaving like strangers. But he'd forfeited the right to anything else and was now paying the price. It was hellish, making polite conversation when he'd adored every inch of her way back in what seemed like another life.

Fresh menus were being brought to the table for the extra diners and as Tessa gazed at the selection of foods available the print blurred before her eyes.

She would have the fish with the creamed potatoes and fresh vegetables, she told them when they came for her order, with a child's portion for her daughter.

Once they had eaten they would go their separate ways, and this would all be over. But soon it seemed that, like everyone else who met Drake, the old man had fallen under his spell and wanted to chat.

Yet Randolph had no problems about them moving on when she made the suggestion at the end of the meal, but to Tessa's dismay Poppy had. She had wriggled down off her chair and gone round to the other side of the table, and climbing up onto Drake's knee was sitting there, sucking her thumb. After a moment of complete astonishment on his part, his arms closed around her.

This is madness, Tessa thought wildly. Not only was Randolph impressed by Drake's easy charm, but her beautiful Poppy must be seeing in him something she hadn't seen in any other man since she'd lost her father. It had to be him of all people, him, for whom babies and mortgages were no-go areas.

Drake was reading her mind as clearly as if she was speaking her thoughts, and putting Poppy gently back onto her feet he led her back to where Tessa was sitting and said softly, 'Yours, I think.'

'You think correctly,' she told him levelly, 'and now, if you will excuse us, Poppy's grandfather always takes us up into the hills when we've had lunch, don't you, Randolph?'

'Er, yes,' he replied uncomfortably, and turned to their host. 'It has been good to meet you, Mr Melford. Maybe next Saturday *we* could take *you* for a meal, if you aren't too busy.'

Tessa noted that he didn't say either yes or no, just smiled, and she thought, Please, let it be a no when next I see him.

When they were clear of the restaurant Randolph asked curiously 'So what is it with you and the man back there, Tessa? What have you got against him? I thought he was most pleasant. We butted into his meal-time with our requests and interruptions and he never batted an eyelid.' He looked down at Poppy's dark curls. 'Whatever *you* might think of him, our young miss took to him like a duck to water.'

'Yes,' she admitted. 'I saw that. It is just that Drake and I had a misunderstanding a few years ago.'

'And you still bear a grudge?'

Not a grudge, she thought. It was scars that she car-ried, mental and physical ones, but she wasn't going to tell Randolph that, so she just let a shrug of the shoul-ders be the answer to that question, and he let the mat-ter drop.

Randolph was very fond of both Poppy and Tessa, whose loving role of a second mother to his grand-daughter took away some of the dreadful feeling of loss that he had to live with, and no way did he like to see her unhappy in any way.

But as he drove the last stretch homewards he was reminding himself that all he knew of her was what he saw now, in her early thirties and beautiful. There had to have been men in her life previously, if not at the present time, and it seemed that Drake Melford might have been one of them, though clearly not any more.

When the little family had left the restaurant after the uncomfortable moments when Poppy had been drawn to him, Drake sat deep in thought. It had been a mis-take to come back to where his roots were, and where he'd had the mad fling with Tessa. Yet what was it he'd been expecting when he did? That nothing would have changed and Tessa would be waiting, patient and adoring, after the abrupt way their affair had ended?

One thing he certainly hadn't expected was that she would have a child in her life. Not his, of course, not a child born of a 'no responsibilities' type of guy, but a sweet little thing that it would be easy to love, given the chance.

He'd liked her grandfather, had been relieved to see that there was someone else connected with Tessa and the child. Whatever the old man's problems with his vision, he would give him his best attention when he came to see him, and with the thought of an empty weekend ahead he paid for their meals and went to see what was on at the theatres and cinemas in the town centre.

There was nothing that appealed and on a sudden impulse he drove to the place not far away where he had lived when he'd met Tessa.

It was an apartment in a block of six and if it had been up for sale he would have bought it for the sake of the memories it held, and to get away occasionally from the big cheerless property in the hospital grounds.

Seeing that it wasn't on the market, he turned the car round, drove back the way he'd come, and settled down for the night in the mausoleum once more.

Back at the cottage Tessa was wishing that they hadn't come across Drake in the restaurant and that she hadn't suggested that Randolph should speak to him about an appointment, because if none of that had happened Poppy wouldn't have gone to sit on his knee and given *her* food for thought.

She had been content in her new life until that moment, but now the future seemed blurred instead of clear, and Randolph hadn't enjoyed their time together so much after that because she hadn't been able to face telling him the truth about how she'd come to know Drake Melford.

CHAPTER THREE

SATURDAYS SPENT WITH Randolph were pleasant and relaxing, but Sundays were precious, when Tessa had
Poppy to herself all day. She did chores in the morning while her small adoptive daughter played with her
toys, and in the afternoon they went to the nearby park,
where they picnicked either inside or out, according to
the weather.

Again Tessa hadn't slept. She'd twisted and turned
restlessly as the memory of their meeting with Drake in
the restaurant had kept coming back to remind her that
it had been a crazy and intrusive idea to confront him
with Randolph's request for an appointment.

But as usual he had brought his charm into play and
come out of it on all sides as the relaxed and understanding host who had been swift to hand her child back into
her keeping. An apology from her was going to be due
when next they met which would be at the hospital in
the morning. That was her last thought before the pat-
ter of tiny feet and a small warm body snuggling in beside her indicated that breakfast-time was approaching.

As the day followed its usual pattern Tessa began to
relax. Worries of the night always seemed less in stature

in the light of day, she decided as she drove to the park
on the edge of the town.

She'd parked the car and as they walked the short
distance to the children's play area she was hoping that
she might have a day without any sightings of Drake.

Her wishes were granted. The day passed happily,
as it always did, except for the fact that she couldn't
help wondering what he was doing in his absence. One
thing she felt certain about was that he wouldn't be
spending the time in his over-large accommodation if
he could help it.

But Tessa was wrong. He was doing just that because
he wanted the arrangements for seeing private patients
to be sorted for Monday morning, with a secretary in-
stalled. Especially after the request he'd had from Mr
Simmonds the previous day.

He was still bemused by his meeting with the three
of them, especially with little Poppy's entrusting climb
up onto his knee, and if he hadn't been so aware of Tessa's dismay he wouldn't have handed her back to her
mother so quickly.

By the time he had finished rearranging part of the
house he was hungry but resisted the urge to dine in
the town again. He knew it would afford a glimpse of
Tessa's cottage on his way there, as well as a sighting of
a certain park bench, so he took a ready meal out of the
house's well-stocked refrigerator and made do with that.

During a long night spent amongst creaking boards
and the smell of mothballs he'd decided that, after looking up Poppy's case notes from the time Horizons had
treated the eye injury she'd sustained in the car crash,

he was going to suggest to Tessa that he should check her over to make sure that all was well with her vision and the surgery that she'd had.

It wasn't anything to do with how he'd felt when the little girl had climbed up on to his knee. It was his job for heaven's sake, to bring the far horizons closer to those who might be denied the sight of them.

On his very first morning there he'd been faced with a child that he might never be able to do that for. A five-year-old boy with an eye missing, born with just an empty socket, had been there for a regular check-up, and if it hadn't been so sad it would have been amusing the way he could remove the artificial eye he'd been fitted with and put it back with so little fuss at such a tender age.

If there had been no sightings of Drake during Sunday it seemed that he was making up for it on Monday morning, Tessa thought when she arrived at the hospital. No sooner had she positioned herself behind her desk than he was there, observing her with a dark inscrutable gaze that made her heart beat faster.

But there was no way she was going to let him see how much he still affected her. It was different from her wild passion of before—now she saw him more as a threat than a joy, jeopardising the new life she'd made for herself with Poppy. As she observed him questioningly, what he had to say took her very much by surprise.

'I've had a look at your little girl's case notes,' he said without preamble, as if he had guessed the direction of her thoughts. 'Would you like me to check the present state of her vision and the area where she had the surgery to make sure that all is still well there?'

'Er, yes,' she said slowly. It was an offer she couldn't refuse for Poppy's sake. Drake was the best, but she didn't want to be in his debt in any way, didn't want any relighting of the flame that she had been burned with before she'd learned the hard way that what they'd shared had meant nothing to him.

She often thought that if they'd spent less time making love and more getting to know each other in the usual way of new acquaintances, if she'd got to know his mind before his body, she could have been saved a lot of hurt and humiliation.

But maybe that was how Drake liked his relationships to be, and if that was the case there was no way she was ever going to let him know the degree of her hurt when he'd taken thoughtless and uncaring advantage of the pact they'd made after those first magical moments.

Tessa doesn't trust me with her beautiful child, he thought. Can it be that the little one coming round to my side of the table to sit on my knee in the restaurant on Saturday is rankling?

'You don't sound so sure,' he commented, turning away as if ready to leave. 'It seems about time she had a check-up, just to make sure all is still well with her vision.'

'I'm sorry if I sounded dubious about your offer,' she told him awkwardly. 'It was just that you took me by surprise. Yes, I would be grateful to have your opinion about Poppy's vision and anything that might be going on behind her eyes. So far she's had a clean bill of health regarding that, but I do worry sometimes.'

'Then do I take it that you will trust me on that?' he wanted to know.

'Yes, of course I will,' she told him hurriedly, and wished that their conversations were less overwhelming.

'Good. I'll get my secretary to ring you to arrange a time when you and I are both free for me to see your child.'

'She does have a name!' she said dryly. 'I suppose you think I'm crazy adopting Poppy after all that we vowed?'

'I'm not in a position to be making judgements,' he replied, 'but as far as that's concerned it's clear to see that you're happy in the life you have chosen, that you have no regrets.' *Which is more than I can say for myself*, he thought. And then, from nowhere, he found himself saying, 'It would be nice if I could take you for a drink somewhere, for old times' sake.'

'I don't go out in the evenings,' she said, her colour rising at the thought.

'You haven't got a childminder, then? What about your friend Lizzie?'

'Lizzie sees enough of me and mine, and after being away from Poppy in the daytime I want to be where she is in the evenings.' With her cheeks still flushed at the thought of being alone with him, she continued, 'My life these days is very different from when I knew you. It has sense and purpose and...'

'All right!' he said. 'You don't have to justify yourself, Tessa. It was only that I thought it would be nice to bring ourselves up to date with each other. How about I buy you lunch one day in the hospital restaurant if you don't want to spend time away from your child? Not very exciting, I know, but it might be more convenient for you.'

'Yes, of course,' she said, smiling across at him, and thought there wouldn't be much time for chatting if they did that, which would suit her fine. The last thing she wanted to accompany the meal was memories of the good times they'd had blotting out the misery of how it had all ended.

At that moment her secretary came bustling into the outer office, ready for the week ahead, and Drake departed, striding purposefully back to the ward.

When he'd gone Tessa felt like weeping. Since Drake had arrived at Horizons he hadn't had a moment to spare from his consultancy, yet he'd taken the trouble to check Poppy's records and offer an appointment.

It was only in his attitude to his private life that she'd ever found him to be less than generous, but she had known the risks that came from that sort of affair. If only she hadn't been so mesmerised by him, and remembering his startled questioning about whether Poppy was his when he'd seen her that night at the bottom of the stairs, she wondered what his reaction would have been if she'd had to tell him that she was.

Would he have been horrified at the responsibilities that would have come with her and dealt with them from afar?

Jennifer in the outer office was fidgeting to get started on the day ahead, so putting her mind games to one side Tessa called her in and the mammoth task of keeping the hospital clean, hygienic and well supplied with food and clothing began.

Meanwhile, somewhere else in the picturesque old stone building that had once been a wool mill Drake and his staff were preparing to perform what would have been impossible in bygone days, and as he scrubbed up for whatever surgery lay ahead after his stilted conversation with Tessa he would have been grateful for a minor miracle of his own.

If she had shown distress at the thought of him leaving her behind all that time ago he might have taken notice, but the euphoria he'd felt at being headhunted by the Swiss clinic had made him oblivious to things around him, and apart from her being a little quiet and withdrawn during his last few days everything had seemed normal. If she *had* said something, would he have taken notice with his head so high in the clouds?

The time he'd spent in Switzerland had been the coldest and loneliest he'd ever known. The experience and knowledge he'd gained over the three years had been excellent, but he hadn't been able to stop thinking about Tessa and the magic they'd made together, which he'd cast aside as if it had been nothing.

When the position at the Horizons Hospital had been his if he wanted it, he'd accepted the offer without a second thought.

He hadn't flattered himself that time would have stood still for her, had accepted that she might have someone else in her life, but had never expected it to be a child that she'd adopted. He had to admire her for that, while at the same time shuddering at the thought of what it would entail.

As Tessa was on the point of leaving at the end of the day he rang her office and said, 'Sorry to be last minute with this, Tessa, but I haven't had a moment all day. It's just a thought, but how about your daughter coming to be checked over on Saturday? I've given Mr Simmonds an appointment in the morning and have accepted his invitation to have lunch with you folks afterwards. So if she's at all apprehensive, maybe her having watched my treatment of him will help to stop her from being upset. What do you think?'

'Er, yes, I suppose so,' she said hesitantly, with the feeling that since his surprise appearance he already featured too much in her life. She went on to say, 'Although Poppy does know you already, doesn't she?' And isn't afraid of you...and I'm not looking forward to another uncomfortable meal, she thought in silent protest.

He almost groaned into the earpiece and said, 'I'll leave it with you, but it would be better from both our points of view if she came on Saturday as my time on weekdays is soon filled', and rang off.

When she arrived at Lizzie's her friend said, 'You're looking very solemn.'

Tessa dredged up a smile. 'Ashamed would be a better description. Drake is being kind and thoughtful and I'm as prickly as a hedgehog when I'm in his company. He's offered to check Poppy's vision and the back of her eye where she had the bleed just to make sure that all is well there, and—'

'Surely you didn't refuse?' Lizzie exclaimed.

'No, of course not, but I wasn't gushing, and he wants me to take her to Horizons on Saturday morning while her grandfather is having a consultation with him to reassure her if she isn't happy about him doing some tests.'

'I don't see anything wrong with that,' Lizzie said gently.

'No, neither do I.' she agreed, 'except that I feel as if he's too much in my face.'

'And you definitely don't want that?'

'It's a matter of my not being able to cope with it, but obviously I'm not going to refuse anything that's beneficial to Poppy, so when she's asleep tonight I'm going to phone him and accept his offer.'

Randolph rang in the middle of Poppy's bathtime and while she splashed about happily he informed Tessa that a secretary had been on to him, offering an appointment with Dr Melford on the coming Saturday morning, and he'd accepted it with pleasure.

'So that's good, isn't it?' he said. 'And she informed me that he's pleased to accept our invitation to dine with us when the consultation is over. I hope that's all right with you, Tessa, as I know you're not a member of his fan club.'

'Drake has offered to check Poppy's eyesight along with any scarring from the bleed she might have and will generally give me an opinion on the state of her vision,' she replied. 'He wants me to bring her to the clinic on Saturday so that she can watch him examining your eyes, and hopefully she won't be too fretful when it's her turn. Needless to say, I'm most grateful for the offer but that is all. After what Drake has done for you and Poppy I can hardly refuse to join you for lunch. But, Randolph, please don't expect me to be the life and soul of the party on Saturday.'

'So the rift runs deep, then,' he said disappointedly, and having no intention of explaining just how deep it was she left it at that.

She didn't tell him that she hadn't given Drake a definite answer regarding Saturday because in spite of his thoughtfulness in offering to check Poppy's eyes she still felt as if she couldn't communicate with him.

But for her little one's sake she would accept his offer, and take her to his consulting rooms at the same time as Randolph.

When he'd gone off the line and Poppy was asleep Tessa sat deep in thought as the summer dusk that would soon be tinged with autumn colours fell over the town and its surroundings. She'd been so happy in her newly found contentment, she thought as she looked around her. Why couldn't Drake have stayed away?

But if he had it would have been Horizons that would have been the loser, as well as herself, and she couldn't wish that on the patients in need of a specialist eye hospital who lived in Glenminster and the surrounding areas.

She was just going to have to keep a low profile where he was concerned—as if she wasn't doing that already. And if it got to be too difficult? Well, she would just have to move somewhere else where he wouldn't be always under her feet as a reminder of a time in her life that she'd once wanted to last for ever.

When she finally rang Drake there was no reply, so she concluded that he must be eating out somewhere, and for the briefest of moments she let memories of the past, the passionate never-to-be-forgotten past that had left her hurt and aching for him, intrude into the present. But then the sight of Poppy sleeping the sleep of the innocent brought calm to her stressed mind.

When she phoned again and said that Saturday morning would be fine for her to bring Poppy for a checkup he said, 'That's good. If she watches me with her grandfather first, she should be happy enough when it is her turn.'

'Er, yes,' she said hesitantly, and waited for a comment about the four of them doing a repeat of the previous week's lukewarm meal together, but there wasn't one coming, so maybe she was exaggerating its importance.

When she told Lizzie about Drake's suggestion, that they catch up for old times' sake, her friend said, 'So what do you think it means, that he's sorry about the past? Or that he's just trying to mend fences with a colleague?'

'He did refer to the past while we were discussing it,' Tessa told her. 'A mild comment along the lines of why didn't I say something if I wasn't happy about him leaving, But we'd agreed that it was to be a no-strings affair and he'd been so on top of the world about Switzerland I think he would still have gone, even if we'd been in a proper relationship.' She sighed and finished with, 'So, as far as I'm concerned, Lizzie, nothing changes, and that's how I want it to stay.'

When Saturday came Tessa dressed with care in a blue linen dress and jacket and shoes with heels instead of her working flatties.

She had dressed Poppy in a pretty pink dress with shoes to match and as the minutes ticked by she could feel tension rising inside her at the thought of what lay ahead. But it was also bringing back memories of how badly hurt Poppy had been, orphaned and injured, and those first moments of seeing her when word had been going around the hospital about her plight.

There was also the thought that the morning's events were everything she'd been trying to avoid with Drake as much as possible. An eye examination for Poppy, yes, but dining with him afterwards was a different matter, an ordeal to be faced, and the sooner it was over the better.

There had been no signs of any long-term after-effects of the bleed and bone fracture, but to have him—of all people—check that all was well behind those beautiful dark eyes had been something she couldn't possibly have refused and as she and Poppy watched while he dealt with Randolph's vision, they were all making light of it for her daughter's sake.

But not enough, it seemed. When Tessa would have settled on the chair that he had just vacated with Poppy on her knee she rebelled, and sliding down, said, 'You first, Mummy Two.'

When she seated herself reluctantly into a make-believe position in front of Drake and his instruments she saw amusement in his glance. This wasn't part of the arrangement!

'Don't touch me,' she said quietly.

'Of course not. I have no intention of doing any such thing,' he said smoothly. Pointing to nearby instruments, he said, 'These are what I will be using, my hands don't come into it, but that isn't going to persuade your daughter to do what we want if she's set against it, unless I can rustle up some of the charm that I keep on hand for this sort of fraught occasion.

'But first we have to convince her that you are also having an eye test.' He raised his voice. 'So put your chin on the ledge in front of you, Tessa, and look straight into the green light for me.'

It worked, and after watching Drake actually giving her an eye test Poppy came over, climbed up onto her knee and allowed him to do the same thing for her. When it was over and Tessa had lifted her down and sent her to sit by Randolph, he said, 'I've looked at the backs of her eyes, Tessa, all is well there, and her vision is excellent too.'

He was serious now, amazingly so, very much the ophthalmologist instead of the ex-lover as he said, 'I'll write you a report and let you have it first thing on Monday if you'll come to my office before my day gets under way.'

'Yes, of course,' she told him. 'Thank you for giving us your time this morning, Drake, and I'd like to settle your account at the same time on Monday if you will have it ready then.'

'There's no rush,' he said absently, with a frown across his brow as if his mind was elsewhere, and she hoped he wasn't going to use the occasion to bring them back onto a better footing.

'So, are we ready to eat now?' Randolph was asking. 'I've booked a table at one of the restaurants on the promenade.'

'Yes,' Tessa said, watching mesmerised as Poppy went to stand beside Drake and put her hand in his.

Aware of her reaction, he looked across, shrugged his shoulders and followed Randolph to the car park of the hospital, leaving her to bring up the rear with a strong feeling that the meal ahead was going to be exactly the nightmare she'd feared.

As they neared the cars he said, 'Obviously, I haven't got a car seat for Poppy, so if she stays with you and Mr Simmonds, I'll follow on behind.' The glint in his eyes told her that he could read her mind, but what was she supposed to do when her adorable child made a bee-line for him?

'So Poppy's eyes are good, then?' Randolph said, turning to Drake as they were shown to a table in one of the town's best restaurants. 'That's a relief, isn't it, Tessa?'

'It certainly is,' she agreed, and was ashamed of her reluctance to sit down to eat with the man who had given them such welcome news. For the rest of the time she let her gratitude show by smiling across at him whenever their glances met, but wasn't rewarded by any warmth coming from Drake's side of the table. Just a brief nod in her direction was all that was on offer.

The answer to his strange behaviour was waiting for her when she presented herself at his consulting room on Monday morning. 'I have something to tell you that you won't like,' he said levelly, when she'd seated herself across from him, and he watched dread drain the colour from her face.

'You've found something wrong with Poppy's eyes after all?' she questioned anxiously.

'No, she's fine,' he told her reassuringly.

'So it's Randolph who has a problem?' she questioned as relief washed over her in a warm tide, knowing that he would rather it was him than anything happen to his granddaughter.

'No, all he needs are a couple of cataracts removed,' he said sombrely. 'It's you that I'm referring to. It was fortunate that I gave you a proper eye test, instead of pretending for Poppy's sake, as it has shown an eye defect that may need surgery.'

'Me!' she gasped. 'That can't be right, surely!'

'I'm afraid it is,' he said levelly.

'No,' she said, fear rising inside her. This was what single mothers must dread, she thought, not being there for their child when the unexpected threw their lives into chaos. All right, Lizzie would look after Poppy for her if she was hospitalised, but it wouldn't make it any less agonising to be away from her.

As he observed her dismay Drake thought that her eyes, as blue as a summer sky with golden lashes, were one of the things he remembered so clearly from their time together. During the test his attention had been drawn to the fact that on one of them the pupil had been forcing her eyelid apart, which was an indication that there could be over-activity of the thyroid gland—also known as hyperthyroidism.

As he explained the situation, pointing out that it was a problem that could restrict eye movement and cause double vision, Tessa's pallor deepened and her dismay increased as he went on to say, 'Sometimes it can be solved by medication to relieve the pressure, but it isn't always successful and then surgery is required to bring the vision back to normal. But first I need to arrange some tests.'

'And will I have to be hospitalised if I need surgery?' she asked tightly.

'For a short time, yes,' was the reply, 'but you can always go somewhere else if you don't want to be treated here.'

'Of course I want to be treated here!' she protested, and as her voice trailed away weakly she added, 'By you.'

'Fine, so under the circumstances I am going to treat you myself while the relevant clinics do their bit, and with regard to that will take some blood from you now to go to the endocrine folks for testing. The results should be back by tomorrow morning and when I get them I will know better what I am dealing with. Have you not noticed any discomfort in and around your right eye?'

'Er, yes, I suppose I had,' she told him. 'It felt tight in the socket, but not enough to cause alarm as I haven't had anything like double vision, but I don't have much time to fuss over myself. My world revolves around Poppy.'

Drake longed to take her in his arms and tell her that he would make it all right for her, that he'd been a prize fool to have left her like he had, and since he'd found her again was aware of the depths of her hurt.

But he knew that a few hugs and kisses wouldn't wipe out the past, the decisions they had both made, and the awkward situation they now found themselves in. Even though Tessa had said she wanted him to perform the surgery if the need arose, he knew that she didn't want him in any other part of her life. How did he feel about that, especially now she had a daughter? He shook his head at the thought. How had a simple affair between co-workers become this complicated?

'Be prepared to make yourself available first thing in the morning Tessa, and we'll take it from there,'

he'd told her, and she'd nodded with the feeling that they were being thrown together whether she liked it or not. But there was also relief, a warm tide of it inside her, because Drake of all people would be there to see her through the nightmare that had just unfolded in her life.

'I have to get back to the office,' she said weakly.

He nodded. 'Yes, of course, by all means. I'll give you a buzz in the morning when I have the results of the blood test and Tessa, don't worry, I will be with you all the way'.

It seemed as if she had no reply to that, and nodding she went back to her daily routine with a heavy heart. What was happening to the contentment that she'd cherished so much, she wondered miserably as she sat hunched behind her desk.

First Drake had come back to stir up the past that she'd thought lay buried deep, and now she might need surgery. But there was one happy thought that came to mind. He'd said that Poppy's vision was fine and Randolph's would be too once the cataracts had been removed.

So with those comforting thoughts and the knowledge that whatever was wrong with her eyes was going to be treated by the top ophthalmologist for miles

around, she had to be grateful that he had come back
into her life, if only for that.

About to start his Monday morning clinic, Drake was
imagining the kind of thoughts that must be going
through her mind. How cruel a twist of fate that he
should have to tell Tessa that she had a problem
that might be serious, on top of everything else still
unresolved between them. Yet there was relief in him
too, because it was sheer luck that he had been examining her eyes and had therefore spotted the problem
early. There was every chance that it could be treated
without the need for surgery.

Still hunched behind her desk, Tessa was reminding
herself just how much expertise there was under Horizons' roof, how dedicated these medical professionals
were in treating those who relied on them. Whatever her
personal feelings towards Drake, nothing could compete with that. So as calm settled on her she called Jennifer into her office and began to face the day's duties,
doing her part to look after the health and safety of the
hospital and its patients.

When she called at Lizzie's that evening to pick Poppy
up it was her first opportunity to tell her the results of
their Saturday morning appointment at the clinic with
Drake.

'So everything is fine, then,' she said delightedly,
when she heard what Drake had said about Poppy's eye
test, but her expression sobered on hearing of Tessa's
problem She held her close and told her, 'Between us
we'll cope. Daniel and I will look after Poppy if you're

hospitalised, and this time Drake will be doing what he does best and not disappearing into the sunset. But, Tessa, how do you feel about seeing him so often, about having him feature so much in your life? Do you still have feelings for him?'

She shook her head. 'Not really, but now that I've got some of the hurt out of my system I remember how fantastic it was, being loved by him. Drake appeared in my life from nowhere and went out of it just as quickly.

'Knowing him, his stay at the hospital might be brief now that he's in my company once again. He won't want to be confronted by an old girlfriend everywhere he turns, and I don't want to be reminded of how I became surplus to requirements when Switzerland beckoned.'

Back at the hospital Drake had just finished for the day and was making his way towards his accommodation with little enthusiasm. What to do during the evening, he wondered. A boring ready meal and then an early night was what it would most likely be. He'd had a few of those of late and had lost the taste for them.

His mind kept going over those fraught moments with Tessa. It was typical in the present climate between them that he should have to take the sparkle out of her life with the news about what might turn out to be a worrying problem, with the only good side to it being that *he* was going to be in charge of it.

That was how he saw it, but in spite of her appearing to be happy about the arrangement he'd known that to her it would be just a means to an end, that the sooner it was sorted the sooner her fears that she might be separated from Poppy would be gone. If he could promise her *that*, she might just let him into the life that he now had no part in. But was that what he wanted, especially on such terms?

If ever she let him back into her life he would want it to be because it was him she needed, not his expertise.

In such cases as Tessa's, medication was usually tried first to slow down the over-activity of the thyroid gland. Surgery was only resorted to when it didn't solve the problem, and if he could save Tessa the stress of an operation he most certainly would. Not only because he cared about her as a patient but because he cared about her for old times sake…

CHAPTER FOUR

AFTER PARTAKING OF the inevitable ready meal, Drake felt restless. It was a clear, calm evening. The sun was about to set over the town and the hills that encircled it, making him feel stifled inside the big house. It had been another hectic day and he needed a break. So, prescribing himself some fresh air, he set off to enjoy what was left of the day.

What would Tessa be doing at this time? he wondered, and leaving the hospital behind he walked towards the town. Would she be sitting alone in the cottage while the little one slept up above, with the news about her condition lying heavily on her and no one to discuss it with?

He would be there in a flash if he thought she would welcome it, but at this point he ought to consider himself lucky that she'd agreed to let him treat her. She had been quite willing to hand over Poppy and her grandfather into his care, but he hadn't known what to expect when it came to herself.

The cottage would be coming into view soon and if he had any sense he would pass it without stopping. But sensible he was not, because he found himself pressing the doorbell within seconds of it appearing in his line of vision.

It wasn't opened to him and, restraining himself from going round the back in case Tessa had seen him and didn't want to be disturbed, he went on his way, shaking his head at how disappointed he felt. It stood to reason that she was inside as small children were usually asleep by the early evening, and there would be no opportunity for lie-ins for that small family, with her having to take the little one to her friend's house every weekday before going to the hospital. Why she had lumbered herself with that kind of responsibility he really didn't know.

When they'd met up again a part of him had hoped they might fall back into the easy agreement they'd had before he'd got his values all mixed up. But it was turning out to be a lesson in endurance because there were no signs that she still had feelings for him. Instead, a small brown-eyed, dark-haired child was bringing Tessa more happiness than he ever had.

He was passing the park once again, but this time his glance fell on a group of parents watching over their small offspring in the children's play area. Amongst them was Tessa, looking pale but composed as she pushed her child backwards and forwards on one of the swings.

She hadn't seen him, but Poppy had and she was indicating that she wanted to get off the swing. When she'd lifted her down Tessa glanced up and saw the reason why. It looked like she didn't know whether to be happy or sad, but there were no signs of any inward tumult as she greeted him.

'I called at your place as I was passing and got no answer,' he told her, 'and now I know why.' Poppy held out her arms to be picked up. 'Isn't it somewhat past the young miss's bedtime?'

'Yes and no,' Tessa told him, as he bent to lift the small figure up into his arms with a wary glance at her mother. 'Lizzie said that she'd had a long sleep this afternoon and wouldn't be ready for bed at the usual time so we came out here for a breath of air and some play time for her. Why was it that you called at the cottage?'

'Just to check that you were all right after the upsetting news I had for you earlier today. But now that I've seen you and am reassured, I'll be on my way.'

He put Poppy gently back on her feet and when she was standing firmly said, 'I've been in touch with her grandfather today, and I'm going to remove one of his cataracts some time next week.'

'You didn't tell him about *my* problem, I hope,' she said. 'If Randolph gets to hear about it he'll start concerning himself about my not being there for Poppy as he's too old and frail to take on the responsibility.'

'Of course I didn't tell him,' he told her dryly. 'I would have thought that you would have been around hospitals—and me—long enough to be assured of patient confidentiality. At the moment he doesn't need to know anything as tests need to be done on your eye first.'

His glance was fixed on what lay behind her and she knew why. The bench where they'd once made love in the moonlight when the park had been empty was in view.

'Don't even think of it,' she said in a low voice.

'Why not?' he questioned, 'You're asking me to forget something as special as that?'

'Special for who?' she asked, and when she took Poppy's hand in hers and began to walk away he didn't stop her, just watched her go and continued his walk into the town grim-faced.

With no reciprocation from Tessa regarding the pleasures of the past, Drake brought his thoughts to the treatment of her condition. If it was an overactive thyroid gland that was affecting her eye; it might react satisfactorily to medication, but didn't always. If it didn't work and surgery was needed because the pressure in the orbit area was so severe that it was restricting the blood supply to the optic nerve, possibly leading to blindness, it would become a more serious matter. He had no doubt that Tessa would have read up on it by now and must be tuned in to what lay ahead, so he could imagine just how much she would want some definitive results on the situation, for her child's sake more than anything else.

Back at the cottage, with Poppy now asleep beneath the covers in her pretty bedroom, Tessa was allowing herself some moments of reflection. If she and Drake had been together in the way that they'd once been, and Poppy had been their own child, it would be so much easier to face up to this thyroid thing, she thought bleakly.

But in the present situation she was using him because of who he was—the top man for eye problems in the area—knowing that there was none better. Part of her was imagining it as payback time, when the truth of it was that Drake owed her nothing. He had merely kept to the pact they'd made and had moved on when the Swiss job had come up. Could she really blame him for that?

And now he was back, having gained the expert reputation that he'd sought so eagerly. It was fine, just as long as he hadn't any ideas about taking up with her where he'd left off. It was too late for that. Her life was so different now, she had different priorities and a casual no-strings hook-up couldn't be further from her mind.

The next morning there was a message waiting for her in the office asking if she could spare him a moment. When Tessa explained to her secretary that she would be missing for a while and would Jennifer proceed with the routine of the day in her absence, the older woman was surprised but asked no questions.

She found him seated behind his desk like a coiled spring, ready to face the day's demands. But he was clearly prepared to put her first amongst his commitments as he said with a keen appraisal of the offending eye, 'How are you feeling this morning?'

'Not on top of the world,' she said flatly.

'I can understand that. How is Poppy?'

'Happy. She loves going to Lizzie's to play with her twin boys, who are a similar age,' she told him, and wished he would leave out the small talk.

As if he'd read her mind Drake said, 'I have the results of the first blood test.'

'Yes?' she questioned anxiously.

As she faced him across the desk, what he had to

say was both was good *and* bad. Aware of the distance between them, and how different it was from the intimacy they had once shared, he needed to tread carefully because he knew just how much she didn't want to be in his debt in any shape or form, yet she was having to rely on him because he was the most senior eye surgeon at Horizons. Their past only complicated what should have been a purely professional relationship, and he couldn't let it affect the care he would be giving her.

'Your thyroid gland has become overactive,' he said, 'and that is causing the swelling of the eye socket, which could be dangerous if left untreated. In cases such as yours another doctor would normally be in charge of prescribing the medication to slow it down. But in this instance everything has to be centred on not interfering with the optic nerve. As I've already promised, I am going to deal with every aspect of the problem myself, and if there is no improvement over the next few weeks and the eye problem is worse rather than better, we must consider surgery.'

Aware of her distraction the previous day he said, 'I was sorry that I had to deliver such news, Tessa,' his voice softening. 'I'm tuned in to your opinion of me and all I can say is that protecting your sight will be my prime concern.

'At the sign of any further change in the eye socket please don't hesitate to get in touch. I'm available day and night and I have already sent down to the pharmacy for the medication that you will require. Someone from there will deliver it to your office.'

She was on her feet. 'Thanks for that, Drake,' she

told him steadily. 'Needless to say, I will trouble you as little as possible as my vision isn't affected so far.'

With that she went, trembling after the attempt at calmness that she'd just presented him with, and praying that nothing would stop her from looking after Poppy.

When she'd gone Drake got to his feet. His busy day was waiting and nothing that was to come could possibly make him feel so concerned as the moments he'd just spent with Tessa. So much for a happy reunion. He must have been out of his mind for even thinking of it, but at least the fates had given him the chance to be there for her in her hour of need. For the present, what more could he ask?

He had longed to put his arms around her during the conversation they'd just had and hold her close to let her see that she wasn't alone in the moments of stress and fear that had appeared from nowhere, but he could imagine the kind of response he would have got. Tessa might have thought he was using her distress to hit on her. Aside from being professional misconduct, that couldn't have been further from his mind in that moment. She was a friend and colleague receiving bad news, that was all.

When she arrived at her friend's house that evening Lizzie was watching anxiously for her arrival and her first words were, 'Have you got the test results?'

'Yes,' Tessa told her, dredging up a wan smile. 'It is my thyroid gland that has become overactive and is causing the problem. Drake is going to try me on medication first. If it doesn't work it will mean surgery,' and went on to say with her voice thickening in an unexpected moment of yearning, 'I would have given anything for him to have held me close for a moment.'

Lizzie's eyes widened.

'No, I'm not weakening in my determination never to let him take me for granted again. I'm just so grateful that Drake is on my case.'

'Why don't you and Poppy stay here for the night?' her friend suggested. 'I don't like to think of you on your own after today's news. You know the spare room is always ready for visitors and when Poppy and the twins are asleep you and I could pop out for a change of scene. You need some light relief and Daniel will keep an eye on them.'

'Maybe you're right,' Tessa agreed. 'I need to unwind, and get what is happening into perspective. It will be a few weeks before Drake can clarify any improvement in my eye condition and until then I need to live as ordinary a life as possible. But I'm still in my work clothes, which are hardly suitable for going out.'

'We are the same size,' Lizzie said. 'You can have the run of my wardrobe if you wish.' And while the children were having their bedtime drink the two women went to see what would be suitable for Tessa to wear on her first night in the town for as long as she could remember.

It seemed strange to be out in the nightlife once again, she thought. It brought back memories of the time when she and Drake had lived it up there at every possible opportunity and then gone back to the apartment where they'd made love.

It was incredible how different her life was now,

but she had no regrets. It had more purpose, more giving than taking and she was happy with that, not that it stopped her from remembering what it had been like to be romanced by Drake.

Where was he tonight? Tessa wondered as she and Lizzie approached one of the town's famous nightspots. The Bellingham Bar was a popular meeting place for those who liked to relax in pleasant surroundings with good food and a cabaret for anyone who liked that sort of thing.

It had been a favourite haunt of the two lovers and as they paused outside the place Lizzie said, 'Shall we throw away our cares for a while at Glenminster's top spot? Or will it upset you?'

'No,' Tessa told her. 'Having Drake back in my life is just coincidental, so why not? What about Daniel, would he want you in a place like this without him?'

'He wouldn't mind. Daniel knows I'm safe as long as I'm with you and anyway our marriage is solid.'

Lizzie's throwaway comment hurt for no accountable reason. Tessa guessed she was just feeling fragile and sensitive because of the difficult news. She refused to admit that she was affected by Drake's sudden return to Glenminster, and she couldn't regret the life choices she had made. Poppy was the best thing ever to happen to her and nothing, not even thoughts of Drake, would change her mind on that.

Without further conversation she led the way into the bar and looked around her, almost as if she was expecting to find him there. After all, he was appearing in every other aspect of her life. But there was no sign of him, and she pushed firmly from her mind her earlier desire to have him hold her in his arms and comfort her.

She wasn't to know that he had been round to the cottage to check that she was all right and on finding her missing was at that moment on his way to Lizzie's house to ask if they knew where she was.

He'd had to drive through the town centre to get there and was dumbstruck to see the two of them, smartly dressed, going into the Bellingham Bar as he was passing.

Before he'd had time to think about what he was doing—or indeed, to ask himself why—he'd parked the car and entered the bar. The thought uppermost in his mind was that Tessa wasn't exactly moping after the day's dark moments, and he was some fool to think that it would have been him that she would have sought out if she had been.

She was studying the menu with head bent when he stopped at their table. As his shadow fell across her she looked up, startled. 'Drake,' she breathed, 'where have *you* appeared from?'

'I've come from trying to find you to make sure you were all right,' he said dryly, 'but it would seem that I needn't have concerned myself. I'll leave you to what is left of the evening.' Then a thought suddenly struck him and he blurted out, 'Where's Poppy?'

'She's safe at my house with Daniel and the boys,' Lizzie hastened to tell him as Tessa sat speechless.

'Right, I see,' he commented, and went striding out of the place with every woman's glance on him except hers.

'Would you believe that?' Lizzie breathed. 'How could he have known that we were in here?'

'I don't know,' she said, 'Maybe he was passing and saw us outside on the pavement. I feel dreadful. He will have been working hard all day at the clinic but still took the trouble to drive out to check how I was feeling, and now finds me about to start living it up in this place. How embarrassing!' Tessa put her head in her hands and groaned. Could this night get any worse?

'Let's go home.' Lizzie said gazing around her as the tables were filling up with would-be diners. 'It was a mistake to come here, though seeing Drake was the last thing either of us would have expected.'

'You're early!' her amiable husband said, when they re-appeared. 'What happened to the night on the town?'

'Drake Melford happened to it,' Tessa told him flatly. 'He'd been to the cottage to see how I was after him giving me the results of my test today, and of course I wasn't there.'

'Lizzie and I think Drake was on his way to see if I was here and when he saw us going into the Bellingham Bar he wasn't pleased to find me there instead of being at home having a quiet evening,' she said ruefully. 'Not that it's any of his business what I do or where I go. All my evenings are quiet and I'm happy with that, knowing that Poppy is sleeping in dreamland only a few feet away.' Lizzie nodded and squeezed Tessa's arm in support. 'But tonight was different, Daniel. I needed something to take my mind off everything and didn't want to be alone, brooding over it.'

When she went up to check on Poppy a few moments

later and stood looking down at her sleeping child, Drake's questioning of the little one's whereabouts came to mind and she thought wonderingly that he'd sounded almost father-like in his over-zealous concern for her well-being.

If the next thing he did was take on a mortgage she would have to eat her words, but in the meantime she felt she owed him an apology. His thoughtful gesture had clearly caused him further fatigue at the end of his busy day. It was the least she could do after his numerous attempts to reach out to her, and his kindness towards her little family.

The next morning she rang his office several times and was told by his secretary that Drake would be in Theatre for most of the day and asked whether she wanted to leave a message.

The answer to that was definitely no. What she had to say wasn't for anyone else's ears. But say it she must, and the first opportunity came when Tessa saw him coming towards her in the main corridor of the hospital at the end of the day.

'I've been trying to get in touch with you,' she said, stopping in front of him, 'but I understand that you've been busy. So can I take a moment of your time now to apologise for last night. I'm so sorry that I wasn't there when you called at the cottage and for my rudeness in the bar. If I had known to expect you I would have been there.'

Tessa rushed on, hardly able to look him in the eye as she delivered her rehearsed speech. 'As it was, I was feeling really low when I arrived at Lizzie's house and she suggested that Poppy and I stay the night. When the children were asleep she came up with the idea that we should go into town for a change of scene and some night life—which is never normally on my agenda—and I suppose it was as we were going into the bar that you saw us.'

He was smiling. 'The main thing is that you were safe and *I* owe *you* an apology for being so abrupt when I saw you. Shall we call a truce and make up with a kiss?'

When she took a quick step back he laughed. Taking her hand, he opened a door nearby that led into a quiet rose garden that was rarely occupied, and once they were out of sight Drake tilted her chin with gentle fingers to bring her lips close to his and kissed her.

It was like coming in out of the wilderness, magical and blood warming for the first few seconds, until Tessa pushed him away and with pleading eyes said, 'Please, don't do this to me, Drake. I want a relationship that has substance, one that will last.'

'And ours didn't, of course?'

'No, it didn't,' she told him, holding back tears at the memory of those last sun-kissed moments before he'd gone out of her life.

Turning, she went back through the door and was gone. As he followed her at a slower pace he thought bleakly, So much for taking things slowly.

'Did you see Drake to apologise?' was Lizzie's first question when Tessa arrived that night.

'Yes,' she told her, having scooped Poppy up into her arms the moment she'd arrived. 'But it was a rather hotch-potch affair as he said it was all his fault. He took me into a rose garden at the side of the hospital and I was like putty in his hands.' She shook her head at the memory. 'But the thought of this little one and all she means to me brought me to my senses.'

'What does Drake think about you adopting Poppy?' Lizzie asked.

'I don't know. I can't think he approves but he hasn't said anything. I imagine that he thinks I'm crazy. Part of the pact we made was to stay clear of exactly these sorts of responsibilities and it would appear that his ideas haven't changed like mine have. No doubt he will think that adoption is even more of a trap than an ordinary family. But if he does he's missing so much.' And with that, Tessa gave her gorgeous little girl a hug and silently counted her blessings for the way things had turned out.

Back at the big house that was so not to his liking, except for its nearness to Horizons, Drake was sitting on the terrace at the end of another busy day, reliving the moments with Tessa in the rose garden.

He could have gone on kissing her, kept on kissing her over and over, if she hadn't pleaded with him not to, and it had brought him swiftly down to earth. They were living in different worlds, he thought, and for once it occurred to him that she must be far more content than him.

Tessa had gone into the town for the evening to try to clear her head, and had had to face his bullish interruption just as her night of freedom had been beginning, and yet, incredibly, *she* had sought *him* out to apologise for not being at the cottage when he'd called to check on her. She was different. Tessa seemed sorted, happy. It was starting to make him question a lot of the decisions he'd made way back.

His private life was a lot more carefree than hers, but much less happy. He'd taken one of the theatre staff out for a meal one night after they'd worked late and were both ready for some food. She'd reacted like most women did to his likeable charm and if he'd asked her back to his place he knew she would have been quick to accept which would have made her the first woman he'd slept with since leaving Tessa for Switzerland.

Ironically, the one he did want in his bed didn't want him. Her life wasn't the same as when he'd known her before, and if he wasn't content with what he had now, Tessa was happy with the life she'd chosen. This thought brought to mind the small Poppy's apparent attachment to himself.

Could it be that he resembled her father in some way and it drew her to him? One thing was sure, she was a sweet young thing with a loving mother and no way had he any right to interfere in that.

The sun was going down over the hills that he loved, with villages hidden amongst them that were graced by old almshouses and farms built from the beautiful golden stone that the area was renowned for.

Since returning to Glenminster, he'd never been any further than the hospital and the town centre. He told himself it was because he'd been too busy at the hospital, but he knew deep down it was because the place was full of memories that had all of a sudden become uncomfortable to face.

So a notice in the staff restaurant announcing that the yearly picnic for staff and their families was to take place on the coming Saturday had Drake's interest immediately. The arrangements were that the coaches hired to take them to the picnic area would be waiting in the hospital car park at eight-thirty.

He hadn't mentioned it to Tessa as he'd thought she might run a mile if he told her he was thinking of going on the outing—he had discovered that she was its main organiser—but the yearning to be up there on the hills was strong and he decided that unless an emergency at the hospital occurred to prevent him, he would be there waiting for the coach like any other picnicker.

On that thought he went into the house towering behind him and climbed slowly upstairs to spend another night in the four-poster bed that graced the main bedroom with its creaking woodwork and the smell of mothballs.

Before Saturday there was Randolph's cataract removal to be done and on the morning that he was due at his private clinic Drake had a quick word with Tessa to find out how much the old guy knew about her eye problem.

'He knows nothing as yet,' she told him. 'I so much dread upsetting Randolph.'

'Yes, I can understand that,' he said, 'and if the medication does its job he need never know, but, Tessa, it's early days. There's no guarantee that it will, and then he will have to know.'

'So that will be soon enough, don't you think?' she said, and he had to agree.

'I wanted him to come and stay with Poppy and me

at the cottage when the cataract has been removed,'
she told him, 'so that I can supervise the drops that
he'll need to have and make sure that he doesn't do any
bending down. But he assures me that his neighbour
in the next apartment has offered to do all that, and as
she will be there all the time while I would have to be
at work during the day it seemed to be the best idea.
She will be making him a meal and looking after him
generally, but I will call on my way home each night
when I've been for Poppy to make sure that her grandfather is all right.'

'What did Poppy's father look like?' he asked.

'I've only seen a photograph obviously,' she told
him, surprised at the question. 'He was quite tall, dark-
haired, hazel eyes. Why do you ask?'

'Just curious, that's all,' he replied, and went on to
question, 'Does she ever cry for her parents?'

'She did at first, but not any more. I got the impression that she was very much her daddy's girl, though
she's not cried for him recently, and I've taught her to
call me "Mummy Two" so that her birth mother, Randolph's daughter, isn't forgotten.'

'Yes. I see,' he said thoughtfully, with a glance at
the clock on the wall of her office. 'He will be here any
moment so I must go. If anyone asks for me, I'll be in
my rooms over at the big house. Also, I'm coming on
the picnic on Saturday so will you please book me a
seat on one of the coaches?' He rushed on to add, 'If
there's a problem with that, I shall get a bike and fetch
up the rear.' Without giving her the chance to reply, he
was gone, leaving her to question if his comment had
been a threat or a promise.

She could imagine the expression on the face of the chairman—who always put in an appearance at the event—if he saw his top medic following the coach on a bicycle. It would seem that a ticket for the man who still made her heart beat quicken was going to be required.

But what was he up to? He surely couldn't want to spend time with Poppy—she knew how he felt about children. After that kiss in the rose garden…could it be her he wanted to see? Tessa shook her head. She had set him straight on that front. Perhaps he just wanted to be amongst the beautiful green hills to get away from work. Whatever the answer to that question, nothing had changed as far as she was concerned. Her life was sorted and it didn't include Drake.

CHAPTER FIVE

DRAKE SMILED WHEN he came back after dealing with the old man's cataract in his surgery room. There was a coach ticket on his desk with a note.

With the compliments of the picnic organiser. A seat next to the chairman in the first coach.

He wanted to be seated next to her, he thought. Not beside someone who was going to talk about work all the way there and back. But Tessa had outwitted him, and when he strolled across to the car park on Saturday morning beneath what was promising to be a hot sun he found that the two of them, mother and child in matching sundresses, would be travelling on the last coach to leave, in order to round up latecomers.

As he went to greet them Drake saw that the chairman was already settled in the first coach and he sighed at the thought of joining him. But Poppy had seen him and was approaching fast, dragging Tessa along behind her. He said with a wry smile, 'Thanks a bunch for seating me with his lordship.'

'It seemed the right thing to do,' she said blandly.

'To you maybe,' he said, patting Poppy's dark curls as she gazed up at him. 'Tessa, how long is this thing going to go on between us? I've got the message. You don't want anything to do with me because I treated you badly. I was a thoughtless, selfish clod, leaving you as I did, but you never tried to stop me, did you?'

'No, I didn't,' she said, 'because I kept to the agreement we'd made that it was to be a no-strings affair. So how could I protest when you wanted out? It was the way you did it, as if I didn't matter, as if I didn't even exist!' Tessa stopped suddenly, remembering where they were as one of the nurses came hurrying into view with her children. 'Here are my last passengers, Drake, so if you would please go to your seat we'll be off as soon as I've given the coach drivers the go-ahead.'

'Yes, sure,' he said, and watching him go Tessa thought that she must be insane not to want to him back in her life if that *was* what Drake had in mind after his long absence.

His ambition and career had taken him from her once already, and she hadn't meant enough to him even to discuss the possibility of them staying together, making it work long distance, let alone that she might go with him. He hadn't shown a moment's regret that what they'd had was over, and nothing—not even his dedication to restoring the sight of the blind—was ever going to lessen the hurt.

As Poppy tugged at her hand for them to follow him she shook her head and lifted her daughter up the steps of the coach they were travelling on. When the latecomers had settled into their seats they were off, driving towards a day in the sun.

* * *

'And so how is it going for you at Horizons?' the chairman of the famous hospital asked as soon as Drake was seated next to him. 'No regrets?'

'No. None,' he told him, the vision of the woman and child he'd just left as clear in his mind as the long nights in Theatre and the over-subscribed clinics that were filled with sufferers desperate for better sight.

Only the other day he'd dealt with a woman who had been diagnosed with a blocked blood vessel behind one of her eyes that had been affecting her vision quite seriously. She'd also had a cataract that had been in front of it, and that was going to have to be removed before he could judge if better sight was going to be possible for the patient.

It hadn't had the look of one of his success stories, but she had accepted it quite sensibly when told that the surgery might give her better sight but that there was a real possibility that she might lose sight completely in that eye, and the answer to that would only be revealed when the procedure was completed.

As it turned out she had been fortunate, Drake thought. When she'd removed the eye covering the next day she had cried out that she could see—and therein lay his whole reason for living, as in his life at the present there was no other joy to be had.

'How do you like your accommodation?' was the chairman's next question.

'It's all right,' Drake told him, 'but at the first opportunity I shall look for something else, not so large and more modern.'

'Yes. I suppose that's understandable as you aren't

married with a family to accommodate,' the other man
said. Once again the vision of Tessa and Poppy came
to mind, and Drake couldn't believe that his thoughts
were running along those sort of lines, especially with
regard to another man's child. It was totally opposite
from what he'd always decided about being burdened
with family responsibilities of his own, let alone those
of someone else.

The picnic was to take place in the tea gardens of a hotel
in one of the area's most attractive villages, and when
the last of the coaches arrived at its destination Drake
was waiting for Tessa and Poppy to alight, along with
its other occupants. When she saw him the 'organiser
in chief' groaned.

How was she going to be able to concentrate on en-
suring that all those present enjoyed themselves if she
was mesmerised by Drake's presence all the time? Tessa
thought. And what about Poppy? Was she going to run
to him, as she'd tried to do once already?'

'If you've got things to take care of, I'll watch Poppy
until you're free,' he offered. As her small daughter
was already clinging to his hand it didn't seem like the
moment to argue, so she gave a brief nod and went to
check on the catering that she'd ordered and find out
which chairs and tables had been allotted to them for
the occasion.

When that was sorted she went to look for Drake and
Poppy and found him pushing her to and fro on a swing
in the children's play area. He hadn't seen her and for a
brief poignant moment Tessa let her heart take control
instead of her hurt and it was there, the feeling that the

three of them were bonded together, when deep down she knew that it wasn't so.

He turned in that moment and unaware of what was in *her* mind let her see what was in *his*. 'Here you are,' he said teasingly, 'eager to make sure that I haven't run off with your precious child! Of course I knew it would be more than my life was worth.'

'You needn't have concerned yourself about my thinking that,' she told him. 'I haven't forgotten your views on family life.'

The slight edge of bitterness that he could detect in her voice made Drake swallow his next comment. He'd been about to surprise her with the memory of his casual remark about house-hunting to the chairman.

While she'd been busy he'd taken Poppy onto the field where the other children were playing and, incredibly, he'd found it! It was there, on the other side of the hedge, his dream house, in the last stages of being built in the golden stone that he loved, windows everywhere, a terrace to sit on in the sun, at least five bedrooms at a glance...*and it was up for sale!*

He'd decided that when Tessa came to claim Poppy he was going to go across to get a closer look, let the perfection of it sink in, then find the builder whose name and phone number were on the 'for sale' sign.

Knowing none of that, she wasn't amazed at the speed with which he handed her child back to her, as if he'd had enough and been reminded exactly why he never wanted children. In fact, Tessa thought nothing of it, Drake being far from sharing her joy in parenthood.

When she and Poppy had disappeared amongst the

crowd of picnickers Drake went to get a closer look at the house and discovered the builder was on the site, about to finish for the day. As he appeared around the corner of the house—his house, Drake already couldn't help but think!—the man eyed him questioningly.

'Can I have a look inside?' he asked.

'Yes, sure,' was the reply.

'Would you show me around, please?' Drake asked him. 'But only if you haven't got a sale already.'

'I haven't,' he replied. 'Wait a second, don't I know you from somewhere?'

'Only if you've had cause to visit the Horizons Eye Hospital in recent days.'

'I have,' the builder told him, surprise at the coincidence lighting up his face. 'But it wasn't for me. It was you who treated my lad when his eye was injured during a football match at school.

'We thought he was going to lose his sight, his mother and me, but you sorted it. Goodness! What are the chances? If you decide to buy this house, I will consider it an honour.'

'It's just what I've dreamed of,' Drake told him, 'and if the inside is as beautifully designed as the outside, we have a deal! I'm sure we can come to an agreement on the price.'

'Gee whiz!' the man exclaimed. 'How long have you been house-hunting?'

'No time at all,' Drake told him. 'This could be my first and last time, viewing a property.' Gesturing towards the front door, he said excitedly, 'Lead the way!'

The inside of the house was just as attractive as the outside and when the builder told him what he looking to get for the property, he said, 'You have a deal. I'll give you the name of my solicitor and any other details that you may require. Let's shake on it now.' The builder beamed back at him. 'How long will it be before the house will be ready to move into?'

'I'd say about a month,' was the reply. 'There are a few things that I want to do to achieve the results that I have in mind, and of course if you are going to buy it you can have your say about anything that you would like done. As soon as the contracts have been signed, the keys will be yours!'

They shook hands again on that and as Drake made his way back to the picnic area he wondered what Tessa would think of what he'd just done. Would she even be interested? The last time he'd been this crazy was when he'd knocked on her door in the early morning, having only met her briefly the night before; when she'd asked him in they'd made love and it had been wonderful.

They'd carried on from there with the no-strings agreement, the one that he realised now had been mostly his suggestion. Although it had left him with a get-out clause when he'd been offered the Swiss contract, he'd paid the price with three cold, miserable years to contemplate the mistake he'd made in letting Tessa go.

Now he was back where it had all started and she didn't want him near her. She had a child who was strangely drawn to him…and, even more unusual, he was equally attracted to the little Poppy. But Tessa was doing everything she could to keep him out of Poppy's life and he found he was oddly hurt by this, unexpectedly so.

He found the two of them enjoying picnic food at one

of the tables, and as he looked around him he asked, 'So how is it going?'

'Fine,' she told him. 'This sort of event depends so much on the weather' She glanced at the sky above. 'And today is perfect, especially for the children.'

It had been a good day for him too, he thought, finding the kind of house he'd always dreamed of, and being in a position to buy it. But the way things were, he might be rattling around in it on his own like a pea in a bottle.

At the end of the day, as they walked to where the coaches were parked, Drake said, 'I've spoken to Randolph a couple of times and he's due to see me again next week for a check-up on his cataract removal. He seems quite happy with what he's had done so far, which is a start.'

'Yes,' she agreed. 'I've called on my way home each day and it would seem that he is being so well looked after by his neighbour Joan, I can almost hear wedding bells.'

'Really! Well, they do say that it's never too late,' he commented dryly. But whether Tessa had the same feelings was another matter, and until he knew what the answer to that was he needed to tread carefully.

The first coach was ready to leave, with the chairman once more settled in his seat. As Drake prepared to join him he looked down at Poppy and she gazed back up at him and said, 'I want to go with *you.*'

'Our seats are on the other coach,' Tessa told her gently, but she didn't budge and the chairman called across, 'She'll be all right with us, Tessa.'

Observing the reluctance in her expression, Drake bent down and when his face was level with Poppy's he said, 'No, sweetheart, you belong with Mummy. I'll be waiting when you get back.' And taking her hand, he placed it in Tessa's and went to his seat.

He was true to his word, and when the last coach arrived back at the hospital Drake was waiting, and as Tessa saw him standing there she felt like weeping for the three of them, Poppy for the loss of her parents, Drake for trying to bring back the past that was dead and buried, and herself because his nearness was affecting her the same as it had always done.

'What do you have in mind now?' he asked, as Poppy ran into his arms. 'Bedtime for the young miss? Going for a meal? Or an assisted tour of the mausoleum?'

'The first one, I think,' she told him. 'It has been a long day for a child of her age.'

'Yes, of course,' he agreed, 'but, Tessa, before we separate I hope you don't think I'm deliberately encouraging Poppy to want to be near me. I know it's the last thing you would want. Do you think it could be that she sees her father in me for some reason?'

'I really don't know,' she told him hurriedly, 'and it's been a long day, Drake. Maybe we could discuss it another time.'

'Yes, of course,' he agreed, and cautioned, 'Be sure to give me a buzz if you're getting low on your medication.'

As he turned to go, Poppy lifted her face for a kiss and Tessa turned away. Did he remember the time when all his kisses had been for her?

* * *

Sunday once again was chores in the morning and the park in the afternoon, and from the moment they got there Tessa was watching for Drake to arrive.

She wasn't to know that his intention had been to join them until he'd been called into Theatre at eight o'clock that morning, on his one day off, to deal with the emergency treatment of a guy who had received serious eye injuries on a building site. As the hours dragged by with no sign of him, Tessa had to keep reminding herself that he hadn't said he would be in the park, so she shouldn't be disappointed when he didn't come.

Looking in the mirror that morning, she hadn't been able to see any change as yet in the protruding of her eye and, desperate for reassurance, had wished him near. It must be the reason why his absence was getting to her so much, she decided, and consoled herself with the thought that at least she hadn't had to put up with Drake gazing at the park bench.

As soon as he'd received the message about the injured man Drake had assembled the members of his team who were on duty over the weekend and by the time he'd arrived they had all been in position.

One nurse was monitoring the patient's blood pressure while another was holding his hand and trying to soothe his fears while at the same time warning him not to move his head while being examined or operated on.

Drake's assistant was hovering closely. He was young, intelligent and keen to follow in his footsteps, observing everything his mentor did and said. However, the sight of the man with both eye sockets bleeding being wheeled into their midst on a stretcher and transferred carefully onto the operating table had caused him to pale for a moment or two.

The theatre sister stepped forward and gently wiped the blood away, where possible, to allow Drake the space to use the ophthalmoscope to check for tearing of the iris, or ruptures of the sclera, which could cause collapse of the eyeball or even blindness.

The atmosphere in the operating theatre was tense when he told the patient, after examining both eyes, 'There is a retinal tear of the left eye, which isn't good, but it looks as if the macula is still in place, which is the main thing, and we are now going to sort that out.

'But the damage to your right eye is not repairable because there are ruptures of the sclera,' he said gently. After passing the ophthalmoscope to an older colleague, and then to his assistant for their observations, he told the man, 'All I can promise is that your horizons won't have disappeared completely.'

He rang Tessa in the late afternoon and knowing every tone of his voice she could tell that he was feeling low.

'What's wrong?' she asked.

'I've been trying to save the eyesight of a guy from a building site who'd had his head split open, blood all over the place, and couldn't see afterwards. The damage to one of his eyes was untreatable, and in the other one there was a retinal tear that we just managed to sort out before his vision became impaired.'

'Have you eaten?' she asked with a shudder.

'No. Why?'

'Do you want to come round and I'll make you a meal?'

'Are you sure?'

'Yes.'

'Then thanks, I'd like to. Is seven o'clock all right? I've got some notes to write up, and before that the family of the injured man want a word as they've only just heard about the accident.'

'Yes, seven o'clock will be fine,' she told him, and when he'd rung off she was left to ponder why she'd issued the invitation. Had it been because she needed him near to give her reassurance about her own eyes, or because she could sympathise with Drake's frustration at not being able to save the man's vision? Or was it simply because she wanted him near for a little while?

When he tapped on the kitchen window so as not to awaken Poppy with the doorbell, Tessa was in the kitchen, with steak grilling and an assortment of vegetables bubbling on the hob. When she let him in his hunger peaked at the smell.

'This will be the first decent bite I've had in hours,' he said. He was assailed with the memory that it had been something more physical than food that had always been his first thought every time they'd been together all that time ago. That and prestige. Yet his expertise hadn't been enough today to save that poor fellow's eye; the man's injuries had been appalling. It was a miracle he hadn't lost his sight altogether.

'I need to wash up before I eat,' he said, bringing his mind back to the moment on hand.

'The bathroom is at the top of the stairs and Poppy's room is next to it,' Tessa told him. 'Please don't disturb her. If she knows you're here she will be down in a flash.'

'I wouldn't complain,' he said laughingly.

'Maybe not, but I would,' she told him, 'and you know making friends with her doesn't exactly fit in with your no-family-ties resolution, if I remember rightly.'

'Neither does the huge responsibility that you have taken on single-handed fit in with yours,' he said, suddenly serious. 'Why, for heaven's sakc?'

'I thought you were hungry,' she chided, ignoring the question. 'The food is ready.'

Drake was halfway up the stairs and wishing he'd kept silent. The truth of it was he envied Tessa her life and her child more than he would ever have dreamed possible.

A vision of the beautiful house he was going to buy came to mind and he hoped that he wouldn't feel as lost and lonely in it as he did in the one he was staying in at the moment. It was hard to believe Tessa and Poppy would ever live there with him as she appeared to be content in her cosy little cottage, and was showing no signs of wanting to get any closer to him than on that first day of their meeting at the AGM.

When he sat down to eat it occurred to Tessa that they had crossed another barrier by her inviting Drake to eat in her home. When he'd finished, the feeling was still on her as he said whimsically, 'I think I'll book into a hotel for the night to get away from the smell of mothballs.'

'I have a spare room that you can use if you like that I always keep ready in case of visitors,' she told him. 'I don't like to think of you driving into town looking for somewhere to sleep after the kind of day you've had.'

'Do you get many?' he asked.

'What, visitors? Oh, yes, they come in droves,' she said laughingly.

'Sarcasm doesn't suit you,' he said softly, 'or maybe what you've just said is correct.'

'Yes, well, you're quite capable of working that out for yourself,' she told him teasingly. 'So do you want to stay the night?'

As if, he thought, with her only feet away and memories of how it used to be pulling at him. But he was crazy if he thought Tessa might want him to be part of the new life she'd made for herself.

He'd come back to Glenminster and found that she had her life sorted, not with another man but with a little orphaned girl.

He'd been dumbstruck at the sight of the small, dark-haired child standing sleepily at the bottom of the stairs when she'd opened the door to him that time, and been staggered when Tessa had explained the circumstances of her being there. But he was getting more and more comfortable with the idea of Tessa *and* Poppy in his life, though he was no closer to understanding why that might be so.

She had gone into the kitchen and was clearing away after the meal she'd made for him. With her back to him, she wasn't aware of him approaching until she felt him plant a butterfly kiss on the back of her neck, and as she swung round to face him he held out his arms. Unable to resist, she went into them.

If it hadn't been for Poppy suddenly crying out above it would have been like all those years ago when he'd called at her apartment at six o'clock in the morning and taken her into the bedroom.

But this time it was different, Tessa thought as she withdrew herself from his hold. She was no longer free and easy, she had a child, a beautiful little girl who depended on her entirely, and to reopen the floodgates of her love for Drake was not what she was intending.

The crying up above was becoming louder and moving towards the stairs she said, 'I think you'd better go, Drake. Poppy has little nightmares when the memory of the car crash comes back and she feels frightened but doesn't know why, so I hold her close and cuddle her until she goes back to sleep.'

Moving swiftly upwards, she paused and looking down at him said in a low voice, 'I forgot for a moment where my responsibilities lie. It was crazy of me to ask you to stay, just a mad moment, that's all.' And then she was gone in the direction of Poppy's sobbing.

As he closed the front door behind him and drove back to his own place he relived the moment she had walked into his arms. It had felt so right, until Poppy had cried out. How quickly Tessa had let him see that her child came first, he thought. As if he didn't know that already.

The days, weeks and months after Drake had gone to Switzerland had been the darkest time of her life, she thought as she gazed at the child in her arms, now sleeping with dark lashes sweeping down onto flushed cheeks. It was Poppy who had brought her out of sadness and into joy as they had each healed the other's hurts.

But tonight Drake's nearness had brought back the longing she'd thought she had under control, and when he'd kissed her neck it would have gone on from there if Poppy hadn't cried out. Her daughter's anguish had brought her back to reality she thought as she laid her gently under the covers, leaving the door wide open so she'd hear any further sounds.

Drake was back in the big house and sleepless with everything that had happened at the cottage starkly clear in his mind. The meal Tessa had made him, her offer of a bed for the night had taken him by surprise, considering that she was so wary of him. Then when he'd kissed her from behind there had been her amazing response, but that had lasted only seconds before Poppy's cries had shattered the moment and Tessa had wanted him gone.

So much for the barriers coming down. He could have nursed Poppy for her, soothed whatever it was that had brought her out of her sleep, while Tessa gave her a drink and they checked her temperature. Instead, she had wanted him gone as fast as possible and before he'd known what was what he'd found himself ejected from her home.

He'd been hoping that after tonight she might let him take her to the theatre, or out for a meal some time, or both, but clearly he'd been wrong to anticipate any such thing. She was a single parent, bringing up a child she adored, and everything else came second.

There was little chance that she would want to take

time away from Poppy, and he'd been crazy to think the kiss in the kitchen had meant anything to her, other than a moment's arousing of the senses.

It had been a strange day of ups and downs. He'd been able to save the vision in one eye of a man who had looked likely to lose it completely, then he'd been invited for dinner at Tessa's—and to stay the night!

He'd actually held her in his arms for the briefest of moments until they'd come down to earth and he'd been reminded that he would never come first in Tessa's life, never be her top priority. Perhaps not be in her life at all.

The next morning she knocked on the door of the big house before going to her office in the hope of catching Drake before he left for the day, and was rewarded by the look of surprise on his face as he saw her.

'I'm sorry that you didn't manage a night away from this place,' she told him awkwardly. 'But I am always most concerned when Poppy has one of her bad dreams. She's so little and she's been through such a lot.'

'And you didn't think I might have been able to assist?' he said abruptly. 'I'm not unused to dealing with children and Poppy does know who I am.'

'I didn't ask because I was so conscious of what had been happening between us at the moment of her awakening,' she explained awkwardly, 'and it seemed inappropriate that you should stay when my position as Poppy's mother was being called into account.'

Drake looked at his watch as if time was of the essence and Tessa felt her face warming. 'Yes, I suppose so,' he said dryly. 'I'm due in Theatre in five minutes, can't stop.' And closing the door behind him, he strode off towards the hospital, leaving Tessa to interpret that as she would. The sheer male attractiveness of him once again caused heads to turn, but left her with the awful feeling that those moments in the kitchen the night before meant a lot more to her than they did to him.

Yet she'd learned one thing from them. That she wasn't as far from wanting Drake back in her life as she'd thought.

As he scrubbed up for what lay ahead in the operating theatre Drake was wishing that he hadn't been so abrupt with Tessa when she'd knocked on his door. But he'd been left with the uncomfortable sensation that for the first time in his life he wanted something very much that he couldn't have. The truth was that he had no idea what he was going to do about it.

When Tessa arrived at her office, Jennifer was already there and the first item on the agenda was an event that was to take place on the coming Saturday that the two of them were organising on behalf of the hospital management.

The picnic that had only just taken place had been basically for the children and families of staff members, while this occasion was for staff and partners only in the form of a supper dance on board a floating restaurant on a nearby river.

Tessa's involvement meant that Poppy would have to spend the night at Lizzie and Daniel's place, which they didn't mind in the least, but she, Tessa, did. Her little one had been there all week during her working hours so it didn't feel right to expect more from her friends. And no doubt Drake would be at the party looking absolutely mind-blowing, while she would be bogged down with the pressures of making sure that the organising was perfect.

When she'd invited Drake for a meal and then offered him the spare room for the night it had been because he'd had a rough day in Theatre, and she'd felt sorry for him. But it had been a major lapse of her avowal not to be alone with him except during working hours, and when Poppy had cried out she'd made a big thing of it because she'd felt guilty and ashamed for breaking her promise to herself.

What he'd thought about that she didn't know—probably decided that it was a bit over the top—but he had done as she'd asked, though his manner now was abrupt to say the least.

She and Jennifer had an appointment during the morning with the manager of the river restaurant to discuss menus and floral decorations for the event and to hand over name cards for the guests seated at each table. It was time-consuming and when they'd finished it was almost lunch-time.

On arriving back at the hospital, Tessa found a message from Drake saying that he would like to see her at four o'clock if she was free, to check on the progress of the treatment of her overactive thyroid gland.

She shuddered. It was always there, the thought of what might happen if the medication didn't solve the problem and she had to have surgery. The only good thing about it was that at least she would have the best of his profession to perform it. But there was Poppy, small and defenceless, and she had to be able to take care of her no matter what. If Drake could give her that she could forgive him anything.

When she arrived at his consulting rooms at exactly four o'clock he was on the phone and told whoever he was speaking to that he would get back to them shortly.

It was the builder, as it happened, wanting to discuss the décor in one of the rooms in the house of his dreams and, pleasurable though it was, it came a poor second to having Tessa near for a short time, even though it was clear that there was no joy in her.

'It's early days as yet,' he said when she sat facing him across his desk, 'but I don't see any harm in checking to see if the treatment is working,'

It was true, he didn't, and after their lacklustre exchange of words at the start of the day he'd been wanting to do something to make up for his surliness.

CHAPTER SIX

So far she hadn't spoken and as he beckoned her to position herself across from him, only inches away, with her chin resting in the required position, Drake thought ironically that this was probably the nearest he was going to get to Tessa after their very brief encounter of the night before.

Once he had finished his examination he asked, 'How does your eye feel now? Does it seem any less pressured?'

'Just a little maybe,' she told him, with a feeling that what he had to say next wasn't going to be uplifting.

'Mmm,' he murmured thoughtfully. 'I can't see much improvement yet, but it is early days, Tessa, so don't be discouraged.'

'It's Poppy that I think about all the time,' she told him tearfully. 'I need to be able to take care of her, Drake. She has no one else apart from her grandfather and he is way past looking after her if I should lose my sight.'

He came round to her side and looked down at her. 'Why don't you let *me* worry about that?' he said softly. 'I do have my uses.'

'Yes, I know,' she said. 'I'm aware of how fortunate I am to have you as my ophthalmologist.' 'But how do I know that you aren't going to move on to pastures new just when I need you?'

'I didn't leave any of my patients in the middle of treatment when I went to Switzerland. There was no one left behind to fret about my absence.'

'Except me,' she said. 'I was just a plaything for you.'

'I can't believe that you remember it as such,' he said sombrely. 'You were beautiful, divine, and I let my dream of being at the top of my profession spoil what we had.'

'Oh!' she said with surprise. 'I didn't know you saw it that way.' After a short pause she continued, 'But did you have to come back from your Swiss idyll and shatter the contentment that I'd worked so hard for?'

'That was never my intention, Tessa. I love Horizons, this place is my home, and when I was offered this position I couldn't resist coming back to where I belong.'

He glanced at a clock on the wall above their heads. 'I've got a consultation in five minutes, Tessa, but before you go will you promise me that you will trust me with your eyes?'

'Yes, of course,' she replied, and thought she would trust him with anything…except her heart.

As she was on the point of leaving he said, 'What about the event on the river boat on Saturday. Are you going?'

She was going all right, Tessa thought. There was absolutely no way to get out of it since she and Jennifer were the organisers. Drake was waiting for an answer so she told him, 'Yes, I am. Poppy is staying at Lizzie and Daniel's.'

'So, will you save me a dance?' he wanted to know.

'I can't. I'm booked for the night.'

'What?' he exclaimed. 'You must be in big demand.'

'Yes, I am,' was the reply, and she left Drake's office overwhelmed with regret for what could have been.

When Tessa took Poppy to her friend's house on the Saturday night and Lizzie saw that she was wearing the smart navy suit that she had to wear for work she said, 'What a shame you aren't allowed to wear a dress, especially since *you know who* is going to be there.'

'It's regulatory that staff involved with organising efforts away from the hospital wear work clothes,' she told her laughingly, 'and the person in question will be too occupied with his fan club to chat to skivvies.'

After watching Poppy playing happily with the twins, Tessa went, making her way reluctantly to the riverside where the fashionable restaurant that they'd hired for the night was situated.

She hadn't seen Drake since he'd checked the progress of the eye treatment and wished herself far away from a situation where the two of them would be at the same gathering. She was apprehensive about his reaction when he discovered she was far from the belle of the ball she had presented herself as, but since she and Jennifer would be there quite some time before the guests arrived, she hoped by then to have everything under control—including herself.

It was a vain hope. They were greeted with the news that the head chef was in hospital after being knocked off his motorcycle on the way to work that evening and that the manager had gone away for the weekend. So instead of organisation there was chaos in the kitchen, with Tessa assisting the missing chef's two assistants and Jennifer doing the last-minute setting up of the dining room with the help of the bar staff.

She had taken off her jacket and was wearing a long white apron and white hat as she obeyed the orders of the two remaining chefs, and was praying that all would be ready in time. So much for being in big demand that she'd teased Drake about. She would be lucky if she even saw the dance floor.

In evening dress with a corsage of lily of the valley and pale pink roses in a florist's box on the back seat of the car, Drake had intended on arriving early to make sure he got the chance to spend some time with Tessa if possible, and as he pulled up by the riverside he smiled to see that her car was already in the restaurant's parking area.

What would she be wearing? he wondered. Whatever it was, she would look divine, and with hospital and family commitments put to one side for a few hours, maybe they could spend some time together.

When he went inside, up the gangplank's gently rocking timbers, he saw that apart from her secretary, who was chatting to a couple of bar staff, there was no one else in sight from the hospital. It was still quite early, so it wasn't surprising, but he was sure he'd seen Tessa's car parked on the river bank and was determined to catch her alone for a moment before the event kicked off.

Jennifer had seen him and when he asked where

Tessa was, he was pointed in the direction of the kitchen, and in a few swift strides he was pushing back its swing doors and coming abruptly to a halt.

'What on earth!' he exclaimed, as she swung round to face him while in the process of testing a large joint of beef that looked as if it had just come out of the oven. All around her was food of one kind or another, with the kitchen staff having returned quickly to their tasks, as if his interruption was not the most pressing of demands on their attention.

Tessa was still wearing the long white apron and shapeless hat, and as it deserved an explanation she said, 'The head chef was involved in an accident on his way here and is in hospital. I was just another pair of hands, but the crisis seems to be over now.'

'Why you?' he questioned. 'Who is supposed to be in charge?'

'I am,' she informed him. 'It's part of my job.'

'So when you told me that you would be otherwise engaged when I asked you to save me a dance, it was this sort of thing that you meant?'

'I'm afraid so,' she informed him, as she took off the hat, undid the apron strings and revealed that she was wearing work clothes underneath.

He groaned as he passed her the corsage of flowers that he had hoped to see her wearing and said, 'So much for that, then.' He turned without another word and went back into the restaurant area, which was gradually filling up with hospital employees.

When the band began to play Tessa surprised him a second time by appearing beside them and their instruments—with the corsage firmly pinned to her jacket—

to announce that the meal would be served in half an hour's time and there would be dancing before and after.

When Drake glanced up from reading the menu at a table at the far end of the bar he observed her, slack-jawed. She was standing before him, smiling with hand outstretched and asking, 'Can we have this dance?'

'Yes, of course,' he said, 'though what about your duties?'

'I feel that two hours over a hot stove should cover that.'

'I'm quite sure that it will,' he said laughingly, 'but aren't you forgetting something?'

'What?'

'I can't dance with you without touching you and I thought that wasn't allowed.'

'Maybe just this once,' she said, smiling back at him, and he thought how beautiful she was despite the plain navy suit bedecked with his flowers.

'So let's do it,' he said, holding out his arms, and she went into them like a nesting bird under the surprised glances of those present.

Drake was holding her close when he felt her stiffen. 'There's Daniel!' she said. 'Something must be wrong with Poppy.'

'We had better go and find out,' he said, and hand in hand they hurried towards Lizzie's husband.

'Poppy jumped off a stool with a metal whistle in her mouth and it has cut open the roof of her mouth quite badly,' he said, wasting no time. 'Lizzie and the boys are on their way to A and E with her, but needless to say it's you that she wants, Tessa. I've left my engine running so we'll soon catch them up.'

'I'm coming with you,' Drake said, and after leaving Jennifer in charge of the rest of the evening Tessa, Drake and Daniel piled into the car. Tessa was holding tightly onto him and praying that it wasn't as bad as it sounded and that Poppy wasn't afraid.

As he observed the pallor of her face and the fear of what awaited her in her eyes, Drake was debating whether parenthood was worth it, taking on a lifetime burden of care, and for someone else's child into the bargain. The enchanting Poppy had almost made him change his mind about that, but tonight was going to be the testing time.

Lizzie and the twins had arrived just before them, with Poppy crying loudly while a doctor attempted to assess the damage to the inside of her mouth, which wasn't easy under the circumstances. When he saw that Tessa had arrived he said, 'I'll leave you for a few moments while your little girl calms down and then we'll see what will be the best way to deal with the problem.'

'If you can coax her to stop crying and open her mouth while I have a look, we might be lucky and find that the injury is of such a nature that it might suction back up into position while she sleeps, as I have known it do sometimes in similar circumstances.' And off he went to see someone else who needed his attention, with a promise to be back shortly.

Since arriving, Drake had kept a low profile, standing apart from those closest to Tessa, and as she held Poppy and soothed her gently he felt that she was probably wishing him miles away right now.

They'd been sharing a precious moment of togetherness back there on the dance floor, he was thinking, but within moments the magic had gone with the news of Poppy's accident.

He supposed there was a chance that she would let *him* see inside her mouth because she knew him and so save Tessa more upset. But would she want him to try, after making it clear that she didn't want him there when Poppy had woken up from a bad dream that night? His professional instincts kicked in—the little one was hurting and he couldn't stand by and do nothing.

Tessa went weak with relief when he appeared by her side and said, 'Maybe Poppy will open wide for me. Shall I try?'

'Yes,' she said desperately, as the crying had stopped since he had appeared.

When he held out his arms Poppy went into them and gave a little whimper, but didn't cry when he said gently, 'Open your mouth wide so that I can see where it hurts.' After a gulping sort of sob she obeyed.

The doctor who'd been attending her was back and gazing in amazement at the sight of his young patient co-operating with someone he recognised as Drake Melford from his much-publicised top-ranking position at the Horizons Hospital.

'If you will take my word for it, I think you could be right about your suggestion that the roof of the mouth might suction up again when Poppy goes to sleep and is still,' he told him.

The other man nodded. 'It would save the child a lot of distress if we try that first, and to have your opinion is much appreciated.'

He turned to Tessa. 'If you are willing for that to be done, I'll phone the children's ward and make the arrangement for an overnight stay for her and we'll see what tomorrow brings.'

When he'd gone, Lizzie, who had been hovering anxiously, said, 'Thank goodness for that, Tessa. It may not be as bad as it seemed at first.' Glancing across at Drake, who was still holding Poppy, she said, 'As Dr Melford is here to give his support, we'll be off. I've got to get the boys home but I'll ring you later.'

After they'd gone he said, 'I'll carry her to the ward then I'll go, as I'm sure that you must be feeling that you've seen enough of me in the last few hours. Give me a ring in the morning when you have an answer as to whether the damaged area of Poppy's mouth has gone back into position, and I'll come and pick you up.'

Tired in both mind and body, she nodded. It had been a long, exhausting day. There had been the preparations for the event on the river boat in the morning, followed by a couple of hours in the heat of the kitchens in the afternoon, which had been quite exhausting, and then the few magic moments when they'd danced carefree and happy had been shattered by the news that her child was hurt. After that nothing else had registered, except Drake being in her life once again, and this time he had been so very welcome!

By the time they reached the ward Poppy was asleep in his arms and as he laid her down carefully on the bed that had been waiting for her, with a smiling nurse standing by, Tessa was filled with thankfulness that the first part of the nightmare was over, and if the fates were kind there might be better news in the morning.

She longed to ask Drake to stay but wasn't going to.

He had been there when she'd needed him. What more could she ask?

'You know where I'll be,' he said with a wry smile. On the point of departing, he added, 'Amongst the mothballs in the big house, but not for much longer. You may find it hard to believe but I'm in the process of buying a house and can't wait to move into it.'

· If she hadn't been so tired Tessa would have wanted to know the details, but she merely nodded wearily and said, 'I hope that you will be happy in your new home.' As if it was a minor item of news amongst the other matters in her mind, she pointed to the sleeping child on the bed and said, 'If you should have any reason to speak to Randolph, please don't tell him about this.'

'Of course not,' he said dryly, with the feeling that he had been chastised for bringing mundane matters into the moment, and that much as he wanted to stay he needed to relieve Tessa of his presence and let her sleep. So, with a last glance at Poppy, he went.

The night staff had found her a comfortable chair beside the bed and every so often came to check on their young patient, and in the meantime, as the hours dawdled by, Tessa was able to take in the surprising news of Drake's about-turn on his views of the time they'd spent together.

She had changed her ideas long ago—the no-babies-no-mortgages idea was long gone. All right, it was someone else's child that she loved, and her home was a small cottage, yet it all felt so right, and until Drake had come back to unsettle her she'd been content.

The moments she'd spent in his arms on the dance floor of the river boat had been exactly how she'd known they would be. They'd brought memories of that other time back in full force, and if it hadn't been for Poppy's accident she would have given in to them.

At the worst possible moment Drake had told her that he of all people had bought a house and now in the quiet night her mind was adjusting to the news. Now she was filled with questions—where? What? How…? But most of all, why? When she saw him again she hoped to get some answers.

Maybe he'd taken the step because he loved Glenminster and the villages dotted around it that were a source of delight. If the house he was buying was local, the very fact of what he was contemplating had to mean that his wanderings were over, and she didn't know how she would feel about that. Would she be able to cope with Drake at Horizons for the rest of their lives?

Poppy stirred in her sleep, gave a little moan, then opened her eyes and said croakily, 'Drink, Mummy Two.'

The nurses had left some water by her bed and when Tessa raised her up against the pillows Poppy drank thirstily, looked around her and said, 'I'm hungry.'

One of the nurses had appeared and she said, 'Not until the doctor has had a look at the inside of her mouth, I'm afraid, but she can have plenty of liquids.'

Drake was deep in thought. While Daniel had been driving them to Accident and Emergency he had told himself that tonight he would finally know what he wanted in his life, and he did.

He'd tried to stay on the edge of things and let Tessa, her friends and the doctor in charge deal with what had happened to Poppy. But he loved the child too much to stand by when she was hurt, and by taking over had admitted to himself how much she meant to him.

As for Tessa, he wanted her back in his life completely, but he knew she had doubts about how she felt about him, and like a crazy fool he'd told her about the house he was buying at the worst possible moment. Naturally she hadn't been in the least interested, with her little girl hurt and crying. He had made a proper mess of the whole thing.

When he rang the hospital in the quiet of a bright Sunday morning, ready to set off immediately if the news was good, he wasn't disappointed, at least not right away.

Tessa's voice had a lift to it as she told him that Poppy had slept through the night and what they had hoped for had happened, the roof of her mouth had suctioned back into place and the doctors there were allowing her to be discharged with an instruction that for the next few days she have only soft foods and liquids.

'Fantastic!' he cried. 'I'll come and get you.'

'There's no need,' she told him. 'I've got a taxi waiting outside, but thanks for the offer, Drake.'

'All right.' It was an effort to sound casual but he felt her rejection to his core. Tessa was clearly on her guard again.

Surely he didn't think that what had happened the night before was going to bring them back to how they used to be? Tessa thought. It would always be there, the magnetism they had for each other, but she'd lived without it for three years...no, it was nearly four, and she had no intention of altering the arrangement.

As they walked slowly towards the waiting taxi Poppy was looking around her and Tessa didn't have to question who it was she sought. Knowing that Drake had been there the night before, she would be wanting to know where he was now.

The answer to that was he'd gone to seek comfort in the only place where he could find it. In one of the villages up in the hills was the house where he'd been hoping to bring Tessa and Poppy one day.

It was only during the long night that the thought had become a certainty in his mind, and it had taken just one short sentence when she'd rebuffed him to wipe it clear.

The builder was on the job when he got there, at the top of a ladder, putting some finishing touches to the house, and Drake thought that whatever else he might have got wrong this was not it. His job at the Horizons Hospital wouldn't leave him much time for leisure, but however much it did he would spend it here in this beautiful house...lonely as hell.

'You don't look too happy,' the man said. 'Is it something to do with this place?'

'No, not at all, it's fabulous,' he told him. 'How long will it be before it's finished?'

'Three weeks, a month at the most.'

'So I'll soon be free of the mothballs.'

'I can guarantee that,' the builder promised laughingly. 'So why don't I take you for another tour of your new home, show you the progress?'

* * *

On the way home in the taxi Tessa felt like weeping. His casual acceptance of her decision to take a taxi hurt. She sighed at how foolish she was being. Was she so afraid that he would shatter her contentment? Could she not let him in just a little?

Were its foundations so feeble that she couldn't let him share in the joy of discovering that Poppy's accident had proved not so serious as they'd at first thought? Some of it had been due to him because her small daughter liked him, trusted him—which was getting to be a problem—and it was that thought that had prompted her to phone for a taxi, and which was why she was now on the way home with Poppy cuddled up close, asking where Drake was.

To add to Tessa's unease there was the moment when he'd told her about the house he was buying, and now that Poppy was fine she was burning with curiosity about where it was, when he would be moving in, what it was like—and, of course, what had prompted him to buy it.

It was Sunday once more. No chance of seeing Drake again until Monday morning at the clinic to try to make amends for her rudeness after everything he had done for her and her family, and Tessa resigned herself to a day of keeping watch over Poppy's intake of light foods and liquids, even managing to coax her to have a sleep in the afternoon.

It was evening after what had been a long day. Poppy was asleep up above when a car she didn't recognise pulled up outside the cottage with Drake behind the wheel.

With her heartbeat quickening, Tessa watched as he uncoiled himself from the driving seat and walked slowly up to the door. When she opened it to him he said quizzically, 'I waited until I was sure that Poppy would be asleep before coming, as I didn't want to be any more intrusive than I was yesterday.'

As she stepped back to let him in she swallowed hard. Drake had been there when she'd needed him and was describing it as an intrusion. She wanted to throw herself into his arms, let him back into her life totally, but couldn't because he was saying breezily,

'I got your point about the taxi, so spent the afternoon with the builder at the house I'm buying and then went to the garage to pick up the car that you see at the bottom of your drive.

'It has been on order for a few weeks and they phoned yesterday to say that it had arrived, so today I got the chance to do both of those very pleasing things.'

'Yes, I see,' she said stiffly. 'I'm sorry I didn't get the chance to ask about your decision to become a homeowner. I suppose it's because you are so weary of your present accommodation?'

'Partly, but not entirely,' he replied. 'It is more that I fell in love with it and had to have it. You may recall that I am rather inclined to be like that. But, in general, I'm learning to hold onto precious things, am changing some of my views on life.'

'And so where is it, this house that you've fallen in love with?' she asked, without taking him up on that last comment.

'In one of the villages. It will be ready soon and I shall commute daily to the hospital, but I didn't come to discuss that. I'm here to ask about Poppy's mouth. Any problems?'

'No,' she said flatly. 'It seems all right. We've had a quiet day, unlike your own, and I will be at my desk as usual tomorrow.'

'Fine, but the place won't fall apart without you. Why not take another day to get over the weekend's traumas?'

'I'm aware that my position at Horizons is much less important than yours,' she told him wryly, 'but I'm a working mother and take my responsibilities seriously.'

'I do know that, and I admire you for it,' he said easily, 'but there must be times when you need a helping hand. You have only to ask. And now that I know that Poppy is all right I'll be off.' And before she could think of something to say that would delay his departure, he went striding back to his new car with the sheer male charisma of him turning her bones to jelly and her heart to lead.

Upstairs Poppy whimpered in her sleep and as she hurried to her Tessa was aware of the irony of the situation she found herself in. Poppy already loved Drake and would be happy to have his presence always there, but her own love for him was a battered and bruised thing that was reluctant to be brought back to life. The only cure for that was to avoid him as much as possible, but that strategy could hardly be any worse!

And as if a prod in that direction the voice of conscience was there to remind her that he wasn't the one who hadn't kept to the vows they'd made. She had been that person, and as the last rays of the sun slanted across the hilltops like the bands of gold of that other time, the memory hurt now just as much as it had then.

CHAPTER SEVEN

THE NEXT MORNING Tessa was treating it as back to normal, with herself at the hospital and Poppy at Lizzie's for the day. She would have liked to inspect the inside of Poppy's mouth before she left her, just to be sure that all was well, but was getting no co-operation as the light breakfast she'd made for her was of more interest than obeying the request to 'open wide'.

Just as she was about to give up the phone rang and Drake's voice came over the line. 'Would you like me to call round to check Poppy's mouth before you take her to your friends?' he asked. 'Or have you already accomplished that?'

She almost groaned. Here he was again, her daughter's favourite person. It went without saying that Poppy would oblige for him.

'No. I haven't,' she admitted, 'but not for want of trying. I would be grateful if you would come, Drake, as I'm concerned that there might be some damage that isn't obvious.'

'How long before you leave for your childminder's?'

'Forty-five minutes.'

'I'll be round before then.' So much for avoiding him.

But she couldn't fault Drake's concern for her child, even though he was continually turning *her* world upside down.

'Looks fine,' he said after Poppy had opened her mouth to its widest for him. 'I'll drop her off at your friend's house, if you like, to save you the journey into town after the harrowing weekend you've had.'

'It's kind of you to offer,' she told him, 'but, no, thanks, we'll be fine. I have a suggestion of my own, though, that I'd like to put to *you*.'

He was smiling, unabashed. 'Let me guess. Could it be a request that I stop interfering in your life?'

'No, it isn't. It is connected with you having some breakfast while you're here because I'm sure that coming to check Poppy's mouth means that you haven't had time to eat.'

'It's a tempting thought, but I ought to be off,' he protested weakly. 'I really haven't the time to wait while you prepare me a meal, Tessa.'

'It's ready,' she informed him calmly. 'I cooked bacon and eggs while we were waiting for you to come, and tea and toast will only take a matter of minutes, so take a seat.'

'Why?' he asked, obeying the request. 'Why are you doing this when you've made it clear you don't want me in your life?'

She was placing the food in front of him and said, 'I don't know. I must be crazy, but I do owe you an apology for the way I behaved about the taxi. It got shelved when I heard what a lovely day you'd had.'

'Yes, it was a riot,' he said dryly, with the memory of

gazing at the house he was buying and thinking again that he was going to be as lonely as hell in it.

When he'd finished eating Drake said, 'I need to see how the medication you are on for the eye problem is progressing. When are you free?'

She shuddered. The mere mention of it made her feel nervous, but he was waiting for an answer and she told him, 'Not today if you don't mind. I left my secretary to clear away after the event on the river boat and feel that I must be available to sort out any loose ends that I may have left before anything else. Would tomorrow be all right?'

'Sure,' he said easily. 'I'll give you a buzz when I've sorted out a suitable time. And, Tessa, don't feel so apprehensive at the thought. It's a trifle early for results, but we'll see… And now I must go, I've a busy day ahead of me.'

He longed to hold her close again, if only for a moment. It had been magical having her in his arms as they'd danced on Saturday night, but it had been short-lived and he wasn't going to risk a rebuff at this hour of the day. The new Tessa could be unpredictable and he needed a clear head to get through what looked to be a very busy day.

So, bending to pat Poppy's dark locks as she came to stand beside him, he smiled across at her and said, 'Thanks for the breakfast. It was a lifesaver.' And when seconds later his car pulled away Tessa felt as if the day had lost its meaning.

Drake's face was set in sombre lines as he drove the short distance to the hospital. A quick glance while at the cottage hadn't shown any big improvement in

Tessa's eye, but he needed her where his equipment was to decide about that. He understood her anxiety about caring for Poppy and maybe underneath was the dread that he might muscle into their lives if she couldn't cope for any reason.

She had softened towards him, though not to the degree that she wanted him back as before. So it was going to be a case of treading carefully and doing all he could to allay her fears. Being too pushy wasn't the answer. He had to face up to the fact that the future still held a lot of questions.

Horizons had just come into sight, the old stone building that had once been a wool mill and was now used for a far worthier purpose. As Drake glanced at the hills above the thought came, Would Tessa ever want him again, need him like he was beginning to need her, and want to live in that lovely house with him?

With that thought uppermost he parked the car and the day closed in on him, with a clinic in the morning, Theatre in the afternoon and a special appointment for Randolph in the evening to discuss his next cataract surgery, which was coming up soon.

He liked the old guy and when the consultation was over said, 'Can I ask you something personal?'

'Sure, go ahead,' was the reply, because Drake was liked in return.

'Do I resemble Poppy's father in any way?'

'Yes, you do,' Randolph told him without hesitation. 'The dark hair and hazel eyes, the bone structure of your face and your height. I think Poppy is confused—sometimes she seems to think you *are* him, but then she doesn't understand why you and Tessa are so at odds. The two of you don't get on, do you?'

'We had an affair before I went to Switzerland to take up a promotion, and I hurt her a lot by behaving like an idiot and leaving her behind.'

'Ah! So that's it,' Randolph said. 'I did wonder. So are you going to do anything about it?'

Drake's smile was wry. 'I'm working on it.'

If he hadn't promised Tessa that he wouldn't mention her eye problem to Poppy's grandfather he would have told him that the unromantic but vital task of sorting out her vision had to come before anything else, and that he was hoping that tomorrow might have some answers for both of them.

Yet it *was* still early days to expect significant improvement in her eye. First the treatment had to disperse an accumulation of debris behind the eye that had built up over recent weeks before being seen to have any effect. Only time would tell if surgery was required.

When he saw her the following day she looked pale and tense and greeted him with the news that her Aunt Sophie, the younger sister of her mother, who had died when she'd been in her late teens, had phoned for a chat, and on discovering that she had an eye problem had said that she'd once had something similar and so had her mother, that it ran in their family.

As he listened to what she had to say Drake wanted to reach out to her, hold her close, and tell her that he would always be there for her, but Tessa's expression was indicating that it was strictly a doctor-patient moment, and she was hardly likely to believe him anyway, with his track record of disappearing when the mood took him.

'Yes, hyperthyroidism can be hereditary,' he agreed, 'but so are quite a few other illnesses and the medication for this one can take a while to clock in, so shall we see what it's been up to?'

When he'd finished checking the eye from all angles and had measured what was a minor reduction of the problem with the orbital area of her eye he said gently, 'We have a small success. Does your eye feel more comfortable at all?'

'Yes, a little,' she told him, and smiled for the first time since appearing before him. 'I've been reading up on these kinds of conditions and they can be quite scary, so thank you for being here for me, Drake.'

'Thanks aren't necessary,' he said, smiling across at her, and took advantage of the moment. 'How about you let me take you for a meal to celebrate the slight though most welcome improvement? To somewhere more upmarket than my previous suggestion of the staff restaurant in this place.'

There was silence for a moment of the kind indicating that the other person intended to be firm but polite. 'I'm sorry,' she said. 'I can't ask Lizzie to have Poppy more than she does already, and don't you think the two of us see enough of each other already? From a distance, maybe, which seems the most sensible arrangement, but nevertheless...'

'Oh, by all means let's keep our distance!' he said tightly. 'All I am doing is asking you out to lunch, Tessa.'

She swallowed hard. Didn't he see that her unwillingness to dine with him and take their frail relationship a step further was because of her dread that he might do the same thing again if the mood took him? Leave her behind? Which now would hurt Poppy as well as herself, and she couldn't bear the thought of that happening.

But to reject what on the face of it was just an invitation to take her for a meal had the sound of playing hard to get over something of minor importance. Finally she caved in and said, 'Yes, all right about the meal, but in the daytime during Monday to Friday so that I don't put any extra pressure on Lizzie.'

He nodded. 'All right, I'll take a couple of hours off around midday tomorrow, as long as you're able to do the same. We'll drive into the town to a smart restaurant somewhere. And now, if you'll excuse me, I have work to do.'

'Yes, of course,' she said weakly, and went back to where Jennifer observed her curiously.

In spite of her reluctance to socialise alone with Drake, the next morning Tessa had an insane longing to dress up for him, because apart from on the odd occasion he hadn't seen her in anything but her office clothes since he'd come back into her life, and putting the dark blue jacket and skirt to one side she surveyed the clothes in her wardrobe.

Gone were the days when she had revelled in making herself look beautiful for him with smart clothes and jewellery. A turquoise dress of fine linen caught her eye, mainly because he had always loved to see her in it.

If she wore it today it would have another message,

one that told him she wasn't just the single mother of a small child having to work to survive, but a beautiful woman, just as he was a man who had heads turning wherever he went. If he ever asked if she had forgiven him for walking out of her life so uncaringly, she was beginning to feel that she could truthfully say that she had, but that was as far as it went.

Yet it didn't stop her from being afraid that he might come knocking on her door early one morning like that other time, and with her melting in his arms carry her upstairs... But this time she wouldn't be alone. Poppy would be there, sleeping in her pretty little room, and he would never do anything to upset the child who sometimes thought he was her father.

In the end she chose not to wear the turquoise dress. If Drake got the wrong signal it could be harder than ever to stop him from thinking it was just a matter of time before she melted into his arms again. So it was a top of apricot silk, slim-line cream trousers and high-heeled shoes that she arrived in at the office, to Jennifer's amazement.

'What's going on?' the other woman asked laughingly. 'Are you going out straight from here tonight?'

'No,' was the reply. 'Drake Melford is taking me out to lunch. I have an eye problem that is worrying me and he wants to discuss it in more relaxing surroundings than these. It will be just a matter of taking an extended lunch break, and the clothes are...er...'

'To let him see how beautiful you are out of the clothes that we spend our working days in?' Jennifer teased. 'Because when he sees you it's going to knock him out cold.'

Better cold than hot, Tessa thought wryly, so why was she doing this?

There was no sign of Drake during the morning, just a brief phone call to say he would be waiting in the car park at half past eleven, if that was all right. When she'd assured him that it was he'd rung off, and now it was just five minutes to go, and she was making her way there, wishing she'd worn her usual work clothes instead of dressing up like a Christmas tree.

He followed her outside seconds later and when he saw her his eyes widened. As far as he was concerned, the occasion came from a longing to be with her, even for just a short time, disguised as a working lunch in the middle of a busy day. The last thing he'd expected had been that Tessa would have dressed up for it. Was it a sign of forgiveness, temptation or a moment of mockery? He wished he knew, but it was as if the sun up above was shining just on them and maybe the hurts of the past would be forgotten for a while.

'It's nice to see you out of your usual work clothes for once,' he said casually and left it at that as they drove out of the hospital grounds, having no wish to say the wrong thing in the moment of meeting.

'It's good to have a change sometimes,' she said in a similar tone, and with a glance at what he was wearing thought that no one could fault Drake's appearance. His suit had the style and quality that he always kept to.

'I've booked a table at the new hotel in the gardens at the end of the shopping promenade,' he said, as the town came in sight, and thought Tessa couldn't fault that for tact. No going to one of their old haunts to pull at her heartstrings. They were too far apart for that sort of thing.

'So how is little Poppy?' he asked, when they had been shown to a table in the restaurant. 'Is her mouth still all right?'

She smiled. 'Yes, thank goodness.'

He nodded. 'It was fortunate that it was the roof of the mouth, which in such cases can suck back upwards easily, instead of the bottom of the mouth, where injuries can be more serious.'

With a change of subject he went on to say, 'When Randolph came for an appointment the other day I asked him outright if I resembled her father in any way. He said yes and was quite definite about it. So, Tessa, I do hope you don't still think I'm using Poppy's attraction to me to ease myself into your life again.'

As their glances locked she said, 'I did, but I don't any more, Drake. It's just a most unusual coincidence and if it makes Poppy happy, it's all right with me.'

'Just as long as I don't want to take it to its natural conclusion,' he commented dryly.

'Yes, you could say that. She has already had one father who through no fault of his own disappeared out of her life, another would be just too much for her young mind if you decided to move on again to pastures new.''

There'd been nothing green about his time in Switzerland, he thought grimly. It had been cold outside and he'd been cold inside with the misery that had always been there when he thought about how in his arrogance he'd left behind the special woman in his life.

But this getting together for a meal was supposed to

help put Tessa's mind at rest as much as possible about the thyroid over-activity that was affecting her eye.

Blood tests were showing a slight improvement in the condition, but there was some way to go before he would be able to tell her anything definite. An under active thyroid was easier to deal with by far than one that was the opposite.

He could remember some years ago having to remove the four parathyroids from an elderly woman's neck because they were overworking and causing her calcium levels to rise dangerously, making such things as benign tumours appear, and causing serious kidney defects along with other life threatening illnesses, and it could have been the same with Tessa's problem.

So far there had been none of the hazards associated with the problem except for the eye protruding from the socket and there had been a very small sign of improvement the last time he'd done a blood test but there was a way to go before the problem was sorted.

So he didn't let himself be drawn about her lack of faith regarding his reliability and said, 'The medication is beginning to work and now we might see a reduction in the pressure around the optic nerve and your eye feeling more comfortable. Then it really will be time to celebrate.'

The food had arrived, it was time to eat, and they talked about minor things until she said, 'So where exactly is the house that you're buying, Drake?'

'Why don't you let me take you to see it instead of talking about it?'

She didn't reply to that, instead asked casually, as if she wasn't bothered one way or the other, 'Are you intending living there alone or will someone be sharing it with you?'

'A couple of folks might if I can persuade them, but it will be a few weeks before it is ready for occupation,' he explained, 'and then it will be goodbye to where I'm living now, thank goodness. Would you feel like giving some advice when it comes to furnishings?'

She was observing him, startled. 'Er, yes, I suppose so, but I don't really want to be involved in something that might be wrong for others.'

He was smiling across at her and she thought he was still the most attractive man she had ever met. It wasn't surprising that from the first moment of their meeting she'd adored him and that it was taking all her will-power not to let it happen again.

The moments on the dance floor, the time when he'd kissed her in the rose garden and the brief moments of desire they'd shared in her kitchen were like an oasis in a dry land. But there was the new life she'd made for herself and Poppy with its special kind of contentment that she couldn't risk.

'It's what I like that counts, anyone else doesn't matter,' he was saying, safe in the knowledge that if they ever did have a fresh start and she and Poppy lived with him in his house up on the hillside he would be sure to like the furnishings because she would have chosen them, and if that wasn't reaching for the moon he didn't know what was.

They'd finished the meal and the clock in the restaurant said there was a short time left before they had to return to the hospital, so Drake suggested a walk in the hotel gardens and said, 'When I passed a couple of days ago there was a wedding taking place and I thought what a beautiful setting it is.'

'Yes, all right,' she agreed reluctantly, having no wish to be reminded of such things while they were together, and was amazed that he who had scorned matrimony had commented on it so favourably.

There was his obvious love of Poppy, he was buying a house, and now Drake was speaking admiringly about a wedding he'd seen. Could this be the same man who had left her all those years ago?

The gardens *were* lovely, the moments together in them filled with promise, but a promise of what? she questioned. Their time had been and gone long ago. She had branched off into a different kind of life since then, separate and fulfilling. Did she want to change?

This isn't working Drake thought, casting a sideways glance at her expression. If you are going to woo Tessa you have to come up with something better than this. Why don't you ask her to marry you outright?

The words were forming themselves in his mind, but on the point of saying them he saw that in Tessa's expression there was nothing but the wish to get back to the hospital and reality. It wasn't the right moment, he decided, far from it, and led the way to where he'd parked the car, unable to ignore the relief in her expression.

He was expecting a speedy departure from her when they arrived back at the hospital, but instead Tessa turned to face him in the confines of the car and said, 'I'd like to return your hospitality. When would it be convenient for you to come for dinner with Poppy and me at the cottage?'

He was observing her sombrely. 'You don't have to do that because I took you out to lunch. If you remember, it was to celebrate that the over-functioning of your thyroid gland was beginning to slow down. So don't feel that you have to invite me back.'

'You don't want to see Poppy, then?'

'Of course I want to see her, but not on sufferance!'

'What makes you say that?' she protested.

Drake, the memory of his aborted marriage proposal still fresh in his head, had his answer ready. 'It might be because you were so obviously bored back there.'

'If that is what you really think you are so wrong,' she told him. 'I feel as if I don't know you any more. Your thinking is different. All the things that you didn't want as part of your life then are acceptable to you now.'

'And is that not allowed?' he asked.

'No, of course it is, but my life was sorted long ago. As I picked up the pieces of what I'd thought was a love that would last for ever I discovered that there was a lot less pain in loving a child than loving a man.'

'So you intend to stay as you are, just you and Poppy in your safe little cocoon?'

Tessa didn't answer. Her glance was on the clock on the front of the hospital building and she said hastily, 'I have a new food supplier arriving in ten minutes, Drake, I must go.'

'Yes, me too,' he agreed. 'I have a cataract removal this afternoon.'

'I do hope it goes well,' she said softly. 'That is so much more important than what I will be doing.'

'You know our patients need nourishment as well as eyesight, and Tessa, I'd like to accept your dinner invitation, if it still stands.'

She smiled. 'Yes, of course it does. I thought of lunch during the weekend so that you will have more time to be with Poppy than in the evening. Which day would suit you best?'

'Sunday would be fine if that if that is all right with you. I usually work on Saturdays.' On that promise they went their separate ways into Horizons, with their own skylines looking momentarily brighter.

When Drake arrived on the Sunday morning Poppy was on the drive, playing on a small scooter that was her latest treasure, and as his car stopped outside the gate she became still until she saw who was in it and then as he eased himself out and came towards her she began to run towards him, and as he swung her up into his arms the name was on her lips for the first time... 'Daddy!'

For Tessa, who was following close behind, it was the moment of truth. As their glances met above Poppy's dark curls the quiet contentment she had so treasured with just the two of them was disappearing. She would have to talk to Poppy about it once Drake had gone, to help clear up what must be a very confusing situation for her little girl.

Drake's smile was rueful as he placed Poppy back onto her scooter and when she'd gone whizzing off he said, 'I told you what Randolph said about the likeness, but I didn't tell you that I asked him if the poor guy would be upset if he knew that his little girl thought another man was him and he said, no, not at all, that somewhere in the ether his daughter and son-in-law would want what would make their little girl happiest. That her father, who'd been a great guy, wouldn't mind someone else taking his place if it brought comfort.'

She looked white and withdrawn, as if a cold hand was squeezing her heart. It would be so easy to give in and let Drake back into her life for Poppy's sake, but that wouldn't do. She had made a good life for the two of them out of sadness and hurt, and it hadn't always been easy with the memory of what it was like to be in Drake's arms, in Drake's bed, the kind of things that were only ever going to happen again in her dreams.

'I want us to carry on as we are doing,' she said, 'with you living in your lovely new house and Poppy and me in our home. You can see her whenever you want, but you know that it works both ways, Drake. She has to be able to see you when she needs you—you have to be there for her too.'

It was a hurtful thing to say, and she wished she could take it back the moment she'd said it. His glance was cold as he told her, 'I know how it works, Tessa. You and I had an agreement—you can't hold that against me for ever.'

Yes, but I do, Tessa thought raggedly. Can't Drake see that? I've had the foundations of my life crumble once. I couldn't face it again. But he is so confident, so keen to make sure I remember that I wasn't entirely blameless all that time ago. Should I try a second time round?

She had cooked foods that she knew he liked and watching his enjoyment of them brought back memories of the two of them arriving home from their different work-places and while the food was cooking making love wherever the mood took them.

They had been days of reckless rapture and even more reckless promises about the lives they intended to live devoid of responsibilities. But all that had come to Drake living alone in a rented house in the hospital grounds and her a single mother with a child that wasn't his.

He was reading her mind and when the three of them had finished eating he said, 'Let's fill the dish-washer and go out into the garden for some playtime with Poppy. I see no reason why she should suffer for our lack of rapport.'

'Yes, you're right,' she agreed, holding back tears at the thought of such a farce. What Randolph had said about Poppy's father made her feel trapped. Nothing was clear and uncomplicated any more, and after Drake left in the early evening and Poppy was asleep, Tessa watched the sun go down and tried not to think about times past.

CHAPTER EIGHT

WHETHER IT WAS because of that she didn't know, but in the stillness of the night she dreamt that she was in Drake's arms and it was magical. Consequently, when she awoke the next morning she felt tired and low-spirited.

Lizzie didn't miss her lacklustre appearance when she dropped Poppy off, and wanted to know how Sunday lunch had gone. Tessa could only manage to give a silent thumbs-down as she departed to face Monday morning at the hospital.

After the trauma of Sunday she was hoping that Drake would stay out of her radius and wasn't happy to find him perched on the corner of her desk chatting to Jennifer, when she arrived.

'Hi, there,' he said in greeting. 'Just stopped by to leave you an appointment card for next week. Now that the treatment is working I need to see you more often.'

The phone rang, her secretary answered it, and while she was taking the call he said in a low voice, 'We need to talk. When can I see you alone?'

'I don't know. I'd rather not,' she told him.

He frowned. 'I'm getting a little tired of being cast as the archvillain in your life.'

'Lunchtime, then, at the big house?' she suggested reluctantly, and he nodded and went on his way, leaving her wishing that she hadn't been so obliging in agreeing to his demands. But wasn't that how she'd always been?

When she rang the bell Drake greeted her unsmilingly and invited her to take a seat in its huge sitting room. She obeyed with the feeling that what he had to say was unlikely to be good, and waited to hear what he had to say.

It was brief, to the point, and incredible.

'When I got home from your place last night there was a message waiting for me from a clinic in Canada, offering me a similar position to the one I have here, and I've arranged to go over there in a couple of weeks' time to see what's on offer.'

He was about to take temptation out of her way, and relief was washing over her, but only for seconds until reality took over. 'You can't leave us now!' she said in a strangulated whisper. 'Poppy doesn't want a father figure who is there one moment and gone the next. She has had enough hurts in her young life.'

He didn't reply to that, just commented, 'I notice that there's no concern at the thought of my departure with regard to yourself?'

'I don't care about myself,' she cried. 'You've already messed my life up by coming back, but she's so small and defenceless.'

Tears, warm and stinging, were forming behind closed eyelids as she tried to shut him out of her vision, because Poppy wasn't the only one who was defenceless when it came to Drake. So far she'd been able to cope with his return and the effect it was having on her life but not any more.

She'd already had to pick up the pieces after one of his departures, had she the strength to do it again, this time with a child to think of?

'I'm only considering the Canadian offer because you've made it clear you don't want me here,' he said, 'and Poppy will soon forget me once I've gone. If you marry at some time in the future she will have an adoptive father to go with an adoptive mother and all will be well.'

'I can't believe that you could be so smug about something so important,' she said, fighting to maintain her self-control. 'Is that it, you have nothing more to hit me with?'

'That's it,' he said levelly. 'I didn't plan it. The offer came out of the blue at what seemed to be just the right moment in both our lives.'

'Yours maybe,' she told him, 'not mine and Poppy's. Apart from anything else, you promised to be there for me with regard to treating my eye problem. What are you going to do about that, shuffle me on to whoever takes your place?'

'I'll sort something, don't worry. If I take this offer I won't be living on the moon. There *are* airlines, you know.'

'Don't come back out of limbo again for my sake,' she told him flatly. 'What about the house that you're buying?'

'I shall still buy it and use it for holidays if I accept the offer. Or rent it out.'

Tessa was on her feet, holding onto the arms of the

chair as she asked, 'And is that it? No other me, me, me kind of news you have to pass on?'

Drake shook his head wearily. 'No, nothing else. But, Tessa, you can't have it both ways. You don't want me around, but you don't like it when I'm prepared to oblige and get out of your life.'

The door was wide open, flung back on its hinges, and she had gone. As he closed it slowly behind her the room felt cold, as cold as it had been in Switzerland.

The rest of the day dragged on. She forced herself to concentrate on hospital matters with Jennifer's chatter in the background about what a lovely weekend she'd had with her new man friend, and all the time Tessa was imagining the pain of yet another separation from Drake. He was treating it as if she was to blame— maybe she was.

He'd been nothing but kind and caring and supportive since coming back into her life, and what had she been? Mistrusting? Unpleasant? It wasn't surprising that he was ready once again to go his own way, and ahead of them was an uncomfortable fortnight until he flew to Canada to investigate what was on offer for him out there, which was certain to be spectacular. It would need to be to lure him away from Horizons.

When she arrived at Lizzie's house after a dreadful day her friend's first words were, 'You look ghastly. What's happened?'

'Drake has been headhunted by a hospital in Canada and is going to see what's on offer in a couple of weeks, and it's all my fault, Lizzie. He's tired of me keeping him at arm's length and being so mistrusting and…well,

I have to admit, sometimes I've been rude and hurtful—when that other time was just as much my fault as his.

'Poppy called him Daddy yesterday, which was fine by me until we got our wires crossed as usual and ended up putting on a big pretence of playing in the garden with her. Then he went, with things as bad as they've ever been between us, and as if the fates were weary of our lack of trust in each other the Canadian offer was waiting for him when he arrived back at the big house.'

Lizzie was observing her sadly. 'Tessa, when are you going to admit that you still love him?'

'Why not ask me when I'm going to climb Everest or something equally difficult? Why couldn't he be any man instead of Drake Melford? He loves Horizons and I'm driving him away from the place. The only way that I can admit to myself that I still love him is to do something that will make him stay.'

'And what might that be?'

'Move out of the area. Give him the space that he deserves without judging him all the time. Then he can carry on with his plans to buy a house in one of the villages and live there in contentment.'

'You can't do that!' Lizzie exclaimed in horror.

'I can. Before Drake leaves on his visit to Canada I shall tell him that if he proceeds with his crazy plan of moving there to be away from me, he will find me gone when he comes back to say his goodbyes to the folks at Horizons.

'The hospital needs him, Lizzie, and if I can't persuade him to change his mind I will appeal to his conscience by having left when he comes back after looking the Canadian place over. Once he is airborne I shall put

the cottage up for sale and find somewhere not too far
away to move to, and once that has been sorted Poppy
and I will go into temporary accommodation until the
sale goes through.'

'Where have you got in mind?' Lizzie asked unbe-
lievingly.

'Maybe Devon, or somewhere not quite so far away,
so that I can visit you regularly and keep an eye on Randolph, and once I've found somewhere to live please
don't tell anyone except Daniel where I am, will you?'

'Of course I won't,' she assured her, staggered at the
scenario that was unfolding before her. 'We shall miss
the two of you so much,' she told her sadly.

'Please don't make it any harder,' Tessa begged, with
her glance on Poppy playing happily in the garden with
the twins.

Driving past the park on their way home, she brought
the car to a halt. Workmen were delivering new benches
and putting the old ones into a truck. The one that had
such sweet and sour memories was the next one to go.

'Can I buy it?' she asked, pointing to the bench in
question.

'Yes,' she was told. 'Unwanted things such as these
are sold and the money goes to charities. This lot are
fifty pounds each, including delivery.'

'You have a deal,' she told them. 'I live on the road
that goes past the eye hospital.'

'Right, we'll drop it off now if you like,' one of them
said, and with a sick feeling that both she and the bench
were surplus to requirements she led the way.

'Where do you want it?' he asked, when they arrived at the cottage. 'On the patio at the back, please,'

Tessa told him, having no wish for Drake to see it if he should happen to drive past. When they'd gone she stood observing it in silence as Poppy whizzed to and fro on her scooter.

It was a strange thing to choose as a memento of a dead love affair, she thought, but if every time she sat on the bench it brought Drake near in her self-imposed exile, it might take some of the hurt away.

Randolph rang in the late evening. It seemed that Drake had told him about his proposed Canadian trip and he wanted to know what if anything was going on be-tween them.

'Nothing is going on,' she told him uncomfortably. 'He has the chance of a fantastic opportunity over there and is flying across to see what is on offer.'

'Surely you don't want him to leave you and Poppy back here while he goes to live and work in another country?' he questioned.

'It has happened to me before, Randolph, and what Drake does is his own affair. We have no claim on him.'

'No, of course not,' he agreed vaguely, and rang off, leaving Tessa with another problem to worry about. Randolph wasn't going to want to be far away from his granddaughter.

After Monday's day of despair Drake rang her office the next morning and said in clipped tones that he would want to check her eye once each week before he left on his Canadian trip, so how about on the mornings of the two Fridays before he flew out in the afternoon of the second one?

'Er, yes,' she agreed, remembering how she'd accused him of leaving her in the middle of the treatment if he took a job abroad.

'So shall we say first thing on each Friday?' he suggested. 'I'm going to be pushed to get all my commitments here dealt with before I leave.'

'How long do you expect to be away?' she asked, as if only mildly interested, when, in fact, she was aching for him to stay.

'I have no idea, but does it matter?' he questioned. 'You aren't going to miss me.'

She didn't reply to that. Just rang off and sat gazing through the window to where the hills that they both loved so much and the gracious town nestling beneath them seemed to be saying, If you can persuade Drake to refuse the Canadian offer and stay here, you won't have loved in vain.

She rang him back a few moments later and said, 'You shouldn't leave Horizons because of me. The hospital needs you, Glenminster needs you. So I've decided to leave the hospital and the area in order to give you some space. Perhaps you could keep that in mind while you're being shown around the Canadian set-up.' Tessa rang off before he could comment. *Coward*, she thought.

But he rang back only minutes later and said, 'I'm free for a short time and am hoping that it will be long enough to tell you what I think about your ridiculous idea, Tessa. I am quite capable of sorting out my affairs without you offering yourself as a sacrificial lamb. Don't even think of taking Poppy to some strange place because of me!

'I made a mistake coming back and I'm going to

rectify it. It's as simple as that, and I'm expecting that by the time you come for your appointment on Friday you will have seen sense.' Drake put the phone down without knowing that she was going to proceed to Plan B regardless.

It was a week of miserable activity: putting the cottage up for sale without a 'for sale' sign until he had flown to Canada on the second Friday, searching for a place to move to that would meet her needs and Poppy's, somewhere that was not too near and not too far, and when she'd found the right sort of place—if ever there could be such a thing without Drake—starting afresh with little enthusiasm.

She'd spoken to the chairman and explained that she might have to leave without the usual month's notice. He'd been surprised but quite amenable as Tessa had served Horizons well over the years, and when she'd asked that the possibility of her leaving be kept private he'd also agreed, and wondered at the same time if it had anything to do with his top man being headhunted by a Canadian hospital.

When Tessa went for the check-up early on the Friday morning of that first week, Drake was waiting. She'd had a blood test the day before in the endocrine clinic with better results than before and once he had done his examination of the offending eye he said, 'It begins to look as if I won't need to cross the Atlantic to check progress. The medication that you're on seems to be working fine'.

For a moment she felt weak with relief. But that thought was swiftly followed by the realisation that everything had its price. His next and last consultation would be her final goodbye to him, and it would be beyond bearing.

It was early September. Poppy had a place reserved at the nearest pre-school, but now it was beginning to look as if she was going to receive that part of her education elsewhere. Tessa still hadn't found a suitable place for them to live until she saw a house similar to the cottage for sale in a Devon coastal resort. It had a good pre-school nearby, and she decided to drive down there during the coming weekend to look the place over.

The idea would have been great if it hadn't been that with every mile in that direction on the Saturday her concerns regarding Poppy being separated from Lizzie's twin boys, and Randolph fretting because he wasn't going to see enough of her, were assuming gigantic proportions, and halfway there she stopped the car in a lay-by and decided to turn back.

Not because she'd changed her mind about leaving but because the place she'd been heading towards was too far away for an easy relationship to be maintained with Lizzie's boys and, of course, Poppy's beloved grandfather. How could she be so cruel as to contemplate taking his granddaughter so far away?

Yet those thoughts didn't solve the problem of leaving Horizons and Glenminster and all that they stood for to stop Drake from moving to Canada. Tessa knew that she had only herself to blame for the situation she found herself in. How had it come to this? At first she would

have been delighted that he was leaving her alone—
when had she changed her mind?

When she pulled up in front of the cottage the
thought came that one week had already gone before
Drake flew out there and she was floundering with no
idea where to go before he came back.

The phone was ringing as she put the key in the lock
and on answering it she was surprised to hear her Aunt
Sophie on the line once again. But when Tessa heard
what she had to say it was as if someone, somewhere
was looking after her.

'I did so enjoy our chat,' said the sixty-year-old keep-
fit fanatic, 'even though I caused you alarm when I mentioned the thyroid connection between the women of our
family. I would love to see you and Poppy and wonder
if you and your little girl would like to come and stay
with me for a while. I have lots of room and you'd be
most welcome for as long as you'd like.'

'We'd be delighted,' Tessa said weakly.

Sophie, her mother's younger sister, lived on a part
of the coast not too far away for Randolph to see his
granddaughter quite often and Poppy to see the twins,
yet distant enough for them to be away from Glenminster as far as Drake was concerned. If she liked
it there, maybe she might see a house that would be
suitable for them with a school close by, and even a
hospital not too far away where she could put her training to good use.

'So when can you come?' her aunt was asking.

'Would next weekend be too soon?' she questioned.

'Not at all,' was the reply, and Tessa sank down onto

the nearest chair, relieved yet tearful. Everything would work out for the best now, wouldn't it?

During the week that followed, the talk around the hospital was that Drake would be crazy not to accept the offer from a much larger and more prestigious hospital than their own, but would be sorely missed. As Tessa listened to the gossip she prayed that her departure would keep him where he belonged, enjoying life in the house that he was so set on buying, instead of having to give up the dream.

The fact that she also was involved in departure plans wasn't known generally as the chairman was keeping his word and Jennifer was too head over heels in love with the new man in her life to take much notice of what was going on anywhere else.

The more Drake thought about a move across the Atlantic the less he was looking forward to it. He'd gone to Switzerland for prestige and had got it, wrapped around with regrets over what he'd lost in the process.

It had stood to sense that in the time he'd been gone she would have found someone else to fill the gap he'd left, but nothing could have prepared him for the enchanting small child that Tessa had adopted who had all her love and devotion.

She had offered in recent days to move out of the area so that he would stay, but no way was he going to allow her to do that. He wanted her in his life now more than ever, and would be devastated if she wasn't there when he got back from Canada.

If he hadn't already agreed to attend the appointment

with the Canadians he would forget the whole thing. He hadn't seen anything of her in days, and when she came for his last examination of her eye this Friday he was going to repeat what he'd said about her not leaving Glenminster.

Almost everything Tessa possessed was going to be put into storage once Drake had gone until she found the right place to live, and when she called at Randolph's on the way home on the Thursday night before her last Friday of residence in Glenminster there was a chill in the air that indicated that Poppy's grandfather was not pleased with her plans for the future.

'We aren't going to be too far away,' she told him reassuringly. 'I will bring Poppy to see you as often as I can.'

'And are you going to give me a new address where I can get in touch?' he asked crustily.

'I will when I've got one,' she promised, 'and in the meantime I've made a temporary arrangement with my Aunt Sophie and will give you her phone number.'

'So what has Drake to do with all of this?' he wanted to know.

'Everything and nothing,' was the reply, and he had to be satisfied with that.

That same morning Tessa had told Jennifer that the following day would be her last at Horizons and her secretary had gazed at her in astonishment.

'So no fanfare of trumpets at *your* departure,' she'd said incredulously. 'I wouldn't be surprised if there's a

brass band if Drake Melford decides to leave us. The
general feeling is that no one wants him to go, but you
can't begrudge him what has to be the opportunity of
a lifetime.'

Tessa had turned away. What would everyone think
if they knew she was responsible for him considering
the move to Canada? She prayed that her leaving Glenminster would not be in vain. That when Drake came
back and saw she was gone he would stay and be happy,
and perhaps having given up on her might one day meet
someone less difficult to love.

It had come, the final check-up for her eye problem with
Drake, and she made her way to his consulting room
with dragging steps.

What she was hoping was that he would return to
the place they both loved and that, whatever decision
he'd made while in Canada, he wouldn't leave Horizons
once he discovered that she'd gone. She wanted him to
be happy in the house of his dreams and fulfilled with
the work he did at the hospital, while she would seek
a return to the contentment of sorts that she'd found
while they'd been apart.

Tessa looked tired, he thought when she appeared.
There was a crease across her brow and a listlessness
about her that indicated inward weariness. But one thing
was sure, she would be relieved to see him go after the
telling off he'd given her.

Yet there was no way he could let her disappear from
his life, he loved her too much. He was going to make
one last attempt to show her how much he cared when

he came back from Canada, and if she still didn't want him near, well, he would just persist until she did.

For one thing, his beautiful house was meant to be lived in, not used as a holiday home, and for another was the knowledge that a little girl wanted him as her daddy and he wasn't going to let her down on that.

He'd told Tessa that he was going to accept the offer from the Canadians in a moment of frustration and ever since had wished he'd kept silent.

'What time is your flight?' she asked in a polite but disinterested kind of voice. She didn't want him to call at the cottage later in the afternoon and find her in the middle of moving.

'Half past three,' he said, and with a wry smile, 'I imagine that you are just being polite with that question as the only real emotion you are feeling with regard to my departure has to be relief.'

She flashed him a tired smile. 'I thought I was here for an eye check. Is the mind-reading a freebie?'

'No, just an observation. so if you would like to open wide we will see what has been going on behind those beautiful eyes over the last week.'

Tessa could feel tears rising, and when Drake had finished the examination she said, 'Before you tell me the final results, whether they be good or not so good, I will never forget how you have been there for me with this whole unexpected eye thing.' Before he could answer she took a photograph of a happy, smiling Poppy out of her bag and, giving it to him, said, 'I thought you might like this.'

'Yes. I would indeed,' he said, as he looked down at it. 'But I would have liked one of the two of you more.'

'I'm sure you are only saying that to be polite.'

'Not necessarily,' was the reply, and cut that discussion short. 'Your results, Tessa. The eye is back to normal. Keep on taking the medication for another couple of months to be on the safe side and it should be fine. If at any time you are worried about your vision let me know immediately.'

'Are you definitely going to accept the position if they offer it to you?' she asked, choking on the words. 'I meant what I said that day on the phone.'

'Maybe you did, and maybe I won't take the job over there. What matters is that irrespective of whatever I decide to do I find you here when I come back in two weeks' time. Don't make any sacrifices on my account, Tessa. The Canadian job is already mine if I want it.'

'And you are going there because of me?' she choked.

She held out her hand to wish him goodbye, but ignoring it he looked down onto her upturned face and kissed her just once, then, releasing her, opened the door for her and closed it behind her with a decisive click.

Speechless at the finality of the moment, Tessa went back to her office to watch for Drake's departure from the big house in time to catch his three-thirty flight.

When a taxi arrived and his baggage had been put in the boot he paused for a moment before seating himself in the back of the vehicle and glanced across to where her office was. It took all her willpower not to rush outside and beg him to stay, but thankfully it wasn't his final departure.

That, she hoped, would not come, and she prayed that when he returned Drake might forget about Canada on finding her gone and decide to stay in Glenminster where he belonged. Otherwise what she was planning to do would be a waste of both their lives.

Her furniture would be going into storage in the late afternoon and the park bench, which was covered by waterproof sheeting on the patio at the back of the cottage, was going to be transported by haulage to her aunt's home, later in the day.

All that she would have to do at the end of her last working day at the hospital would be to check that all was secure at the cottage and collect Poppy from Lizzie's house for the last time before they went to the bed and breakfast place where she had booked them in for the night.

It had been a painful farewell for the two friends, who had kept what was happening in the background from the children to avoid tears, but she was determined to make a fresh start with Poppy, and Lizzie at least understood her reasons, even if she didn't agree with the decision.

Tessa had brought a snack with her to serve as their evening meal at the bed and breakfast place and once they'd eaten she consoled a fretful Poppy, who didn't like the strange place she had brought her to with the assurance that the next day they would be at the seaside. Then she'd tucked her up in the big double bed that graced the room and, once she was sleeping, eased herself in beside her daughter and tried not to think about those last moments she'd spent with Drake in his consulting room.

After an early breakfast she stopped off at the cottage to see if the bench had been picked up yet and was relieved to see that it had. Then one of the strangest days Tessa had ever known got under way, and as the miles flashed past the enormity of what she was undertaking was beginning to register.

It was fortunate she'd managed to leave while Drake was away, she thought. She couldn't have done it with him being anywhere near, and now the die was cast and the future that not so long ago had looked contented was in front of her. She tried not to think of it as bleak— indeed, thinking of Poppy's joy at going to the seaside helped her to smile.

She had been anxious to make sure that her scooter was in the car boot before they set off, and now she was asleep after such an early start when she'd been bewildered by what was happening but excited too because they were going to be staying at the seaside and she had brought her bucket and spade on the promise of it.

Tessa had found her looking wistfully through the window at the front of the cottage a few times since the day when she'd invited Drake to lunch, but she hadn't mentioned him, except for one night when Tessa had heard her cry 'Daddy' in her sleep.

But now in the excitement of what was going on in her life he wasn't mentioned and Poppy didn't watch out for him as before.

They received a warm welcome from her aunt, who had prepared a double bedroom for the two of them, and had a lovely meal ready for the travellers at the end of a long day, and when Poppy was asleep later in the evening Sophie said gently, 'Tessa, you have the look of someone who is running away from something. Is it a man?'

'Yes,' she said. 'The love of my life left me, then he came back, and now he's leaving again. I can't cope.'

'Did he leave you for another woman?' her aunt asked.

Her smile was wry. 'No, it was his career that I had to compete with.'

'And what was that?'

'Eye surgery, ophthalmology.'

'And where is he now?'

'Debating whether to accept a position in Canada to get away from how I've been pushing him away. I felt that if I left Glenminster he might decide to stay as he loves the place.'

'It sounds as if you care for him a lot.'

'Yes, I do. But I hurt so much when he left me that I'm afraid of it happening again, and to make matters worse Poppy is drawn to Drake like a magnet. He and I feel that she thinks he's the father that she lost in the car crash as we are told that he looks very much like him.'

'So stay here as long as you like,' Sophie said. 'Let your hurts heal by the sea and the golden sands, and, Tessa, you will know when the time is right to decide who you want to spend the rest of your life with.'

When the plane touched down in the UK Drake gave a sigh of relief. The journey had seemed to take for ever and he wanted to get back to Glenminster with all speed. He was going to ask Tessa to marry him, and if she refused he was going to keep on asking until she said yes.

The Canadian set-up had been excellent and he'd thought a few times that not so long ago he would have accepted the offer immediately, grabbed it with both hands like a precious gift. But he was no longer the same person as the one who had left Tessa with scarcely a word of goodbye and had spent the next three years wishing he hadn't.

He had bought a ring of sapphires and diamonds while he'd been in Canada, regretting all the time having told her that she was the reason why he was contemplating leaving Glenminster. It had been said in a moment of frustration. He loved the place and dreamt all the time of sharing his new house with her and Poppy.

On leaving the airport, he hired a taxi to take him straight to the cottage. It was late evening, but not so late that he would expect Tessa to have gone to bed, and he didn't want to waste a moment before being with her.

But as he turned away from paying the driver Drake saw that it was in darkness. There was a 'for sale' board on display in the front garden and his heart sank. Unconvinced, he rang the doorbell several times but got no response, and then went round to the back, only to find no signs of life there either. He thought grimly that it was going to be his turn to be left in despair and it served him right, but where to start looking for Tessa and Poppy?

Were they staying with Lizzie and Daniel? It seemed the most likely place. He checked the time. The autumn dusk was falling over the town. It wasn't fair to pressure Lizzie for Tessa's location until he was calmer, and maybe she wouldn't want to tell him where she was even then.

A better report on what had been happening while he was away might be available from Horizons tomorrow.

Surely someone there would know where Tessa was, either the chairman or her secretary maybe.

He unpacked, had a shower and sat outside on the terrace of the house he had found so depressing and soulless, though it felt almost cosy after seeing Tessa's cottage dark and empty in the autumn night.

That day in his consulting room when he'd told her that if he liked the set-up in Canada he would take the job to get away from her was starkly clear in his mind and he'd never stopped regretting making the comment. Now he knew it must have pushed her too far.

CHAPTER NINE

THE NEXT MORNING he rang the chairman at home to ask if he had any knowledge of where Tessa had moved to and was told he had no idea, that the only thing he knew was that Tessa had asked him if he would allow her to skip the usual four weeks' notice.

He'd agreed reluctantly, and she'd left the same day that Drake had flown out to Canada.

'And since you're back, have you come to a decision about the job in Canada?' finished the chairman.

'I'm staying here,' Drake told him. 'I care for Horizons too much to go elsewhere.' And amidst the other man's relief he thought, and that goes for Tessa too when I find her. I care too much for her to ever want to be anywhere other than here with her. She has given up much that meant a lot to her to make me stay. But surely she knows that if she isn't with me, life will be meaningless?

After that he went to what had been Tessa's office to have a word with her secretary and saw that a temporary replacement was already sitting behind her desk, which added another ominous note to his enquiries, and when Jennifer said that she hadn't known that Tessa was leaving until the very last moment and had no idea where she was planning to move to he gave up on that one.

He could no longer ignore the fact that Lizzie and Daniel were the only people who would know where she was, and he hoped he could persuade them to tell him. He'd had an exhausting day, bringing his appointments up to date and taking the clinic that his staff had been in charge of during his absence, but like the cottage of the night before there was no answer when he rang the doorbell. Luckily, a neighbour told him they were on holiday. So using the moment to ask a question he said, 'Have Lizzie's friend and her little girl gone with them?'

'No, just the four of them—Lizzie, Daniel and the children,' he was told.

So much for that, Drake thought grimly, pointing the car back towards Horizons. As he was driving past the park his eyes widened: the bench had gone! All the benches had gone, and been replaced by new ones. Was it a sign, telling him that it really was over between the two of them? He wouldn't take no for an answer this time, he was going to find her and tell her how he felt. He should have done it ages ago, but somehow his pride and her prickliness had got in the way. This time would be different.

After his unsuccessful visit to Lizzie's house Drake rang Randolph, who told him that he didn't know where Tessa and Poppy were, but she had promised to be in touch the moment they were settled somewhere new, and that was it.

'What is it with the two of you?' he asked. 'Anyone can see that you are meant to be together.'

'Not quite everyone,' Drake told him. 'Tessa doesn't, and I'm to blame for that.'

The old man sighed. 'So work your magic on her. We both want her back here, don't we?'

'Yes, we do,' he told him flatly. 'I'm doing my best. I'll find her.'

They were having a picnic on the beach, Tessa and Poppy with Lizzie and her family, who had just arrived in the area for a short holiday further along the coast so as not to draw attention to Sophie's house guests, though it was unlikely that anyone from Glenminster would be visiting the isolated coastal village.

Her aunt had gone to a keep-fit class in the village hall, and the children were splashing in the shallows after making a sandcastle.

But the adults were having a serious talk as Lizzie reported that Drake was apparently back from Canada and hadn't been tempted by what was on offer there, from the looks of it. She had rung the hospital in the guise of a prospective patient and been told that Dr Melford was back and was taking appointments as he would be staying on the staff of Horizons for the fore-seeable future.

'So Drake is back where he belongs,' Tessa said. But the relief at his decision to stay was complicated by not knowing how she was going to endure a future that was grey and empty, like that of an exile from a promised land, and as if Lizzie had read her mind she had a question to ask.

'So are you going to go back there now you're sure that he isn't leaving?'

Tessa shook her head. 'No, not unless I'm asked.'
And for the rest of the afternoon she picnicked and
played with the children until the light began to fade,
then Lizzie and her family, who were leaving the next
morning to travel further along the coast for another
few days, said their goodbyes with a promise to see
her again soon.

Almost a week had gone by and it was as if Tessa had
disappeared off the face of the earth, Drake thought. No
one at the hospital had seen her or knew of her whereabouts. There was no sign of Lizzie and Daniel having
returned from their holiday, but he would try again tonight, he vowed, and if they were still away he would
ask the obliging neighbour if she'd had any messages
from them that might point him towards locating Tessa.

The house had the same look of being unoccupied as
on the other occasion when he'd called, but this time
he rang next door's bell and the same woman as before
appeared.

'I've been looking out for you,' she said. 'They'll
be back tomorrow. I got a card a couple of days ago.
It seems they've been staying at a place called Bretton Sands.'

'Fine!' he said. 'I'll call round tomorrow night and
surprise them.' And went on his way thinking that
he'd heard the name before, but it didn't sound like
somewhere Tessa would make a beeline for. The kind
neighbour had also said the first time he'd called that
Tessa and Poppy weren't with them, so he was still
none the wiser.

It was in the middle of the night that he awoke wide-eyed and raised himself up off the pillows. At the time of Tessa's aunt phoning and mentioning that the women of their family were prone to thyroid issues he had recalled that she was the one that Tessa had once told him lived in a remote village miles down the coast. Was it possible that was where she'd gone?

There was no way he could set off now to find out. A full day in Theatre and on the wards was ahead of him, but he could set off the moment he'd finished, and if he found himself to be mistaken he could drive all night and get back in time for the next day's duties.

If Tessa was to be found in the place that he was heading for, someone else would have to take his appointments until he came back down to earth... And there was the ring. If he took it with him it might bring him his heart's desire, the woman he loved as his beautiful bride.

The day that followed seemed never-ending but Drake's attention to his patients was faultless. Blindness was everyone's terror and if it was possible to prevent it, he had the skills to help.

His last case of the day was a middle-aged woman brought in as an emergency with an eye injured from the cork of a bottle of home-made wine flying off explosively when she'd been trying to open it, and was in a state of shock.

This time he decided to let his second in command take over while he watched, and while he inspected the eye with the ophthalmoscope Drake listened to his comments, and then took over to see if he agreed with his findings that the blow from the cork had been prevented from doing serious damage by the eyelid's reflex action, and that the bruising and soreness would disappear in a few days.

It seemed that his findings were correct and he said, 'Well done!' and left him to give the good news to the anxious patient.

As soon as he had been home to change Drake set off to find what he now knew was real love, the kind that Tessa had wanted, the kind that was ready to give rather than take, and prayed that he'd find her at the place off the beaten track called Bretton Sands.

Poppy was asleep, sun-kissed and wind-blown after all the fun she'd had with her friends on the beach, and as Tessa moved restlessly from room to room, with Lizzie's news uppermost in her mind, her aunt said, 'There's a full moon and the tide is out. Why don't you go for a stroll along the sands while I keep an eye on Poppy?' and because of all things she needed quiet and the time to think, she followed the suggestion.

Outside it was warm, with moonlight turning the sea to silver, and when Tessa left the sand behind and came to rocks she perched herself on the first one she arrived at and sat silhouetted against the night sky.

Drake had parked the car and was moving along the short promenade, seeking someone to ask where he might find Tessa's Aunt Sophie. He wasn't sure of her surname, which would make the questioning tricky. Even trickier was the fact that there was no one to ask, the place being deserted.

As he approached the end of the paved area and was about to turn back he saw her, seated on a rock, gazing out to sea. He said her name softly, and the wind must have carried it out towards her for it could not have been loud enough for her to hear.

Tessa turned, startled, and as their glances held she exclaimed, 'Drake! How did you know where to find me? No one knows I'm here except Aunt Sophie, Lizzie and her family…and Randolph.'

He was smiling. 'I'd tried everywhere else and no one knew where you'd gone, until on a second visit to Lizzie and Daniel's place yesterday their neighbour said she'd had a card from a place called Bretton Sands, which didn't ring a bell at first. But in the middle of last night it dawned on me that your Aunt Sophie lived somewhere along that coast, and as soon as I'd finished for the day I was on my way, praying that I hadn't got it wrong.'

'Why did you change your mind about leaving Horizons?' she asked softly from her perch on the rock.

'Because I love you, and know that you love me, or you wouldn't have left Glenminster for my sake.' He produced the ring and said, 'I bought this while I was in Canada. Will you let me put it on your finger and in the near future place a wedding ring next to it? Will you marry me, Tessa?'

'Yes,' she said, finding her voice, and when she stretched her arm across the divide that separated them he put it on her finger. Looking down at the sapphires and diamonds, she said, 'It's beautiful, Drake. I shall feel truly blessed wearing it. The only way I knew to show you how much I loved you was by moving out of Glenminster to give you a reason for staying.'

'Yes, I know,' he said softly, 'but you overlooked one thing. I can't live without you.'

He opened his arms and took her hands in his and as she stepped down from the rock and was safe inside his hold he said laughingly, 'What do you think Poppy will say when she hears about this?'

'It goes without saying, she'll be delighted,' she told him, and then he kissed her and at last life was how she had longed for it to be.

CHAPTER TEN

THEY HAD TO sort out where Tessa and Poppy were going to sleep when they arrived back in Glenminster the following day. Drake had spent the night in Bretton Sands' only hotel and had been greeted rapturously by Poppy the next morning.

There was no way they could sleep at the cottage as even the bedding had gone into storage, but there was one thing that hadn't, and it had been an emotional moment when he'd seen the park bench on Aunt Sophie's patio.

'Where on earth has that come from?' he'd asked huskily.

'I was driving past when the workmen were taking them away and I bought it from them as I had to have something to remember you by,' she'd told him.

'What a lovely surprise,' he'd said, holding her close, 'and when we get back I have a surprise for you.' Turning to her aunt, who had been beaming at them in her delight at seeing her niece so happy, 'You must come and stay with us, Aunt Sophie, when we are settled. I'm indebted to you for looking after my precious ones.'

* * *

And now Drake was inside the hospital, rearranging his appointments so that he could take a couple of days off while they arranged their wedding. It was, of course, going to take place in the gardens of the hotel where he'd taken Tessa for lunch that day, and she was making up the other four-poster bed in the big house so that she and Poppy would have somewhere to sleep until the night of the wedding.

When he came in and saw what she was doing Drake said, 'For once this place won't seem so cheerless tonight, we might not even notice the creaking. Are you ready for the scenic tour?'

She smiled across at him. 'Of course. Is it the surprise that you promised?'

'It is indeed because I don't want you to get any wrong ideas that I might be expecting you to live in this place.'

He couldn't wait to take her and Poppy to see his new home, and was hoping that they would love it as much as he did. Tessa would adore the idea of planning the furnishing of its empty rooms in the short time they had before the wedding, and the large garden was just crying out for some children's swings and slides.

When they arrived at the village that Horizons had chosen for its yearly picnic that day, Tessa recalled how Drake had been quick to pass Poppy back into her care after minding her and had strolled off casually towards a house that was for sale in the last stages of construction.

She'd thought nothing of it at the time, but now here he was, turning the key in the lock, sweeping her up into his arms and carrying her over its threshold, and as she looked around her it was easy to tell why he loved the place.

It was light and airy, with clean lines, spacious rooms and fabulous views from the windows. All it needed now was to be furnished, for them to put the finishing touches to it that were their choice. As Poppy gazed around her in wonderment he said gently, 'This is where we are going to live. Do you like it?''

'Yes!' she cried. 'Can the boys come to play?'

'Of course they can. We are all going to have a lovely time living here, aren't we, Mummy?' he asked Tessa.

She nodded, and told the man who had once held her heart in careless hands, and had come back to give *his* into *her* keeping, 'Yes. We are. It will be wonderful beyond words.'

'We have such a lot of time to make up for, Tessa,' he said softly. 'Does that make you glad or sorry?'

'Just so glad,' she whispered. 'Happy that we are together at last.'

Lizzie and Poppy were the bridesmaids on the day of the wedding with Randolph giving the bride away and the chairman in the role of Drake's best man, while the vicar from the local church was to marry them.

It was autumn and the day had dawned with fruit ripening on the trees and everywhere to be seen were the bronzes and golds of the season.

The wedding wasn't a big family affair as neither bride nor groom had many relatives, their parents having been lost to them at different times over the years, but plenty of staff from Horizons who weren't on duty were there to offer their best wishes.

Tessa's white wedding dress had lily of the valley looped along the hemline and she was carrying a bouquet of the palest of pink roses. As Drake, standing beneath an archway of the same kind of flowers, watched her walking slowly towards him along the main walkway of the hotel gardens, he recognised them.

Lily of the valley and pink roses had been the flowers in the corsage he had given her that night on the river boat when she'd fastened it to her suit and asked him to dance, and the thought brought even more joy to a day that was already overflowing with it.

The marriage had taken place. The gold band of matrimony was in place next to the beautiful sapphire and diamond ring. The festivities were over and Poppy was asleep in the back of the car after all the day's excitement. But when they arrived at the house, she opened her eyes as Drake carried her upstairs and said, 'Can I sleep in my bridesmaid's dress, Daddy?'

'I don't see why not,' he said, and when he'd laid her gently against the pillows they watched her eyelids droop, and before they'd got to the door she was asleep again.

It was late afternoon and a September sun would soon be setting on their special day. As they strolled around the garden of their new home, with the park bench safely inside a flower-decked arbour, Drake said with laughing tenderness, 'How long do you think we should wait before we give Poppy a brother or a sister?'

'No time at all,' Tessa suggested laughingly, and she could tell that he thought it was a good idea.

EPILOGUE

THEY HAD MADE love with the evening sun laying strands of gold across them while Poppy slept in dreamland. It had been as good as it had always been, wild, sweet and passionate.

But instead of it being the end for them, it was only the beginning of lives that would be built on the rock of their love for each other, instead of the shifting sands of desire and a need for acclaim.

* * * * *

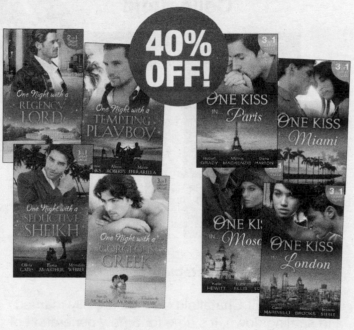

MILLS & BOON®

The Chatsfield Collection!

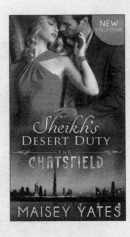

Style, spectacle, scandal…!

With the eight Chatsfield siblings happily married and settling down, it's time for a new generation of Chatsfields to shine, in this brand-new 8-book collection! The prospect of a merger with the Harrington family's boutique hotels will shape the future forever. But who will come out on top?

Find out at
www.millsandboon.co.uk/TheChatsfield2

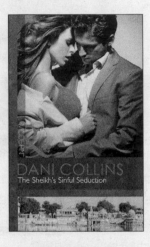

MILLS & BOON®

MEDICAL ROMANCE™

THE ULTIMATE IN ROMANTIC MEDICAL DRAMA

A sneak peek at next month's titles…